A
WEEK'S
WORTH

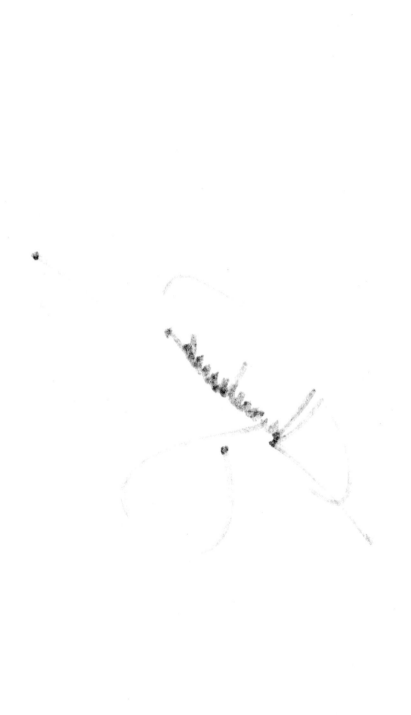

A WEEK'S WORTH

THYME LEWIS

Charleston, SC
www.PalmettoPublishing.com

A Week's Worth

Copyright © 2023 by Thyme Lewis

All rights reserved

First Edition

Paperback: 978-1-64990-566-6
eBook: 978-1-64990-565-9

Thyme Lewis
29090 Robinson Canyon Road
Carmel by-the-Sea, California 93923
www.ThymeLewis.com

Mac is embedded deep with FEMA, the Federal Emergency Management Agency, when another disaster strikes. His mother is in trouble, and he must fly cross-country to save her.

MacGuffin, or Mac. No middle name. Under the branch of Homeland Security, he provides disaster assistance to individuals, families, and businesses whose properties have been destroyed. But like everything else in Mac's life, he goes further. He can't help it. In the midst of crime, deceit, and corruption, time and time again, he risks everything to right the wrongs of the world.

Your mom is your mom no matter how far you want to get sometimes. She bore you, nourished you, influenced you, then released you out into the big blue world.

CHAPTER 1

DAY 1

California was burning, but that wasn't why Mac was going home.

In late September, Mac had been operating ninety miles east of Fort Walton Beach, the hardest hit by the latest hurricane on the panhandle of Florida. Natural disaster work had been slow going, methodical. His tools were four-fold. His FEMA tablet, his work phone, his skillset of repetition acquired over many years, and an innate ability to sense liars miles away or face to face. All civilian communication was down, so Response Force One had their generator powering a satellite link within its secure network. Unless you were a first responder, had your own satellite or walkie talkie, communication between rescue teams was nonexistent. As were most roads, utilities, and everything resembling normalcy.

Mac had been sleeping in his fifth tool, his rental car. It was no big deal. He'd done it before. He preferred it over the two-hour commute to base camp and another two back to the zone he was working. A waste of time and energy, which was precious to Mac. Something he'd learned growing up in Big Sur and applied in Puerto Rico when the roads in his sector hadn't been cleared. *But we'll save that data dump for another time.* When he returned to base camp to shower, eat a hot meal, and catch up with fellow inspectors, an urgent message was posted on the board.

Mac's sister Nadine had rung the family alarm, which was rare. She never cried wolf, especially to her older brother. When she couldn't reach Mac on his personal phone, she got word to Mac's Response Force One Team Section Chief, which was a feat unto itself. He contacted the Urban Search and Rescue Task Force Leader Dawn McKenzie, who posted the notice on a board in the commissary at base camp. It annoyed Mac because McKenzie could have rung him directly on his FEMA phone. The message was thirteen words, all caps: MACGUFFIN: MOM HAD HEART ATTACK. YOU ARE CLEARED TO GO HOME: ONE WEEK.

Mac read the message a second time, then looked at the posting date. It was seven days old.

He hustled back to the barracks, numb. His legs felt like dead weight, two pillars of cement at the bottom of the sea. Each step jarred as his spinning mind hoped for the best but anticipated the worst. When he got his sister on the phone, she informed him Mom was alive and recovering at home. Three stents inserted into her clogged blood vessels and a defibrillator. He packed his belongings, put away his badge, and caught the next transport west to a state that was on fire.

Now, twenty-four hours after receiving Nadine's message, Mac clenched his leather steering wheel tight. His knuckles revealed hairline scars on brown skin. He was in his early forties, lean and fittingly proportioned at just over six feet. His intense hazel eyes looked straight ahead under dark-furred brows. But he wasn't seeing the evaporating moisture on the windscreen nor the soot from the forest fires. He was far away from the here and now as he sat in his little sports car facing the wrong direction on the Seaside, California street.

Mac's mouth was turned down like the letter *N* without the arms. His eyes had been looking outward, but now they were somewhere between the wiper blades and abyss of what he imagined inescapable.

This town was like any small seaside conurbation: a grid of blocks that paralleled the shoreline and could be stamped anywhere, USA. The location was all that made a difference between skyrocketing real estate and affordable housing. That and the epidemic of opioids, homeless, and a mosh of other society debacles. This grid happened to be on the north end of Monterey County, one hundred miles south of San Francisco and forty miles north of Big Sur.

This town was affordable by California standards compared to some of the neighboring area codes. The general consensus along the bay and inland was the homeless population hadn't flourished due to colder winters and lack of food programs. An overall sense of harsh conditions made homeless living on the fringe of society rougher here than other counties. The lack of food programs doled out by government, churches, and retirement groups hadn't happened, unlike Santa Barbara and San Francisco, where homeless habitats thrived.

Mac crossed the third intersection and slowed when he saw the rear end of a Volkswagen Passat sticking out from a green hedge. The car was white, had four doors, and from Mac's line of sight, fit nicely in the small space. The hedge was ten feet tall and towered over the little car, its leaves jutting at various angles, unruly and overgrown. In contrast, the other neighbors' hedges appeared orderly and manicured, like children lined up at primary school. Mac granny-geared past the car and pulled tight along the fence line. The property stretched fifty feet wide and appeared equal in size to the other properties on the block. When Mac opened his door and stood up, he wiggled his shoulders and did an upper body shake.

Mac's keen eyes took everything in as he turned 180 degrees, surveying the street. More cars on it than parking spaces per house, typical of families with kids parked in front and rented guest houses out back.

Mac walked around his car and kneeled, looking at the soil beneath the hedge. The earth was a mixture of sand, salt air, and pocked black dirt with a light blanket of gray ash from the fires that had been raging for weeks. He imagined urine saturated into the pickets of the fence from passers-by walking their dogs. All the nutrients created a variety of gardens. However, his mother's hedge was taller than all the others.

He knelt forward and slipped his hand through the pickets, grabbing a healthy clump of grass and pulling. Rich black soil appeared underneath with white flakes of nutrients. Mycelium. Two red worms and some ants scurried through the underbelly. He watched one ant crawl along his finger's ridgeline, and he gathered it with his other hand, returning it to the grass, then lightly pressed the soil down.

"Twenty years," he repeated while crouched, peering into the garden. From his position, he couldn't see anything through the fence line but hedge. He stood up and walked the property width on the street side. Both edges, east and west. The inside was completely hidden from the street, maybe the whole town. Only a drone would penetrate this fortress or an intruder with a key. *What lies beyond is a mystery,* he thought. Mission accomplished.

Mac pressed the key fob, and his car lights flicked. He went to the Passat and checked the tires. Their tread was thick and rubber good. He looked inside her car's windows. A little dog pillow lay upon the passenger seat and a spill-free water bowl on the side floor. A braided red and gray leash lay among dog hair, whiskers, kibble bits, and a worn horse brush.

Mac paused a moment to lay his hand gently on the driver's window before making his way to the tall brown lattice gate that fortified the entrance. He slipped a brass key into the gate's lock and turned a click before returning the key ring to his pocket.

Inside, the garden was an overgrown habitat of plants and trees. It could have been mistaken for a jungle in Central America. There seemed to be no rhyme or reason of placement. Flowers in pots sporadically placed. Trees, bushes, shrubs growing everywhere like seeds thrown in the wind during a good tropical rain. Small piles of dead branches and wilted leaves scattered the underbrush of grass-patched earth. A wavy cement path adorned with little colorful stones for borders split in two directions. One went right along the side of the house, and the other curved left to the front porch. Mac remembered picking the pretty stones and hand-pressing them into the wet cement's edges twenty years prior.

Mac went left and stopped at a Meyer lemon tree. It stood nine feet tall and seven feet wide, branches full with ripe lemons invading half the path. He turned and looked back at the champagne vine. It, too, blocked the path as it wound its way

up and over the eight-foot gate in the other direction. Mac
ducked right to avoid being stabbed in the face by a branch's
thorns, and grabbed a plump lemon as he passed.

The home was a cottage by design, white and square in
shape with a Cape Cod feel, only miniaturized. Its roof was
pitched in two places, and it had an outer porch that was
converted into a painter's studio with multi-pane French
doors facing outward.

An aluminum ladder leaned on the house to the left of
the front door and a broken solar light hung off the roof
above it. Farther left, a large single-pane framed window
protruded from a stepped-out wall. Once clear of the plants
and various obstacles along the path, Mac could see art and
trinkets hanging inside.

Mac stepped past the ladder and peered through the
window. The view revealed a brown desk cluttered with
drawing papers, knickknacks, and a record player. Several al-
bums leaned against it, and a soft smile appeared on his face
when he recognized the closest. Art MacGuffin Jazz Trio.

The album cover presented three men standing, all in
black suits with embroidered vests. The middle man had
broader shoulders than the others, chiseled features, and
kind, happy eyes. All three men exuded joy, but Mac held his
focus on the middle man holding a pair of drumsticks. "Take
it light, do what's right," Mac repeated twice before answering, "I'm trying, Dad."

Mac rubbed his face and knocked on the window, calling out, "Mom, I'm here. It's your son." Nothing stirred inside the house. He turned and scanned the yard again. A few
knickknack doggie toys lay dirty between the grass patches
and rooted soil.

Mac turned away and walked back to the French doors and gently pushed. A silver hook attached inside held the doors from opening, so he knocked again, slightly louder. "Sadie, I'm here. It's Mac."

Twenty seconds later he heard footsteps, and the inner door opened. At first look, the woman that appeared didn't resemble the man before her at all. For one, she was white and he brown. Two, she was wearing a blue medical mask, he wasn't. The woman took a good look at Mac's face before continuing forward.

Sadie was seventy-one years old, five foot nine, and stout. She was wearing a white robe over a flowery dress of blue and red. Her Scots-Irish heritage could be seen in her smart, curious eyes and high cheekbones, but she looked tired and swollen. Her skin was blotchy, and her streaked gray hair was held back with brown wooden barrettes above her ears.

She unlatched the hook, and the door fell open. Her movements were focused and precise: identify nonthreat, allow crossing of threshold, inform present condition.

"Mac. I'm so hot. Be nice if we could open these windows again and bring some more air in."

"Hello to you too, Mom. I'm so glad you're okay. How about a hug?" Mac replied, stepping forward, arms outstretched.

"Oh, I'm sorry. I just feel terrible." She shrugged, discouraged, putting her hands up.

"I can imagine," he said optimistically.

Sadie had concern on her face. "My house is a mess. I'm really not prepared for company."

"Are you kidding me, after what you've been through? I'm sorry this happened. Can I hug you?"

Sadie kept her hands up, blocking Mac's approach.

Mac stutter-stepped cautiously, looking at her chest. "Does it hurt?"

Sadie let her gaze fall and shook her head. "Not anymore."

Mac stepped inside the enclosed porch, reached out, and gently pulled her toward him. The embrace was awkward, and neither surrendered to the other. When she pushed away, he countered, stepping farther into her. It was futile, and the tension remained. He searched for eye contact, but she looked toward the far wall of the enclosed porch.

Mac shrugged, asking sympathetically, "What can I do to help?"

"You can open these windows for starters," she replied, making a face.

Mac stared at the windows and the painting pinned to them. "But what about when winter comes?"

"Then we will shut them again." She emphasized *again* as if he were hard of hearing.

He turned back to face her. "Do you want to sit down?"

"No, I want you to open these windows."

"But I sealed them with caulking and screws, remember? You said the weather stripping wasn't working."

Sadie said nothing.

"It was drafty, and you wanted them shut for good is what I recall."

"Well, what do you want me to say? I'm hot."

Mac smiled. "Everybody's hot, Mom, including me." He looked around the room. "What about the fans I bought? Don't you use them?"

"I need an air conditioner," she replied definitively.

Mac just stood there, staring at the unplugged cord to a shiny black tower fan in the corner. Its cord's teeth were bent sideways like it had been pulled at a right angle from the outlet, then stepped on. The room wasn't far from that feeling of disjointed desperation. A need of connection and direction. The only thing that matched was the calamity of the colors on canvas surrounding them inside the stark white porch. So much had been inserted into the space; even the beautiful white multi-pane windows were obscured by paintings.

Mac peeked past his mom into the next room. A large vintage armoire stood away from a wall, its doors bulging, paintings peeking out. There were more stacked tight behind, filling the gap. Sadie followed his eyes. "I know," she repeated. "Don't say anything. I just—it's been really rough for me. Dying has made me not want to do anything." She broke down. "I really don't want to go anywhere. I've been crying every day, and I don't want you to see the inside of my home."

Mac took a deep breath and stepped forward to embrace her again. This time she didn't resist. As he held her, he let his gaze drift away from the living room past another window that separated the inner room from the porch. He turned slowly and found the flowers and ripe lemons again on the tree outside, then remembered he was still holding the lemon from her garden. "It's okay, Mom. We aren't in a rush," he replied, rocking her. "I saw you pulled out the ladder." He handed her the lemon. "I'll see what's wrong with the light." Mac gently patted her shoulder before turning away.

When his mother retreated back inside, he turned and tried to take the setting in with fresh eyes and an open mind. Immediately, he wanted to pick up all the pieces of chewed animal toys on the floor. He wanted to sweep up the ash and brush the dog fur away. He wanted to toss out the beaten couch covered with a throw blanket.

But he knew that would upset his mom if he told her this. And he knew she'd just fill that space with more stuff.

He stayed on the porch listening for her return as he scanned what he thought could stay and what should go. It was easy for him, his right eye twitching like a laser beam incinerator every time he saw something dated or decayed. When he scanned the room a second time, he saw through items he'd vaporized as if they were already gone. Within a few minutes, it was decided. Except for her desk, armoire, and art on the walls, most of her things could go. Those staple items were the only keepers.

He stepped outside and eyed the solar light above the ladder. He wondered if his mom had actually moved the ladder since returning from the hospital or if it had been there for years. He didn't know.

As he began to climb, his mom called out to him, but it was indecipherable, so Mac called back, "What was that? I can't hear you."

Sadie appeared at the door beneath him. "What are you doing here?"

Mac stopped fidgeting with the light and looked down. "I'm doing what I said I would do, Mom. Nadine and I talked about this."

"Oh, Mac." She sighed. "I don't wanna go to LA. I'm having a hard enough time trying to keep it together here."

Mac's heart sunk. Dropping his head, he replied, "But it will be good for us."

"I haven't seen you in two years. You think you can just show up and everything will be great. Look who is here! Yay," she said sarcastically.

Mac took a deep breath and replied, "Yeah, I do," matter-of-factly. "I just came from the other side of the country to be with you, Mom."

"I don't think you have your priorities straight. Look around—there's a lot to do here."

"And we'll do some of it before we go. And we'll do some more when we get back."

Sadie stood silently, looking at her garden. After a beat, she asked, "Why is it so convenient that you come now?"

"Who said it was convenient?" he replied. "We love you. Just because we don't live here anymore doesn't mean we don't care."

Sadie said nothing and remained stone-faced.

"And what is going on in the neighborhood? I just had the most bizarre encounter at the off-ramp near Home Depot."

"What are you talking about? The homeless people?"

"Yeah. When did they show up?"

"I've been feeding them."

"By yourself?"

Sadie said nothing and clenched her jaw.

"I don't feel good about that, Mom. A lot of these people are dangerous."

"Don't be ridiculous. You don't know what you're talking about. We need to save these people."

"Save these people? These people you wanna save are not stable."

"Not all of them."

"No, just most of them. And depending on their mood swing and time of night, maybe the rest. What I saw at the corner was aggression. Did you see their eyes and missing teeth?"

Another long silence.

"This is a whole new level of addiction. Heroin, meth, drugs I've never even heard of. This is bad. Since when do homeless people sleep at the off-ramp? It's quite a tactical adventure coming to see you, Mom."

"Don't you watch the news?"

"I didn't know it had gotten this bad in California."

"You're always somewhere saving people. Why don't you go save them?" Sadie said, pointing her thumb west.

"Those folks look like they need rehab."

"You should pay attention to the news."

Mac rubbed his forehead. "A third of those people are drug addicts, Mom. And another third, mentally ill. I don't need the news to figure that out."

"Did you give them money?"

Mac took a deep breath, his patience draining. "Don't you know what I do for a living, Mom? I don't support drug addicts. I help people whose homes have been destroyed. From hurricanes. Tornadoes. Cyclones. Earthquakes. Natural disasters. Like the fires we're having here."

Sadie raised her hands above her head. "Oh my God, this is gonna be a hell of a trip." Then she moaned as agony spread across her face.

Mac came down the ladder.

She grimaced and waved him off. "Don't touch me. I'm fine."

Mac took another look at her and obeyed. "You're not fine. You just had a heart attack."

"Hardly."

A stalemate.

"FEMA work is eighteen-hour days, seven days a week, four-month stints at a time, Mom. At least for me. First boots on the ground, saving lives. And I came here to save yours."

There was a long pause before Sadie spoke. "Will it be smoky in LA?"

CHAPTER 2

The beady eyes hovered over the man like a cat watched for mice. Anxious with anticipation, calculating and salivating until its mouth became drools of saliva. The blueprints that lay beside him were not unique. They were ordinary and urban, repeated everywhere in the world a million times over. The colors would change, but the palette was always the same with anonymous rental apartments. The exits to stairways, emergency doors, fire alarms, smoke detectors, parking ratios to occupants. Minimums and maximums and code violations and everything else not exciting with such undistinguished buildings.

At least for him. The only thing that made sense was the money that flowed. And that was what he was waiting for. The money.

The plan had been close to perfect, and no laws had been broken. At least none that could be traced back to him. He reminded himself that things take time and time was on his side. The plan took place in a transient environment, which meant people came and went and could easily be manipulated.

He coughed. The biggest obstacle that had been in the way was about to die. Just a little more time.

CHAPTER 3

Mac closed his phone and slipped it into his back pocket. He'd been fidgeting with the light when he heard his mom's footsteps return. "I checked the AQ index. Only fifty in LA. Two fifty here."

"What's an AQ?" Sadie asked from somewhere on the porch below.

"Air quality index, Mom. We're lucky ash isn't blowing today."

"There's been plenty, trust me," she replied sarcastically. "Probably why I had to go to the hospital."

Mac rolled his eyes. "Lucky the wind isn't blowing this way or the air quality would be much worse. Fires can start their own weather storms." Mac rubbed his eyes with his free hand. The other was holding on to the roof for leverage. "Are your eyes burning like mine?"

Sadie didn't reply. She'd disappeared inside.

Mac opened the brown sleeve of the solar light. The seal was broken, and an orange-brown rust covered the end of the corroded spring and battery sleeve. Mac pulled the Phillips-head screwdriver from his pocket and unscrewed the harness. He undid the thin black wire connected to the solar light, unscrewed the light, and tossed the whole contraction to the spotted lawn below.

As he climbed down, he saw his mom through the kitchen window. She was packing a bag of food. He continued down, retrieved the light fixture, and walked out past the gate to the trash can on the street.

There were three bins in total, all at the far corner of the property tucked into an insert in the fence line. Green, brown, and blue. He pondered the blue and opted for the brown, saying to himself as he scanned the yard, "When brown, flush it down." But then he immediately reached back in to retrieve it and place the junk in the blue can, letting the lid fall closed.

He returned to the gate and looked around. The yard still had remnants of Tintin's turds scattered about randomly. The making of his last tiny shits before he dove into the afterlife.

Mac continued around the back of the house and found a pitched shovel against one barren peach tree. Like the tree and fence, the shovel was gray and bleached by the sun. He grabbed the faded shovel and made his way around the yard to the most obvious and alarming poops in full view.

After he collected five turds, he made his way back to the bins. This time he contemplated placement of Tintin's turds, brown or green. Balancing the spade with his left hand, he reached to the top of the green bin and opened it with his right. Swiftly, he swung the spade up and over the opening, snapped his wrist, and the poop was gone.

Back inside the gate, he surveyed the yard and quickly scouted more poops. A repeat performance ensued, ending at the green bin. Returning to the garden, Mac closed the ladder and returned the shovel to the peach tree. Proceeding on to the back of the house, he tucked the ladder up under a plastic awning and opened the blue door beside it, the laundry room.

To the right side of the dryer, on the ground, lay two rat traps with fresh peanut butter smushed on each lever. Mac thought to himself, "Cats that don't catch mice. *No bueno.*"

Beyond the traps, two green poison cubes lay untouched. He knew the type well. A slow rodent death ensued within twelve hours to two days, depending on how much they ate, how long between meals, and their size. Mac knew anticoagulants like brodifacoum, diphenadione, and warfarin were key ingredients preventing rodents' blood from clotting. Cheap, effective, and terminal.

Mac wondered if those same ingredients were in the processed food his mom had been eating. Then he thought about the correlation between toxic ingredients, meals per day, time on Earth, weight, and so on. It was a despicable calculation that left a grimace on his face and guilt for the judgment placed. He closed the door tight, exiting the room and the guilt with it.

Twenty paces along the side of the house, he was at the rear kitchen door. Gingerly, he turned the handle and entered the house. She was still standing in front of the old stove, brown grocery bag in her hands. "God, it's hot," she complained again to herself.

"Yes, it sure is," he replied, eyeing the grocery bag curiously.

Startled, she turned. "I've put some things together for our drive."

"That's nice. Anything else I can do that's quick and easy?"

Sadie didn't answer him. Instead, she asked, "I wonder how hot it will get at the beach today?"

Mac pulled out his phone, punched two buttons, and asked, "What's the weather in Venice Beach today?" The phone responded in a robotic voice Mac directed toward her. "Today's forecast for Venice is eighty-three degrees and mostly sunny."

"Apparently, it's going to be a lot more comfortable in Venice than here. It must be ninety already. One of several reasons why we should head south sooner than later."

"Oh, Mac," she replied, folding the bag closed. "Don't rush me."

"No rush, Mom," he replied, opening his palms to her. "Can I help with anything else before we go?"

She laughed sarcastically. "I've got a long honey-do list."

"I imagine you do, but we really should get going."

"I'm doing the best I can," she replied, scanning the kitchen.

He followed her eyes. "You gonna wear that mask all the way to LA?"

"Shouldn't you be wearing one?"

"In the field, yeah. But this isn't work, Mom. This is personal. Not our government telling us we have to wear one or we lose our job."

"But you're vaccinated, right?"

"Of course. I have to be."

"It's all so confusing. The news keeps telling us to wear them everywhere."

"I know, Mom. Where are the cats?"

"Hiding under the bed." She pointed in the general vicinity of her bedroom. "Keep the door closed."

Mac took the hint and stepped through the separating door, closing it behind him. Looking behind it, he saw the litter box was clean and tidy. It was a win for Mac—his mom was prepared. All the unnecessary drama of pretending not to go. A small break in the tension, and reassurance that hope and luck and gentle persistence were in play.

Mac pulled out his cell and punched some digits. When the phone lit up, the picture of a cinnamon woman with deep red hair and glasses that screamed "Look at me!" appeared. In bold font below her chin was written *Nadine*. Mac's sister.

The call went to voicemail. Mac smiled as a swaying, energetic voice sounded impenitent from his speaker. "You've reached Nadine. Can't get to the phone. Leave a message." A woman on the move, getting things done, nonapologetic.

He returned the phone to his pocket and rounded the tight corner through the cramped square. "You've got Nadine coming to check in on the house?" he called out before stepping into the bedroom.

"She is going to come down twice while we are away," she called back.

"So she'll check on the cats?"

"Yes, she will check on my babies."

Mac stepped inside and saw the big television that hung from the wall, beaming Fox News Alert without sound. He walked over and turned it off then knelt and looked under the bed. "Where are they? I don't see them."

"Oh, Mac," she replied, sounding irritated. "Then they are out doing what cats do."

Mac surveyed her bedroom. One queen bed with a huge, matching armoire. A matching dresser, two chairs, and a table near the corner window. And paintings on the walls. Lots of them.

The paintings were a variety of sizes and bursting with fantastic color. But they'd been crammed against each other next to the one corner window. The art created one big, borderless collage. It was overwhelming, and Mac cringed at the thought of this resembling any part of his future. "Anything I can help you carry out to the car?" he asked his mom. But to himself, he thought, *What gallery can we drop all these paintings off to?* and *Can we repaint these walls?*

"Yes. My bag next to the bed."

Mac saw the bag at the foot of the armoire and picked it up. "Let's get going. We have to make a quick stop on the way out."

CHAPTER 4

Sadie and Mac were eastbound on a two-lane highway numbered sixty-eight by 10:15 a.m. They were doing forty in a fifty-five-mph zone. Sadie behind the wheel of her Passat with sunglasses on. Mac in the passenger seat without. Neither wore masks.

What Mac did have on his face was fur, not his own. It was accumulating on his five-o'clock stubble and slowly growing into a beard, the Passat going just fast enough to get the hairs airborne but not fast enough to suck them out the window.

Oblivious at first, he had brushed a few tuffs from his face when they tickled his nose. It wasn't until he caught some thicker hair in his hand that his interest piqued. He pinched the course hairs between his fingers and examined them. His mom hadn't been anywhere exotic he was aware of in quite some time. That canceled out yack, llama, and camel. He assessed horse by process of elimination. Then he felt another tingle on his right nostril, and his cheek began to itch.

Half curious and half annoyed, he flipped down the visor and looked in the mirror. Unbeknownst to Mac, hairs had stuck to the thick stubble along his jawline like Velcro to yarn and accumulated into a beard. A few stuck to his eyebrows too. Big hairs and thin hairs in a variety of colors, the most prominent being black. The thin white and curly ones he assessed as Tintin's. They gave a sort of aged appearance. The thicker ones were a colorful blend of pitch black to light brown.

He wondered if his mom knew this was happening and had chosen to say nothing. Or was she oblivious, like the diet she'd given Tintin—and herself? Fifty-fifty either way. Mac didn't know.

The unruly fur was swirling about the car like hay wafting in a storm. He looked down at the speedometer and had an idea. *If I jam my foot on the gas pedal, we can speed up to seventy. Technically not even a Category 1 hurricane. But if I could get her out of the driver's seat and put myself behind the wheel, we might hit a Category 3. That would give the inside of this VW Passat a proper vacuum and clear up this mess.*

He chuckled to himself and flipped the visor up, deciding the beard was an interesting look and would make great conversation. That was if Mom ever looked over at him. He imagined his mom looking at him and seeing twice the amount of fur that was actually there. This image brought about more chuckles.

His mom's love for animals was extensive. "Mom, did you feed horses?"

"No. I don't go on Sundays," she replied, not looking over.

"Oh, what days do you usually go?"

"Whenever I want. They need their treats."

He remembered the horse brush on the floor from this morning. He reached down, felt around, and found it under the edge of the seat at his left heel. It was full of thick black hair. He grabbed a clump from its metal bristle pad and released it out the window, then grabbed two more handfuls and watched them fly away. Then he gripped his beard in one fell swoop and released the hair into the wind.

Mac wondered if his mom noticed these things from behind her glasses, fur flying everywhere when she drove with the windows down. It must have been a sight for tailgaters passing by, clumps of hair flying out the windows like wafts of pot smoke from stoners. He looked in the side mirror. There was a car tailgating them.

Now, Mac's eyes kept darting between the VW's speedometer and the rearview mirror. A canary-yellow Camaro behind them kept speeding up, then drifting back, then speeding up again, like it was building up momentum to pass but was anxiously waiting until safe. When it finally zoomed by, the engine roared loud and guttural. It quickly skated the oncoming traffic and shrank into the distance. As Mac scraped more hair from his chin, he said, "You sure you wouldn't prefer I drive? We've a long way to go."

She bit back, "I know how long it is."

"Okay." He looked back at the thick black hair at his feet and pinched another tuft between his fingers. "Well, it feels good to be moving," he said with glee.

"The air feels good," she said, upbeat.

"I just wished I'd shaved and brought goggles."

Another silence.

Again, Mac felt deflated because Sadie didn't take the bait. Instead, she gave a deep sigh. "I never liked air conditioning."

Mac was thrown by the subject jump but went with it. "Makes my nose run," he replied, hoping for a truce.

She barely glanced at him. "But maybe now at my home because of the heat."

"Right," he replied, squinting his eyes as more hair whirled below. Truth be told, he felt a little dumb. He'd let his mom steer him into agreeing a need for an air conditioner instead of countering with humor. He'd been thinking about the yellow Camaro and how nice it would be to be speeding alongside it, tracking it or taking turns leading the charge all the way to LA with radar detectors blasting in all directions and miles flying by to clear the smoke.

"But not in the car," Sadie said. "The natural wind is better."

"Organic, even," he replied, hoping.

Sadie remained quiet. A few minutes passed before either spoke. Then Mac said, "He was a good dog, and he was good for you."

"Oh, Mac," she burst out. "I feel like this has been the hardest thing for me ever."

"That's why I'm home, Mom," he replied, trying to be sensitive. "To help you tackle this."

"It's been so difficult."

"Maybe I should drive."

"I want to drive."

"But you're feeling emotional. I think it would be best if—"

"I need to drive," she replied, firmly cutting him off.

"Okay." He paused a beat. "I get it. I know Tintin was your best friend. You've been buddies a long time."

"He was such a huge part of my life!"

"I know," Mac repeated and sat another beat. "But he was in poor health. Really bad, right?"

Mac watched Sadie let the question sink in. Slowly, she came around to nodding and chewing on the inside of her lips.

This conjured up images for Mac of Tintin's teeth. In his mind, they were horrid. He couldn't bring himself to comment. The dog had just died. So instead, he said, "He had the perfect name, though, for a mini schnauzer."

"Yes, he did."

"You gave me all those Belgian cartoon books when I was little. Big Sur, no television. All we did was read. And play outside. Tintin and his faithful companion Snowy."

"You remind me a lot of him."

"Who? Tintin or the dog, Mom?" Mac replied with a sharp look.

"You're always getting into all sorts of adventures. Traversing here and there."

"I'm on an adventure with you right now." He laughed, scratching his cheek. "So I'm Tintin and you're the dog, Snowy?"

Sadie said nothing.

"Truth be told, you spoiled him rotten. Rotten to the jawbone, to be exact."

"Oh, Mac, it wasn't that bad," she said, brushing it aside.

"Wasn't that bad, you say? Let's review. Rotten teeth. Horrible breath." Mac waited, then, "Did you have any guilt about Tintin's health?" throwing the question away as if it were light as the floating fur.

"No…"

Mac glanced back, then quickly straight ahead again. "Tintin was eating people food a long time. Little bits of oven-roasted chicken. Sautéed baby carrots and peas with lots of butter. You two were eating the same things for years, Mom."

"That's part of his diet, Mac. Look it up."

"Everything but dry kibble, which would have cleaned his teeth from tarter and plaque. That same clogging-arteries plaque in your system that the stents are for."

She snarled, "My teeth are fine."

"The reason your teeth are fine is because you brush them. Tintin didn't get that luxury. I think what happened to Tintin's arteries will happen to yours if you don't make big changes going forward."

"This is not the time to talk about it."

"When is the time? Let's schedule that."

Sadie didn't reply.

CHAPTER 5

Mac watched the burned mountains as they crawled at a snail's pace east. He'd cleared most of the wafting animal fur but knew an increase in speed would bring rise to more. A quagmire. He hadn't driven this slow on a highway since he was in a military convoy halfway around the world.

After a little time had passed, Sadie said, "Your brother. When was the last time you saw him?"

Mac shuffled, adjusting in the seat. "It had been a while, Mom."

"Hmm. He didn't call me at the hospital."

Slowly Mac replied, "That… would be difficult for him. Theoretically."

"What's that supposed to mean?"

"Never mind. When was the last time you saw Nadine?"

"I saw her at the hospital when I woke up."

"Yeah, you had us all worried."

"You never called me."

"I apologize, Mom. I didn't know until yesterday."

Sadie paused, then said, "While at the hospital, your sister and I had a serious conversation. We talked about you coming here."

"And how did that go?"

"Are you listening or talking?"

"Both. That's how conversations work."

"Why are you being difficult?" Sadie said, gripping the steering wheel with her fists.

Mac hesitated. "I'm sorry."

"I didn't want you here."

"I figured you'd say that. But you can't do this alone. I know that, and so does Nadine. And she has her hands full with her own family. She can't hold your hand through this from a hundred and fifty miles away."

"But you can?"

Mac took a breath. "I can try."

They stared at each other, neither giving way until Mac's eyes softened. He looked ahead at the road and gently put his hand on the steering wheel just before they drifted into the yellow bumps on the highways edge. Sadie followed. "Okay. Can we talk about something else now?"

"Sure."

"When was the last time you spent time with Nadine?"

"Before she was pregnant."

Sadie reacted as if the answer wasn't sufficient and sniffed. "What were you up to?"

"We took a trip to Jamaica."

Sadie looked surprised. "I don't remember you telling me about it. Was it nice?"

"Truth be told, Mom, we tried to tell you. But you were so absorbed in the artists you were meeting there, you never gave us the chance. So we never got around to it. And maybe"—he paused—"you never asked?"

"I'm sorry," she replied, pursing her lips. "Did you enjoy it?"

"You're asking now?" he replied sarcastically.

"Better late than never."

Mac's mind began racing through what he could tell his mom and what he needed to edit out. He had become accustomed to this process, as it made their time shared easier. Less argumentative. "We drank coconut rum and swam in the ocean. It was fantastic."

"Sounds wonderful. Caribbean warm waters." She beamed and began tapping the steering wheel to imaginary music.

"Yeah, the flight took forever, so we started with rum as soon as we landed. Then when we got to the hotel, we just walked right into the ocean."

They both smiled, enjoying the commonality of the harmonious moment shared, then Sadie asked, "You have a nice time overall?"

Mac pondered the question. "Yes. Like we are gonna do on this trip."

"It's dangerous there. You know that."

"It was good at the time." Mac said slowly, "And we never left the resort."

"There were things I really liked about Jamaica and"— Sadie dropped to a serious tone—"things that annoyed the shit out of me."

"*Really?*" Mac replied. "Like what kind of *shit?* And when were you there?"

"Don't be so naive. You know what I'm talking about," she snapped back.

"The extremes of wealth and poverty?" Mac asked.

"And racism."

"You don't really see it in the resorts, Mom."

"But you do with some of the whites that have been there for generations," she fired back. "We were lucky to get out of there when we did. Your father was so brave marrying me."

Mac thought about his father and what they'd endured, then softly said, "Yeah, you two were beautiful together."

"I miss what we stood for. What we fought against together."

"You two were a big part of the equal rights movement back in the day."

"I am now too—for horses."

Mac laughed.

"Don't laugh," she replied, wagging her finger. "They add more value to our lives than you know. And dogs as well."

Mac turned to look at his mom. "We just went from men to dogs in a flash."

"Man's best friend," she replied, smiling. "They're really genius in fighting depression."

Mac thought back to the ranch where she'd raised him and his siblings in Big Sur. "Fourteen cats, five dogs, geese, chickens, a peacock, and doves. Plus, one spirited billy goat. Fun times in Big Sur. No time for depression."

"I had to keep you kids busy doing something. Learning responsibility and caring for animals was a big part of becoming who you are."

Smiling, Mac replied, "I wouldn't have had it any other way. And you protected us by moving away from all of that prejudice."

"I was running away, but you're right. I was protecting you too."

"I didn't even know what racism was until I was eleven."

"What happened?"

"Sixth grade. I was waiting in line for my music class, and one of the kids called me a nigger. Kid named Brandon. Trumpet player."

"Ouch."

"No. Not really."

"Why not?"

"That's what's funny."

"Why? What did you do?"

"At first, nothing. I didn't know what the word meant."

"And when you did learn what the word meant?"

Mac smiled. "After I asked the librarian, I punched him in the mouth. Couldn't play the horn for a week."

"Good for you." Sadie shook her head. "I don't remember that happening, but good for you."

"Yeah. Everyone's got an opinion until they get punched in the mouth," he said reflectively. "A different time then. You could do that in sixth grade. But it gets more complicated as you get older."

"That's part of growing up."

Silence fell. Mac wondered what his mom was thinking about as he looked at her profile before she said, "You can drive when we stop for gas."

He smiled. "Sounds good," he replied, though he'd found momentary solace in the slow pace.

CHAPTER 6

A t that exact moment, in a medical building three hundred miles south, two doctors shared news. It was disappointing. Numerous tests had been taken, exploratory surgeries performed, sophisticated equipment inserted, and all had failed. The bloodwork was the same. No improvement.

As pragmatic surgeons, they'd exhausted all known medical procedures and explored a few others still in development. They had been hopeful, optimistic, and tactful in their execution. One after another, each of their efforts had failed, and now they'd incurred another setback. The pandemic. The abyss of doubt was beginning to rear its ugly head.

Telling someone they should get their affairs in order was not an easy thing. It meant their life was over and death was imminent, overhanging and without escape. It meant every option to extend life had either been exhausted, wasn't affordable, or was an unrealistically painful and tragic existence.

Once the patient accepted that, who would he tell? Those closest to him? Would they already know? Did they need to know? Could they even suspect?

What if his dying wasn't obvious? The physical signs were nonexistent on his exterior. But his interior was an inferno of infested organs. It was not cancer, but something doctors had never seen before. There was no name for it because it'd never been diagnosed. Ever.

That was the issue being discussed with these two doctors. The time allotted for life wasn't long at all. Under three months. There would be certain tells that would signal organs shutting down, and once that happened, things would turn dire rather quickly. Not that they weren't already. The pandemic was in full swing and the rate of contagion skyrocketing. But both doctors believed miracles were possible. Even though scientific evidence wasn't present, miracles had happened before.

Yes, they wished the pandemic weren't in the way. Didn't everybody? It had every medical person on the planet scrambling to find a cure for COVID. And that limited the scope of what was possible for these two doctors sending samples to colleagues around the country. Their efforts were thwarted at every turn.

The curly-haired doctor adjusted his round glasses. "I thought I'd live a lot longer." It was a sad statement. A reflection of the condition he was in. His clothing looked too big on him and his demeanor was nervous as he sat in the patient's chair across the big oak table.

"Lot of people dying right now. Seems the 'in' thing to do."

"Like I said before, I'm gonna go home and listen to the waves. Play my horn. Some Coltrane or Miles maybe."

"You still drinking?"

The doctor smiled but didn't answer.

"It would be nice to give your liver a chance."

"What's the point?"

* * *

Now the minutes flew by as Mac and Sadie scooted sixty-eight past her favorite hole-in-the-wall cowboy diner to the 101 south. Through Spreckels, the smoky air thickened, lying stagnant on the Salinas Valley floor. They quickly rolled up their windows. The smoke continued past Chualar, past Gonzales and Greenfield, and beyond. A massive billboard read, "It's happening in Soledad." Mac and Sadie weren't sure of what was happening in Soledad other than a maximum-security men's prison. But the sign was there, so apparently "it" was. Then came King City, the last of the Salinas Valley, the smoke still thick and heavy. All the while, they kept gazing west at the scorched mountains in silhouette, burned black by the River Fire that had raged just a week before.

"How was my childbirth, Mom? Did I come out screaming and angry, or was I easy?"

"Oh, Mac. What is going on?"

"I wanna know, and we've a lot of road ahead," he answered optimistically. "Plus, I was your first," he said proudly. "I'm the oldest. What was it like?"

"Painful," she moaned. Then a relaxed smile crossed her face. "It's *still* painful."

Mac chuckled. "Did I come out kicking and crying? Like I'd been in a fire?"

"No!" Contorting her face, she asked, "Where do you come up with these ideas?"

"I'm half you, Mom. You have a fantastic imagination and heaps of experiences. I want to squeeze it all out of you before you're gone." He followed with a sinister grin, "While we have the time. We are going to explore all sorts of things. You haven't been down to LA for years, and a lot has changed. It'll be good for us."

He poked her shoulder with his pinky finger.

Flinching, she said, "Aren't you done with LA, Mac? Haven't you moved on?"

Mac sat back and looked into the smoke. "Yes and no. Part of that life, those experiences, I'd like to write about. Like you do, only different. I'm no poet, but I enjoy writing about things, sometimes."

"What kinds of things?" she prodded.

"Well, characters for one. People I've met or worked with. I was only in LA five years, but the navy too. My travels, I guess."

"But you can't talk about a lot of that stuff," she said, cutting him off.

"Not everything, no," he said, rubbing his knees. "But some things." Then he took a deep breath. "I guess it all goes way back to childhood, really. Growing up in Big Sur. You."

"Me?" she shrieked.

"You as my mom. And Dad too, of course," he continued. "Summers in New York maybe, but Big Sur was... better for me."

"It was important you spent time with your father."

"Absolutely, Mom. I wouldn't change it for the world. Those experiences, you pushing us, the juxtaposition between Big Sur and Dad's three-level apartment in Brooklyn."

"Williamsburg."

"Yes. Across from the old Miller Beer building on Broadway."

"It was a nice place."

"It was. I wish he'd bought it. Probably worth a fortune now. That whole area is really hip and just a bridge away from the city."

"What bridge is it?"

"Williamsburg Bridge. Seventy West Broadway."

"You remember the address?"

"I remember most things, Mom," he said matter-of-factly. "Elephant brain." He tapped his skull. "Good genes," and pointed at her. He looked down at her left foot and up at her thick legs. "How are your legs this morning? I forgot to ask."

"They hurt. But it's really my left wrist that's bothering me today."

Mac looked at her wrist, which was now wrapped in a beige brace. It looked like a cheap fix from a pharmacy. "Then let me drive, Mom. This is silly. I'm willing and able. We could have taken my car, for Chrissake."

"Too flashy."

"The truck?" he questioned back.

"Oh, I thought you meant the sports car."

"I knew you wouldn't want to take that. You'd say we were a target."

"We would be. There's entirely too much poverty right now, and this president isn't helping the situation."

"I don't want to talk about the president right now."

"I don't either."

"Cool, just saying. No politics, no religion, and whatever the third thing is we're not supposed to talk about."

"You trying to be funny?"

"No."

Mac knew bringing up two years ago wouldn't help anything. The thought spiraled through his mind with waves of dread and made him feel small. He imagined short periods of sunshine and relief, then suddenly without warning, dark clouds summoning torrential downpours of uncontrollable tears from his mom. Losing Tintin had brought it all back to the surface.

Part of his mom was wise and evolved, while another was still a little girl in a bubble. That part existed in a world of animals and butterflies. A child's world. And maybe that was the age when her conscience began to comprehend what was happening, so she blocked out what was scary. The frozen part of her was stuck in that time.

Mac wasn't a psychologist, but he knew a few and had done some therapy of his own. It was his sister Nadine's idea and helped him navigate with perspective between those he felt worthy of his time and those not capable or permitting. The sessions' work made him very conscious and protective of his boundaries with people.

Mac said, "You're lucky you got the time that you did with Tintin. He was a great dog. Taking this trip will be really good for you. For us. And we will get healthy together. Get right back to the way it was—"

"You can never go back," she cut in. "Only forward."

"Yes, I know, Mom. But what I meant was maybe we will find another Tintin."

"It's too soon."

"No, of course."

"I feel like those mountains right now," his mom added.

Mac looked up at the mountains, burned black and ominous. "You do?"

It was hard not to acknowledge the fire's wrath driving south on the 101. It loomed constant and kept creeping back into their conversations. A scarred footprint a mile dead west. Below, among once-green fields of spinach, cabbage, and artichokes, lay vineyards stretched as far as the eye could see, right up against the charred black foothills of soot and ash.

"Something else is bothering me, Mac."

"Yeah. What's that, Mom?"

"Your brother."

CHAPTER 7

Sadie held the wheel firmly as she steered the little car down the highway. A few times her lips moved, eyebrows raised, but nothing came out. Mac thought his mom was searching for a way to present what was bothering her as diplomatically as possible.

It was weighing on him. A complex tug and pull full of speculation. And Mac had been gone two years. A lot could happen.

A lot *had* happened.

Being absent strained their relationship. So, Mac was running blind, having alienated himself. Disappearing into work to avoid family drama felt good on one hand but irresponsible on another. Plain and simple, it felt wrong, which was odd for Mac. He was usually right about most things, but as time went on, he'd been less right and more uncertain. Specifically, about his mom's mental state. Her beliefs, views, and direction.

All the telltale signs were there for his mom, though. Mac could see it a thousand yards away. Abuse, neglect, depression. Void of proper contact, and unwanted. The abuse and punishment constant through time and space. Then she left the space, and anything which was left was a flag. A trigger. Which created an impulse to further move away from it.

So she ran. Far and wide, the arc heavy and burdensome. And it was depressing, plain and simple. Who wanted to be around that? Not anyone in their right mind.

So he ran too. Back to his job.

But he wasn't conclusive about his brother's doings. He hadn't spoken to Tristan recently and was skeptical of conclusions his brother had last presented. He knew whatever he foresaw his mom asking, it would be deep, and he wanted to tread lightly.

"Can you open that bag? I'm getting hungry."

"Sure. Why don't we stop at the next gas station? I've got to use the bathroom. We can fill up the tank and switch seats."

"Okay. I want to know what's going on with Tristan," she said, looking over at Mac.

He smiled back, the box in his mind checked. "I don't know, but I'm sure we can figure it out."

They took the next exit and pulled into a Chevron. The station was basic, two islands and four pumps and a cement box with a flat roof. The exit circled the building, with an access road along a field that quickly darted back onto the highway. Mac climbed out and stretched. The air still smelled foul. He pulled a credit card from his back pocket and inserted it into the pump. He looked back at Sadie, who was digging around in the grocery bag.

"Where's the cheese I put in here?" she asked. He could barely hear her over the sound of cars whizzing past on the highway. "I can't seem to find it."

"Because it's not in the bag," Mac replied gingerly, leaning toward the passenger window.

"Why not? Where is it?"

"I gave it to Greg."

"Greg?" she gasped.

"Yes, when we dropped off my car at his shop. I gave him one of the apples and the cheese."

"Why? Why did you do that?" Sadie asked, dumbfounded. "I bought that cheese for us."

"Yes, but we're going to do the juice diet—part of the health plan, remember?"

"But we are not in LA yet! That was goat cheese."

"And Greg will enjoy it," Mac replied, pushing the gas nozzle into the hole. "He's not on our diet."

She scowled. "That cheese was expensive."

"Doesn't Greg deserve something for changing my oil while storing my car a whole week?"

"That's not the point, Mac. That would have been delicious with the apples. I would have shared it with you."

"Yes, it would have... if it was part of our diet."

"Apple is a fruit. Fruit makes juice."

"Yes, but the juices during the day are pressed juices mainly made up of water. Not fiber. It's very specific, and there's no dairy involved. That means no goat cheese."

"This is terrible. My body hurts."

"Mom, part of the reason you are needing all these surgeries is because of the food you've been eating."

"You don't know what you are talking about! My wrists hurt from carrying cameras my whole life, Mac, not the food!"

"And if you were vegan, you'd have less arthritic pain as well."

"How dare you tell me about this. I know my body."

"Do you? The pain in your legs is from clogged circulation, which is related to your diet. I've seen you binge on food that clogs your arteries."

"You're an asshole. That was sneaky what you did."

"An asshole who cares, Mom."

"Tristan wouldn't have done that."

"Tristan was fifty pounds overweight the last time I saw him. Just like you."

Sadie's face turned fire engine red. "We can turn around right now," she demanded, looking back over her shoulder north. Then she crumpled the bag like a bitter baker kneads bread.

"We are not turning around," he said calmly, then shifted his posture and dropped his shoulders. Ever so gently, he added, "I'm sorry, Mom. I shouldn't have said that. That was reactionary, and I apologize."

Sadie scowled, and Mac shook his head. She turned back and dug into the bag again, retrieving two apples and some salted almonds. Mac looked up to see the gas had stopped. He clicked the lever to restart the flow, then headed toward the stand-alone building. Halfway across the lot, he realized he didn't have a mask and turned around.

Sadie was eating the almonds when he arrived. She bit into her apple while scanning for keys. The look on her face told Mac it wasn't a great pairing in the valley of wine and cheese. "Sorry again, Mom. It will get easier, I promise."

"That was really rude."

"I'm sorry, please forgive me," he replied. "Let me make it up to you and drive the rest of the way." He pulled her car keys from his pocket.

"Seriously, you took the keys?"

Mac nodded. "Jump in the passenger seat and I'll drive. It's better."

"Are you really sorry?"

"I am," he replied solemnly. They considered each other for a few moments.

"So what's really up with Tristan?" she shot back.

"My brother. The man of grit, guts, and gumption?"

"Gumption?"

"Yeah. He's super resourceful."

"Are you being sarcastic?"

"No, but I do gotta go to the bathroom, so we can dig into that when I get back." He leaned in, grabbed his mask, and was gone, keys still in hand.

Mac crossed the short parking lot and came to the boxed building's single glass door. A handwritten sign on a taped cardboard box read "bathroom around back." The bathroom was disgusting, a slurry of unmapped terrain navigating through trash on the floor and uncleaned urinals.

Mac immediately spun around and exited as soon as the waft of germ-infested muck hit his face. He surmised the only reason it didn't stink from the outside was because of the burned cinder smell permeating the warm breeze.

He headed for the nearest tree in the back parking lot that separated the building from the highway. In the valley surrounding the structure, there were plenty. In the mountains in the distance, not so much.

Sadie was nibbling away on her apple and more almonds when Mac returned. "I'm going to drive a bit more," she said, still seated in the driver's seat.

"Okay," he replied.

CHAPTER 8

Sadie was still driving as Mac said scathingly, "No, Mom, that's not how it happened. It didn't go down like that."

"Then tell me," she said. "What started it?"

"I brought a gallery person by, and she didn't like the paintings."

Sadie thought a moment. "Was she a critic?"

Mac took a breath and, on the exhale, said, "She was the woman I'd been seeing. It started with an insult Tristan said about her, and it spiraled from there."

"You didn't tell her what he said, did you?" she asked, eyes widening with concern.

"Are you trying to get a rise out of me?" Mac asked. "No, of course I didn't tell her. I defended her." Mac shook his head. "Every time you open your eyes wide, you try to raise the narrative to drama. All I'm doing is trying to tell you what happened."

"Oh, go ahead, then," she clapped back, her tone sounding derogatory.

"Tristan is stubborn. He's half of you—"

"He's half of you too."

"Can I finish please?" Mac paused. "He's stubborn, and so was the woman I was seeing at the time. They butted heads. That's all. But I do not see the point in talking about someone that is no longer in my life. Lesson learned, moving on."

At least that's how Mac took it, sitting stiffly in the passenger seat. He knew every bone in her body felt this subject reeked of emotional danger for her. Like a pull-and-release sawed-off shotgun shooting huge metal targets at close range. Knowing shrapnel could ricochet back and tear both their eyes out. He didn't like being vulnerable either.

The truth of the matter was Mac's relationship with his mother was very much like his relationship with his brother.

Strained.

The idea of conquering these two subjects with one drawn out conversation during the long drive made him hopeful but not convinced. It was risky too. He didn't like the idea of being left on the side of the 101. And he'd ditched the woman shortly after the altercation anyway. He'd defended his brother.

He started in again. "Each time we share a meal or get together for some art event, the meal or event feels more important than getting any understanding of how we feel for each other."

Sadie looked over at Mac and smiled. "You don't always have to tell someone you love them for them to know."

"Thank you, Mom. I only want whatever Tristan wants for himself, and I don't know what that is. I'm sure it's something beautiful. Maybe it's his father's paintings being recognized, maybe to extend his father's legacy. I don't know. And I don't know why he doesn't call you. I can't speak to that."

"What kind of English is that?" she asked.

"What are you talking about? Are we having a real conversation or what? I'm trying to tell you my feelings."

"To that?"

A solemn feeling of sadness moved through his body. "For him. I can't speak for him, but I can speak for me." Mac paused, then pushed onward. "You're not the easiest to be around. Things you don't need to have an opinion on, you seem to push into them anyway. Regardless of being asked not to."

Mac bent forward and put his hands on his knees, rubbing and massaging them in slow circular motions. He closed his eyes and imagined gentle ocean waves breaking on a beach with a waterfall. He pictured his mom on the beach walking along the shoreline, not giving two shits about anything. No complaining. No judging. No gossiping, nothing. Just walking and observing.

He smelled fresh salt air and watched seagulls and sandpipers along the shoreline. A waterfall and an imaginary stream flowed into the sea. He saw wildflowers and poppies in the grass at the fall's edge. He rolled his view to the right and saw a red umbrella, its cloth torn and disheveled, blowing in the breeze, and wondered what that was about. Then he looked back toward his mom, but she was gone. In her place were snowy plovers. The little brown-and-white birds were running in the sand.

"What do you think Tristan's mad about?" Sadie's voice startled Mac, and he opened his eyes, wondering how long he'd dozed off. "You think it's because I never married his dad?"

Mac rubbed his eyes, sitting up.

"Maybe that's it," she said. "I didn't marry Castony, and he feels less than because of it."

Mac shook his head, yawning. "No, Mom, Tristan's dad was an asshole. It's good you didn't marry him."

"Yeah, he was!" Sadie exclaimed. "You know, one time he gave me a black eye—"

Mac raised his eyebrows and puckered his mouth in disappointment. "Yeah, Mom," he said, sitting up in the seat. "I remember you telling me about that thing in Choomblahblah."

"Cochabamba," she corrected him.

"Okay. But he beat you up more than once. And unfortunately, you stayed." *There it is, raw and true*, he thought to himself. He watched his mom as she reflected back more than thirty years ago.

"That was one hell of a trip," she continued. "He had us staying on a mountain peak in the middle of nowhere."

"Yeah?" He examined her profile. "That could be cool."

"Every day, he would travel down the mountain to his studio and paint."

"He didn't paint on the mountaintop?"

"No, he'd go down the hill."

Mac furrowed his brows. The fact Art didn't allow her in his studio was interesting. "Was it hot there like it is here?"

"Yeah, I think it was," she said simply.

Mac was elsewhere. "I still can't get past him punching you. Or me, for that matter. I don't think I will ever forget or forgive that," he said reluctantly. "Nope, I don't think I ever will."

"What are you talking about?" she asked, letting off the gas pedal.

"When he hit me. Not deserved." He turned to face her. "Nor when he hit you for a finger in the face or whatever it was you did. Pathetic."

Sadie didn't respond. She appeared confused and turned her gaze back through the windshield to the road. She pressed the gas pedal down again, and the car accelerated.

Mac figured she was either back in the past or forward, away from ugly reflections, broken mirrors, and shattered yesterdays. He continued anyway, but slowly. "I know it because I'd learned way back when I was a five-year-old. In his Oakland studio. When Tristan was pooping on the floor. I thought they were little Indian Choctaw beads. His poops. How was I supposed to know? We were in a house full of art. Everything was beads and necklaces, paintings, sculptures. Everywhere. I was innocent, and he fucking hit me. For those little poops."

"Jeez, Mac, your language."

"I'd never been hit by a fucking adult. I knew right then he was incapable. It didn't surprise me when you told me he'd beaten you up. You know he did some fucked-up things later in life too, but let it go, right?"

"I did let it go. I finally got away. I had to pretend I was going to see some mutual friends. I hid Tristan and snuck off in the night. It was crazy and dangerous."

"Sounds it. Deception. Abuse. Mountain peaks," Mac chirped.

"You're not being very cooperative," she said.

"Neither are you. I've been trying to drive for an hour. I just wanna know how this helps us, is all."

"And I'm trying to tell you in my own way about what I've gone through to raise you kids. Connection. That's what we're doing, Mac. You don't need to be smart with me!" She pointed at him.

"Okay." He looked at her finger. "I apologize. I'm listening, Mom."

"Then I—" She looked at Mac to make sure he wasn't going to interrupt. "My girlfriend helped me escape with

Tristan on a train. A train with chickens and llamas and everything South American you can imagine."

"Wow, Mom. That was the right thing to do. And brave."
Mac meant it.

"Yeah, but the train broke down. Thank God there was a guy on the side of the track with a truck. He let us climb in the back with all his stuff. The men from the train were complaining because he didn't have room for them. But the man defended us, saying he only had room for us. Only us."

"The three of you?"

"Yes." She nodded.

"Didn't that concern you? That he might want to rob— or rape—you?"

"Let me tell the story!" She paused. "Then that night, some men with guns—"

Mac rolled his eyes.

"—tried to stop the truck we were in. I remember the truck slowing and hearing yelling. I looked through the front window of the cab and saw men blocking the road ahead. Our driver leaned over, reached into the glove box, and grabbed a pistol. He yelled for us to stay down and sped toward the men while firing at them. I could see flashes from the barrels of their guns. They were shooting at us. I quickly got as low as I could to the floor. I was so naive."

"Yeah, I see that now."

"I wasn't prepared for the world, but I went out into it anyway," she said defiantly.

A long silence followed. No music; no talking. Just the hum of his mom's tires on the road and the silhouette of burned black mountains to the west.

CHAPTER 9

M ac's phone rang. He pulled it from his back pocket and looked at the caller ID. Dawn McKenzie. Mac pressed the button and accepted the call. "MacGuffin here."

"This is Dawn McKenzie with Urban Search and Rescue Task Force. Is it MacGuffin? I was informed you prefer Mac."

"Mac is fine. Thanks for asking."

"Well Mac, I owe you an apology. Donald Kerry told me you didn't get my message for a week."

"Yeah, that's true. A phone call would have been more effective or an SMS."

"I didn't realize you were working the inspections and volunteering for my Search and Rescue Unit. That's a lot on a plate. Hell of a thing to do."

"I figured you could use the help and being in the rubble at night is often more effective when all is quiet."

"I was told you were responsible for saving three."

"Our team dug them out. Yes, ma'am."

"Please don't call me ma'am. You'll make me feel old."

"Okay. How can I help you?"

"I'm extending your leave another week if you need it. Kerry looked up your punch list and told me you're hovering at the top of the completion list for the whole region. We're offering incentives to make a bigger impact, so you'll be receiving an additional bonus of two thousand dollars."

"Well, thank you. I'll give it to my mom."

There was a pause on the line. "I'm sure she'll appreciate it. Please come find me when you get back."

"Okay," he said and hung up.

Sadie asked, "Were you serious about giving something to me? What is it?"

Mac gazed west to the fields and burned mountains beyond. "My two-thousand-dollar bonus for exceeding the quota within a given period of time."

"Well, that's exciting."

"Mom, do you want me to drive?"

Sadie tapped the steering wheel. "So why do you think Tristan won't return my messages?"

Upbeat and positive, Mac shrugged his left shoulder toward her. "I'd kinda like to drive."

When she didn't respond, Mac rolled his eyes. "Mom, I am not going to call him for you. He has been included in a group text, which probably annoys him. He is a social media guy. Reach out through Facebook. That is his thing, I think. That or Instagram. Definitely not TikTok."

"I don't get it. I apologized to him twice."

"What did you apologize about?" Mac responded, waving his finger. "Did you give him business advice?"

"I told him Charles Boyd was a sham."

"Charles Boyd the flutist? There's a name I haven't heard in decades."

"Yes, Charles Boyd the flutist. I told him he better not trade any of his dad's paintings for anything that guy was offering. Make sure he gets cash when he sells them."

Mac bit his lip and scratched his nose. He knew Tristan had done that very thing. Months ago. Charles had made Tristan some promises, including taking him on tour, and

Tristan had handed him a painting. But no money was exchanged.

Mac treaded lightly and began, "Tristan is a smart guy. I'm sure he created a list of potential buyers that would help grow his dad's value as a painter. Aren't painters' works usually worth more when they are dead than alive, typically?"

"Yes," she replied, keeping her eyes on the road.

"Tristan has an affinity for faces, especially musicians. And his repertoire probably includes Jon Hendricks, Hugh Masekela, and all the guys that frequented our home when we were little."

"That makes sense."

"We were neighbors with the Beach Boys, for Chrissake, Mom. I think Tristan and Al Jardine were still friends when we left Big Sur. All the musicians from the Monterey Pop Festival from way back."

"But they're all dead, son," she reminded him.

"I know, Mom, except for Al," Mac replied. "Maybe Tristan has some of their art now from his dad. Maybe that's part of his plan. To reconnect with those guys from way back—or their kids, because they're dead—and see what art pieces he's got of value. I mean, your art was in the mix too, right?"

"Yeah, but all my things were stolen."

"You gotta let that go, Mom. Past is past and all that."

"Not so easy to do. Do you know—"

"Let's stay on Tristan and his dad. Please," he said. "Whatever he has in his dad's studio must have some value. I mean, Castony was hanging out with arguably the most influential people for equal rights on the West Coast at that time."

"We had a lot of meetings and went to a lot of social marches together."

"Yeah. See, Mom? That could be part of it," he said optimistically.

"That's true," she replied, her right hand tapping the steering wheel. "But why won't Tristan call me? If you know, you should tell me."

"I don't, Mom, but I have a theory. Wanna hear it?"

"I do." Sadie accelerated.

Mac looked at the speedometer and winced. "I think it's so stupid that we as a society at large are still stuck on the color of our skin. I think Tristan is still going through that. It took a lot to move in with his dad for the last four years of his life. I think that had to be amazing and extremely difficult, especially in the end."

He continued, "I think about your old friend Miles Davis. How, for a time, Miles wouldn't talk to white people. And I am sure he had his reasons. And like you, Mom, I despise thieves. I can imagine a lot of music scenarios where Miles was being ripped off like you were ripped off. Like you were ripped off. Except I think he knew it from the beginning." He paused. "I think Castony Monroe painted about it. I think he lived and breathed and fought with every bone in his being to expose it. Tristan is Castony's son. All those cats knew one another's hardships from back in the sixties and seventies. Hell, the fifties and forties, their childhood and their parents. Some of those people picked cotton. That meant something. That resonated."

"Oh, Mac."

"My point is this. Tristan is getting the full brunt of how complex and difficult his father's life was. Especially in the end. He must have gone through the entire gamut of all of the emotions on earth with his dad. If you can't relate to that, he's not going to call you. I know I can't relate to all of it myself. I don't know what happened in there, but I wouldn't be surprised if Tristan is now exploring painting himself. I mean, shit, why not? It's in the fabric of his soul." Mac reached for his water bottle. He offered Sadie a new one as well. "Jon, Judith, their kids, and all sorts of people would come to our house—"

"Yeah, but Charles was a thief," she interrupted. "He stole jewelry from me."

"It was the sixties. Parties, free love, and all. You have to stay alert, or things go missing," Mac replied, trying to calm her. "But not uncommon. Same today." He took a big swig of water. "How many dinners did you pay for when going out with your friends?" The question was rhetorical, and he bulldozed on. "These guys were all looking out for each other. Free meal tickets. Does that make sense?"

"By stealing from me?"

"Not all of them, but obviously at least one of them. So if Charles has a painting of Castony's, so what? Let it be. I'm sure they bled together." He added, "But I didn't know he stole from you. If I did, I would have stopped him."

"Thank you. That's all I wanted to hear."

"You didn't raise us like that. To steal? To take what is not earned? That was never our makeup."

"No, I didn't."

"I've got more compliments if it will help us be on a better path together," he joked. They locked eyes and smiled.

"Yeah?"

"Yeah."

Sadie took her time enjoying the jest. "Like what?" she challenged, a hint of delight in her timbre.

"For instance," he said, raising a finger, "Shakespeare described England as, 'This sceptered isle… This other Eden, demi-Paradise.' Descriptions like, 'This happy breed of men, this little world, / This precious stone set in the silver sea—'"

"Jesus, Mac," she said, "where do you come up with this stuff?"

"I didn't. Haven't you been listening? Shakespeare did."

She laughed. "So now you are quoting Shakespeare? Where do you get this behavior from? Certainly not me or your father."

"Let me have a little latitude so I can get to my point. Shakespeare was describing this special place during a very magical time."

Sadie turned back to the windshield and said nothing.

"The question is, what do these words I'm saying remind you of? 'The sceptered isle… This other Eden.' Off the grid. Utopia."

Her eyes squinted. "Big Sur."

"Yes." He slapped his hands together. "Big Sur and, more importantly to me, our childhood that you created. You put us in that incredible place and nourished us with unlimited possibilities. You get that?"

"I thought we were talking about Big Sur."

"We are, but it's really about you, a healthier you. We all go through hard times. You get stuck, and I don't know why. You have done these incredible things, yet you fixate on silly things like food? It's just food, Mom. Nourishment. Fuel for our body and mind, basically."

"You haven't seen me for two years! What are you saying?" Sadie frowned like she'd bitten into a rotten apple. "I don't wanna be punished."

Tears welled up in Mac's eyes. "I'm not trying to punish you. That is not my intention."

"That's what it feels like."

"I apologize. Let me ask you this, then." Mac paused and shifted tone. "Why do you think I've not seen you for so long? Why don't I come around much?"

CHAPTER 10

It was a complicated question, and Mac watched his mom contemplate her answer. He was careful, though, not to steer. Not to hurt. Not to tease. He didn't know if she knew, but he imagined the thought had crossed her mind numerous times. He loved her and knew he had his own faults to bear. Perhaps he and his mom and brother were more alike than he'd imagined, holding the same frustrations with each other all these years.

"Well, what do you want me to say?"

"That's why I'm asking."

"I'm here, aren't I?"

"Yes, you are. And so am I, finally."

"Whatever people do, I'm sure they have their reasons, like I have mine and you yours. I couldn't have given any more of myself."

"I believe you."

They drove in silence again, the burned mountains long gone and far away like the past. Mac glanced down occasionally to see his mom's little toes tapping beyond the brown straps of her sandals. Mac wondered if she was thinking about what he'd said and for a time believed they had clarity. That they'd agreed to accept where each other had landed and held space for both in reflection.

On the outside, they'd have to drive another three and a half hours before clearing the smoky haze to fresh air. They'd traveled well beyond the Santa Lucia Mountains where everything had burned to the foothills of the

Tehachapi Mountain Range, its shoulders spreading east to west, north to south, with peaks and valleys like a buried cross. Only after passing Pyramid Lake with its fingers outstretched did the blue haze disappear.

Mac had napped most of the drive and awoke to the sound of wind blowing in from his mom's window being rolled down. This happened at Tejon Pass, which traversed the Grapevine Canyon of the I-5. They were close now. Approximately seventy miles north of Los Angeles.

Sadie looked over at Mac. "What are you thinking about?"

Looking over at her, he replied, yawning, "About how bizarre it is going all the way to Los Angeles to find fresh air." He shook his head in disbelief. "Leaving Monterey County, a population of four hundred thousand, to a city of more than ten million. It doesn't make sense."

Sadie didn't say anything, but her eyebrows made some unanswered response.

As they crested the mountain, the sun was low in the sky to the west. Thirty minutes later, the moon hung over the eastern mountains. By the time they hit the valley floor, it was an orange glow through smog, soot, and ash and climbing into the eastern sky. The entire planet felt like it was on fire. Mac wondered if it would ever get away and clear the haze.

CHAPTER 11

They arrived in the night to an uncrowded freeway dipping toward Marina del Rey. Mac directed Sadie west as they rounded the corner from Pacific Avenue and Driftwood. A pungent scent of hydrogen sulfide blowing in on the breeze consumed them.

"Oh my God, it smells so good here," Sadie said.

"Yeah, it's seaweed rotting on the beach. To be more specific, sargassum seaweed."

They rounded the turn at Speedway and slowly drove north on the little sand cay just south of the Venice Pier. Sadie looked around curiously, taking in the dimly lit street.

"You remembering any of this?" Mac asked. "It's been a long time."

"It's too dark. Maybe. Do I turn here?"

"Yeah. See, you remember. And then pull up to the garage on the left." He reached into his satchel bag.

The place was a safe haven, a hideaway from most of Los Angeles. A rarity that if someone asked where he lived, they usually didn't know of the Marina Peninsula. It was kept secret for those who knew, the beach tucked away to the left of Venice Pier. A place to come home to after long days of work fifty miles in every direction but west, where the beach lay. Quaint., quiet, and hushed.

Mac directed his mom to drive the little white VW into the parking area at Catamaran, and they pulled up in front of a parking garage. He pointed the remote-control clicker at the garage gate. "Let's see if this thing still works," he said, squeezing the gadget. A red light flickered, and the rust-orange gate jerked to life and disappeared behind the wall. Sadie pulled in and did a three-point turn to an empty spot. Stepping out like rusted ladders, they stretched and gathered their belongings. Mac insisted taking his mom's bags, which she willingly gave up. She held her purse and the small food bag as they began to climb the two flights of stairs. With two duffle bags and satchel over his shoulder, he followed behind her. At the top of the landing, Sadie stepped to the right, and Mac punched in the door code. The door buzzed open, and he nudged it wide with his knee, then elbowed the light switch and illuminated the room.

The apartment was still warm from the sun. It was rectangular in shape, twenty feet deep. A mirror ran two-thirds the length of the space from the big windows at the front to the kitchen entrance. There was a redwood slab for a dining table that stuck out of the wall and matched the floor. It had two chairs. To the left was a couch in front of a stone fireplace and a space where a television had once been. The holes from the wall mount where still present. And past that, a staircase that went down to a bedroom. Another staircase on the right past the kitchen went up.

He set the items on the table and turned to his mom. It had been a long day. Many miles driven, much smoke inhaled, and the underpinnings of family reminded. He wanted to keep things upbeat. But instead, he simply said, "Shall we brush our teeth, wash up, and go straight to bed?"

"Yes, please. I'm tired."

"Just want to say thank you for driving. You wanna sleep upstairs or downstairs?"

"Downstairs. I don't want to climb anymore."

"I understand. Okay, follow me." He dropped his satchel and brought her bags down the hallway to a second set of stairs. "It was a cool lifestyle I had, being here for five years."

Sadie didn't respond. She was struggling as she navigated herself down each step, holding the railing and taking heavy breaths. Mac asked if she'd like him to run her a bath or shower before bed. She opted for the shower, so he set her up with fresh towels and made the beds, then went to his bathroom and brushed his teeth. Calling down the stairs, they wished each other sweet dreams.

Back upstairs on the third level, Mac lay in bed, then a low hum buzzed with a barely audible double bleep. His cell phone. He looked at the screen. Blue eyes beamed beneath ski goggles of a pretty woman's face in the snow. A soft, raspy voice said hello after several clicks. "This was unexpected. How's it going?"

"You there yet?"

"Just got in. You tracking me?"

"Hardly. You're doing the right thing."

"I sure hope so."

"Did you talk to your sister this morning?"

"No."

"You should."

"Uh-huh."

"I gotta go."

"Okay." And the phone went dead.

Like counting sheep, he drifted off trying to recall all the street names that made up the Marina Peninsula. Anchorage. Buccaneer. Catamaran. Driftwood…

* * *

Not far away in a dark room another phone rang, and a groggy man answered.

"Hello?" he answered, sounding annoyed.

"It's me. Put the old man on."

"He's dead."

"Are you serious?"

"Yeah, I'm fucking serious."

"How?"

"COVID."

"I'm sorry. Ugh."

"It's late. Why the fuck are you calling?"

The caller had a nasal voice with a WASP sound. "He's back."

"Who's back?" the man demanded.

"The guy you warned me about from a few years back."

There was a long silence. "Are you sure?"

"I looked him up. Jack MacGuffin."

"He just showed up?

"Yeah."

"Alone?"

"With some woman. What do you want me to do?"

"Nothing for now. Fuck. I need to think."

"Okay."

"I'll call you tomorrow." And the line went dead.

CHAPTER 12

DAY 2

Mac woke relaxed. He rolled onto his back, pulled a pillow to his chest and stared up at the ceiling. It was lit by the streetlight, which made it glow.

His eyes fluttered with images from the dream he'd had. It was about a little girl, but he couldn't make out her face. Soft sounds emanated from the ocean in the background. Though her face appeared blurry, the young image had felt comforting and good. Then her mother appeared, Mac's grandmother, her details unmistakable. She was thin and rigid with a big black pushpin hat and expensive coat. She towered over little Sadie and began reprimanding her for something he didn't understand.

A wave crashed outside and pulled him further away from the dream images. He took a deep breath before stretching straight and long, pushing his arms far above his head. When he brought his hands down, he touched his eyelashes. They felt velvety.

He thought about the velvety sensation as he got up and descended the dark stairs to the bathroom and turned on the light. Maybe the velvet represented his grandmother's hat, and his fingers were the pins.

Trying to make sense of it, he reached for his toothbrush when thumping began. It was a soft-tone thump, a low frequency resembling a crowded bar scene. Mac stopped brushing his teeth, rinsed out the water, and listened.

From the bathroom, the vibration was subtle, but it was there, permeating the floor with reverb. Mac let his eyes travel around the bathroom over the green-slated countertop and glass-enclosed shower to the far left wall. He confirmed the noise source when he lay his hand on the wall. The music increased decibels as someone pumped up the volume.

He guesstimated the time to be just after two in the morning. He left the bathroom and tiptoed through the living room to the stairway. Holding the railing, he leaned over and listened again. A second sound surfaced directly in the wall across from him. Banging or stomping perhaps, he wasn't sure. More sounds, a singular pop of some sort from the window, which made no sense to Mac. And another sound rose from below. His mom was snoring.

Mac smiled in the direction of his mom. He figured since his mom was snoring, the music wouldn't be an issue, and he waved off any idea of going and having a chat with the unknown neighbor. He went back up the stairs and climbed into bed, wondering when late-night music on weeknights became acceptable during the pandemic.

He woke again at 4:30 a.m. sharp. Not because he wanted to wake at the crack of dawn three thousand miles east of his present position, but because he had no choice. His mind had been doing this since he could remember. Internal clock.

And that was fine. So at four thirty every single day of his life, his mind was alert, straddling a delicate thread between his unconscious and conscious. He was in the balance now, able to tap deep REM and his thoughts. He referred to this time as "magic minutes." And they were. A clear brain without all the noise of a thousand things to do.

Mac decided they would commit to a daily walk that would get them to a smoothie shop at some point along the way. It made sense to Mac that his mom would agree, even though it involved a walk much longer than she'd anticipate. He was paying for everything, and that was always an enticer. And a smoothie would be deemed healthy, reasonably priced, and delicious. A way to motivate his mom when she had other things going on. She needed exercise, so he justified the tactics.

Over the years, when Mac would call his mom and she sounded the alarm, he'd usually assess a victim plea for help, like crying wolf. This time was different. After he'd spoken with his sister and caught the next flight home, he began calling doctors at 7:00 a.m. He began by informing them he was next of kin. One after the other, they all concurred her arteries were clogged and circulation poor.

In Mac's mind, she was a walking heart attack waiting to happen. He knew that two years ago. He knew heart attacks happened for two reasons generally: bad genes or personal choices. He knew his mom had great genes, so it boiled down to her choices.

Twenty-four hours later and four hundred miles south, Mac stood in the kitchen making Café Bustelo coffee. His mom appeared in the hallway. He'd heard her climb the stairs huffing and puffing a little, which caught his attention. He wished he had milk for her and other items that would make her feel welcome. His kitchen was basic. All the accoutrements he'd become accustomed to years ago were gone.

He turned off the small pot of boiling water and poured it into the two bowl-sized cups adjacent to the Bustelo canister. "I might have honey." He opened a cabinet above the stove. The cabinet was bare except for a small honey bear container half full. "What do ya know? We are halfway there, meaning we are here and we've got honey," he said, upbeat. "How did you sleep?"

Sadie's eyes were glazed as she waddled over to the kitchen. Her hair was matted and clumpy, and she resembled a sleepy Santa's helper wearing a red nightgown. "Pretty good," she said, pointing at the wall. "Your neighbor likes to play loud music."

"Yeah, sorry. I heard it too."

"Do you know him?"

"Not sure. I wonder if it's the same guy from before."

"You don't know?"

"Mom, I've not been here in a long time. People come and go in LA. It's a spherical state in flux."

"Well, that's comforting. People coming and going all the time."

"It's a city of orbiting transients. Especially when there's an earthquake. Great time to upgrade."

"How often is that?"

"You never know. There's always one around the corner in SoCal. And this whole beach is built on landfill. It's a man-made peninsula, so it rolls more than it shakes."

"So what do we do about the neighbor? Want me to talk to him?" Sadie replied.

"Like the way you talk to me?" Mac laughed and ran his hands through his hair, scratching his scalp. "I love you, Mom," he replied and handed her one of the cups. "We will get almond milk and a few other things at the store later. But remember, we stick to the juice diet, okay?"

"Okay." Sadie sat down on one of the three barstools at the kitchen counter. "I need to wake up before we go for our walk, though."

"I figured as much, considering the way you've prepared your hair."

They both smiled as she tried the coffee. "Oh!"

"Careful, it's hot!" Mac said. "Want some cold water to cool it?"

"It will be fine."

"Okay, I'll be back," Mac said and disappeared up the stairs.

Upstairs, Mac turned the corner past the bedroom and continued to the balcony above. The door was jammed, so he set his coffee down and forced the lock open. Calcium residue had accumulated in the male bolt, and he made a mental note: lubricate everything at the beach.

When he pushed the door wide, the deck was as he remembered it. A large brown wicker couch ran the length of the far wall, covered by a worn camouflage tarp. He knew a hidden Persian rug lay rolled beneath the tarp. A wooden table that was sun bleached sat perched in front of the couch. And two wooden beach chairs were equally faded by the sun, which made them more desirable in fancy outdoor furniture shops.

Mac unrolled the tarp and tucked it behind the couch. He shook the red rug over the edge and laid it on the floor. Then he tipped the coffee table on its side over the edge and brushed off sand and dust with his free hand. He returned it to the deck, only now it was edged over the carpet and created a warm, inviting outdoor living room.

He grasped the railing with one hand and the back corner of the couch with the other and scanned the rooftops, windows, and decks across the street. He figured it was an early weekday morning and very logical people might be sitting having coffee or rushing off to work, but he didn't see a soul.

Carefully, he leaned down as close to the railing as possible and peered around the corner. At first, he saw what he remembered, a small refrigerator covered in cheap, fake grass, the kind found at Home Depot or other commercial building supply chains. He leaned farther, and an outdoor firepit, a six-foot heating tower, and three chairs entered the frame. These he didn't remember, only the mini refrigerator. Maybe the neighbor invested or someone new was living there. He didn't know.

Returning to his bedroom, Mac changed into shorts and a fresh T-shirt. Rummaging through his bag, he grabbed short socks, then walked downstairs and waited in the living room for his mom.

Sadie appeared a few minutes later with a colorful summer dress on, her gray hair pulled back in a ponytail. She wore a tan straw hat, open-toed walking shoes, different from the sandals she driven in, and a fanny pack around her waist. A true tourist, Mac thought, only missing a camera to complete the look and make her a fantastic target to rob.

Nothing would happen with him at her side. He opened the door and gestured her through. Outside the door, she grabbed the handrail and began her descent. When Mac stepped out and turned to close the door, he noticed a white surveillance camera tucked up high in the corner. He hadn't noticed it when they'd arrived in the night because it had been behind his head as they climbed the stairs. Only descending the stairs would it be noticed unless someone was actively looking for security cameras.

"That's new," Mac said, looking at it.

"What is?" Sadie replied.

"The security camera above our heads. It wasn't there before. Oh, and here's another one," Mac said, looking up. "Missed that last night too."

"That's good, right?"

"I guess. Helps deter crime."

At the bottom of the stairs where the cement met the gravel driveway, they turned right and headed straight out toward the beach.

A voice called out, "Hey, mister, do you live here?" The voice was thin and nasally, with a lot of air escaping the nose. Like a shallow breath speaking from inside a tin can.

Mac turned back and saw a wispy-looking thirtysomething guy standing next to the mailboxes. *Cast this guy in a film as the narc,* Mac thought immediately when he laid eyes on him. He was dressed like a carpenter who had swung penny nail hammers most of his adult life. He wasn't short, just lean, maybe six feet tall but didn't eat his pancakes to bulk up.

"Sorry?" Mac said, looking back but still proceeding toward the beach.

"Do you live here?" the guy repeated. This time he dropped his voice, adding some sort of authority, more macho than anything else.

"You work here?" Mac replied, stopping.

"Yeah, my name is Ribbit. I'm the manager."

"Nice to meet you. I thought Jim was the manager?" Mac asked, looking him over like a beach rat.

"He was fired or let go, I don't know. But it's my building now."

"Is it?" Mac asked, looking past his tool belt to freshly stacked timber lying behind him. A few boards leaned against the side of the wall. "What are you doing?"

"I'm fixing the mailboxes. Framing them."

"I see." Mac stepped closer. "With pine?"

"Yup. I'll paint it after. What unit are you in?"

"Three," Mac replied sharply.

"Do you live here or vacation renting?"

"Vacation renting?" Mac answered, more of a question, and shook his head before walking away. Ribbit stood there, having watched Mac dismiss him, a perplexed look on his face, like a mouse struggling to decide whether the cheese was real or imitation.

"Who was that guy?" his mom asked as Mac approached her waiting patiently on the path.

"An idiot. Guy used eighteen nails for something needing six screws."

"Was he using pine? Won't that get termites?"

"Like I said. Idiot."

They turned right at the sand's edge where a beach path ended or started, depending which way a person was coming or going. No one else was around, and that was fine to Mac. The sky was clear, no haze, and he estimated the temperature to be seventy degrees. A little makeshift succulent garden was planted along the parking lot's edge as they approached the access path. A sign posted on a two-by-four post read "Second Chance Park" in dark blue paint.

They turned right and started walking north. A gray-haired man with a blue medical mask covering his mouth approached from the opposite direction and began pointing his finger at Mac.

"Long time, buddy," he said. "Couldn't forget your face. Even with the mask on."

"Do I know you?" Mac replied.

"It's Stevo!" the guy blurted back, excited.

Mac squinted and turned slightly. "Sorry, the mask and hair threw me. Been a long time."

"Yeah. I let the hair go gray. No sense hiding it. Know what I mean?"

"I guess not. Nice to see you, man."

"This is your mom?" he asked.

"Yes. Mom, this is Stevo. Stevo, this is Sadie."

Sadie didn't step forward, but Stevo did and extended his hand. She repelled it, putting her hands up apologetically.

"Oh, right, COVID. Sure. Nice to meet you." Stevo turned to Mac. "Boy, you're lucky."

"Why?" Mac asked.

"They just fixed the garage after leaving this gate broken for nine months. The new management really sucks here."

"I wouldn't know," Mac replied. "I'm not around much."

"How long you in town for?"

"Only a week."

"Cool. Well, good to see you."

"Good to see you too."

"And nice to meet you, Sadie. Wow, Mac's mom. Cool."

They parted ways, and Sadie looked back in Stevo's direction once he was gone. "He sure likes you."

"Nice guy. He looks a lot older with that hair."

Sadie didn't say anything, and they continued onward. Mac looked at his mom's gray hair. The pandemic had put a pinch on everybody in its own way.

CHAPTER 13

They'd walked fifteen minutes when his mom suddenly gasped, "Mac. I need to rest." They were on the pathway between beachfront homes and the sand.

"Really, Mom? We haven't even reached the halfway point yet," Mac said, looking back at his home less than four hundred yards behind them.

"How much farther is the smoothie shop? I need to sit down."

"Mom, you really don't want to sit anywhere here," he replied. "It's pretty dirty."

Sadie brushed her sweat-damp bangs with one hand and pointed at a nearby park bench with the other. "But there are benches right there."

"And they are filthy," he replied, looking at the benches with disregard. "Definitely slept on last night. We have a huge homeless problem here, and now with COVID, I imagine it's even worse."

Sadie stopped walking. "Well, isn't there somewhere to sit down?"

Mac looked around. "Not really. We can stand here and rest in the shade. Or go out on the beach. But there's no shade out there. Unless we walk to that lifeguard tower way over there."

Sadie looked across the beach. "Forget it."

They stood for several minutes while Sadie caught her breath. Mac wished he'd brought water for her. His mom was winded and beading sweat. Her small hat wasn't helping much. "We can walk a little and rest intermittently."

Sadie gave a deep exhale and a stern look. "You sound like a trainer, Mac. I'm not in a gym. I'm old. I can't do this stuff."

"We will go slow, Mom. I promise."

"You never slow down. You're always rushing to get somewhere."

"I slow down all the time, Mom. You just don't see it."

"I don't believe you. Just wait with me, please?"

Mac didn't say anything, just nodded and stood by patiently.

"Ugh. My legs hurt," Sadie replied with hands held on her hips.

Mac bit his lip and didn't say anything more. They stood watching the seagulls fly down the beach looking for trash and a free lunch.

After five long minutes, they pushed on and soon were among the early-bird fitness walkers, the tourists with cameras, the vendors setting up, and the street people. Rows and clusters of tattered tents. The enclave of tents were wall-to-wall like a shantytown of a Third World village. There was zero social distancing, and the homeless who sat around one another were itching, scratching, and some were twitching.

Mac watched his mom's anxiety building. She was noticing everything with her keen eyes and was subconsciously beginning to itch herself. It started on the back of her hands. Then her wrists. Forearms were next. Then a homeless dog came sprinting out from somewhere. It startled Sadie as it darted by, sniffing her leg. She screamed, "Ahhhhh!"

"Just a dog, Mom," Mac tried to comfort her.

"That poor dog. Where's its owner?"

"No idea. Not sure it has one."

"Don't be ridiculous." She scowled.

Mac turned to his mom. "We could catch the dog. I'll pick it up and carry it. And you can walk around asking if anyone has lost their dog. Then we can set up a soup kitchen and serve food all week. What do you say?"

Sadie paused, gave Mac a look, then started laughing. She was still itching when she replied, "That's not funny."

On the next block, a homeless woman sprang out of a tilting blue tent, yelling obscenities at a man they had just passed. He yelled back, "You crazy, lazy, hazy, bombastical bitch!"

Mac veered his mom forty-five degrees to the right. "Best to keep clear." The man appeared too clean to be part of the enclave, but he yelled back just the same before passing them, "You should go back to Mars, you bitch!"

Sadie's covered her ears. "Is this the normal deal here?"

Before Mac could answer, the woman appeared from inside the tent, wearing panties and not a stitch more. Her eyes were saucer-wide while she spouted, "Mo fo' mutha' sucka' bah-bah ahhh!" It seemed as discombobulated as the man's first rant.

Mac steered them back onto the main walkway after they passed her tent and said, "She must be schizophrenic, Mom. Lots of mental illness here."

"Do you even know what schizophrenia is? I don't think so," Sadie replied in a pointed, stinging tone.

"Sure I do, Mom. We just saw it," he replied, emphatically gesturing his hands like a man at a lecture. "They make up imaginary people to talk to, including themselves. They're in a fragmented reality. Kind of like multiple personality disorder. But different."

"I don't think so," she said in finality, not looking his direction.

"Okay. Schizophrenia… maybe?" It was an empirical thought based in no theory or logic, really. A shot in the dark. For all Mac knew, these two yellers had a daily sound off.

But Sadie and Mac walked on. No sense in debating a clear definition of schizophrenia. They had been getting along fine, barely. They'd made the long six-hour drive to LA yesterday. No reason to mess that up. They were on a roll. Let other people argue.

But was that possible? Sadie had an opinion about everything, and as the apple sometimes doesn't fall far from the tree, Mac might as well too. He was aware of that. He was trying to break the chain of overreacting without breaking her.

The massage booths at Windward Circle were not yet opened. Sadie looked at them in disdain. "I used to love those massages."

"You remember." Mac beamed.

"I wouldn't ever think about doing that again after what I've seen today."

"I can understand that."

"Why did you let me get on those tables when I was here before?"

Mac recognized the setup but answered anyway. "Because it was a safer time then," he replied.

"The hell it was. I must have been out of my mind thinking it was safe. This is a dirty place."

Mac didn't say anything. He was wondering about massage places he often utilized when he discharged from the navy. He spent most of his rehab in San Diego, but when he was done there, the move to Venice Beach had been exciting and the daily visits during the backside of rehab easy.

His shoulder.

His knee.

His wrist.

His hip.

Injuries incurred from a training accident; they'd called it.

Yeah, right. He smiled to himself, rubbing his shoulder.

They passed the skatepark where kids of all ages from under ten to forty skated and slid across the terrain and jumps. Then the rollerblade area where the skaters circled and danced. This was the older crowd of twenties through seventies with ponytails and pom-pom skirts, hipster sunglasses and funky hats. The music normally blared, not yet pounding like the afternoons. Instead, scraping sounds dominated the eardrums. Cheap wheels under hardwood boards filled the air. Rubber, plastic, and wood slid aggressively over curved cement. A marriage of desired skill and constant rehearsal repeated.

Mac looked past the park to a breakwater that Abbott Kinney had constructed a century before. He remembered swimming in the surf with a bunch of Black surfers' years before—the Black Contingency, they called themselves. A group of watermen trying to make an impact in the world and stretch stereotypes. So many groups making a statement in Venice. Or at least trying.

The place had lost its luster for Mac. The homeless scene had exploded. The once-prestigious Venice Beach Boardwalk that had been renovated just five years before was now dirtier than what he remembered twelve years earlier. The lifestyle that was once funky and hip had turned dirty and sour. It seemed many things in California had shifted too. The political landscape had slid so far apart that families argued and became more divided than he could remember. The middle class was evaporating quickly as the rich got richer and the poor desperate.

Of course, the pandemic didn't help any. In Mac's mind, it just added to the stench of unwashed people wafting in the breeze. Yet as horrid as it was, specks of the possible dream he'd imagined still existed in fragments. He remembered what his mom had said years ago.

Mac turned to his mom. "I want to thank you."

"Thank me?"

"Yes. Thank you for coming. Thank you for trying. Thank you for always supporting me with encouragement. All of us. Nadine, Tristan, and I."

"Well…" She paused.

"I appreciate you."

"It wasn't easy. I didn't know what I was doing."

"I know. But you did a lot. I wasn't always easy on you. I put you through hell, and I tested you a bunch."

"Yes, you did. But you were my baby boy. You're still my baby. You were my first."

"I remember you sending me fruit baskets at college, and I'd say, 'Send me money, and I'll buy the fruit. Save the shipping costs.' It was expensive."

"Well."

"I know. It was the thought."

"It was."

"When I came here so many years ago, you supported me going for it. Not financially, of course, but emotionally. I remember you saying, 'I don't care what you do. I care that you love it. That you give your all. And that you are proud of it.' "

"Sounds like something I would've said."

"I knew you meant it."

* * *

In a room that was now light, a man stood looking out the window at rows of double-wide trailers symmetrically placed. One after the other, they neatly aligned with precision accuracy like headstones in a military graveyard. They were equal in size and shape; only the coloration varied. A palette consisting of red, white, blue, yellow, and green made up the neighborhood.

"Here's what we're going to do. Nothing."

"Nothing? Why?"

"Because the timing is all wrong," he said, turning with the phone. "Everything is frozen while we're in lockdown. There's no way we'll get him served during COVID, and even if we did, the system is backed up."

"But you filed the case two years ago, right?"

"He never got served because we couldn't find him. So it's been dead in the water."

"I see," he replied, sounding disappointed.

"Besides, there are other problems now, and I think it's best we wait and see what happens."

"So do nothing?"

"Does he have a car?"

"Yeah. A white one parked in the garage."

"Run the plates. Maybe there's another address assigned to it. We can track him that way if he disappears."

"Okay."

"Everything else the same?"

"Yeah. I keep pushing buttons. They keep complaining."

"Good. Pressure is good. It's all we can do for now unless some opportunity presents itself."

"And they always do."

"Exactly." The man pushed "End" on the phone and put it in his pocket.

CHAPTER 14

Mac's mom only complained twice more about the walk before rounding the corner to the smoothie shop. They'd opted to stand in shade and rest both times. The masks were on tight, and they were careful not to touch anything. This included walls when they rested, items for sale, or anyone approaching them like panhandlers and vendors, which happened several times. Mom put both hands out like a passing guard stopping children, and Mac steered them clear when passageways presented themselves.

As they turned the corner, a unique-looking elderly man sat alone at a table wearing land roller skates and a guitar placed across his lap. He was brown skinned and wore a Middle Eastern head wrap with ginger-gray dreadlocks sporting out the top. Mac beelined toward him, his eyes darting between the coffee and water on his table and his headdress.

"Mom, this is a Venice Beach icon. A real boardwalk busker."

"I don't care who he is. He is itching his scalp. Do you see that?"

The man looked up past Mac, did a second glance at Mac, and dove back into his phone as they approached. Mac turned back to her and whispered beneath his mask, "Calm down, Mom." Then Mac changed direction, and they passed in a wide arc, hers much wider than his.

"*Tranquilo, mamasita,* I was only kidding." Mac laughed as they stepped past him to a small storefront trimmed in green. "This is the place. A little hole-in-the-wall packed with deliciousness. We are lucky they are open!" He used his pinky and pulled open the screen door. Sadie hesitated, insisting Mac enter first, so he did.

Inside the small space, Sadie found barely enough room to stand. It was tiny, approximately four feet deep by six wide, most of which was covered in unopened, stacked cardboard boxes. Mac scanned the room as the screen door slammed behind them. He looked at his mom, acknowledging she didn't bother to stop the slamming door from closing. Sadie shrugged her shoulders and pushed to the right of Mac.

To the left was a glass-door refrigerator filled with fresh coconuts and some sort of blue-packaged items unrecognizable unless opened. To the right was a small table, perhaps for to-go orders to be placed. Ninety percent of the space, all behind the counter, was kitchen. The side walls had shelves stacked high with kitchen cutlery.

The barista was behind the counter at a prep table. He was Hispanic, in his early twenties, and appeared tired. When he looked up from cutting apples, Mac nodded hello. Sadie didn't. The barista set down the chopping knife and wiped his hands with a kitchen towel before approaching to take their order.

Up close, Mac could see his nose was pierced because the purple mask he was wearing fell below his nostrils. His long, greasy hair was pulled back, and ripe pimples adorned his forehead. Mac looked over at his mom to see how she was taking this all in. She was bug-eyed. He figured it might be affecting his mom's take on organic staff hygiene. Not the best smoothie day kickoff.

"You okay, Mom?"

"Yeah," she replied. Mac couldn't read her response.

"Good morning," Mac said to the barista, stepping forward an inch. "May I order a large muscle beach smoothie and a large tropical smoothie please?"

"We are all out of smoothies today," the barista replied, deadpan, flat as a pancake.

Mac paused in disbelief, then asked, "Are you sure?"

"Yup."

"All out of smoothies?"

"Well, out of frozen bananas."

"Oh, I see. That doesn't make you all out of smoothies. There are bananas piled high behind you."

"But we are out of *frozen* bananas."

"Sure. I heard you the first time. My mom and I don't need frozen bananas. In fact, I don't even like ice in my smoothie. We'll just use the room-temperature ones."

"I can't do that."

Mac pivoted to look at his mom again. Her eyes revealed her thoughts like a giant billboard on Sunset Avenue, beaming: *This guy is an idiot. I knew this was a bad idea.*

Mac pivoted back. "Sorry?"

"I can't make you a smoothie because we don't have any smoothie bananas."

"You've got what seems to be like a hundred and fifty bananas behind you," Mac replied sarcastically, pointing with his finger like a gun. "Am I offending you?"

"No," the guy blurted without looking at the back wall. "It's just that those bananas are for acai bowls. The frozen bananas weren't delivered today, so we are not doing smoothies." Mac did his darnedest to make sense of it. "You're going to turn down business because your bananas are supposed to be in another dish?" It was a jab straight to the young man's mindset.

"Yeah. I'm not allowed to make those."

"Says who?" Mac looked around the room.

"My boss," he explained.

Mac squinted, searching his mind for some sort of recognition. "Is your boss the nice woman that also works here? Because I'm pretty certain you can skirt the issue today and make us some smoothies."

"No. She's not the boss," he replied down-toned, his face wrinkling.

"Well, can you put your boss on the phone?" Mac tilted his head with curiosity.

"I can text him."

"Great. Please do that."

Mac and Sadie stood at the counter, both shoulder to shoulder. The guy retrieved his cell phone from his front pocket. "My boss usually doesn't respond for five minutes," he said after he finished his text and set the phone down. The barista tapped his fingers, waiting.

They were at a standstill. Mac wondered if the guy was going to wait for five minutes. He must have had other food prep work to do, so Mac said, "Okay. We will wait outside." And with that, Sadie and Mac stepped out while he held the door with his elbow.

His mom, upon clearing the door, asked, "Are you kidding me, Mac?"

"Mom, I've never seen anything like this before," he said, sounding apologetic.

"This is ridiculous. Let's go somewhere else."

"I know, right? But let's just wait. The smoothies here are really good."

"Why don't we go next door?" she replied, looking at the adjacent café.

"They don't have smoothies. Just coffee and stuff like what the busker is drinking."

"He went in there?" she replied, her tone dropping in surprise.

"Probably."

"Then I don't want to go."

Sadie's back was to the busker's table. Beams of sunlight shot through her tan sun hat, casting light speckles on her cheek. Mac looked at his mom thoughtfully. At seventy-one, she was still pretty, her facial features sharp, elegant. The little girl that had become a debutante. The prettiest girl at the ball who was compared to Grace Kelly. The mischievous girl who got into all sorts of trouble when she'd cross the bridge to the other side of the city.

Mac, smiling, went back into the smoothie shop. The guy was back at the kitchen table cutting apples. "Hi, buddy. What did your boss say?"

"He said we can't use the other bananas. But you can have a smoothie. You just have to substitute another fruit in place of the bananas."

"Really?"

"Yeah."

"Okay. What are my choices?"

On his fingers, he counted out, "Strawberries. Blueberries. Pineapple. Apples."

"But no bananas. Not even half a banana in each so we use less banana. It would make the smoothie taste better."

"No." He was definite, like he didn't want to repeat the interrogation.

"Blueberries, please, in both. Thank you."

Mac walked back outside. Sadie was talking to a goldendoodle that was tied to a chair. "Who's this?" Mac asked.

"This is Tucker. Isn't he cute?" she said, rubbing his chin.

"Adorable," he agreed happily.

"What did he say? Are we leaving?"

"He's making the smoothies," Mac replied, now petting the dog's shoulders.

"Really?" Sadie sounded surprised.

"Without the bananas. He's using blueberries as a substitute," he replied. "Antioxidants, but I'd prefer a banana or two."

"Me too," Sadie confirmed.

"Ridiculous," they spouted in unison.

CHAPTER 15

The smoothies came and, they both concurred, were delicious. The consistency was thinner than Mac liked but full of flavor. But they were healthy, thirst quenching, and loaded. Coconut water was the base.

They walked east away from the boardwalk, past Main Street, nicking the corner of Abbott Kinney Boulevard, onward to Indiana Avenue, and stopped at Fourth Street.

"Why are we stopping here?" Sadie asked.

"Just to rest."

"Oh, that's nice," she replied, placing her hands on her hips. Mac stared at the southwest corner of the street. A 1912 Sears catalog double-story home sat behind a green hedge with a stone wall at its foundation. Purple bougainvillea blossomed at the corners of two gates inlayed with redwood, and security lights perched above. The home was white with dark green–trimmed windows that could only be seen on the second story because the ivy hedge was dense and private.

Mac wondered if his mom remembered the home, but her attention was down the street at a clump of palm trees nestled high in the air above the treetops.

"Does anything here look familiar?" he asked.

She looked around at the Sears home and across the street at the apartment building. Then back the way they'd come. "No. Am I missing something?"

Mac looked down at the stone wall surrounding the home, disappointed. "No, not really," he replied. "Ready to continue?"

"Yes, thank you."

They turned right two blocks later and looped back across Abbott Kinney Boulevard. They'd finished the smoothies, so they tossed their empty cups in a bin that had been spray-painted with graffiti. It read: I LIVE HERE. A blue-and-white sticker was there too. BIDEN—HARRIS. Mac turned to his mom. "Do you remember any of this?"

"I do. It's been a long time."

"I know. We passed our old house a while back."

"The one you and Nadine bought? Why didn't you tell me?" she said, disappointed.

"I was wondering if you recognized it? It didn't look as nice as when we had it," he replied, hoping she still might see it behind his left shoulder.

"You made that home beautiful," she said tenderly.

"Built the rock wall too."

"I wish you would have pointed it out."

"Next time. We have a week here."

"Yes, we can walk this way again if you like."

Mac didn't say anything.

"I have to go to the bathroom."

"So do I," Mac replied, looking up as they passed the palm trees. "Maybe we can stop in the canals first?"

"Mac, I really have to go. I haven't walked this far in a long time."

"Okay. Let's see what's open up ahead."

Nothing was open. No restrooms available anywhere. The pandemic had closed most of the businesses, and every single place open was not letting patrons use their restroom. It was absurd.

Mac wondered how long his mom could last. He guessed the non-banana smoothie must have done a job on her insides.

He didn't know all the food she had been eating prior to his arrival, but he imagined a combination of cheeses and nuts and desserts that would bring most digestive tracts to a slow crawl. Now, with a juice smoothie loaded with lean fruits and cleansing powders after a strong coffee, she was sure to explode.

Here he'd wanted to make this walk as easy as possible and just push her cardio a little, clipping her unhealthy, weight-gaining diet. Now his efforts were about to backfire, and he had no solution in sight. Improvising, he began trying to keep her mind off of it. "Remember when I was in London and met George Michael?"

"Do I know him?"

"George Michael, the singer who had that song—the 'Faith' one?"

"Remind me," Sadie replied, grimacing. She seemed to be clenching. Mac noticed her walk had definitely changed. She was swinging her arms forward and outward, more of a fast walk than casual walk.

"We were at a party, and I was standing in a circle, talking with some friends in a band. I turned and saw George Michael behind me."

"I know who he is now."

"Was. He died."

"Oh, he did?"

"So, he is standing there with two women, and I said, 'Hi.' He looked at me like I was interrupting him. He literally turned up his nose and glared before turning away."

"Oh, yes," she replied, clutching her belly.

Mac spoke faster. "I remember grabbing his arm and saying, 'Hey, we love your music, man. Don't be snooty. You're George Michael, and we love you.' "

"What did he say?"

"Nothing at first. The women were shocked. I remember their jaws dropping, but he apologized, saying something along the lines of he was sorry. In a bad mood, something like that. And you know what I said?"

"No."

"'Don't come out to parties. Get your rest.' Then I turned to open my circle to his." Mac mimicked his movements as if reenacting it. " 'They think you're awesome. We are all your fans.' "

"And he was nice then?"

"Yeah, he was cool."

Sadie paused in thought. "Not everyone can do that."

"I know. What I'm trying to say is treat everyone equal and with humility is all."

"Not realistic."

"Maybe not, but it would be nice if we could, wouldn't it?" Mac replied optimistically, looking up at the sky.

"Do you think you did that with the guy at the mailboxes this morning?"

"I tried, but he had a funky vibe."

"Wasn't there a famous painter that lived next to you?"

"Lots of them. But I think you mean Dennis Hopper."

"Yeah."

"Supposedly a great actor as well."

"Yeah, that's him."

"He's dead now."

"Oh, I didn't know."

"Yeah, he died a while ago."

"What was Dennis like?"

"I never met him."

"But you lived next door?"

"Owned the house next door but wasn't there very much. Besides, I couldn't exactly grab Dennis Hopper by the arm. He always drove by with his window up and never said hello."

"Probably a good thing. You can't go around grabbing people. Lucky George Michael didn't call security."

"Yeah, I suppose you're right. But still, sometimes it helps when you are direct and real. Everyone comes from somewhere, Mom."

"Yes, we do."

"You know, part of the skill to talk to anyone comes from growing up in Big Sur," Mac said, turning to her as he spoke. "All the people we grew up around. And all the tourists coming through. All the artist characters you surrounded us with. It takes a village."

"I know." She smiled back. "I was running away."

"You may have been running away from your mom or whatever. From that snooty life of privilege, ball gowns, and finishing school. But the universe was on our side." Then Mac quickly corrected himself, "*Is* on our side and always will be if we stay open to it."

"I don't believe that."

"I know, Mom, but I do. And I believe in you whether you see it or not. Even if I have to keep saying it over and over until you do." Mac knew they were working toward something, but he didn't know what, exactly. And he wasn't sure his mom knew either. She had a propensity to think she understood everything, when that was impossible. But what was attainable was believing that positive change could happen. So he did.

Since nothing was open, he continued to use distraction. He would comment on every furry animal they passed. Every architectural home that was unique. Anything interesting that had something distinguishable he could call out.

And it worked. Soon they were in the canal zone headed to the first car bridge.

"Keep walking, Mom. We're almost there."

CHAPTER 16

Sheriff Dean Kootz wasn't a tall man, but his lack in height was made up tenfold by the width of his shoulders and keen sense of calling bullshit on people. He'd put in twenty-four years and was less than a year away from retirement when he'd lost all sensation in his right arm. The injury had happened to his neck when he'd been hit by a woman armed with a frying pan. It wasn't tin and light like the ones you buy at a convenience store. This pan was cast iron and could stop a bullet, with an eighteen-inch diameter spreading across half-inch of bacon cooking goodness.

And it had hurt. So much so that he knew upon impact he was going to be knocked out. But before the impact happened, and as he was stepping through the door to help his partner already entangled with the husband—assailant—he got a glimpse of the wife to his right and the dark object descending toward his head. He had no helmet on; no riot had been issued. Just a simple domestic dispute, like any other typical day with threats made and doors usually broken.

But this one he'd let his guard down, and right then and there he knew there'd be consequences. He spun, trying to push off his left heel, and punch with all his might. The iron pan barely made an audible sound as it bounced off his ducking head. He spun, fist clenched, aiming for her face. Then his peripheral vision shrank to tunnels, and the walls came crashing in and everything went black.

Kootz didn't know how long he'd been unconscious, because suddenly his partner and the assailant were wrestling on top of him. He had his back to the floor, and he could see the woman standing nearby holding her jaw. He immediately grabbed the assailant by the back of his Afro and pulled with all his might. The man yelled and twisted and kicked. Then the man tried to turn away, and Kootz was able to put a choke hold on him. A few moments later, his partner gained control of the man's arms and administered handcuffs.

The Black woman, mid-forties, with fifty extra pounds around her midsection, was clutching her jaw and screaming, "You punched me! You freaking punched me! I wanna file a complaint!"

Kootz got to his feet, spun her around, and wrestled her to the wall. "Lady, you hit me! I'm arresting you for assaulting a peace officer," he growled and physically manhandled her into cuffs. Twisting her hands away from her jaw wasn't easy. The room was still spinning, and his head and neck hurt. But also his pride. He'd let his guard down by not checking his right side as he entered a domestic dispute call and was distracted when he saw his partner get kicked in the balls.

Simply put, the man didn't want to let the officer in, but it was customary practice for officers to walk in and assess the safety of both parties before they could leave the scene. Rarely did it get into a physical altercation.

Because of it, Kootz was reduced to doing paperwork in the station while he closed the gap to retirement. And at this very moment, his right arm was numb from typing and he could still smell the grease from that frying pan. A smell that never really went away.

He'd been rubbing his arm for a long time, trying to get the circulation going. But he couldn't feel it, could barely move it. It was working intermittently an hour before. Suddenly, it'd gone numb again. He wondered if he would have to pretend to his wife that nothing was the matter.

He didn't want that. Not at all.

Who would?

So he kept rubbing just like the therapist had done. Rubbing and hoping and tapping his fingers on the desk. They felt like lead.

Both Kootz and the only other person on duty at the station, Officer Russo, watched the television on the far wall in the little squad room. It had CNN on, and Anderson Cooper was asking questions of a health official for the US Navy. The spokesperson was backpedaling, trying to alter his reply that had been taped a day earlier and shown to him for clarification.

Russo shook her head and peeked over at Kootz, then her eyes darted back to the television. She was sipping a coconut water and had her feet up on the counter.

"How's your arm?"

"I don't want to talk about it," he replied sternly. "They couldn't figure out my arm. How they gonna figure out this virus?"

"You got me there," she said, making a sucking sound as she emptied the carton. She stood up. Her short butch hair flipped as she turned, looking back at Anderson Cooper. She was a fan.

Both were still glued to the television as she tossed the carton and grabbed another. With each new question, Kootz's chest expanded as air went in, but none was exhaled. Then the radio squawked, and Russo slid her wheeled chair left ten feet to the dispatch radio and plugged her headset in.

"Pacific division. This is Officer Russo. How can I help you? Yes, patch it through."

Kootz stayed at his desk, eyes glued on the television as Russo took notes in the background. Russo turned to Kootz as she hung up the phone.

"Remember that building down on the peninsula where they were throwing all those Fourth of July lalapalooza parties?"

"Yeah. Lots of noise complaints," he replied, looking over at her. "The tenants were playing hide-and-seek every time we got called out there."

"Yeah. We've got a DOA, possible homicide."

Kootz's chest deflated. "This is a mess. I got three detectives down, more than half the patrolmen sick, and we don't even have an antiviral yet. We just don't have enough manpower. What we need is the National Guard down here. The governor has got to do something."

"Sure, Sheriff. As soon as the navy figures out what happened to all those sailors. This thing is spreading. No question about it."

"Send units. Police and sheriff."

"Copy that."

"Yeah, I better head down there. Shit," he answered and stood up. He shook his right arm at the shoulder and sucked in his cheek. "Worthless."

CHAPTER 17

The Venice canal bridges ran along Dell Avenue and totaled four. At the top of the first canal for automobiles, Mac and Sadie could see the other three in a straight line looking south. To the east and west, the canals traveled a few hundred yards, intersecting waterways running north and south. Some of them had walk bridges. The entire area was residential and created long blocks of calm water with canoes and pontoons along the shore.

Mac knew the bridges were a throughway for tourists, but due to the circumstances, most businesses being closed, and the scarcity of anyone not homeless, the canals were desolate. A perfect time to not be hindered by cars, bikes, and lookie-loos passing through.

Mac and Sadie turned left from Venice Boulevard onto Dell Avenue and soon were climbing the first of the four bridges against the nonexistent traffic. The sun was shining brightly on the water below, and its reflection glimmered and sparkled on the bordering homes. The colors exuded charm, and a variety of homes lined the banks. Small cement paths shot off left and right at the entrance to the bridges that went along the water's edge. Some homes had little wooden docks, some painted white, others left natural to wash out in the hot, drenching sun.

Walking up the bridge, Mac asked with a curious look on his face, "Do you know who Abbott Kinney is, Mom?"

She turned. "No."

"Really?" he asked, sounding alarmed.

"Sounds familiar," Sadie replied.

"You can sit there, I think," he said, pointing to the flat top of a cement arc.

"Tell me." She stopped to rest.

"You really don't know?" he asked, adding big gestures and a wide, bragging grin like a display. She shook her head, sitting down.

Mac wondered if her focus was still getting to a bathroom or if the twister in her belly had subsided. He chose not to ask and keep up the distraction. "Abbott Kinney's vision and how he flipped a coin to choose this area instead of the more desirable Santa Monica is a fascinating tale."

Sadie grinned, referring to his body language. "Is all that necessary?"

"Oh, yes, most definitely," Mac replied and continued. "His trenching canals in 1905 to reproduce Venice, Italy, was genius at the time."

Sadie shook her head. "Am I entertainment for you?"

"Maybe," he admitted, smiling. "There used to be a lot more canals before the crash in twenty-nine. Then automobiles became popular. The city decided to fill a bunch of the canals for roads."

"Okay."

"Do you know what crash I'm talking about?"

"No, I don't. Did the cars crash?"

"No, Mom, the Wall Street crash. The stock market collapse. Nineteen twenty-nine."

"I do not want to talk about money, Mac. It pains me."

"Sorry. Anyway, as the story goes, Abbott Kinney allegedly flipped a coin and won this area to build his wild dream."

"And that's the story?"

"Never too late to dream."

"I dream of a bathroom," Sadie said, standing up.

They continued to walk through the tightly knit community. Mac weaved stories and complimented homes with eclectic gardens bursting with flowers. Sadie tried to keep up but was often distracted by petunias, marigolds, and impatiens, naming them as she went. Most of the waterfront homes had a little porch or deck, and some had stone patios. Large lawns were rare.

As they crossed the third bridge, Mac pointed to a row of homes across the canal. "This is where the annual Venice Garden Tour starts, Mom. You'd like it."

"Yeah, I bet I would," Sadie replied, looking across the canal. "This is such a departure from the beach, isn't it?"

"Magnum opus means having a great body of work. The canals are that to me. Peaceful, isn't it?" Mac nodded, looking back at her reflectively. "And more colorful with flowers. What does it remind you of, Mom?"

"My garden in Big Sur," she exclaimed. "Surrounding the homes like ours did."

"Yeah, a nice feeling being surrounded by sweet smells of deliciousness." He beamed, looking back. "The only bummer to me is the lack of privacy. You're very exposed here."

"Yeah, it's a choice, I suppose. I like your place except for the homeless situation when you step outside. That is not good. I wouldn't feel safe at night without you."

"Yeah, I think something's gotta give to resolve this mess and get things cleaned up. I don't think that it will happen anytime soon. Gonna get worse before it gets any better."

They continued on and waved to people sitting in their gardens having morning coffee. They talked to children playing in their front yards with grandparents watching close by. They talked to cats that wandered the path and dogs on leashes with wandering owners. It called into question whether the owners were walking their dogs or their dogs were walking them.

Some of the dog owners were pressed into their phones, sucked deep into the slippery rabbit hole. It as a social dilemma Mac was guilty of himself. But he wouldn't do that with his mom. He'd made a conscious decision to leave the phone at home. He saw others using their phones as a portal. Transported somewhere he didn't want to be. Far from beach life, perhaps across town, perhaps across the country to a colder place in the north where snow had fallen. And perhaps even farther, where different languages were spoken and the day had become night.

Mac stopped at a little white gate just off the path, his mom trailing behind him. At a small dock to his right, a lazy rope held a canoe with enough room for two and a small pet. He called out to the front door of a rustic single-story white cottage with nine-pane windows. The door was open, and inside lay a goldendoodle. Her ears immediately perked up, and she bolted across the lawn to greet them.

"Hi," Mac said, reaching over the gate, taking the dog by its collar, and reading the brass name tag. "Charlie dog."

The dog jumped on the fence with its front paws and barked back, "Ruff. Ruff, ruff," excited and wiggling.

Mac leaned down. "You're a girl, I see." She was jumping like young puppies do.

Nathan, a handsome, vibrant man in his thirties, strolled out the open door of the home, a look of surprise on his face. He resembled Ryan Gosling with his facial features and coloring, tall and lean. He wore denim jeans and a periwinkle T-shirt.

"Hey, Mac, I didn't know you were in town!" His smile was happy and eyes gentle.

"Yeaaah. Thought I'd do a getaway with my mom. You've never met her, right?" Mac turned as Sadie arrived.

"Wow. This is your mom?"

"Yes. This is Sadie. Mom, this is my dear friend Nate."

"So nice to meet you," he replied, extending his arm. He had no mask on. "What an honor."

"Nice to meet you." Mom smiled, extending her hand, mask crooked. Then in an instant she turned to Mac, all expression of joy from her face drained. Suddenly Sadie looked catatonic and in a trance seizure, her body rigid. As if her head was on a swivel, eyes crossed and holding, through clenched teeth, she gasped, "I really have to go to the bathroom."

"Oh, sure," Nate replied, switching gears, "please come right in." Nate quickly opened the gate.

"Do you mind?" Mac asked apologetically. "I'm so sorry."

"No. Not at all." He brushed it off.

"We've been walking all morning," Sadie cried.

"Please. No problem. Come right in." Nate was polite beyond measure, adding, "I think you'll be able to find the bathroom. Inside on the left, second door in the hallway. I'll walk you there."

Mac stood back as Nate trailed Sadie down the path and inside. He thought if another minute had passed, his mom would be squatting in the nearest bush of Nate's garden.

Now by himself, he stood admiring the cottage as he heard doors rush open and close inside. It was a beautiful scene as sunlight poured into the home from all directions. There were long skylights and big mirrors in the living room. The mirrors extended the length of the house to its kitchen, where a big window sat over a white porcelain counter front sink. The cottage's furniture was a blend of shabby chic and modern, with white walls and tan mid-century furniture.

When Nate returned from the hallway through the living room, the big smile on his face was gone. He appeared expectant, apprehensive.

Outside, Mac asked, "All good?" But inside, he was thinking how close to a disaster he'd come.

"Yeah, why? Was it bad?" Nate replied, concerned.

"It could have been," Mac huffed.

"Wanna beer?"

Mac flashed a light, forgiving smile. "It's a little early, thanks."

"Yeah, I suppose," Nate joked, half laughing. "I'm stoked you're here. You got to meet Charlie."

Mac frowned. "Dogs are cool, but Mom's the animal lover."

"Oh." He beamed back, eyes wide. "How long you in town?"

Mac sensed something was amiss and answered. "Not too long and not long enough..." He trailed off, petting Charlie.

"Well, that's an interesting response." Then Nate turned toward the deck chairs. "Oh, sorry, wanna sit?"

"Sure."

They moved the chairs into the shaded area under the eave, facing west to the lawn and canal. Mac opened his chair with an adjusted angle so they were facing each other. "It's a nice place you have."

A pregnant pause. "How did you know where I was?"

"You're not hard to track."

Nate lowered his eyes but quickly came up bright. "Of course. You make it your business to know things."

"Mom's visiting for the week." And in a sigh, he added, "I actually brought her down."

"Oh. Does she not come often?"

"No, she doesn't." Mac reflected a moment. "It's been four years."

"Oh, geez. That's a long time." Nate began fidgeting. "But you've not been here in a year yourself?"

"More or less. I've kept the place in case I ever wanted to live on the beach again."

"I see."

"Yeah."

He gestured, opening his hand to ask what was up. Nate missed it. Mac looked at Charlie and considered Nate was lonely and needed a companion, hence the dog. They sat quietly for a moment, then Mac added, "It's changed a lot here, hasn't it?"

"Besides the pandemic? Yeah, but it's still great, though. Especially here on the canals."

"Hiding out in the canals maybe?" Mac asked leaning towards Nate.

"I haven't been back to the peninsula, if that's what you mean."

"You feel more protected here?"

"We get a lot of walk-bys, but it doesn't attract the riff-raff. You know what I mean?"

"Still, the environment has changed out there so you gotta wonder who is wandering around at night." Mac watched his assessment land. Nate nodded in thought.

Mac continued, "People are desperate. The lifestyle and safety element has shifted. I could see it today. It's not good."

"Yeah," Nate admitted, tapping his fingers on his knees.

"You're fidgeting," Mac said, looking at Nate's hand. "You're very nervous, Nate. It's not like you."

Nate rolled his eyes. "I am," he replied, eyes widening. "We need to talk."

CHAPTER 18

Mac and Nate sat looking at the canal. Neither one said anything or looked at each other, but whatever Nate was about to tell Mac, it held the forefront of both their minds.

"About what exactly?"

"Your mom doesn't suspect anything?"

"Why would she?"

"You brought her down here?"

"Yeah. She had a heart attack."

"Oh, shit! And you've got her walking all over Venice?"

"Best thing for her, really. What do you want to talk about, Nate, that's so important?"

"I don't want to talk out here."

"Well, we can't talk in the house, obviously."

"No," he replied, looking in the direction of the bathroom.

Mac took another beat and sized Nate up. "I think I understand. I think, mind you, not that I know, because I won't assume what you're about to tell me. We haven't rapped deep in a while. But I presume it has to do with Catamaran."

Nate nodded. "It's been so long, yet…"

"Hmmm." Mac nodded, sensing shame or guilt. He wasn't sure but knew the conversation would be longer than the time afforded by his mom in the bathroom. Still, it concerned him. Nate was a good friend. They hadn't served together. But they had gone through a rite of passage, per se, and Mac knew not everyone came out the other side without wounds.

"You didn't do anything, Nate. I did." Mac squeezed Nate's shoulder to reassure him. "I'll be here a week. We can talk about it." Then, grabbing his seat by its sides, he lifted his body off the chair for a moment, airborne before setting his feet down on the deck. "I'm gonna check on my mom." He stood and walked inside.

"Mac, is that you?" she replied.

"Yes, Mom. Do you need anything?" He waited, holding his breath.

Silence followed, then, "No, I'm fine. I'll be out in a few minutes."

"Okay, then. Take your time," he gasped, stepped away, and rejoined Nate on the deck. "Mom's fine. She is working it all out."

"That's good."

"I'm on a weeklong health cleanse with my mom. If we can last that long. I'd like to have that conversation now. Otherwise, we can go out in the ocean for a swim and do it there."

Nate paused a beat, his mouth agape.

"Why don't you turn on some music."

"Sounds good."

Nate turned on some classical music, and suddenly Chopin filled the air and the vibe changed. The serious look was back on his face. Mac walked straight in front of the speaker and turned up the volume louder.

"I don't feel I should go over to your building anymore in case someone would see me from management," Nate said.

"Fine by me. There's cameras everywhere now anyway. It's like my dad use to say, sometimes it's better to leave and let things cool off. I've been gone for two years. That's a lot of cooling."

Nate nodded.

Mac leaned in, "I don't have any regrets Nate. I'd do it again if it saved you."

Nate nodded again. "I'll never forget that. I just can't go back inside. Once you're in the system, you're done. I wouldn't survive it again."

CHAPTER 19

Kootz **drove northwest on Culver Boulevard,** then swung onto Washington, heading straight to Marina del Rey. He had the lights on but no siren. The streets were empty, traffic nonexistent, the way he liked it.

What was bothering him was that he hadn't been completely honest on his injury report. And now the injury had come back to haunt him. It was a major inconvenience. He loved his job, and he wanted to finish strong with full benefits. Retirement would be sweet, and he'd earned it. Ten years at the prison ward, duty in the field, and later investigative work. But that was before the accident.

He really enjoyed being a sheriff. He'd climbed the ever-pressing ladder serving jail riots, cartel hits, and one cast iron frying pan. A little desk time was fine by him. One more year. One more call. It was literally just a matter of months to retirement and he was done. Kaput.

But Kootz had his hands full. One of them, anyway, because the other one wasn't working. He was in a big-city beach town, and right now he wished he was retired and living off his pension in a small, quiet town somewhere far away.

But it wasn't meant to be. Not yet, anyway. He had another year to go. Then it was green grass and ocean tides far away from LA County.

Pacific Division in Culver City had his attention now. He swung the car hard onto Panay Way before realizing he should have gone straight. He flipped the car around with both hands and suddenly felt a plop in his neck, and circulation returned to his arm.

"What the hell is that about?" he said to himself and wiggled his shoulder. "This is one weird day that's getting weirder!"

* * *

Mac and Nate stood in front of the speaker.

"When did the cleanse start?" Nate asked.

Mac stepped closer. "I'm glad you're so fascinated with my mom's poop. Technically yesterday, but really this morning. That's why she needed to use your bathroom."

"I see," Nate replied seriously, then burst out laughing. "I'm sorry. I'm being silly, I suppose."

Mac whispered, "I hope she can't hear us."

"No, of course not. Thick doors," Nate replied, pointing to the bungalow's woodwork. Mac nodded reassuringly. The woodwork had nothing to do with sound reduction, and the living room to the hallway was wide open.

"So what am I missing here?" Mac asked. "Because the suspense is killing me."

"I'm feeling weirded out."

"About what exactly?"

"About what happened. What we did."

Mac put his forefinger up to Nate's nose. "You, my friend, should have flushed these feelings out a long time ago. You would have been past this now."

Nate's jaw dropped. "You don't have any remorse?"

"Nope."

"Because of your experiences?"

"Because I got my mom with me. I don't have time for it," he said matter-of-factly.

The bewildered look on Nate's face made Mac start laughing. "I'm serious, Mac."

They both stood face-to-face in front of the speaker, much like outside on the deck. A bleak emotion in Nate's eyes. A curiosity in Mac's.

Then his focus drifted to the art on the walls. They were covered in beautiful Japanese prints depicting local villagers and common city scenes. Nature and safari were also there. An overall sense of Zen filled the space, simplistic and clean, uncrowded.

The prize that held Mac's attention was a Japanese katana. It hung on the wall behind glass above the dining table. It was curved, with a single-edged blade and circular guard with a long black grip to accommodate two hands.

Mac reached over and turned the volume down. "That's new."

"Yeah," Nate replied, following his eyes. "I remembered that cool King Arthur sword at your place in Venice and thought this was right for mine."

"Subconsciously, it must weigh on you too."

"Huh?" Nate replied.

Mac did an exaggerated head tilt and moved on. "Tell me about these other pieces," Mac replied, turning away from the sword.

"They're called block paintings. Do you know about that era?"

"A little. It was the time of the samurai. A lot of intense sword making going on. Folded steel and all that."

"Yes, exactly," Nate agreed.

"The images are hand carved into the wood blocks, and the process to make washi paper is super intricate.

It involves water and stretching, then framing, the paper. It shrinks while drying, making it super tight, strong, and lasting."

"How do you know this?"

"I studied at a dojo when I was stationed in San Diego," Mac replied and turned to look directly at Nate. "You don't have to worry about anything that doesn't concern you. I was thorough."

"I haven't gone over there because it freaks me out."

"Listen to me. You've got a lot going on. Your future is bright. Don't mess it up by stirring up a past that can't be fixed."

Nate looked baffled. "I try not to, but you showing up here out of the blue kinda freaked me out."

"I apologize."

"I thought you were full time with FEMA."

"I'm trying to be a good son."

"Did anything ever come up about what happened?"

"Not that I'm aware of."

"Nothing ever?"

"Nate, I've been away working for a long time." Mac gestured toward the encased sword, "Christ, brother, look at that sword. No wonder you are having second thoughts." Mac looked over at Nate and casually asked, "Did you tell anyone?"

Nate's eyes went wide. "No, of course not."

"Okay. But you're considering?" Mac replied, not satisfied.

Suddenly, Sadie could be heard struggling to open the bathroom door. Several rattles ensued. The door popped open, and Sadie appeared. It was an awkward moment as she froze in the doorway.

Mac turned away. "And you're out. Good." Mac clapped his hands together. "We were concerned." He turned back to the art on the walls.

"What's going on?" she asked.

"Nate's art, Mom," he replied.

Nate chimed in, "We are looking at the block collection from the Edo era of 1603 to 1868. I'm kinda into printing stuff that's collectible."

Sadie looked at Mac and rolled her eyes.

"Details, Mom. We like the details," Mac chimed in. "He owns a 3D printing company called Kapow. The name reminds me of Batman cartoons, but it's actually Japanese."

Nate spent the next three minutes pouring information out that seemed to fly over Sadie's head like birds on a beach. Mac watched her struggle to catch up as her eyes squinted and blinked. *Confuse me anymore and I'm gonna explode*, was Mac's interpretation.

"And so on and so on," Nate rhymed back, folding his hands over each other like a dance routine. Or perhaps an ancient Japanese block artist making paper, as Mac recalled.

Finally, Sadie smiled and nodded in a circular motion to stop. She was burned toast. "They are beautiful. Very unique," she added politely. "I was a professional photographer years ago and did a lot of my own printing. Interesting work."

"That's so cool," Nate replied.

They looked like three Weeble toy heads from the seventies. Making funny gestures, celebrating mutual interests. Mac didn't think about the generation gap of thirty years between them. Never entered his mind. But he was aware she seemed distant and measuring at times.

Luckily, Charlie Dog wandered in from the garden to check out the excitement. Her presence changed the dynamic, and Sadie smiled, leaning down to talk to her.

She was trying to adapt and go with the flow. Out of nowhere, she said, "It's not always so easy, you know. My dog died."

Nate looked at Mac for confirmation. He nodded and gave a gentle smile, followed by kneeling down to pet Charlie too.

Nate asked with heartfelt concern, "What kind of dog was it?"

"He was a schnauzer," she replied.

* * *

Across Venice Beach at the condominium, Mac's phone beeped. On the screen read a series of fourteen numbers. The phone beeped for twenty seconds before going black.

CHAPTER 20

Back on Washington, Mac and his mom turned west toward the beach. They'd been walking about ten minutes when Sadie asked, "Are you sure it's this way?"

Mac barely turned to her. "AWOL, Mom."

"What does that mean?" she asked as she fell farther behind, looking east.

Mac slowed to wait for her. " 'Always west of Lincoln.' I lived here for five years. Don't you think I would know which way to go?"

"Well, it sure is taking a long time to get there is all," she replied apologetically. "Are you sure we're not lost?"

He spread his hands wide. "I want us to see pretty things on our walk. This is a pretty place if you know where to go." He pointed west. "The house is this way, as is the beach and everything else we'd like to do. See the sun in the sky? Beach is that way. Shall we?" He finished with a curtsy and smile but said to himself, *Stop being a jerk. Just be patient and flow.*

Sadie stepped up to Mac, and together they walked west down Washington toward Venice Pier. When they arrived at the northeast corner of Washington and Pacific, a closed flower shop held the corner, catching Sadie's attention. Its eerie windows were empty, and Sadie stepped up to the glass. Both peered into the dimly lit room.

"They left the lights on in the refrigerators," Sadie said, examining them.

"Yeah, I noticed that. Waste of energy," Mac replied, focusing on a center display.

The display was a round table with an open red umbrella. Mac imagined flowers on the table now gone.

"That's a waste of energy too," Sadie said matter-of-factly.

Mac looked at his mom, not knowing what she was referring to. A moment passed, then he said, "The cold. Yeah, it is. Maybe they thought the pandemic would end quickly so they left the refrigerators on."

"Well, it didn't," she replied.

"No, it's still here. I remember that table filled with pretty white orchids."

"Not anymore," she said, leaning in.

"No, not anymore." Mac turned to check the crosswalk. "Come on, the light's green. We can cross now," he said, stepping forward.

They crossed the street together and Mac looked over at the Cow's End Café. A huge rear half of a black and white dairy cow protruded out the second story wall, an iconic mascot on Washington's restaurant row. Mac pointed to the café below. "Remember the Cow's End?"

Sadie looked across the street and frowned. "I do. There was a good-looking guy that owned it. He liked my turquoise."

"Yes, exactly!" Mac replied joyfully. "He was wearing some turquoise himself the day you met."

"Yeah, he was. Bracelets and rings," she said, trailing off in memory. "How is he?"

"I don't know. Haven't been here in a few years."

Sadie shook her head and slowed. "My legs are tired, Mac. Slow down. You push me too hard."

"I apologize. We are almost there," he replied and waited impatiently.

Sometimes Mac would block out words she punched with discontent or bitter sourness and replace them with birds chirping and harmonious waves caressing the surf. This was one of those times. He smiled as he watched her waddle toward him, forcing love in his eyes. When she got to him, he nodded in some invisible mother-son agreement and walked beside her.

Inside he was thinking, *Love comes in all shapes and sizes. But this has gone way too far. This has got to get better or I'm going to go bananas.*

When they got to the corner liquor store, he said, "Be right back," and cut through to the medical section. He quickly went through the limited items, skipped past the brand name painkillers and swell eliminators, and found some generic aspirin. He looked at the dosage, checked the price, and walked up to the counter.

Mac didn't recognize the Hispanic guy behind the counter as he pulled out a wad of cash, but the guy recognized him.

"Hey, buddy. I remember you. Long time no see."

Mac looked up from the cash he was counting in his hand. "Yeah, how's it going? You're working today, huh?"

"You know me. Beach life is a happy life," he said and punched in the cash register.

"Dig it," Mac replied, counting out four singles after looking at the register. He laid the money down and said, "Save the pennies for someone that needs them," and walked out.

Sadie was standing at the corner with her back to him. She appeared to be assessing which direction to go, but that idea was dismissed when she turned to face him with an expression of disgust. "I don't need to be here," she blurted out.

Mac stepped to the corner beside her and calmly replied, "I don't need to be here either, but I'm trying very hard to make this work for the short time we have together."

"What's that supposed to mean? By punishing me. This is abusive behavior, and I won't stand for it," she continued, her fists pressed against her hips. "I will drive home and leave you here. How about that?"

"I think you got this backward, Mom. We were just getting to a comfortable place of friction."

"You're a real asshole, you know that?"

"You are correct. But I'm trying really hard not to be."

"That's exactly what I'm talking about. You have no compassion for what I'm going through. Do you want me to leave? Is that it?"

Mac contemplated the thought, and it actually didn't sound half bad. He could enjoy his day and probably the week with some surf and reading. Maybe sort out what belongings at the condo he wanted and what he would throw in the trash or donate. Then he could catch a flight back, faster and less of a burden. In fact, he could skip the whole week, leave everything up for grabs, and fly home that afternoon. Probably be home before his mom even got to Monterey County.

But he didn't say that. Only thought it. Instead, he said, "No, Mom, of course I don't want you to go. I'm sorry for pushing my health habits onto you."

"Not everyone is you, Mac. It's not just health. It's the way you treat me sometimes." She scowled. "You're no angel. You're not."

Mac winced as he stood looking across the last of the parking lot to the ocean beyond. The water was so close yet far away. He could see several colored umbrellas on the beach, the faded blue awnings blowing gently in the breeze. He sucked his top lip and imagined what the water would feel like against his skin. Would it be silky clean or dirty with silt and human grime? Between him and the water were a lot of homeless people, and he wondered where they were defecating. The answer came as quickly as the question, and it brought disgust to his face that sunk every imaginable thought of swimming. He turned to his mom. "You wanna walk back on the beach or down the alley? I'd prefer the beach if you don't mind."

Sadie looked into the distance past the parking lot. "That looks far and hot, Mac." She winced.

"Take the alley, then. It's right there. You know how to get in. I'll meet you at the house," he replied flatly and unapologetically.

"What do you have in the bag? Want me to carry it? Is it food?"

Without missing a beat, he replied, "Oh, these aren't for you. They're for me. I know you're gonna be fine, but me, I'm definitely screwed."

"What's that mean?"

"I don't want to fight with you," he said, brokenhearted in ways he only partially understood. "I'll see you at the house." He turned and continued toward the beach. Gone.

Mac walked west one block to the end of the road and turned south. He walked four more blocks through the homeless crowd littered along the edge of the parking lot and trail. It was on his own terms. Acknowledging but not engaging, polite but not hopelessly naive. And lost in his thoughts.

He knew many people on the street had contracted strains of COVID in one form or another and, like stray dogs, had other ailments prior to the pandemic that typically ran rabid among wild animals. But these were human beings, he reminded himself, feeling horrible. People who were sick and not any of them completely sane.

At the end of the parking lot, he turned right, removed his shoes, and walked straight out to the ocean. Thirty yards before the water, the beach shelved downward to the water's edge. A young Asian man sat meditating with his eyes closed. No one else was around. Mac stood nearby, pushing the paper bag deep into his rear pocket. As he looked at the man again, the guy opened his eyes and said, "Beautiful day, isn't it?"

"Yeah," Mac replied. "Great day if you know where to go." He turned his gaze back to the sea.

"You take care," said the man as he rose and walked away down the beach.

Mac wasn't sure if he'd interrupted the man or was just arriving as he was leaving. "You too," he called out oddly.

Mac thought about sitting in his car this time yesterday. Knowing the struggles he would encounter. Wondering if he could find the path of least resistance and help his mother who quite possibly didn't want to be helped. She might only be doing this to appease him.

As these fragmented thoughts bounced around in his head, his hearing was pierced with a loud whining. Then the thumping of a helicopter overhead. He squinted his eyes and was thankful he didn't have PTSD from his time abroad. He had a homegrown version from right here in the golden bear state of California.

His mom.

He turned and walked out of the wet sand and up the shelf, breaking the barrier that separated the water from the flat beach. At the top of the rise, the sand was soft and yellow, unscathed and powdery. It was soothing and felt good on his feet.

Then he looked up and froze.

CHAPTER 21

It looked like a massive five-alarm fire with trucks, police cars, sheriff department cruisers, an ambulance, and a coroner van surrounding his building. Pacific Division policemen had the streets blocked and were spreading yellow DO NOT CROSS crime-scene tape around the perimeter and out into the parking lot. Venice policemen were pushing back spectators as lookie-loos gathered. The police were shouting, "Clear away. Get back!" and forcing them back across the street to clear it and make the perimeter bigger for more emergency vehicles.

Mac started jogging. He crossed the sand to the parking lot in dismay. He looked for smoke. There was none. Now he began dreading the possibility that somehow his mother was involved. She had walked into oncoming traffic on a one-way street. It was only four blocks and three alleys. Seven blocks total. What could possibly go wrong?

Access to the apartment looked bleak. No one outside the building looked familiar. He skirted the crime-scene tape to the side of the building, pushing past several people on bicycles, and he found his mom in the alley near the rear of the building at the northwest corner. She was irate.

First, they were directed to stay clear of the building. Then Mac showed the closest officer his driver's license, so he was redirected to take a statement, then redirected again when he said he wasn't present all morning. Then the first officer came back, saying if he or his mom were present last night or anytime before sunrise, a statement would be required by both of them. Separately, of course, and Sadie wanted nothing to do with any of it. She was pissed off and blurted, "Jesus, Mac! This is what you bring me to? This is all your fault!"

"Excuse me?" asked the first officer. His tone was direct, and he looked at Sadie suspiciously.

Now people were starting to take notice as another officer walked over. It was as if Sadie and Mac had something to do with the matter at hand, and whatever plan they had to evade police was foiled by his mom's temperament. Regardless of the new predicament growing, Mac wondered what had occurred. Obviously, it wouldn't top the fury on his mother's face in that moment. Her cheeks were bright red, and her hair was lifting off from some sort of static cling fury in reverse.

"Excuse me, but I'll need to bring you both over here right now for questioning," the second officer replied, separating them from everyone else.

Sadie stiffened.

Mac said nothing. As he complied, he kept thinking about the coroner's van and what the hell it was doing there.

Finally, two officers had them separated and protocol kicked in.

Who are you?

What are you doing here?

Where were you last night?

Do you know the victim?

Why would anyone?

Mac nailed down the who, what, and where, but the police struck out on the do and why. The victim's name didn't sound familiar and was ambiguous, so Mac couldn't tell if it was a man or woman. There were so many denominations now, Mac just said, "No," across the board.

He couldn't tell what information was being divulged by Sadie. He was two-timing the officer questioning him, answering the questions while trying to read Sadie's lips from twenty-five feet away. Her lips were moving, but her body language told the story. Frustration, disbelief, judgment, anger, bewilderment, and overall general curiosity for some answers the cop wasn't willing to give. Mac knew the cop probably didn't know anyway, and it would be twenty-four to forty-eight hours before any real assessment of gathered intelligence could be formed into any real answer.

Thirty minutes later, after the stories were cross-referenced, driver's licenses were written down, and they were told not to leave town, they were released. They walked from the back of the building around toward the front and were quickly intercepted by another officer, this time a sheriff. He was large with broad shoulders like a fireman but with a standard-issue Glock holstered to his side and baton hung on his left.

"Excuse me," the sheriff demanded in a gritty voice. "Where are your credentials to be in here?"

"I have a unit in this building," Mac replied.

"Have you been questioned yet?"

"Yes."

"By whom?"

Mac glanced down at the name tag pinned to the sheriff's shirt. It read Bean. "Police department."

"Who specifically?"

"Why is that important?"

"Because I said so," he replied, pulling out a notepad.

"Officer Bleeker. My mom was questioned by Officer Ran."

"Where are the officers now?" he asked, scanning a three-sixty head turn.

Mac noticed the jagged scar on the side of his neck, and when they locked eyes again said, "Right now? I couldn't tell you. But two minutes ago, they were at the back of the building, northwest corner, questioning us."

"Let me see some ID," he demanded.

"Sure." Mac pulled his driver's license from his pocket and asked his mom for hers. She fumbled with her fanny pack, which at first she couldn't find. Then when she did, layered between the folds of her dress, she realized it was backward and upside down. She looked up to see if Mac had noticed, which he had, and she scowled, then struggled to unlatch it and reattach it right side up. The sheriff watched with amusement, took both licenses, and did a double take when he read Mac's before writing down the information.

"You got a DB?" Mac asked, taking his driver's license back.

"Yeah."

"Where?"

"Unit six," he replied, still making notes.

"Any idea on COD?"

The sheriff was willingly giving information, which wasn't normal during an active investigation. Mac knew that and thought maybe the cop was newly appointed to the field. Usually, sheriffs had jail duty and jury safety in the courts. In Mac's mind, if the sheriff was willing, he'd continue asking questions. He wasn't current on the latest protocol, but he hadn't been talking with sheriffs in a long time. Not much changed in the judicial system, and when it did, it usually took a long time. Since the pandemic hit the states, everything seemed more relaxed.

It was the term "COD" that made the sheriff tilt his head with curiosity. COD meant two things. To the general population, it meant cash on delivery. But to the medical, military, and judicial system, it meant "cause of death."

"Probably a heart attack. Who knows? I wasn't there," he replied.

Neither was I, Mac thought. "Can I take my mom upstairs to my condo?"

"I've been asked to wait for the detectives."

"Might we wait upstairs in the unit? My mom has a bladder infection, and waiting out here could be problematic."

The space between them went dead quiet. The cop looked uncomfortably at Sadie, then caught himself letting his eyes fall to her midsection.

"It's just around the corner, middle stairway all the way up," Mac added. "We'll be inside waiting for him or her, whoever needs to question us."

"I do not have a bladder infection!" Sadie huffed under her breath as the cop turned to look in the direction of the apartment or perhaps for the detectives. Mac wasn't sure. What he did know was waiting outside for a detective could take an hour. They were probably inside the unit where the body lay doing crime-scene analysis and belting out orders to the uniforms.

Not Mac's concern. Not his circus. Not his monkey.

He turned to Sadie. "Mom, if we wait out here for an eternity, you may get a bladder infection because it could be hours. Let's just say I was doing us both a favor."

"I don't need any favors like that, thank you very much."
The sheriff turned back. "Yeah, that'll be fine. But don't leave the condo."

"We will be there waiting. Thanks."

"Follow me. I'll walk you to your door," the sheriff added.

Mac turned. "Let's go up, Mom."

As the sheriff led them through county crime-scene examiners, more cops, and orderly mayhem, Mac thought about death. It came for all, no getting around that. *It is just a matter of time*, he thought as another cop waved them through.

To him, the question wasn't how long people wanted to live but what they did with their time. Time was precious. He'd seen a lot of people's lives cut short for one reason or another. Most he didn't know, and for the ones whom he'd cared about, he was grateful and appreciative for the time they'd shared.

There was a small batch of people he felt the planet was better without. But he didn't dwell on them or the horrible things they'd done. The thought that came to his mind when death was imminent was: had they reached their full potential? Had they experienced everything they wanted to during their lifetime? Had they found true love? Had they lost it? Did they give up hope or go back out into the world inspiring others? Then, given the choice, how did they want to die—slow and painful, or not know and it be instant and done?

Unit six had a small balcony extending out about eight feet that was equal in width to the width of the unit. Like half of the other units one through six, they were cramped, rectangular, and one level. He'd not been in all six units over his five-year stint in LA, but he had been in three, and unit six was one of them. The layouts were basic. A small bathroom at the back, a tiny bedroom, and a makeshift living room-kitchen area. Small and cheap, one would think, but not so at the beach. And now as they walked past the garage, a small herd of police and medics gathered on the balcony of unit six.

The sheriff they were following was halted by a policeman, this time a sergeant from Venice's finest. He was medium build, not big or small, but pointy in the face and missing his chin. Like a V shape from way back that never developed. Maybe his mom squeezed too tightly when he came out of the womb. Maybe the doctor pulled him out by his chin with forceps; Mac didn't know. But all these thoughts raced through his mind when he looked.

The sergeant's voice was pushed, almost forced, and nasal sounding. Some compensation to make up for it. He asked the sheriff, "Are they the ones?" and the sheriff confirmed with a nod. The sergeant turned to Mac. "May I speak with you?"

"Me? Sure. What's up?"

"Do you live in this building? What unit?"

"I do, part time, in unit three."

"What is your name?"

"MacGuffin."

"What's your first name?" he asked, pulling a notepad from his front pocket and flipping it open.

"Friends call me Mac."

"Mac MacGuffin?"

"Just MacGuffin. Like my driver's license."

The sergeant paused. "No first name? No middle name?"

"Correct. Just MacGuffin. M-A-C-G-U-F-F-I-N."

It took the officer a second to grasp it. "You serious?" He looked over at the sheriff, who nodded.

"As a heart attack. What's this about?" Mac asked, taking on a serious tone.

"Stay right here."

"We need to get to our bathroom. We have a bladder issue," Mac replied, gesturing to his mom.

Sadie said nothing, but her eyes said everything. Embarrassment. Why me? "Asshole," she said under her breath.

"Who's this?" the sergeant barked, looking at Sadie.

"My mom. I gotta get her upstairs," Mac replied, taking her arm and turning her toward the stairs.

"We'll get back to you. Stay in the unit," he commanded and wrote "MacGuffin" on his pad of notepaper.

Another officer gave Mac a hard stare and waved him onward. Mac was going anyway but turned back to say, "I'm a renter on vacation who wasn't here, so I don't think I can be of any help."

The original sheriff stepped aside and waved Sadie and Mac up the stairs like they were in the way. Like they were annoying.

"You're welcome to speak with me at the top of the stairs after I walk my mom up. Unit three is on the left."

The officer looked up the stairs, then nodded.

Mac's place was different because the lower unit connected to the upper unit via a staircase that went along the west-facing wall. Unlike some of the other condos, they had to climb to the top landing because the lower door had been double locked from the inside. It was a security measure Mac had made two years prior due to some alleged break-ins. It wasn't clear whether the thieves had entered units from the balconies or doors, but Mac found the extra locks appealing.

Then he left town. End of story.

Upstairs, Mac opened the front door and guided Sadie inside. She began ranting immediately as she entered the condo.

"This is ridiculous, Mac. I'm going to pack. We need to get out of here."

"I don't think they'll let us. As of right now, they'll want to question all of us."

"I don't believe this," she said and headed to her bedroom.

"Did you see the way they were looking at us like we had something to do with this?"

Sadie spun around. "Preposterous. Why would they think that?"

"I've no idea, but it might have something to do with you saying it was all my fault in front of the officer a few minutes ago."

She spun away and then quickly turned back. "Do you know the people that live in that unit?"

"I did, or at least I thought I did."

"Do you or don't you? Simple question." She made an angry face.

"I don't know. What I do know is if we try to leave, they'll think we're running. You can count on it." Mac went to the refrigerator. "Want some cold water?"

Sadie didn't say anything, so Mac pulled a water from the refrigerator and set it on the dining table, then said, "I'm not sure who it is they are talking about, but I think we are about to find out."

"Are we in trouble?" Sadie called up.

"We haven't done anything wrong, Mom."

"I know that. We just got here and I'm ready to leave."

Mac looked at the typewriter placed on the table next to the front door and turned the corner, descending the stairs. "Let's let this play out, Mom. Besides, we really don't have a choice."

"I don't know. All this is upsetting."

"I agree. But we said we would spend the week together." Mac opened the water and handed it to her. "We didn't know we'd be stepping into this."

Sadie said nothing and sipped her water.

"Look, Mom, I'll take you anywhere. Fires or no fires. It would be great to go to Yosemite. But it's closed because it's an ashpit right now." He took a deep breath. "I say we stay here. This will all be over by the end of the day."

"How do you know?"

"I don't," he admitted. "But things usually work themselves out. It will go back to normal. It always does."

Sadie looked out the window. "This is far from normal."

Mac offered nothing and remained quiet.

"I don't like all these policemen. It makes me uptight. I wanna go home." She took another swig from the water bottle.

"I'm going to go up to the deck. I've made it nice and we can hang up there. Bring your writing or painting things." Mac hesitated. "Actually, I'll carry up your typewriter."

"What do you think they will ask us?"

"I don't know," he replied, returning to the stairs.

* * *

Back in the double-wide, the television was on. A soap opera played with no sound.

"I was wondering how long it would take you to call!"

"We got a problem? The lady in unit six died." The nasal voice sounded irritated but not as irritated as the man watching TV with a phone jammed to his ear.

"I heard. The police called, wanting to speak to my dad."

"What did he say?"

"I run things now, remember? My dad didn't want to deal with it."

The nasal voice kept quiet.

"They wanted to know what was on the cameras. I told them I'd get back to them, which means you will give them access to the footage. But be selective. I don't want them thinking we're cherry-picking tenants. It can't be obvious. You follow?"

"So this is the opportunity we needed?"

"Maybe. Depends on what they see. What happened to the person in six?"

"I don't know. I don't have cameras inside that unit."

"Thank goodness. The cops will go through it with a fine-tooth comb. What do you think happened in there?"

"I can't be certain. She was a weirdo, remember? Difficult."

"She was squatting, is what she was. She wasn't on the lease is what I remember. Just get them the footage and see what happens. Maybe this will make everybody wanna move out, which is what we want anyway." He hung up.

CHAPTER 22

The upper balcony was approximately fourteen feet wide and ten feet deep. It wasn't big, but it wasn't small either, exactly twice that of the lower balconies. It had an outstretched tan awning that formed the letter *V* with the bottom exactly at the center of the railing. The top of the *V* ran the width of the deck and attached at the roofline.

The balcony looked down onto the beach, and at the far-right corner, a large red-and-white striped umbrella attached to the railing created more shade. It was slung into a makeshift bracket attached to a three-by-five teak coffee table.

Mac set the antique Corona typewriter down on the table, then retreated inside while his mom stood and watched him. A moment later he returned with a bouquet of plastic summer flowers and wedged the bundled stems into the aluminum bracket attached at the table's edge. At quick glance, it all looked very pretty with the flowers matching the red-and-white umbrella and the green typewriter set against the faded gray table. Something out of a mid-century novel with Hemingway ready to tickle the keys of the typewriter with thought-provoking storytelling.

But a radio squawked from the street forty feet below, and quickly the Caribbean dream disappeared and the Venice Beach nightmare came blasting back. Mac leaned forward, turned the palms of his hands up to press his eyes and brows, then scratched his head with his fingertips. Resting his elbows on his thighs, he spoke with thoughtful clarity.

"I want to share something that's been bothering me. I've been thinking about it a lot. I'd like you to know I want to arrive at a place where I'm not the asshole. Where you don't call me the asshole because that person doesn't exist." Mac slowed. "We never arrive at that place. And only then, I think... I think will our relationship improve."

"Well, you're no psychologist. But it's interesting."

Mac paused a moment, letting it sink in. He stood up and looked over the railing to the street below.

His mom watched him. "This will pass. The police will finish and go away like you said."

"You're forgetting about the detective," he replied.

"Oh," she said, her brow furrowed as she looked down. "You really think he'll come question us?"

"Me, definitely. You, I'm not sure."

Sadie pulled out a small pouch and set it next to her typewriter. "Why do you say that?" she asked, fumbling with the pouch.

"The cop's energy, especially the sergeant. Plus I'm technically a tenant. You're not."

"I'd rather not talk to them," she replied, lighting up a small pipe. "Anyway, you were inside with me all night, so you've nothing to be worried about."

"I'm not worried, but I wasn't inside all night."

"What are you talking about?"

"I woke up and went down to get your typewriter."

"You did?"

"Yeah. I forgot to bring it up."

"Well, don't tell them that."

Mac gave her a look. "It doesn't matter, they've got it on camera."

"Camera? What are you talking about?"

"They've got new cameras everywhere. They weren't here before."

Sadie pondered the information before asking, "When did you go downstairs?"

"It felt like 2:00 a.m., but I can't be sure. The cameras will know."

Sadie took another puff. "Well, you've always been good with time. Just tell them what time you think it was."

"Thanks, Mom," he replied with a hint of sarcasm.

Mac sat back down on the long red couch next to his mom. The question hummed in his mind, and he hesitated to ask, but he pressed on.

"So, Mom, when?"

"When what?"

"When did you know about your arteries?"

"It doesn't matter."

"It does. It raises questions for me."

"What questions?" She squinted.

Mac wondered if the squint was from pot smoke or something she was amused he was asking about now. "Didn't you wonder if we would have guilt about you going through this alone and not wanting our help?"

"I didn't want to bother you with this."

"You're my mom. There are tedious things, and there are bigger, more relevant things. This is one of those more relevant, life-ending possibilities. Didn't you wonder if we would miss you?"

Sadie said nothing.

"I know I can be a difficult son. I know I don't come around often. You seem to have a good thing going. You have created an interesting life for yourself with your art, your painting, your horses. Right?"

"Tristan won't call me. And Nadine doesn't have any time for me."

"Why am I supposed to have all these answers? Mothers and daughters are supposed to be tight. Have you taken any responsibility in figuring this out yourself?"

Sadie said nothing.

"It's a fair question, Mom."

"I've done the best I can."

"I'm not questioning that. I'm asking you to not give up so easily with Nadine and stop defending Tristan all the time, they get mad then they push you away. These are separate things. Separate relationships. You act as if Tristan owes you something and doesn't reciprocate for all the times you've defended him."

"He doesn't!"

"There you go. So that's it, then."

They both sat in silence, Mac's fingers interlaced on his chest, Sadie's hands at her sides, fingers tapping.

"So it's my turn now?" Mac asked.

Sadie looked at Mac, eyes narrowed. "I'm tired, Mac."

"Of course, you are. We just walked all over Venice Beach." They looked at each other drearily.

"What do you want?"

"I want to know what bothers you about me."

"What do you mean?"

"I want to hear your critique, Mom. Maybe I can fix it. Maybe I can't. I don't know."

Sadie took a deep breath and put the pipe away. She cinched the lace on the small pouch and took her time before responding. Finally, she said with tenderness, "I know you think about things bigger than yourself. I know you push yourself to do things for people that are extraordinary. I know you care. I know bringing me here should be easy, but it isn't. And yet you did this. That means a lot. I know I wasn't the best mother."

"You did fine, Mom."

Sadie said nothing and fumbled with the laces between her fingers.

Mac took a moment and replied softly, "Thank you."

"I know your work with FEMA is important to you."

"That's true." He shifted his weight. "Still is. It keeps life interesting. Making a difference."

"I just wish you'd slow down more. You are always rushing."

Mac's eyes wandered out to the beach. The little blue lifeguard tower in the middle of the sand, alone. "I slow down all the time, Mom."

"I don't believe that."

"I procure those times for myself. You just don't see it."

"Why can't you slow down with me? That's called compromise. How do you expect to keep a relationship if you don't compromise?" Sadie threw her hands up in an exaggerated manner. "Well?"

"I know. I get it. And I love you, but—"

"But what?" she demanded.

"You chose a nervous dog that barks all the time. And jumps on your legs. And isn't trained. It's annoying. It's hard to be around that."

"You're upset with Tintin?"

"I'm upset with you. You chose the dog and didn't train it."

"That's not fair! He's not even here to defend himself. He couldn't help it if he wanted to."

"Sure, he couldn't, but you could. Stop defending poor behavior. But it's your house and your rules, so I limit my time because it's nonsense to me."

"I'm nonsense to you!"

"We go places, and your dog pees on people's carpets. That's not okay, Mom."

"Well, he tries—"

"Tries what? To hold it? He pees, and you tell me not to say anything. That's wrong on all sorts of levels. Not cool, Mom. Not cool. Why do you think we don't get invited back to people's homes?"

Sadie said nothing.

"Did it ever occur that they knew it was your dog Tintin peeing on their carpets? Or were you too embarrassed?"

Sadie went to speak, but Mac cut her off.

"It's a rhetorical question, Mom. Obviously you're embarrassed because it shows a lack of responsibility as a pet owner. But what about me? What about how I feel? What about that?"

CHAPTER 23

The knock on the front door was loud and driven. Like knuckles wanted to bust through into the kitchen's back wall. Mac bounced his eyebrows. "Don't get up. I got this."

Sadie returned the look with no intention of getting up. She opened her paint box.

Downstairs, Mac pulled the door open wide and stood looking at what some might call a fireplug. "Hi," Mac said plainly. "How's it going over there?"

"I'm Sheriff Kootz. Are you Mr. MacGuffin?"

"I am."

"Do you reside here alone?"

"Part time."

"Are you alone now?"

"No. My mom's upstairs."

The fireplug lifted a handheld tablet attached to his waist and began jotting down notes. It was a Motorola MC9090 Windows model, and Mac noticed him struggle with his right arm function.

"So you got a DB and you wanna question us?" Mac added.

"Not 'us.' " Kootz squinted. "Just you."

"Okay." Mac smiled flatly. "My mom would appreciate that."

"Can I see your driver's license?"

"Yeah, sure." Mac reached into his rear pocket. He pulled the license from his wallet, letting the fold fall and his federal-issue ID hang facing the officer. He handed the sheriff his DL specifically across his body to the right hand. "Do you want to come in?"

Kootz took it. It wasn't easy for him. "How do you know there's a dead guy?"

"Call it a hunch." Mac stepped back so Kootz could enter his home.

"This isn't the time for a fuck around," Kootz barked.

"My thoughts precisely," Mac answered. "Why don't you step inside?"

Kootz took a breath then stepped through the door out of the camera's line of sight. Inside, he kept his brash demeanor, though Mac hoped the room with all of its Zen spaciousness and Buddhist pieces might bring calm to the fireplug. The home usually had that effect on people.

"How do you know the deceased?" Kootz asked with a neutral stare.

"I don't."

"Others say you do."

"What others?"

"Are you aware that you currently have a warrant for assault and battery?"

Taken aback, Mac replied "I am not."

"No one has tried to serve you?"

"No, sir. Not that I am aware of."

"I noticed your federal ID. Which department do you work for?"

"FEMA. Homeland Security Six."

"And no one has notified you of the warrant?"

"No, sir."

"Been out of state for two years?"

"Most of it. And overseas."

"I see. Well, it wasn't a warrant initially. But it went to a warrant, so you'll need to address it. Technically, I could haul you in, but I'm not going to do that on account I trust you'll take care of this right away. May I have your word on that?"

"Just give me the information and I'll get on the phone now."

"Do you know a Brandon Patterson?"

"I don't recall that name."

"Grab your phone and take a screenshot of this."

"Okay." Mac ran upstairs and grabbed his phone and came back down. Kootz was rubbing his right forearm.

"So how do you know him?" Kootz asked.

"Who?"

"The deceased."

"Did Hutch die? Hutch lived in unit six."

Kootz gave nothing.

"I didn't know Hutch, not formally."

"Is that what you called him?"

"I think his name was Hutch."

"So you did know him?"

"He died?"

"No, Hutch didn't die."

Mac looked perplexed. "You're not making this line of questioning very easy, and now I'm confused. I only just arrived on vacation."

"I see. How long you been living in the building?"

"I've leased it about seven years, more or less."

"And you say you're on vacation?"

"Yes, that's right."

"Must be nice." It was the first time Kootz hinted at a smile. "Aren't we all living on the beach?" The latter came out more a sarcastic statement than a question. Kootz looked over Mac's shoulder, scanning the room again.

"With my mom. She's upstairs."

Kootz shifted his weight.

"You single?" Mac joked, looking up toward the balcony. "You wanna meet her?"

Kootz sighed. Mac thought maybe Kootz didn't like his sense of humor. Or maybe it had been a long day. Something in his body language suggested he was suppressing agony, but Mac couldn't be sure.

"You all right?"

"I'll be fine. Stick to the main subject here."

"Which is what, sir?"

"Hutch didn't die. But the tenant in unit six did. How did you know it was unit six?"

"Because the sheriff told me. And all the commotion was over there when we got here."

Kootz grimaced. "The officer shouldn't have done that."

"You mean the sheriff," Mac corrected. "I'm just trying to be helpful."

"Do you have a beef with the deceased?" Kootz gave that hard stare again.

"Sir, I don't know who the deceased is. Like I said, I just got into town with my mom and haven't been around for several months."

"How do you know Hutch?"

"Hutch is the boyfriend or husband of Jizzy."

"Have a beef with anyone else in the building?"

"Not really, no. There is a guy in unit two that plays his music loud, but other than that, no issues."

"What's his name?"

"I can't be sure. I haven't been here in several months. The beach changes occupants like I change underwear."

"What is your mother's full name?"

"Sadie Elizabeth MacGuffin."

"Date of birth."

"Christmas."

"Which year?"

"Same year Pearl Harbor got bombed."

Kootz scribbled it down. "When did you and your mom arrive exactly?"

"Not too long after sunset yesterday. We are in a white Volkswagen Passat parked in the garage underneath. It should be recorded on the cameras outside."

"Anything out of the ordinary since you arrived?"

"Only the security cameras. They weren't here last time I visited." Mac paused as Kootz took the information.

With that, Kootz ended the interview. When he stepped outside, he looked at the two security cameras before continuing down the hall.

CHAPTER 24

Mac returned to go through the grocery list with Sadie and found her deep in her phone. On a Google search for dog rescue apps that listed mini schnauzers. Mac told her he would be willing to buy one from a breeder trained. He also offered to buy an older, trained dog that needed a new home. Sadie's eyes lit up with excitement at the possibilities.

Then she remembered shopping and demanded a special milk named Horizon. Mac preferred oat milk. But images of oats being squeezed made no sense to his mom. At the same time, Kootz questioning Mac on a victim he didn't know made no sense to him. Yet letting him go on an assault and battery warrant did. Bizarre circumstances.

The walk downstairs to the parking lot was uneventful. Not much had changed. The emergency vehicles had thinned, the slab wagon was gone, as were the firetrucks and paramedics. But the sheriff and patrol cars were still there, as was the yellow tape which left an eerie feeling in is gut.

The neighbor from unit two was there also, standing at the bottom of his stairs as Mac turned the corner. He was medium build, stocky, a mullet haircut, and dull look in his eyes. But his presence was confident, almost cocky. He stood on the stoop, which sat four stairs higher than the parking lot, so Mac had to look up to speak to him.

"Hi. You still live here, I see."

"Yeah," the neighbor replied.

"Is it Finn? I forget."

"Penny," he replied.

"I'm here with my mom and would appreciate a little courtesy on keeping the music turned down late at night. If you don't mind?"

"Oh, sure. No problem."

"Thanks," Mac replied politely and turned to walk away.

"How long you in town anyway?" Penny called out.

"Me?" Mac asked, turning back. "Just a week or so."

"Okay," he replied with a salute.

At Washington Boulevard, Mac turned right and walked four blocks east to Allan's Market. It was a one-level affair with a glass slider at the front. One way in. One way out. He could see two checkout lines at the door. The cashier could monitor who came in and out from the register. A sign posted on the glass read WE RESERVE THE RIGHT TO REFUSE SERVICE. Dame straight, Mac thought.

Inside on the right was a wall of magazines of the variety sort. *Homes & Gardens* to filth. Walking left, Mac passed the cashier, a middle-aged man who was alert and polite. They nodded at one another as Mac picked up a little green shopping basket and continued left through a decent amount of specialty items. There were fancy jams and sauces, all sorts of breads, an assortment of pastas, followed by more heavy carbs. All things that were not on his list. He worked his way to the far-left corner where the fresh vegetables and fruits gleamed under fluorescent lights.

Right alongside the celery, parsley, and radishes, a variety of exotic juices perched on display. Apricot, pear, some blend of melon juices. Even kiwi and kumquat. The others Mac hadn't heard of, like haskap berry from Canada. It had a pretty blonde on the carton, holding the berries in her hands. Across the bottom of the picture was her signature, Kris Frieberg. The rest were staple regulars like orange, grapefruit, lemon, banana, and others. It was overwhelming. The Mecca of juices.

He hadn't seen such a variety in his entire existence. He wondered what the world was coming to with so many choices. Temptation beyond temptation. He reached out and picked up the apricot juice and turned his wrist to read the label on its back. First ingredient, high fructose corn syrup. Lots of it. Delicious on a fast track to diabetes. A smorgasbord of refined sugar with heavy repercussions. Walk over and get your sweet fix.

How could it be, he wondered, that we have let sugar dominate our world? Where you are what you eat equals diabetes? And marketing the American way, where every freedom becomes an imaginary necessity. Gluttony.

He set the bottle back on the shelf. He wouldn't be getting his mom any of these juices. A comforting feeling washed over him, and he smiled to himself underneath his black face mask.

He was thankful his mom had come on the trip. Thankful she was brave to travel. Thankful the store was open and, frankly, surprised. He knew people had to eat, and the pandemic was being treated differently from town to town. County to county. Definitely state to state. There was a lot of misinformation. Fake news, they called it. FEMA kept him abreast of that with a stream of alerts.

Returning to the celery, he began loading his basket. He found coconut water behind him on a low, nonrefrigerated shelf. They came in carton containers that measured one quart. It read "not from concentrate" labeled underneath and had an image of a fresh coconut with a straw sticking out. Its ingredients read: coconut water, ascorbic acid (vitamin C) to maintain color. That was it. Nothing else. It had seven grams of natural sugar, zero carbs, and no additives. He filled his basket.

He set the basket at the front of the store and picked up another, then wound his way down the aisles to find protein powder and gluten-free superfoods. The store had plenty.

With two full bags of groceries and extra house items under his arms, he made his way back. This time he wandered along a short canal and approached his home from Eastwind Street. More apartment buildings than homes lined the street. It wasn't visually appealing, so he didn't appreciate the walk as much.

At Pacific Avenue, a small group of guys and girls were talking, and he recognized a loud, obnoxious chuckle that stood out above the rest. More a hackle sound, like that of a wild animal after a kill. It was Penny. Then two of the gals gasped, and feigned shock and disgust filled the air.

When Mac passed, one of the gals called out to say hello, but he didn't recognize her, so he politely nodded and didn't slow his pace. Then he heard Penny say, "What does he care? He's not Black."

Mac turned around and stopped. "Sorry?"

"I was just saying, what do you care? You're not Black," Penny replied.

"What does that have to do with anything?" Mac asked back, perplexed.

"Apparently a Black girl got gang raped under the pier last night. That's all I'm saying."

The human jaw can only take so much blunt-force trauma before it dislocates at what's known as the temporomandibular joint. Mac didn't know the exact amount, but at that moment, he imagined Penny's becoming lodged somewhere near the rear of his skull.

Mac looked at Penny, then let his gaze go around the group with disappointment. "Anyone in this circle that holds any resemblance of human kindness or self-dignity should stay away from this vile rube."

Few had stood up to Penny because he was the type who offered lip service all the time and hoped a reactive attack might fund the next twenty years of his bar tab. Mac remembered that hubristic quality about him from years ago, so Mac hadn't bit, not physically.

Instead, he finished with "You're disappointing on so many levels," and walked away.

CHAPTER 25

Inside the condo, Mac put on some classical music, placed the groceries away and washed windows. Once finished, he climbed the stairs up to Sadie, who was in the late stages of painting a portrait from memory. The painting was Tintin in heaven. Colorful puffy clouds surrounded him, and ornate wreaths of gold embellished his head. The clouds were soft pinks, pale blues, vibrant peaches, and soft creams, giving a sense of wonderment reflected in his eyes. Mac pushed the urine stains of Tintin aside.

"What do you think?"

"It's beautiful, Mom. He looks happy."

"I know, right?"

Mac smiled. He understood the polarity of it all. The delicate balance, magnetic and emotional pulls that could ruin the precious time they were sharing. Why ruin a sweet moment forever fleeting and jettison his mom to another migraine that would upset her? He wasn't going to do that now. There was no need to push, no need to judge, no need to remind her of shortcomings. Just chill and let her be in her world with Tintin.

"We have pressed juice or a smoothie. Which would you like?"

"I'm kind of hungry, Mac."

"Then smoothie it is. Heavier and more filling. Would you prefer milk based or apple juice with coconut water base?"

"Oh, I don't know. I'd really like some food," the pitch of her voice rising.

"These juices are food. I'm on it. And maybe we could do a light walk on the beach before sunset. It will be dark in an hour or so."

"My legs really hurt. Maybe we can watch a movie instead?"

"Sure. We can see what's playing that's new."

Back downstairs in the kitchen, Mac poured oat milk into his blender and added a pinch of cinnamon, then peeled a banana and threw that in. He added some spinach, organic Sunwarrior protein powder, maca root, hemp protein, a handful of raw almonds, two scoops of collagen powder and one of spirulina, and hit blend. The high-powered blender hummed, and the sludge quickly became a brown froth. Mac pulled out two tall glasses, removed the carafe from its motor, and climbed the stairs.

Sadie was rubbing her right leg when he arrived. Her right leg was twitching on the outside just below the knee, and she had her hand in a fist, pushing her knuckles against it.

"My leg is cramping, Mac. You pushed me too far. I can't handle it."

"Here, drink this, and I'll stretch your legs for you."

Mac quickly poured his mom a heaping glass of the brown froth and set the rest down. He pulled the table away and straightened out both her legs, then went to work. He held both legs by the bottoms of her ankles and began simultaneously rubbing with his fingers and thumbs.

"Ouch, too hard. I'm sensitive! I can't take it."

Mac lightened his touch and continued kneading with his fingertips and thumbs.

"Drink the smoothie, Mom. How does it taste?" he asked, trying to distract her.

Sadie took her focus away from her legs and reached for the smoothie. She would have to concentrate not to spill it, and Mac knew that. He gently slid his hands higher up her legs toward her calves, digging harder into her right leg with his left hand where the muscle spasm had been and was now gone.

"How is the smoothie?"

"It's thick."

"Is it good, though?"

She paused tasting it. "Yeah, it does taste good. Like dirt and spinach."

They both laughed.

"I want you to set the drink down and try to put your hands on your ankles while I hold your legs straight."

"Mac, I don't want to do that."

"Just try. That's all I'm asking."

"Please keep rubbing. That's all I want right now."

Mac nodded. "Okay, Mom, that's what I'll do."

Mac rubbed her legs for the better part of an hour until the sun dipped below the sea and darkness set in. He knew this was important to help her circulation. He was surprised at how strong his mom was, given her prognosis, and it was encouraging to see her going through the motions without massive upheaval. *Good genes*, he thought to himself.

That evening they watched a documentary about a man and an octopus living in Australia. The octopus taught the man life lessons, but Sadie saw it the other way around as the man always wanted to glorify himself. Like he created all these situations when they already existed and just needed to be acknowledged. It was a nice story either way and made them not want to eat octopus anymore.

That night Mac woke to pee only once, and the building was quiet. No bass-bumping music from next door. No homeless shouting in the streets below. No crunching of late-night passersby in the back alleys. No bicycle bandits trying to break into garages. Just peaceful quiet and soft rolling waves breaking along the shoreline.

CHAPTER 26

DAY 3

When Mac woke for the second time, his left hand was arched high above his head like a barrel monkey clinging to a branch, or something believed but not seen. He was more Buddhist than Catholic and thought maybe it was more a reach for help in the general direction of something physical and not spiritual. His body was relaxed, and yet as he lay there, he pictured the barrel monkey as a piece of a chain, a pawn of numerous proportions just hanging on and being held by a bunch of matching figures.

His eyes fluttered open, and a yellow light from the streetlamp cast a faint glow across the wall. When he looked up to the window facing his upper deck, a hue of sky still dark waited for the sun, as Roberta Flack yearned for when she sang her song "Here Comes the Sun." But the sun wasn't coming, not for an hour yet, so he rolled over and went back to sleep.

This time Mac woke to annoyed grunts and heavy breaths and sighs. Because there were no doors between rooms except the bathrooms, the openness allowed the house to be a sound box, easy to hear everything. In his mind's eye, he followed the sound of his mom rummaging in his guest room downstairs and smiled.

Mac rolled over, pushed his pillow from beneath his head, and pulled his right knee up to his shoulder. Then he repeated the stretch with his left knee and continued to listen. The kicker was when she said, "Where is it? What did I do with you?"

Mac grabbed his toes and flexed, doing a happy baby yoga move, and called out, "Good morning, Mom."

"I'm sorry. Did I wake you?"

"No, I was already awake," he lied. "What are you looking for?"

"My medication. I don't think I forgot it, but I can't find it anywhere, and I need it."

Mac said nothing and continued stretching. His morning ritual. Several minutes passed, and more grunting ensued.

"Can you call it in?"

"No, Mac. I need to find it!"

"But if you don't find it, can't you just call your doctor? I'll give you the pharmacy info down the street."

"Oh. Yeah, we could do that. But—"

Mac waited, and the room below went quiet.

"Yes, Mom?"

"It's prescription, and if I have it at home, my insurance won't pay for it twice."

"What is it?"

"It's for circulation, and it's expensive."

"I'll pay for it if you can't find it."

"I need to find it first."

Mac released his right knee and pulled the left up to his chest. He'd already deducted from the circular conversation that it was probably in his mom's medicine cabinet at home. Either that or the kitties had gotten hold of it and knocked it under something. Maybe her sink or bed or any of the hundred other things that cluttered her home.

Mac optimistically bounced up from his bed and descended the stairs two at a time. Sadie was wearing a loose-fitting white jumpsuit, a red scarf tied around her waist as a belt. Her colorful bags were lying on the bed wide open, along with her clothing, toiletries, and miscellaneous belongings. In a pile at the foot of the bed were several medications. Mac bent down and collected them.

"Mom, could any of these be what you're looking for?"

Sadie stopped pilfering the empty bags. In dismay, she said, "No, Mac. I've already gone through all those, and it's not there."

Mac set the plastic bottles back on the end of the bed and asked, "Would you like some coffee or tea?"

"Coffee, please."

"How do you take it?"

"I'll do it myself," she replied, frustrated. "Just let me know when it's hot."

"Okay."

Mac disappeared one floor up. When he returned, he had piping hot coffee mugs in both hands. The mugs were oversized and could double as cereal bowls. Sadie was still at the foot of the bed, though now she was sitting, looking perplexed.

"How important are these pills?" he asked.

"Very. Each one has a purpose, you know," she answered as if he needed it explained in detail because he wouldn't understand. She looked down at the black liquid. "Did you get that Horizon milk?"

"They didn't have that milk, but we can get some when we go out. Tell me about the pills you take."

"Oh, Mac, it's complicated."

"Try me," he replied, not affected.

"I don't want to talk about them. I have to have these surgeries, and it's upsetting."

"Can you tell me what the pills you're missing are for?"

"They're for circulation," she justified. "And I'm supposed to take one every other day." She seemed frustrated, still staring at the liquid in the mug.

Mac bounced back with, "Don't worry about it. I got you covered the entire time you're with me. Have your doctor call it in. We will walk to the pharmacy and grab milk on the way back."

"Can we drive? My legs really hurt from yesterday."

"Motion is lotion. We're gonna walk. It's not far."

"This is torture, Mac."

"I know, Mom. Anytime you use muscles you haven't been using, they'll hurt. You just gotta get back in the groove."

"It's not easy for me! You're too hard on me." she cried.

"It will get better, I promise. I can rub your legs again if you like?"

Sadie paused, then blurted, "I need coffee!"

Mac looked at her huge coffee and retreated upstairs when his phone pinged.

The phone was on the armoire at the door. It pinged three times before Mac lifted it to his ear. He retreated upstairs and lowered his voice. "I was hoping to hear from you sooner."

The voice on the other end was raspy, raw, and female. "Hello to you too," Simelane replied.

"We on a secure line?" Mac asked.

"Is there any other kind?"

"I suppose not with you. Did you get my text?"

"I did. If FEMA finds out you have an A&B, you'll be discharged."

"No shit, Sherlock. I was hoping you could get it expunged."

"Easier said than done. You think I have a magic wand?"

"I know you've got a magic finger."

"I can vouch for that," she replied.

"And a magic tongue, the way you bash men around," he said firmly.

"Only those who deserve it," she countered. "I'll need the information. Let me set up an access-encrypted email so it's untraceable, and I'll text you when it's done."

"Can't I just read it to you now? Easier, no?"

"Sure, but it's a lot of numbers and letters, plus there's a barcode I'm gonna need."

"I memorized everything except the barcode, which is sequenced. The sequence I know, but that doesn't help, does it?"

"Now who's in intelligence?" she joked. "Let me do my thing. But give me the case number and jurisdiction anyway."

Mac repeated the case number from memory and the Santa Monica courthouse where it was filed. Then he said, "Brandon Patterson is somehow linked, and I do not know who that is. Please get anything you have on him."

"Do you have a DOB?"

"Sorry? I do not."

"That could be a shit ton of people."

Mac paused a moment, then added, "Run California residents born between 1960 and 2000. That should narrow it down some."

A few seconds went by, and Simelane said, "Three hundred and thirty-one."

"Add weight over one hundred and eighty pounds."

"Why?"

"Because I have an issue with bullies. I don't see myself getting tangled up with someone that weighs less than I do."

"Okay." A few more seconds passed. "One hundred and fifty-three."

"Now add police records. Even traffic stops. Everything in the PND. If this guy was linked to an investigation, I want to know about it."

"Give me a minute," she replied then said, "I gotta go. I'll call you back," and hung up.

Mac dialed another number, and the cinnamon girl with the loud glasses appeared on the screen. His sister, Nadine. The phone rang five times before she picked up, and the sound of wind was heard in the background.

"Hi, sis. How's it going up there?" he asked.

"I'm on my way. I should be there in an hour."

"Great. I hear wind in the background. I thought you were bringing the truck?"

"My lovely husband broke the back window, and we haven't gotten it fixed yet."

"I see. For a second, I thought you'd taken the Saab."

"No, sweetie. We got rid of that last year. The kids destroyed all the buttons on the dashboard. It was time."

"What did you get?"

"A Volvo," she replied dismissively.

"Very family of you."

"What do you think of Mom? Did you see how big she is?"

"She's packed on some pounds," he replied, sounding disappointed.

"She's obese! She is easily a hundred pounds overweight."

Mac said nothing.

"Did you hear me? Hello?"

"I heard you."

"So, I'm gonna be there in an hour to do my thing. Then I've got a cleaning service scheduled tomorrow morning and a gardener too. I'll call you if anything comes up."

"Nadine?"

"Yeah," she said.

"Mom's getting a bit wacky."

"Oh, you noticed that too, huh?"

"Yeah. Not too bad, but she jumps subjects a lot and she's argumentative. Likes to fixate."

Sadie laughed, "She's challenging you."

"Why?" Mac asked. "I'm here to help her."

"Welcome to the next chapter of aging. I'm glad it's you with her and not me this time. I've had it."

"That's reassuring."

"You're doing a great thing being there. I appreciate you."

"I appreciate you. Thanks for coming down."

"Love you."

"Love you too."

CHAPTER 27

Twenty minutes later, Mac and Sadie exited the condo into the parking lot below. The east end of the building was still taped off. A big police notice was plastered to the door of unit six with crime tape and DO NOT ENTER. The rest of the building was back to normal, like nothing had happened. All the emergency vehicles were gone, and several resident cars were parked in the gravel at the base of the stairs.

Mac and Sadie walked to the beach-facing side of the building and turned north. They skirted Second Chance Park, where dog owners and their animals chased a tennis ball in the sand. After five blocks, they turned east on Washington.

"How far is the pharmacy?" Sadie asked.

"Not far. About a mile."

Sadie stopped in her tracks. "A mile. I can't walk that far."

"You can, Mom, and you will," he replied optimistically. "Don't give up so easily. Come on." He waved her onward.

Sadie sauntered forward, sneaking a glare at Mac.

"I'd like to talk to you about my dad."

"Oh?" she replied, expressing interest.

"Yeah. I think Dad was ready to pass on, ya know? He'd made his concessions and was at peace with his decision."

"I think he was scared to death of dying."

"Maybe," Mac replied. "Are you?"

"What?"

"Scared of dying?"

"I thought we were talking about your dad."

"We are," Mac lied.

Sadie said nothing, so Mac adjusted his tactic.

"Dad told me a lot in the months leading up to his passing."

"You did the right thing taking care of him as you did."

"Of course, Mom. I think I'm doing the right thing now too."

Sadie kept walking and said nothing.

"Did you know he'd already paid for his funeral service? He had no debt. He owed no money to anyone. He didn't want to inconvenience any of us."

"Your father was a good man. You're very lucky."

"I know. As are you."

"I always believed your dad's conscience was clean."

"He lived life without regrets."

"You shouldn't have taken his car away. I'd be furious if you did that to me."

"It wasn't my call."

"He was a sweet man."

"Who had had a stroke."

"He only got lost once."

"That we know about."

Sadie said nothing.

"Come on, Mom. After a stroke, things can get dicey, and we all know that. Dad was great at hiding it."

"He seemed fine to me."

"Are you taking your daily aspirin?"

"I take something else."

"What?"

"Don't worry about it."

"He was forgetting words all the time. One of the flags was his giggle." Mac looked at Sadie and squinted. "He'd start laughing when he couldn't remember things. He really slowed down that year. You didn't see him in the last two months. I did. I was with him."

"What did you talk about?"

"Being prepared for death and what he wanted."

"Which was?"

"His savings split equally among us. Nonsensically, he wanted his car back."

"I would too!"

"Do you know why he told me he wanted it back?"

Sadie looked at Mac blankly.

"He told me he had a lot of gigs to play around town. That he needed to load his drums in the back."

Sadie started laughing.

"Seriously. He hadn't played those drums in years. All of a sudden, he's getting calls to perform all over the city?"

"He did?" Sadie kept laughing.

"Yeah, gigs everywhere. He said he was in high demand. One of the terms he used."

Sadie laughed even harder. "I didn't know that."

"It was precious. And difficult too."

Sadie shook her head.

"He was confused as to whom he could trust. He became ultra paranoid."

"About what?"

"His plan to commit suicide."

Sadie stopped walking and stood there with a confused look on her face.

"It was simple. He planned to put a hose and duct tape in his car and head out," Mac said, nodding matter-of-factly. "Dad had chosen the place. An old road nearby that ended at a cul-de-sac surrounded by tall redwoods."

"Really?" Sadie's expression saddened, and Mac learned something at that point. His mom had no intention of ever doing that to herself.

Joyed with the information from her reaction, he continued onward. "Sad, but true. Selfish? I'm not sure," Mac replied.

They looked at each other, mutual sorrow in their eyes.

"I never thought Art would do something like that."

Mac nodded. "So I asked him, 'What about the pipe?' "

Sadie listened, saying nothing.

" 'The pipe, Dad.' And he asked, 'What about it?' And I said, 'It's gonna be hot. You could burn your hands.' "

"What did he say?"

"He said he better bring gloves."

Sadie leaned back with her hands on her hips. "Are you kidding me?"

"I'm telling you, Mom. He got really funny and loopy in the end."

"Do you think he really meant any of it?" she asked.

"I think he didn't remember who he'd told the story to and who he hadn't. I don't know if he was serious, though. I think he was trying to find out who was on his side and who wasn't. Each conversation in his mind held brutal consequences if he got it wrong. And I believe he got it wrong numerous times because Nadine was on to him right away."

"Are you for real?" she asked, turning to him and stopping.

"He was my dad like you're my mom, and this is stuff we should know."

Sadie started laughing again and stepped forward to continue. After a block she asked, "Was any of this true?"

"All of it."

"How do you know to ask this stuff?

"You know, I asked him when these conversations were taking place when he wanted to do this. And he said, 'Before Nadine takes my car away.' He knew I could keep a secret, but he wasn't sure about anybody else."

"Yeah?"

"I remember asking him when he thought she would try to take it. And he said, 'Soon.' Tristan asked to borrow the car, so he hid the keys. Then he couldn't find the keys. Then his car was gone."

"I remember that part," she chimed in, amused. "Why were you encouraging him?"

"I wasn't," Mac replied dismissively. "I was merely supporting. Holding space for him. Keeping his trust. Dad and I talked about everything, like you and I do."

"Yes."

Mac studied Sadie carefully. "So, what do you think about dying? In the end?"

"I don't want to be in pain, that's for sure. And I…" She trailed off.

"What?"

Sadie shook her head dismissively. "Nothing."

Mac reached over and touched her shoulder. "Do you miss him like I miss him?"

"I do," she replied tenderly. "Your dad was a sweet man. It just didn't last. But he was wonderful."

Mac let her shoulder go. He wondered what it was like when they'd split. What they'd fought about or if they'd fought at all. Maybe it was mutual, where the obstacles that broke them apart couldn't be overcome. "We don't have to talk about it if you don't want."

"Okay," she replied.

Mac swallowed when his mom replied so quickly. He'd given her an easy out. Too easy. "We all gotta die sometime. No getting around that."

"I know."

"He had other funny ideas he kept presenting me on ways to end it, if you're curious."

"He did?" Sadie said, surprised.

"At first I didn't buy into it, but it was his life. He didn't want to be helpless or comatose, and he knew his abilities were declining fast."

"And you listened?"

"Of course. It was his choice. He'd lived a full life. Realized his dreams. Eighty-four is a ripe age. Plenty of time on this planet to experience all it has to offer."

"It is."

"You're barely seventy, Mom. You've plenty of adventures ahead. Look at us here now. This is fun, right?"

Sadie smiled. "What else was he scheming?"

Mac paused and looked at his mom.

"He talked about crashing his car over a cliff. I told him he had a nice car and that would only ruin it. One of the grandkids might need that car one day."

"Aw."

"Then he talked about crashing head-on into a big truck. I told him that was selfish, and what about the other driver? I told him I'd be very disappointed if he did that."

"You shamed him?"

"I did. Then I asked him, 'What happens when some-body finds you? It's a pretty heavy-duty thing to find a person that's committed suicide. Scary and scarring too. Especially if you know them.'"

"And…"

"Yeah. He said he'd been thinking about that. That's when I mentioned Oregon. They've got a pill up there that's legal. Told him he could do that. Take it and go to sleep."

"Hmm. Is that true?"

"It's the Dr. Kevorkian pill."

"Who is he?"

"He was the doctor who helped people with terminal diseases die immediately. He didn't believe people should suffer."

"What did Art say?"

Mac changed his voice to mimic his dad. " 'Where is this guy? I need to meet him.' "

They both laughed.

"Did he really ask that? Is there really a guy?"

"Why? You want to meet him?"

"No, I don't."

"Good. I think he died anyway back in 2011."

They crossed an intersection and continued east in si-lence. Finally, Sadie asked another question. "What else did you say to him?"

"I told him I wanted to help him but that I was conflict-ed. That he could be helpful with the grandkids for as long as possible. Plus, I didn't wanna deal with Nadine's wrath. What would happen if she were to find out I had anything to do with helping him commit suicide? She would never forgive me."

"Well, that worked out nicely."

"It worked out perfectly. She got to be with him just before he passed, and he did it on his terms. Kinda beautiful."

"Nadine seems like she has closure."

"It's good. His stories were hilarious but disturbing. Especially about his car missing. When he learned the title had been changed? That was painful. Watching his brain navigate that."

"I didn't agree with that," she bit back. "You kids took away his freedom."

"Mom, he was thinking about going back on the road because his phone was ringing off the hook. Yet he didn't recognize his own ringtone, let alone know how to operate it." Mac shook his head.

"Oh my gosh," she said, surrendering.

"Oh, yes, and tasks he'd forget to finish. Once he left the bath running with a washcloth in the tub, and it blocked the overflow drain. Ruined the floor. That was a big one. It got dangerous when he started leaving the stove on."

Sadie smirked, a bit of guilt on her face. "He could have gassed himself with the stove," she said.

CHAPTER 28

The pharmacy was a Walgreens like every other Walgreens and CVS: located at a big intersection, lots of square footage, loaded with items, and a pharmacy in the back. Mac stepped up to the front and the glass doors slid effortlessly wide. He moved aside and let his mom step through into the air-conditioned store.

The store wasn't crowded, rather the opposite. A rail thin Armenian girl stood behind the register waiting for nonexistent customers to appear so she could tally their items and send them on their way. Sadie seemed confused at where to go with all the aisles, so Mac led her to the pharmacy in the far rear corner.

Behind the pharmacy counter was a thirtysomething woman with a plump face. She looked like a Tootsie Roll, with short, curly hair and eyeliner. She stepped up as Mac and Sadie approached.

"Sorry I took so long. How can I help you?"

"Not long at all. We just arrived," Mac said, smiling.

"I need to get my medication." Sadie said muffled behind her mask.

"Sure," the woman replied. "What's the name?"

"MacGuffin. M-A-C-G-U-F-F-I-N. First name Sadie with an *S*."

"Okay."

Mac looked at his mom and wondered why she had explained the *S*.

The woman struggled at the keys as she typed in the information.

"Do you have it?" Mac asked.

She struggled again and took a deep breath.

Mac took a glance at the computer, but he couldn't see the screen, so it was futile. "It should have been called in this morning."

The woman shook her head, appearing overwhelmed.

"Are you doing okay?" Mac asked.

"Yeah," she said and shook her wrists. "I took a two-month leave. It's my first day back. A lot of deaths in my family."

Mac and Sadie leaned away, purely reactionary. She saw it.

"Nothing to do with COVID," she spouted reassuringly.

"Oh," Mac replied, relieved. Sadie had kept retreating and now stood six feet behind Mac's left shoulder, watching. Mac turned back and frowned.

"I feel like my eyes are permanently swollen," the girl continued.

"I'm sorry to hear about your loss. Everyone is going through something these days."

The girl nodded. "Found it," she said and darted away. She went to the rack of shelves and thumbed down to the letter *M*. "Here it is," she replied, returning. "That will be $143."

Mac pulled out a wad of cash. She made change, and they parted, wishing each other well.

Sadie and Mac made their way toward the exit when Sadie turned to him. "I want to grab a few personal items."

"Sure, Mom," he replied and paused to consider items he might need too.

Sadie peeled off down another aisle as Mac wandered the empty store. He turned a corner and suddenly got a horrible whiff of stench. He grimaced, looking down at the floor, wondering where the source of the smell was. He turned and went back the other way. Two aisles later he turned and headed for the far wall of refrigerators.

Mac found the beverage section but deemed it worthless. Everything contained high fructose corn syrups and salted items for flavor. When he turned away from the refrigerator, the source of the stench appeared. A homeless guy wandering toward him. Medium height, slim, not poised, not groomed. Tattoos rode up his neck from beneath his crumpled shirt, and his grimy green pants were a blend of dirt and this morning's urine still dripping. Like his own private bubble of foul stench being served for public consumption.

The shortest distance to the exit was blocked by the homeless guy, so Mac turned away and backtracked. He found Sadie with a small red shopping basket hanging from her arm. She was looking at items in the hygiene area.

"You almost ready?"

Sadie practically jumped. "Yeah. What is that smell?"

"Vagrant."

"In the store?" she asked.

"Obviously. I'll meet you at the front door."

Sadie made a squinty face and looked away.

The pungent smell was still piercing through his mask as he darted down another aisle. He found what he was looking for in the form of a little black bottle toward the front. When he arrived at the checkout area at the front of the store, a thin, frail girl stood behind the counter shaking. She was clutching a phone in one hand and the nose of her mask with the other. The homeless guy was there filling his pockets with Rocky Road marshmallow bars.

She yelped from behind her pale blue medical mask, which Mac deciphered as *help*. The vagrant paid her no attention and continued like a kid on a rampage in a candy store. The girl threw up her arms in surrender as if her day couldn't get any harder. She looked like she was about to quit. Whatever they were paying her wasn't enough, and this store, as big as it was, didn't have a private security officer at the front door.

At least not today. Maybe they were on rotation with other branches, or maybe security only came on the weekends. Whatever the case, there should have been a guard. Especially since they had a pharmacy in the back with all sorts of high-target amphetamines and opioids.

Mac went into automatic mode. Retrieved two black latex gloves from his rear pocket. He stepped straight to the homeless guy and went for his ear, simultaneously slipping his free hand onto the man's left wrist, grazing the hand's forefinger, and reversing it so the wrist took all the torque. Guy went from chocolate scavenger to screaming maniac lightning fast. Mac walked him out the front door like a bad kindergartner headed to the principal's office.

Of course, if that were true, there would be all sorts of reprimands and paperwork. Probably a lawsuit would follow, and a countersuit, all leading to some settlement and a new law enacted in the county, then the state, and maybe the nation.

But the vagrant wasn't a kindergartner, just some mentally off-base person probably looking for attention and a free meal and thought the rules didn't apply to him. Or didn't know the rules. Maybe he couldn't read. Maybe he needed glasses. Maybe he came to the right store but forgot the money to buy the glasses and got distracted.

Maybe, but not likely.

Sadie was waiting for Mac at the counter. She and the girl exchanged glances. They both looked shocked. Mac walked up with no mask on as he removed the rubber gloves.

Do you always walk around with rubber gloves?" Sadie asked, astonished.

"There's a pandemic going on, in case you hadn't noticed," he replied. "Need me to pay for that?" He pulled a credit card and the black bottle from his pocket.

"You can have it," replied the girl.

"Thank you," he replied, turning to Sadie. "Mom, you ready?"

"What happened to all the candy he took?"

"I wasn't going to go through his pockets to retrieve it, as attractive as that sounds." He turned toward the door.

"What did you do with him?" Sadie asked, hesitant to follow.

"Who cares?" Mac headed outside. He returned the card to his pocket and waited for his mom out the front door.

Sadie kept looking at Mac with a perplexed look on her face, followed by looking around, expecting to see the homeless guy.

"Mom, what's up?"

"But you weren't wearing a mask?"

"Sure I was. I just took it off to talk."

"But you breathed the air inside."

"Says you."

"You didn't breathe the air in there?"

"Ever heard of the three-three-three rule?"

"No."

"Three-three-three: Three minutes for air. Three days for water. Thirty days for food."

"What's that—"

Mac continued, "Or you die."

Sadie said nothing. Astonished silence.

"It doesn't apply to me. I can hold my breath longer. Wim Hof Method and all that."

Still, the perplexed look plastered her face. She looked around again.

"Nothing to see, Mom. Let's continue on our walk. Did you take your meds yet?"

"Yeah. Inside at the counter."

"Then you may have breathed the air as well," he said, glancing her way.

Sadie's face drained of color, and her eyes went wide.

CHAPTER 29

On the walk through Mariners Village, the backside of the Marina, and toward the jetty, they kept an even pace. Twice Mac asked to carry her grocery bag, and twice she declined.

"You're not going to wear your mask outside anymore?" She asked.

"No, Mom, not outside."

"But it's the law, Mac," she pleaded.

"I don't have it with me," he replied matter-of-factly.

"What happened to it?"

"I donated it to the homeless guy."

After a moment of dismay, she blurted, "That makes no sense."

Mac glanced at his mom and switched subjects. "I spoke to Nadine this morning. She was on her way to your house."

"That's good. You should have told me. I would have liked to talk to her. Did you talk to Tristan too?"

Mac shook his head. "I take it he didn't call or text you either?"

"No," she replied, looking up at the street sign. They were passing Tahiti Way.

"Did you check his social media page?"

"I should do that when we get home."

"I'm sure he is fine," Mac replied reassuringly.

"Tristan needs to be checked on more than you and your sister. He is the youngest and needs extra attention. I think he sometimes gets stuck."

"Okay."

"So you should do that now."

"Mom, don't you think I have? Don't you think that maybe he resents me pushing too much or criticizing his choices? He holds grudges. People have done horrible things to undermine his successes, and he doesn't forget that. I just hope it doesn't hurt his path climbing back up."

"But don't you feel obligated as his older brother?"

"Tristan is his own man. As much as he is you, he is Dad too, the stubborn parts. He has accomplished great things and will accomplish a lot more. I'm sure he has wise people around him. He's a people person and always attracted talent and wisdom, you know that."

"I don't know. Some of his friends—"

"Stop, Mom, please. Just let him do his thing. He's one of the most hopeful optimistic people I know."

"He trusts too easily."

"Well, that's been true for all of us."

Sadie said nothing.

"He's gonna be fine. He is exactly where he is supposed to be. He'll figure it out."

"I hope so."

"You know, it's funny. When I told him I'd give him my portion of your home, he said he didn't want it. He didn't want it, but for different reasons. I wanted him to own a home, because I already owned one. I think he didn't want it because he hadn't earned it himself."

"You think he was too proud?"

"At the time, maybe. But later he changed. He is seeking life experiences. I think that is why he liked moving to the city so much."

"I agree."

They turned on the slow curved bend and came upon Mother's Beach. It was the end of a waterway stuffed with boats, like a cul-de-sac.

"I used to run this beach pretty much every day. And on days when I'd have to be at work early, I'd run it at 4:30 in the morning, rain or shine."

"Who are you, and could you please slow down?" she puffed.

Mac could tell his mom was tiring, so he slowed his pace. "Mom, a lot of people live this way."

"Not me."

"Exercise is good. Life is beautiful. It's what we make it," he replied. He took a big breath of air and looked up at the blue sky. "I bet you can see the Himalayas from space now."

Sadie looked at her son, perplexed, like he was from outer space.

"It's hard to imagine all this air being contaminated with COVID. I can see being in closed rooms and crowds of people. But outside? Hard to imagine."

As they walked, they came upon a young man sitting on the cement wall that made the curve. He appeared to be in his twenties and was looking at the boats docked on the piers. He was Asian, had medium brown hair, was clean cut, and had a nice appearance. As Mac and Sadie passed, he looked up. Happily, he said, "Nice day, huh?"

"Yes, it is," Mac chimed back, taking a double look at him. The man had features like a Japanese anime superhero and reminded Mac of someone he couldn't place. You never knew who you were going to see or meet. Even in the pandemic. He turned to Sadie. "How do you feel, Mom?"

"Right now, my feet hurt. Can we sit down somewhere?"

"Of course. Wanna sit here?"

Sadie looked at the young man suspiciously. Once she determined he wasn't homeless or weird, she said, "This is good," and stepped a little farther away to create distance.

Mac took the middle position ten feet from the man and began stretching.

The man gently asked, "What are your names?"

Mac turned and replied, "This is my mom, Sadie, and my name is Mac. You?"

"Chad. My name is Chad," he replied with a pleasant smile.

"Nice to meet you," Sadie replied. "We've had some weird experiences, so apologies if we are cautious."

Chad nodded. "No worries. First time in LA?"

"Me? No," Sadie replied.

Mac continued his small talk. "There's so many homeless now. It seems a third are mentally ill. Another third are drug addicts, plain and simple." He turned toward his mom. "And another third or so are people trapped in a bad predicament trying to get out."

Chad said, "It's terrible. And our government isn't helping much."

Mac looked back at Chad. "Not everyone on the street is bad, but some are."

"Yeah, I guess so, huh?" Chad returned his gaze out to the boats.

Mac leaned down, putting his arms straight out onto the cement, and stretched. He flinched and stood up, rubbing his left shoulder joint. Then he rolled his shoulders and asked, "Wanna stretch over at the bars, Mom?"

Sadie followed Mac's gaze and saw a sandpit with a variety of monkey bars, pull-up bars, balance beams, and swings with rings. Three people were there working out. They appeared clean and in a routine that kept them rotating. Sadie surveyed the sandpit, then looked farther away at the grass, tents, and a few homeless milling around.

"Those rings must be filthy. I don't think I want to touch anything. And those people aren't wearing masks."

Mac looked back at Chad. He wasn't wearing a mask either. "Well, they are outside, Mom, and I've this alcohol spray that I bought at the store. We can spray our hands afterward." Mac smiled and pulled out the small spray bottle he got from the store.

"That seems so difficult. I don't think so," she replied dismissively.

"Just don't touch your face. We'll be fine."

"No, I'm gonna pass. Let's go."

"Okay," Mac replied and turned. "Have a nice day, Chad."

"You too," he said, sincerely nodding to them as they departed.

Mac and Sadie walked another fifteen minutes. It was a bit farther around the bend, and the waterway where the boats entered and exited the marina was beside them. "How about here, then? Let's sit here and stretch a bit." Mac turned away and sat down on a low wall facing the water. Sadie looked at it, nodded, and sat down next to him. Her movement from standing to sitting looked painful, and she moaned as she sat down. "Need help, Mom?"

"No, I got it. I just want to sit."

Mac began a series of stretches that made him moan and groan as well, letting his mom know it wasn't easy on him either. He was exaggerating the moans, and she knew it. But he was dedicated and hoped his mom would follow along.

Sadie looked out at the boats, then quietly reached forward and touched her shins. She didn't moan like she had yesterday, and she consciously made an effort to straighten her back.

Mac thought things were looking up until a man approached them from behind, his foreboding shadow piecing their bubble. The guy stood over them, and the stench returned. Mac turned first and looked up at what appeared to be teeth that hadn't been brushed in a year. That's all he could see.

There are many shades of orange and yellow, like when the sun sets and the colors of birds' feathers. And then there was this yellow. Like oil paint drying in blots. This yellow was crude and greasy. It filled the man's teeth like remnants of tinted mud. It moisturized the teeth like a film of liquor and fungus. It was so pulverizing, Mac shuddered before standing up.

Sadie looked up when she smelled the booze. Mac helped his mom to her feet. But he really wished he'd rolled away from the bum. A gentle tug was all she needed, then he looped his arm into hers and swooped her away.

"That was beyond gnarly," Mac said beneath his breath as they walked. "Remind you of anyone?"

"Not that I know," Sadie replied.

"You sure? Anyone from Big Sur days?"

"No, Mac. Jesus!" she screeched like an uptight owl.

"What about Big Sur nights, then? Maybe somebody that's been living off the grid out in the woods?" he teased.

"Nooo!" she howled, pulling Mac closer.

They both started laughing and kept laughing until their bellies hurt.

Mac knew there was an invisible line in the relationship with his mother, and rarely did he cross it. Only in dire times had he done that, and the results were usually futile and left both his mom and him frustrated, angry, and not speaking to one another for extended periods of time.

But this was different, and he teased her with joy. He wanted this to be one of those moments where dredging up the past might throw absurdity into chaos and tailspin into their walk, sending them back to joyous times. Two years had been too long, and he missed howling with laughter only a son and mother could know.

"I was never that bad," Sadie cried.

"You dated some characters, Mom. That's all I'm saying."

"Oh, Mac! You better stop."

Mac slowed at another bench block, and they stretched for fifteen minutes more. Occasionally they'd break out in laughter and struggle to get back into their stretches.

Soon they continued their walk around the slow turn in the road without any more interruptions. The area beyond had low-lying foliage between the waterway and the path that ran parallel the road. When another enclave of tents appeared in clusters, Mac beckoned Sadie to cross to the other side. She complied, and they continued on.

After some zigs and zags, they came out on Lighthouse Street, which T-boned into a little bridge. The bridge was ten feet wide and sixty feet long, intended for foot traffic and bicycles. It crossed the canal that separated them from the peninsula. Beneath it, stretching left and right, was a slough of saltwater. Birds and other wildlife were plentiful, chirping above and scouring below the shrubs that ran its banks.

"How do you feel?" Mac asked, stopping at the center point of the bridge.

Sadie rested against the high, thick, poured concrete railing. She smiled. "Better now."

CHAPTER 30

Back at Pacific Division, Officer Russo was brewing coffee and watching Sheriff Kootz eye what was left from the Krispy Kreme box on the table. She dumped the used filter and poured a new batch of grounds into the funnel. Then she crossed the room, skirting the donuts, to her post, where her coconut carton waited. She looked at Kootz again and said, "They're not going to go away on their own."

Kootz rubbed his chin. "They will. As soon as a few more—"

They were interrupted when two patrolmen walked into the room, followed by a third with a nasty scar on his neck.

"Just in time, boys," he said, grinning. "There're some donuts in the box and fresh coffee brewing."

Both cops went straight to the box, but Bean went straight to Kootz instead, who was eyeing Russo in admiration.

Bean dropped the medical examiner's report in front of him. "Came back suicide," he said matter-of-factly and headed to the coffee machine. It was still brewing, so he spun around and looked back.

Kootz was opening the file. "What was the COD?"

"Fentanyl, and a lot of it. Look at the readings," he said, pointing to the file, then tapped the coffee machine like his touch would make it brew faster.

"Eight milligrams. Lethal dose is two."

"Yeah. Guy must have built up a tolerance. If he'd been taking it awhile."

"She."

"Huh?"

"She. *He* was a *she*," Kootz corrected.

"If you say so."

Bean looked over at Russo, who watched with nonjudgmental eyes. Then he pointed to her and asked, "What are your thoughts? He or she? The whole sex-change thing?"

Russo shook her head slowly, and if she'd had long hair, it would have fallen over both shoulders. But she didn't. Her hair was clipped short and tight around the ears.

"No comment, Russo?" Bean asked.

"No comment, sir," she replied from behind her post. "Happy to be happy."

"What does that mean?" Bean asked, but Kootz interrupted.

"The recommended serum concentration for analgesia is one to two nanograms per milliliter and for anesthesia is ten to twenty nanograms per milliliter. Blood concentrations of approximately seven nanograms or greater have been associated with fatalities where polysubstance use was involved." He turned to Russo. "Get the coroner on the phone so I can understand what I'm reading here." Kootz turned to Bean. "Hell of a detective you are. If this person was undergoing surgeries for a sex change, they may have had traces of this stuff in their system. We need to know that."

Bean fired back, "Haroun or Irene, whatever its name was, was in a building known to be a drug house. It was on a watch list of ongoing buyers."

Kootz returned fire, "Why do I not know this?"

"Because you are a desk jockey on loan from another department. It's called a declaration of cooperation between divisions. This is my investigation. I'm the acting detective who was first on scene."

Russo's eyes went wide as she watched the fireworks.

"I get it," Kootz replied, trying to be sympathetic yet maintain some sort of dignity. "But I'm trying to help. I didn't know it was a watch building."

"Because we are short-staffed, we were not surveilling it. This DB was a drug addict who was very confused. Obviously."

"Understood, but these loose ends can come back to bite us if we are not diligent. I am here and capable, so I will have input on this."

"Oh, that's ripe, considering you let the guy with a warrant walk."

"MacGuffin? He's a federal agent embedded with FEMA."

"Federal agent, my ass. Let me handle MacGuffin from now on."

"It is possible he didn't know about the warrant, so I gave him some leniency."

"And you believed him?"

Kootz felt a moment of doubt and wondered if he'd been suckered. Then he dismissed it and picked up the phone. He dialed an extension. "Any word on the recordings yet at Catamaran?" He turned to Bean and said, "Give MacGuffin twenty-four hours to address the warrant before you pick him up."

"Why?"

"I gave my word, and that still means something. Besides, county jails are full. What do you want to do, give him COVID?"

Bean replied by throwing up his hands. Then he looked at his watch.

Kootz looked at Russo, who was suddenly busy on the phone. When she caught his eye, she put her hand up and set the phone down.

"Sorry," she whispered, not wanting to be involved.

Kootz mulled over his thoughts on the case and the questioning of MacGuffin. He was a good judge of character, and when he'd busted MacGuffin's balls, saying it wasn't the time to fuck around, MacGuffin took it with a grain of salt. He didn't get rattled or spooked or even respond like a perp. He responded like a seasoned vet. Like he was a man who had seen action and was passive for the most part. But capable. Very capable, which meant he could be dangerous if he needed to be.

Kootz remembered looking at MacGuffin's eyebrows and seeing a slight scar over the left one. It was mostly hidden by his eyebrow hair, but there it lay. He wondered what other injuries MacGuffin carried and which ones burdened him the most.

Then Russo called over, "Line four, medical examiner."

"Hi, Doc, this is Sheriff Kootz at Pacific Division. I'm going over your autopsy report of the DB yesterday morning, a Haroun Petar, and I was wondering how long fentanyl stays in the blood after use."

The man took a breath. "That depends on several factors. Depending on the dose, blood tests can detect it between five and forty-eight hours after use. For a urine test, basically twenty-four to seventy-two hours after last use. And hair tests can detect the drug for up to three months."

"And what tests did you perform on Petar?" he asked, flipping the pages.

"All three. That's customary for cross-referencing. Let me pull up the file, though. I'm not at my desk, and we've been backlogged with COVID deaths. May I call you back in fifteen minutes?"

"Yes, you may. I'm at Pacific Division in Culver City. Officer Jennifer Russo will patch you through."

"I'll call you back shortly," he said and hung up.

Kootz turned to Bean. "So 'he' was a 'she.' And when was the last operation she had? She was obviously in transition because I thought she was a woman as well. Didn't you?"

Bean nodded. "Definitely." And kept nodding well past replying.

Kootz watched him pour a coffee, then looked over at Russo again. "You want a little detective work, Russo?"

"Sure," she replied.

"I want you to find out who her doctor was. Any examinations she may have had at clinics. The whole nine. And if she was getting those testosterone shots."

"You mean hormone shots, sir?"

"Yeah. Whatever it takes to transition." Then he turned to Bean, who was listening. "We can all work together on this, see? We're a team."

"Oh, yippee-ki-yay and all that."

CHAPTER 31

When Mac and Sadie arrived back at Catamaran, a silver four-door car was stopped in the street with its rear door open. The driver, an elderly man, was turned in his seat to an equally elderly passenger in the back. The passenger, maybe mid-seventies, was tall, dark skinned, and wispy. When he tried to get out of the car, it was a struggle. He had one bag of groceries slung over his forearm, which was gripping the car door. The other arm, grasping a black walking cane, was trembling as he strained to stand up.

Mac stepped forward and asked, "Can I help you?"

The man, who wore round hippie prescription glasses, looked up and seemed relieved by the gesture. "Sure, that would be wonderful."

The man's reaction wasn't exactly warm and fuzzy but was appreciative.

Mac stepped in, took the man by his thin elbow, and pulled him upright. "Why don't I take that bag from you too?" Before the man could respond, Mac grabbed the plastic handles and slipped them free from his arm still clinging to the door.

"There's another inside on the seat, if you don't mind," the man replied, this time a bit more engaging.

Mac looked past the man to the back seat. The way the man was struggling to navigate everything, he was surprised the guy was expecting to get home at all.

"Sure, be happy to do that."

Mac leaned in and looked at the driver, who had a mask on, crumpled, blue, and weathered. He was old and unwilling to help, regardless of his passenger's inabilities.

"Nice to see another brother in the building," the man with the cane said, gaining his balance.

Mac closed the car door and waved the driver away. Sadie stood back fifteen feet, observing.

"Do you live in this building?" the man continued gaining charm.

"My mom and I are just visiting." Mac didn't think the man saw Sadie standing clear out on the street. "How about you?"

"Temporarily," he replied in a sarcastic tone.

"Well, my name is Mac, and that is my mom over there, Sadie." Mac gestured with the grocery bags in each hand. "Where can I put these for you?"

"Unit two. I'd say follow me, but I'm a little slow these days." He turned to Sadie. "Nice to meet you."

"Nice to meet you," she replied.

His mom had a quizzical look on her face. Mac looked at her with his own perplexed look, concern growing. *Unit two*, Mac thought.

Loud music.

Banging noises.

All hours of the night.

Mac wondered if his mom had heard the man say unit two. This was the culprit next door.

"My name's Theodore, but friends call me Teddy."

"Then I'll call you Teddy, and you can call me Mac."

"Deal."

"So you're in unit two, huh?"

Teddy didn't answer. Instead, he used every part of his focus to navigate the parking lot with his long cane in route to the building. He wasn't strong and the driveway with dirt, gravel, and potholes seemed treacherous for him. It took two full minutes to get to his stairway and another four to walk up the short flight of stairs to the first level.

It wasn't unit two upstairs as Mac had presumed. It was unit 2A downstairs, the separate unit *under* two. The wall opposite Sadie's bed.

Teddy unlocked the door and beckoned Mac to walk inside first. Mac gave a polite smile and peered into what appeared like a yard sale at the end of a long day. Teddy's place was more disheveled than the man himself. A messy, chaotic home. A good match for the wiggly, mad scientist fellow, Mac thought.

Being the unit was separate made matters worse. Mac didn't have one noisy neighbor. He had two.

Mac navigated across the dirty floor toward the kitchen. A catastrophe. The kitchen counters were covered in spices and herb containers, and the sink was full with dirty dishes. He searched for a clear landing zone amongst the onslaught of debris littering the kitchen and settled the two bags on the barstools outside the small kitchen. When he turned around, Teddy was still struggling to navigate his way off the landing into the room.

A saxophone and several other wind instruments were strewn about. A bicycle lay against the wall in the corner. Various ornaments hung from the ceiling, which appeared to have chips in it at various places.

Teddy finally navigated to an armrest on the couch and sat down. That's when Mac noticed the odor. Sour milk maybe? He wasn't sure. He smiled and asked, "Walnut or imitation plastic?"

"The real McCoy," Teddy fired back, looking at his cane.

"So it's got history?" Mac asked.

"Oh, yeah. Just like the man who made the train parts."

"I'm picking up what you're laying down." Mac replied.

"You know the origin of the real McCoy?"

"I do," Mac said. "The genuine article. Elijah McCoy was a brother who made a lubricating device for steam engines, and every white man trying to make a quick buck attempted to imitate him."

Teddy smiled, removed his glasses, and wiped them clean with a handkerchief.

Mac looked at Teddy's eyes, they were glazed and red. Then he pointed at the ceiling. "Those chips in your ceiling have anything to do with the white scratches on the handle of your cane?"

Teddy nodded. "You're very observant."

"You been hitting the ceiling in retaliation to a neighbor upstairs?"

"Been two years going now."

Mac pondered a moment, the sour stench of milk in his nostrils. "And management hasn't done anything about it?"

"Nope. They're a joke. You didn't know that, being as observant as you are?"

"I'm not around much."

Teddy took a moment, then softly said, "That's too bad. You seem like a nice lad."

Mac and Teddy shared a moment, holding the space. Mac found it odd Teddy had used the term "nice lad."

"Tell you what," Mac added awkwardly. "My mom is sleeping on the other side of that wall. So when I hear that music get loud, give your cane a rest. I'll walk over and talk to the guy upstairs. What's his name?"

"Xenophobe."

Mac said nothing but looked peculiar.

"Redneck. Asshole."

Mac smiled, pondered a second thought, then dismissed it. The stench was foul. "Well, gotta go. You take care."

"Oh, too late for that."

Mac stepped out the door, closing it behind him. Sadie was at the base of the stairs, looking bewildered. She had a look on her face like she was really upset. Even with the mask, her body language screamed Mac was in trouble.

"That man was sick, Mac. Didn't you hear his cough?"

"Yeah, but he needed help, and I didn't breathe in his air if that's what you're worried about."

"I'm worried about you as much as I'm worried about me. He probably has COVID," she hissed.

He urged her up the stairs. "Whatever he's got, it was in his body long before COVID."

CHAPTER 32

When they arrived at the second floor door, Mac asked his mom to punch in the code. She looked at him blankly, then pursed her lips. She pushed the keypad, and to his surprise, it went green and unlocked.

Sadie walked inside and went downstairs with her grocery bag. Mac set the hand spray on the ledge at the door and went to the kitchen to wash his hands. After that, he went to the bathroom and grabbed a pair of nail clippers, then returned to the living room and checked his phone.

No missed calls.

No texts.

Sadie stood at the edge of the living room looking at Mac, his back to her. "You expecting a call?"

"Kind of. Looks like we both are waiting for the phone to ring."

"I appreciate what you said, but it doesn't make it any easier. I wish Tristan would call."

Mac took a deep breath. "You really don't remember, do you?"

"No," she replied matter-of-factly. "Remember what?"

Mac looked at her, then at the red painting on the wall. "I'm going to take a shower. Rinse off."

"That sounds good. I'll do the same."

They parted ways. She went back downstairs, and he went around the corner, sat down, put his head in his hands and wept. His love conflicted with his mother's inability to be disciplined on her own and take care of her health. The tears rolled down his cheeks and disappeared into the carpet. A few minutes passed, he gathered his thoughts, and showered. Then walked back downstairs toward his mother's room wearing only a towel.

His phone chimed. He picked it up and opened the text app. It was his sister Nadine, her bright red hair and glasses leading the charge.

Before opening it, he scrolled to a series of alerts and hit the newest one. It read, "Highly contagious variants of the virus that causes COVID-19 are on the rise in Los Angeles County. The new variants tend to spread faster, especially among African Americans and Latino Hispanic populations." He frowned and continued reading: "Please stay vigilant. Los Angeles County is again requiring everyone to wear a mask when you are outdoors and indoors in all public settings. This has always been and continues to be the case at all hospital locations and medical facilities."

Mac set the phone down and wished he'd not opened the news feed, then realized he'd forgotten to read his sister's text and quickly picked the phone back up. It was a series of photos Nadine had taken. The series started with the front gate of his mom's home and systematically went through the property like a garden tour. Everything was trimmed back and neat. The ground was swept and clean. The lemon tree was shapely and manicured. The garden was beautiful, unencumbered, and orderly. Then the front door was opened and looked inviting for the next photograph. Inside, Sadie's studio paintings didn't hang on the windows anymore. The glass was clean and unencumbered. The studio looked organized, orderly, and fresh.

Mac continued the photographic tour through the living room, kitchen, and into his mom's bedroom. The bed was neatly made, and the room appeared less cluttered. The paintings on her walls had a matching theme of forms and colors, rhythmic brushstrokes that brought a smile to Mac's face. There were no doggie toys scattered about on the floor, and the rugs looked washed.

He wondered what Nadine had done with all the other paintings. His curiosity was answered when he got to the second bedroom. Nadine had arranged them in stacks along the far wall. He double tapped one image and zoomed in where a kitty-cat tail disappeared into the shadow beneath the bed. This brought a chuckle, and he replied with several hearts of gratitude and hit send.

He was excited and wondered if he should show his mom the photos. He also thought there might be a better time to tell her. An opportune time when she might be upset and showing her photos would be an appreciated gesture. He also knew the invasiveness of what they'd done could blow up in his face. And his sister's. He hoped not. He crossed the living room, phone in hand to the top of her stairs, looked down, and froze.

His mother was at the edge of her bed, her back to him. She was wearing pale blue underwear, the panties barely covering her bottom. Mac saw the dimples of fat in the backs of her legs. The legs that carried him as an infant, strolled him as a toddler, and chased him as a child. The veins were there, varicose and swollen. As was the fatty tissue that clumped, as it did on her arms, twisted and ugly, cumbersome. They robbed her of fine lines and gentle curves as the fat robbed her of her youth and vigor.

Awkward guilt consumed him for staring at her body and he turned away. His upper lip curled inward, sadness on his face. What he wanted to say, he couldn't. He looked back over his shoulder, wishing for a different outcome. Then she grunted, a guttural groan that landed between frustration and irritation. He realized he was staring again and stepped away, saddened and lonely.

When Sadie returned upstairs, she was wearing a new mask. It had fresh folds and stretched open to cover her nostrils. Mac sat at the table with two small water bottles. He was staring again at the red painting hanging above the dining table. The painting had variations of layered reds in abstract forms with underlayment, creating texture. Along the left edge, burned orange surfaced from top to bottom. The center had streaks of white.

"Who painted this?" she asked.

"A woman named Charlotte," he answered flatly, without emotion.

"It's basic."

Mac looked at his mom and back to the painting and grimaced. "Don't you like it?"

"Futile."

"Futile or fertile?" he asked, hopeful.

She looked at Mac and back to the painting. "Hardly."

"How does it make you feel?"

"It could be turned."

"Sure, which way?"

"Any way."

"Up to interpretation, don't you think?"

"No comment."

Mac took a moment, then asked, "Are you telling me you don't like my art selection?" Inserting humor to lighten the mood. It wasn't effective.

"I don't like a lot of things about you right now," she replied.

Mac felt deflated, and they both stayed quiet for a spell. He looked at the phone lying on the table before him and back to his mom. He gestured to the chair where he'd set a water bottle for her. "Why don't you sit down? I'm going to cut your toenails for you."

She looked at her toenails, then at him curiously. She pushed the bottle that separated the space between them to the side and slowly, cautiously, took a seat opposite him.

Mac reached out, and she lifted her right foot. He removed the rubber walking sandal and held her bare foot in his hand. It felt rough. Her nails were long and feet dry with little cracks and spider veins.

"She's a different painter than you are, Mom," he said softly.

"Yeah," she replied, looking back at the painting.

"And she's trapped in her own way. I think it's reflected in the painting."

Sadie looked back at it. "How so?"

"Don't the white lines and circles with the soft squiggle at the center seem to balance the painting?" he said without looking up. "All the red and orange symbolizing power and the white trapped inside?"

Sadie said nothing.

Mac began clipping her toenails with care. "She hasn't the life experiences you've had. Nor the time you have now. She's a worker bee."

Sadie said nothing.

"I imagine your paintings are much more complex than the paintings you did three years ago."

"I imagine so." Then Sadie's tone changed. "What's it gonna take for you to take this seriously?"

"What are you talking about? I am here, aren't I?"

"This virus is serious, Mac."

"So is your diet and weight problem, Mom. Is that your way of saying you love me?"

"Don't be silly."

"It's a real question. When death looms, it—"

She cut him off. "I'm not dying, Mac."

Mac stopped trimming and looked up at her. "We are all dying, Mom. I meant metaphorically. What happened affects you." He looked at her deterioration with undeniable concern.

"You think it's so easy? It's not!" she cried, eyes filling with tears.

"Not at all," he said softly. "I just don't understand why you want to fight me all the time. There's no reason for it."

They sat in silence a moment, then he looked back down at her foot. "We should get some sesame seed oil. It will heal your skin and take away the cracks. Your feet will feel better."

He looked at the fungi growing along the lower edges of her swollen foot held in his lap. "I'm not perfect. I'm no painter, but I appreciate the art."

Sadie said nothing, just wiped her tears away.

"I'm half you, but I'm half of my dad too," he replied, sounding empathetic. "I don't have that vision or stroke of the brush. Just my own interpretation." At that moment, he felt pathetic. He didn't know why she was crying exactly.

"You might if you tried," she replied.

"Try painting mom? It doesn't interest me the way it does you. I'm glad for that."

"Why?"

"Because I know what I don't want to do. It doesn't stir my soul."

Sadie sniffled.

"Having you here with me now. Connecting. Sharing. Talking things through. Helping, if you will let me. That makes me feel good. Not fighting with you."

"You think I want to fight you?"

"I think you are all too available for the fight. Always ready."

"Really?"

"Yeah. Trust issues, Mom. It's okay. Just accept the answers I give. Or stop asking questions if you don't like what the answers could be. I wanna help you."

"Maybe you're all too eager to fight too?"

"Sure. I get it from you."

"Maybe I don't need your help."

"Well, that's rich. Your weight is horrible and you wanna give up! Suicide by food. This is not okay with me, Mom."

They both sat looking at each other, then down at her feet, then at the floor. Mac felt ashamed. She, embarrassed. Both had matching downward *N* frowns on their lips.

"I'm sorry. I shouldn't have said that. I apologize." Mac's eyes welled up "I didn't need to say that."

"Do I embarrass you?"

Mac put his forearm to his mouth and wiped the tears away with his bicep. "I'm an asshole, but I'm kind too. Not all the time, but usually."

"So it's true. I do," she said.

"Sometimes," he admitted, taking a deep breath. "When you're stubborn and say you can do it on your own, but don't."

"How do you know I can't?"

"Experience. Trial and error. Look at where we are."

"I'm gonna go have a smoke," she replied and stood up.

Sounding disappointed, he said, "I didn't do your other foot."

"Another time," she said and walked up the stairs with one sandal on.

Mac sat alone with the other sandal in his hand, staring at the painting. He thought about his mom escaping to smoke her pipe. It wasn't his thing. It was the last thing he wanted on earth. Something Mac's dad saturated in most of his life. Something his mom dabbled in when making art.

Mac couldn't stand it. Always felt it was a mind shifter that led him astray. A way to dismiss a problem, alter perspective, or drift focus to something else rather than addressing the actual problem. The core issue. Pot's purpose, in Mac's mind, was to avoid issues. And it could become the issue, so the core problem was never dealt with.

At least, that was Mac's opinion on it. Because that was how pot affected Mac. And he'd learned marijuana was much stronger than ever before. All sorts of strands and flavors. It was amazing people got anything done at all, outside of weight training and gardening. He couldn't imagine smoking all day, being way up high in the clouds. Definitely not fully present down on Earth.

He wondered how it had become such an integral part of his mom's life. Then he thought about Teddy, and suddenly it was crystal clear. The mind shift of pot. Change your reality. Don't buy into whatever people were pushing that wasn't agreeable to you.

Xenophobe.

Redneck.

Asshole.

But Mac preferred going straight at the problem. Tackling it head-on. That was Mac's way. Sometimes the hard way.

Mac picked up his cell phone and checked his email. Nothing from Simelane. So he looked at the photo he'd taken of Kootz's tablet confirming he'd memorized the case and courthouse and googled number.

Then a bass thump from behind the red painting vibrated so hard it practically bounced the abstract off the wall. The sound immediately dropped dramatically, but the kitchen wall was still bumping. Mac thought maybe the neighbor did that by mistake. *Maybe he doesn't know*, Mac thought. Then he remembered the silly salute the neighbor had given him. His own gesture of a backhanded "piss off."

So he strolled out the front door, down the stairs, around the stoop, and up to unit two. He hammered the door with three loud knocks, which were answered ten seconds later.

The door swung open to blaring music, much louder than Mac had anticipated. The guy had a neutral expression on his face as if he was expecting someone else, perhaps party guests. Mac didn't know.

"I'm the guy next door, remember?"

"Sure. What's up?"

"I don't think you realize how loud your music is!"

Penny said nothing, a dull look in his eyes.

"Can you turn it down thirty percent? It is a lot louder than you think."

"Yeah, I can do that."

"Great."

The guy went to close the door, but Mac pushed his foot onto the threshold and blocked it. The guy looked down in surprise. When he looked back up, Mac stepped closer and placed his hand on the doorjamb, pinkie high, thumb down, and gripped it.

"I'll wait," Mac said. "You may want to mark the dial on your volume."

"Why?" He looked perplexed.

Mac leaned in closer, past the doorjamb. "Because you're a dumb shit."

The guy stood there, confused, like he'd misheard what was just said.

"I imagine you come from a long line dating back to your Neanderthal lineage."

It was too many words for Penny. His mind was dull behind vacant eyes. Suddenly, it all came together. His face reddened, but nothing else.

No puffing chest.

No peacocking.

No nothing. Just stood there and took it.

"That's what I thought. Now go turn it down."

Mac knew the cameras couldn't read the profile of his lips, nor could they record audio over the blaring music, so he kept his body language relaxed and pleasant. It was the step in and arm raised that shifted the dynamic, and only his neighbor was receiving it as a threat.

Penny retreated over to his stereo and turned it down sixty percent. Mac smiled, pivoted, and descended the stairs, a pleasant, nonaggressive smile of ease across his face. He looked at the second lower camera as he passed and noticed three-minute blinking lights in the camera's lens. Motion sensors. Then he turned the corner and the camera was gone from sight.

Mac reappeared on camera at the center of the building along the hallway that split the building into two halves. He climbed the short stairwell and passed units twelve and eleven. At unit ten, there was a small video surveillance camera screwed to the ceiling above the doorjamb. Mac knocked on the door and waited. He looked farther down the hallway and saw two more security cameras pointed in each direction. The guy in ten must have wanted a close-up, or he had internal monitors on a separate circuit.

The door opened, and the tired-looking building manager leaned around the door. Mac recognized him from the garage project.

"Robert, right?"

"No, Ribbit."

"Ribbit?"

"It's Welsh."

"Never heard of it. Are you really with management?"

"Yeah." He frowned.

"Well, why do I have to tell Penny in unit two to keep the music down? Isn't that your job?"

"I just post notices and fix things."

Yeah, I saw your work on those garage doors, Mac thought but didn't say. Instead, he replied, "I see. Then let me put it to you this way. Fix Penny so both I and the elderly guy living beneath him don't have to endure the noise."

Ribbit said nothing. It was clear he didn't care about Teddy's situation.

"The loud music," Mac threw in. "It's a problem for Teddy and me."

"Mr. Shivelbush is being evicted."

Mac paused. "Why?"

"He doesn't pay his rent. So it's just a matter of time," Ribbit continued.

"For what?"

"Until he is gone."

"So, we're not entitled to peace and quiet? Teddy looks old enough to be your grandfather. Where's your compassion? Sense of duty?"

"He's not, though."

"Not what?"

"Not my grandfather."

Mac looked at him sideways. "What's wrong with you?"

Ribbit stared blankly and finally said, "What do you mean?"

"He did mention something about poor management. I guess that's you?"

"I am not supposed to talk to tenants about other tenants."

"Well, you've already screwed that up, and I don't give two shits either way. You need to talk to Penny in unit two."

"You can write an email to the company. There's a sign on the front of the building with the contact information—"

Mac knew nothing about private citizens and apartment management. This was a far cry from navy housing. Everything in the navy barracks textbook he knew crystal clear. The enforcement had been razor-sharp with those lessons. But he was in unknown territory now. He might have to add a few rules of his own. Ones he'd created from long before his time in the service that dated back to his childhood. Ones that involved thirty-mile bus rides and pain that didn't bruise.

His favorite though was the blunt-force trauma headbutt. Hard to deny and usually a blackout. Which left receivers with shattered noses, short-term memory loss at point of impact, and very unconscious. Totally effective.

The offender could walk away basically unscathed if the nostril blood vessels didn't suffocate the victim. Which was rare. Less than a 0.01 percent. But he would also face legal consequences, which could be problematic.

Mac thought about other ways to dismantle him. He looked at Ribbit's whiny nose. It was thin and unfinished, like a parakeet's beak. Not a lot of blood flow there. Plenty of cartilage. Just looking at him and saying nothing wasn't working.

Ribbit stood quietly looking back at Mac. "Will there be anything else?" he asked.

Mac returned to several things that didn't bruise but turned and stepped away instead.

CHAPTER 33

Meanwhile at the police station, Bean burst into the squad room clutching a memory stick His enthusiasm was electric. A uniformed policeman, with a pointy chin and wickedly long ears that jetted out from beneath his police cap, trailed behind him.

"Guess what I got?" Bean practically shouted, crossing the room.

Kootz was knee-deep in paperwork on his desk. "Video footage," Kootz replied flatly.

"Yeah. And guess who is climbing around on the roof multiple times?"

Kootz looked up, interested. "I don't know. Who?"

Bean grinned. "I thought that might spark your interest," he said and sat down. The V-faced policeman stood by eagerly. "Wanna see it?"

"Yeah. Who is it?" Kootz replied.

"Yours truly, MacGuffin. I got him scaling the wall the second day he's on property and two more times after that. He's a regular monkey. And I've got him knocking on doors. Who's to say what else I find when we press him?"

The V-faced policeman spoke up with a nasal voice. "Tell him the best part."

"Officer Vitali here also has him going into the garage at 2:07 a.m. on the night the he-she died. And the camera at six wasn't working, so there's a likelihood—"

Kootz cut him off. "Wait a minute. Before you start making assumptions, let me see the footage—"

Bean interrupted, "Like you said, Kootz, it's a team effort. We are liking what we are piecing together. I knew there was more to MacGuffin than meets the eye. He's not been straight with us from the get-go."

"And neither has Hutch or his wife Jizzy," he fired back. He held the memory stick and tapped it a few times. "Jizzy is short for Jezebel. Haroun becomes Irene. The owner won't speak with us. Only his son."

"And you've got Penny, which is a girl's name," Bean added.

Kootz looked at Bean, then over to Vitali, the officer with the pointy chin. Vitali spoke up. "I think he's a drug dealer."

"Who?" Kootz asked.

"Penny. There's a lot of traffic in and out of his place. It's all on camera," Vitali replied.

Kootz smiled. "Maybe he's just popular, having a nice place at the beach."

"Maybe, sir," Vitali replied, sounding small.

"How far back did you review video?" Kootz asked Vitali.

"Four days," he replied.

"That's not enough. How far back can you go?"

"Two weeks only. But that's a lot of footage to review. It's a super busy building. Especially in the first and third stairwells."

"And who resides in the first and third stairwells?"

Bean put his hands on his hips as Officer Vitali began to list the tenants. But Kootz cut him off.

"Let's focus on stairwell three for now."

"Okay. That's easy. We got the DB Haroun Petar—or Irene Petar, because she did file to change her name."

Bean rolled his eyes. "Who is not on the lease, I might add."

Vitali nodded and continued, "Then you've got Jizzy, or Jezebel, and her husband, Hutch Bjorn."

"Swedish name," Bean added.

Kootz dismissed the comment impatiently wondering what that had to do with the case.

"Then there's Stevo Heuer. Which is a German name, I believe," Officer Vitali said, nodding at Bean.

Kootz looked at Vitali. "Why is that important?"

Vitali looked at Bean who said, "It's not."

"And that's a busy stairwell according to your camera's detective work?"

"Not as busy as stairwell one. Interestingly enough, all the traffic only knocks, and sometimes enters without knocking, on Penny's unit."

Kootz looked at Bean, then back at Officer Vitali. "He keeps his door unlocked. That's what you're telling me?"

"Apparently."

"So, beach life feels pretty safe?"

No one said anything and let their thoughts merge into concurrence with gradual nods.

Kootz looked at Officer Vitali. "Set up the video on one of those desktops." Then he turned to Bean. "That doesn't explain the black eye Haroun had," Kootz said slowly, pulling another sheet of paper.

"It matched the table, which was a natural path of collapse if, in fact, he did OD. But I don't think he did," Bean spat back.

"The guy was troubled, I'll give you that. But suicidal? Why then? What pushed him over the edge? Or did someone punch him or strike him with something? To me, he looked like a she, and an attractive one at that."

Bean took his time. "We know that head injury was pre-mortem. It was written right there in the autopsy report from the medical examiner. But we know it was the fentanyl that killed him. Not the head injury."

"But maybe the head injury led to the fentanyl." Vitali commented.

"By himself?" Bean asked. "Sounds lonely."

"Maybe two people took it together and one died. The other panicked and left. How many people passed through the camera footage within a two-hour window of the vic's death? Tell me that, and we might find another person in the room."

"We will have to use the surrounding cameras because the one in front of unit six was disabled."

"Is there a path an assailant could take out that front door or over the deck without being seen by that building's cameras? We need to know that as well."

"That's what I've been trying to tell you. MacGuffin was in the vicinity."

"But what's his connection to the body? It doesn't make sense if we don't have motive."

"We do if he was a loud music guy."

"Two units away? Doubtful. It's more likely there was someone else in the unit and the vic was struck and fell. We know it wasn't Hutch upstairs because we checked his bank records and his payments were made monthly with Venmo. He has a clean history with no priors. He's got no motive. He's a pussycat."

"And I interviewed the others on that stairwell. All said the same thing. He played music loud but not excessively, and they had no disputes with him. Ever. In fact, both Hutch and Jezebel stated, and I quote, 'We didn't know him very well. Only had dinner with him once I can remember.' "

Bean turned to Officer Vitali. "Anything yet?"

"Still prepping, sir. The first computer port was busted. Trying this other one now."

"Take him through the footage. I'm going to head down to the building again and see what else comes up. Maybe I missed something." With that, Bean turned on his heel and headed for the door, waving at Russo as he passed.

Kootz looked at Russo as Officer Vitali signed into another computer and loaded the memory stick. "What do you think, Russo?"

She replied, "It's not what I think, Sheriff. It's what I know."

"Which is?"

"Miss Haroun Petar could have been at any number of clinics south of the border. But not north. I scoured the entire database of LA County, Santa Barbara, and San Diego hospitals, clinics, and medical facilities, which were a lot, and came up with zilch. Whether Haroun or Irene, she was saving by subletting that unit. Wasn't costing her much. And she withdrew money in chunks."

"But none was going back in."

"And there wasn't any money found on her premises. Just what was left in her bank account."

"I don't think she was a drug dealer. Just a user."

"Sounds right to me," Russo replied. "And she didn't have to go far if she had a small-time dealer in the building."

"Rules out a robbery. But not a hate crime."

"You think this could be a hate crime?"

"Thought had crossed my mind, but people don't usually leave doors unlocked when there are haters living next to them. Doesn't fit. But I have a feeling I know what does."

Kootz opened the criminal records database and pecked at the keys with his one good hand: *MacGuffin, FEMA*, then punched search.

CHAPTER 34

When Mac returned to his condo, he went to the bathroom and showered. Five minutes later he went to the kitchen and grabbed two juice containers from the refrigerator. He entered the upper deck with both containers in one hand. One was pineapple juice with cayenne, and the other was carrot juice with paprika. Both appeared muted, a hue less bright than their true colors, deep yellow and burned orange. They were faded and heavily watered down in the small, plastic twelve-ounce bottles, their labels listing only a few ingredients.

Sadie had her phone up to her face, glasses on. "Lady Gaga's dog walker got shot while walking her three French bulldogs. Two of them were stolen."

"Who is Lady Gaga?"

"Who is Lady Gaga?" she repeated, taking it up an octave. "Come on, Mac. Thieves stealing dogs! Can you believe that?"

Mac calmly set the drinks down.

Sadie picked both drinks up. "This is not gonna do it, Mac."

"It is what it is," Mac replied.

Sadie looked at them. "It's not enough food."

"The idea is that our stomachs shrink, Mom. Our stomach is only the size of our fist anyway."

"Maybe yours is. Mine isn't."

"Just stick to the regimen, please."

"I'm going to be hungry. I'm hungry now!"

"You got the munchies now," Mac smirked, referring to the pot pipe.

Sadie pursed her lips, set one bottle down in front of her, and opened the other. She took a gulp. Then two more gulps. Gulp. Gulp. Gone.

Mac quickly snatched the remaining bottle up. Sadie glared at him as he reached for it. "That's not for me?" she gasped.

"No, Mom, this one is for me."

"But I'm really hungry!"

"Mom, this is mine. Every three hours. Drink some water if you're hungry."

"I need food."

"The cayenne in your drink squelches your appetite. Just give it a chance. That's what it's supposed to do."

"It's not working."

"Mom, please, you just drank the drink. Give it a rest. Focus on your painting."

"Mac, this isn't easy. I'm starving."

"Do I need to spell it out for you? I bought you groceries for two solid months, and you still cheated on your own."

"Life is temptation."

"Choices, Mom. Own them."

Sadie began fumbling with her nails. Maybe sand had accumulated under the nails, Mac couldn't be sure. But what he did know was body language. Sadie was ripe with avoidance. "Mom?"

"The doctor said surgery would fix it."

"What, stapling your stomach? Did he mention diet at all?"

"I don't want to diet like you all the time."

"I don't diet all the time. I don't even count calories. I'm not extreme. I just know my body and what I can and can't have on a regular basis." With that, he threw his hands up. They sat in silence a few minutes looking out across the Venice and Marina rooftops. "I know you know what's best, Mom. I'm not trying to force anything. I just want you to have a chance if you want it. The best chance."

"I know."

"You used to do your diets every three months, and it kept you in check. I do the same thing. Who do you think I learned it from?"

Sadie said nothing, her eyes wandering from the typewriter to her sketchpad and coloring sticks laid flat on the table.

"What's really going on, Mom? What's the matter?"

"Why hasn't Tristan called?" she replied, lamenting the disconnect. "It's upsetting." Her forehead crumpled. She rubbed the back of her hand against her brows as tears began to well up in her eyes.

Mac sat down and took a deep breath. "Why don't we do the beach today? We can take it easy. Maybe swim a little. What do you say?"

"No more walking?"

"Not today. Today we read and write and paint if you want."

"Okay. I like the sound of that."

"And tomorrow morning, maybe we do a yoga class instead of walking. How about that? I need it. You need it too, and I'm gonna find us one," he said, upbeat.

"During the pandemic? I don't think that's a good idea."

"Trust me. I'll find one outside. I'll find one or we'll make our own."

Sadie sat with a worried look on her face.

So, for most of the day, they sat on the deck reading to each other. Sadie had a novel titled *Walk Away*, part of a crime series with a female badass named Camaro Espinoza. Mac had a thicker book titled *Shantaram* by a first-time writer named Gregory David Roberts. It was a self-proclaimed memoir, but with liberties taken. Sadie found joy in the claim that the author had written it while serving time in prison. Said the sentence must have given the writer plenty of time to think on his sins while trapped in jail. Forced to slow down, time to sit and write about all of it. This prompted Mac to ask, "Are you suggesting I get locked up to write a book about my life, Mom?"

She laughed. "Not at all. I know being with me is a bit of a prison all by itself."

They drank another thin, pressed drink and went to the beach for a swim at 3:00 p.m. They walked out to the beach and south, away from the parking lot and Second Chance Park. Away from the bike path and people. Away from everyone. Just the two of them. They didn't swim very far, but they swam. The waves were small, and the sea was calm. They stayed close to each other and laughed about not separating.

When they returned to the condo, Mac finished cutting the toenails on her other foot. Then they watched an evening movie, *Bridges of Madison County*, with Clint Eastwood and Meryl Streep and they talked about it. Then they slept.

Mac hadn't pushed his mom at all that evening. He didn't try to find out exactly what her medical report said—something his mom wouldn't tell him directly anyway. He knew her better than that. She would be embarrassed. Then she'd feel irresponsible, having put herself in this mess in the first place. There were levels of guilt and deniability, all accumulating in age and experience.

Then there was the flip side. The reflex factor. It wasn't her fault. Children had been doing that spin for years. Mac remembered being one of them when he was really small.

He did wish he knew what was happening to her, though. Both mentally and physically. Getting his mom's password and checking her email for a doctor's report was one way. But he hadn't done that, though the idea floated through his mind while up on the deck as she made tea downstairs. But that would be uncool, an invasion of privacy, and he was having such a wonderful time with her. Why spoil it? No swipes of fingers on her iPhone. No way.

Just let her be, he reminded himself. The doctors he'd spoken with had been direct enough anyway. Heal her with time together and a regimented diet. That was the way, and he was doing it.

CHAPTER 35

DAY 4

Mac woke thinking about Kootz and the promise he'd made to him. Then he thought about Simelane and what she'd said. She would try to backdate the form, but there were no guarantees. What if there were two sets of files with nonmatching dates? That would complicate things, send up all sorts of flags, flares, and maybe explosions, and end with him locked in the slammer. But Simelane insisted he take screenshots as a safety measure in case he were to be arrested. Hope for the best, but plan for the worst.

He could take it a step further and send his screenshots to Kootz and the Pacific Division directly. Mac had his card, and he figured if any officer questioned it, they would presume the system was backlogged and resolve it on the spot, like Kootz had done.

But it still bothered him. Kootz, as rough as he was, was cool to Mac in his own brash way. And Mac liked him back, as one cowboy to another. Mac knew he didn't look like a cowboy. But he didn't look like a frogman either. He felt Kootz possessed the same salt and grit and would be fine sharing a foxhole together if the world came crashing down. Which it had.

He decided he would wait just a bit longer for Simelane. But not past the day's end.

Playa, like Marina del Rey, had a vibe of its own. Cleaner than Venice, but more affordable than Marina. The buildings were the same, systematic and regular. Nothing bizarre or architecturally challenging. And the people were chill, perhaps not as uptight as the peninsula.

The advertisement for yoga had been something posted for two days only. It was called "midweek yoga." All levels welcome. It wasn't. These people were trying to survive and keep the yoga flow going.

Keep the money flow going.

Keep the chi gong going.

And it was needed. So after Sadie's cup of coffee and a fully loaded blackberry smoothie thirty minutes later, they were riding bicycles south, back toward the jetty they'd passed yesterday. Mac was on his silver single-fixie bike and Mom on his red, rusted beach cruiser. Mac didn't tell his mom he'd found the class on Craigslist. Nor that it was all the way south of the boat channel in Playa del Rey, the next town south. But she pushed pedals, and he carried towels without incident.

The vibe when they rolled up to the yoga group was hippie dippy. Mac smiled as they joined a few other bicycles navigating between the parked cars to a small crowd of sun-soaked worshippers. Some in tie-dye. Others in nonmatching yoga gear reminding him of Big Sur. A nest of muted colors.

Mac locked the bikes against a No Parking sign and retrieved three water bottles he'd tucked into the back of his shorts. Then he removed the fourth water bottle from his mom's bike, the beach cruiser, which had an aluminum cup holder. The only thing not rusted on the bike.

"I'm hot, Mac."

"I know. I'm hot too." He replied.

"Can I have my water?"

"Yes," he said, handing her a bottle. "This will be good for us. A nice way to begin the day."

"We should have gone later. It's already too hot out."

"It's called Bikram yoga, Mom. It's supposed to be hot. Usually in a heated room. Look at the group. Kind of like Big Sur, right?"

Sadie didn't say anything, so Mac picked up the two rolled towels he'd set on the ground and motioned her. They followed the eclectic group to several others already set up on the sand waiting patiently. Some were stretching. Others were watching, but none were itching, thank goodness.

The class was set up on the sand as close to a matte gray apartment building as possible. For a reason. It had a cement foot path that bordered the wall. Eight big, four-foot-wide, six-foot-tall sliding closet mirrors had been placed side by side against the wall.

It created a beautiful reflection so the students could see themselves. It also gave a great perspective of the beach and ocean far behind them in the distance. *Creative*, Mac thought.

Then Mac looked at the reflection of the sun on the ground. It was almost eleven in the morning. The glare was hitting the cement path against the wall. The sun would continue to rise. He imagined its peak of high noon. He knew the temperature was hottest around two in the afternoon during this season in Northern California, but he wasn't sure about Southern California. Something to do with an equation involving latitude and physics. Mac chose to guesstimate and look at the sun's shadow and the path it would take.

The reflection of the sun off the glass mirror must have the cement walkway sizzling; Mac imagined the metal frames of the mirrors were probably hot enough to burn hands. In an hour-and-a-half workshop, this could be problematic, Mac thought, but he decided not to say anything to the group. The fellow yogis seemed naive to what the sun could do against glass.

Mac remembered how effective the sun's rays could be through glass to start a fire when he was in Boy Scouts. And how prescription glasses and the bottoms of broken bottles were even better. Bikram yoga was having a cookout, and these yogis were the feast.

No wonder some of them were so dark. They were all Caucasians, yet some of them had olive skin darker than Mac's. Vinyasa. Ashtanga and Bikram. All levels welcome, the advertisement had stated. Mac added to himself: *Come get cooked!*

He looked at his mom. She had no idea how hot it was going to get. That in the sun's direct wrath, every breath would bring a burning so fierce it seared lungs and scorched skin. Mac thought the only thing his mom was probably thinking about right now was seared tuna and scorched kebobs. For lunch.

In an hour, the sun's rays reflecting through the glass would be directly beaming onto the center of everyone on their yoga mats. A real cooker. Mac wondered, *Maybe it's an evolving class?* It started gentle, level-one yoga term, then evolved to another level, maybe two, evolving into "fry you to a crisp and you've no idea until it's too late."

Mac burst out laughing when he walked over to his mom. Not slow. Not fast. Not alarming. He leaned down and said, "Mom, let's move you over this way." When he tried to lead her away from the center of the mirrors, she resisted. Innocently, she fought him, pointing to her towel already set up on the sand beneath her. Mac opened his palm flat and gestured to an area at the far edge, avoiding the sun's path. "We are going to be much better over here."

"But I was making friends." She smiled, looking at the teacher.

To Mac, the teacher looked like a Pandora's box of misinformation, but he wasn't willing to say the price it would cost to learn its contents.

"I want to be where the teacher can see me," she pleaded.

The teacher smiled, but his charms weren't working on Mac. "It's gonna be too hot in the middle when that sun"— he pointed his thumb to the sky—"kicks off those mirrors."

Sadie looked at the sun. Then the mirrors. Then looked at the teacher, who had to touch his metal water container twice before picking it up. She grabbed her towel and followed Mac to the far edge.

Mac set up next to her and began stretching. He noticed the yoga teacher hadn't unrolled his mat yet. Just laid it at the center of the concrete and mirrors. *Probably cooking already*, he thought. Mac nodded and winked at the teacher, then gestured for Sadie to drink some water. He'd given her two small bottles of Smart Water placed next to her mat. Both were unopened.

Finally, the teacher unrolled his mat as a few late stragglers rushed in and set up.

"Not a big class," Mac whispered to his mom as they waited.

"People have to work, Mac," she replied.

"I don't think so, but you may be right."

Everyone was asked to stand at the front of their mats and place their hands over their hearts. The fifteen or so students, or what Mac's mom later described as victims, stood at the center of the mirrors directly in front of the teacher.

Mac thought a short swim might be nice directly after the hour-and-a-half class to cool off, then the ride back to the condo on their bicycles would be more pleasurable instead of walking. The sun's rays changed all that.

At first, the class started with some breathing techniques, deep and long. Then fast-paced, almost hyperventilating breaths followed. By the time they were in warrior one, the reflection of the sun through the mirrors was heating their feet.

Mac looked at Sadie. She resembled a bowling ball. But she was staying the course and trying her best to do the yoga movements.

"You having fun?" Mac jested.

She rolled her eyes sarcastically, then tucked her chin and focused on the teacher.

When he looked back at her ten minutes later during warrior two, her expression had changed to concern. They were both sweating—everyone was. The temperature was rising quickly. Now the sun was on their knees and climbing, its heat significantly higher than the air temperature.

Mac looked around the group, and saw everyone was flowing, then looked at his mom again. He wondered how much sun the group could take. The reflection split between the two of them, Mac in it and Sadie just outside its path. A look of discomfort was growing on her face. She would shake her head every time Mac turned to check on her.

"Do you want to sit and rest?"

"No," she grunted, determined.

"Just let me know. No shame in resting."

The teacher pressed on, as did the class, as the temperature continued to rise.

"It's freaking hot, Mom, I'm not gonna lie. Let me know when it's too much."

Then the teacher had everyone turn position toward Sadie so she was at the front of the class. From this perspective, she looked like a gigantic marshmallow with toothpicks sticking out.

Then the teacher had the group face the opposite way so his mom was at the back of the class. The class went through a series of movements, and when the class bent down to look between their knees, Mac saw Sadie lying down spread eagle.

"Mom? Are you okay?"

"No, I'm not," she replied with excruciating disgust. Mac stood up and went to her.

"This might have been a bad idea," he said, kneeling next to her. Sadie's cheeks were flushed and her face drenched in sweat. One water bottle was empty on its side and the other gone, nonexistent.

"Where's your other water, Mom?"

"I think I sat on it."

"That's okay. Here, drink my extra one," he said and handed it to her.

The next forty minutes passed by rather quickly, at least for Mac. The instructor was wonderfully accommodating. Sadie wasn't the only one struggling, and at several points during the session, several people took breaks in the shade or folded over and rested. The heat was blistering. The teacher took extra care of Sadie's needs and helped her into specific poses to the best of her ability, all the while encouraging her to rest when needed.

After that debacle, most of the class wandered off, their skin tighter than when they'd arrived. But two stragglers followed Sadie and Mac down into the ocean. Not a lot was said. They mainly stood in the gentle sea talking about how tight each other's skin felt.

Mac smiled and looked at his mom. "That was basically the yoga version of Botox. The idea was to get more limber, no?"

Sadie looked at the other two within earshot. "Excuse me. Have you taken this class before?"

They both looked over and shook their heads.

"We may have been tricked," Sadie replied, downtrodden.

Everyone chuckled quietly, as if their ribs had been bruised and jaws broken with their skin so tight. Apprehensive and cautious.

* * *

When they arrived at the condo, it was just after 2:00 p.m. They parked the bikes in the garage next to the white Passat and went upstairs. Mac went into the kitchen and pulled out three fresh-pressed juices.

"Would you like two this time, Mom? You earned them."

Sadie's eyes lit up and she reached for them eagerly. "I'll never do that again as long as I live. I could feel the sun like laser beams burning into my body."

"Imagine how the people felt in the center. It was a Bikram roasting. No wonder they were so tan."

Mac twisted his neck, and it stung. He grimaced. "I watched you breathing in sync with the movements, but that didn't last long."

"It was hard to keep up. I had beads of sweat pouring down my face. Down my arms. Down everything. My crotch!" she cried.

"TMI, Mom!" Mac belted, looking away.

"Thank God we got in the water after."

"I was concerned you were furious with me."

"I was, but I was as much at fault for being in this class as you were for dragging me there."

"I think my eyeballs were sweating," he replied. He stood up and headed toward the kitchen, his belly contracting to hold back laughter. "I think I saw a bottle of aloe vera in the fridge. Let me go look."

As he opened the fridge, his mom called out, "Mac, there's a pinging sound. Not sure where it's coming from."

"Huh?" he replied, looking back to her.

"There's a strange noise coming from somewhere."

Mac returned to the living room with the aloe bottle. They both stood quietly and listened. Another ping and slight vibration were heard. "It's my phone upstairs. I'll check it. I'm gonna shower after, and I'll meet you on the deck. Take this aloe with you and sit in the shade."

As Mac climbed the stairs, his phone pinged with a different sound, this time louder. He picked it up and looked at the screen. "Email. The plot thickens." The subject read "Yours truly."

He confirmed his cloud setting was off and opened the message. It read, "You better go onto the Santa Monica courthouse website and fill out your information. None of the courthouses are taking people in person. I'll try to backdate what you load if I can get in, but no guarantees. Everything is backlogged, and it will be a while before local jurisdictions get caught up. Send the info, and I'll see what I can do on my end. Ciao!"

Mac located the image of the tablet he'd taken from Kootz and hit upload. It immediately began spinning into an encrypted puzzle, with debris flying away from its center.

Morphing, it became a hurricane from a satellite view over a blue planet. It was above Earth and beautiful before worming into a black hole at the center of the frame, becoming ether. "Creative," he said aloud to no one.

He went to his Google history and found the Santa Monica courthouse website. It referred him to a dropdown menu, which he quickly navigated and was redirected to a form. He filled it out and took a screenshot. Then he emailed it to Sheriff Kootz directly and cc'd the Pacific Division front desk with his FEMA badge number and an attachment of two deployment referral emails for time served. In the note column, he wrote: "To Sheriff Kootz, on loan to Pacific Division for an unknown subpoena that went to warrant. TBD." He wrote his direct email and cell number, stating he would be out of state again the following week and to please contact him ASAP if this was an issue.

Mac and his mom both showered and met upstairs on the deck. It was a much-needed affair after the yoga adventure. The Hawaiian Tropic aloe vera was the equalizer. They applied a heavy amount to their faces, neck, and ears first. Afterward, they took turns putting it on each other's backs, arms, and other places they strained to reach on themselves.

Once their hands had dried from the sticky feeling of aloe, Mac continued reading Sadie's book aloud as she painted wild, colorful rainbow squiggles and abstract shapes. At various times, the images became shells, taking form with swooping boundaries. Mac was amazed at the variations and change with each passing hour. Then he pushed forward and started the next chapter, animated and descriptive and free. Not controlled or forced, but natural and relaxed.

That night they went to bed early and slept well. It was quiet, and they had no issues. Music played next door, but not loud, and it didn't disturb either of them.

CHAPTER 36

DAY 5

Mac was enjoying sleeping in, something he hadn't done in a while. When he woke, his mom was standing over him much like an exterminator might eye a pest. Startled, he said, "Mom, you're freaking me out. What are you doing?"

"Do you have a laundry mechanism?" Sadie blurted out.

"Do I have a what?" Mac asked, his eyes fluttering.

"A laundry mechanism?"

Mac rubbed his face and took a moment to grasp the question. "Yeah, I've just never heard it called that before."

"Where is it?" she demanded.

"The laundry mechanism?" he asked teasingly.

"Mac, stop being difficult."

"It's called a washing machine. What do you need to wash?"

"Never you mind. I just need it. Where is it?"

He sat up and yawned. "It's out back on the alley. I'm happy to wash your things for you."

"No, I'll do it myself."

"I'll give you some quarters. I keep them in the drawer next to the front door. I—oh my gosh, Mom! Have you looked in the mirror today?"

"No. I haven't had my coffee yet."

"How do you feel? Is your skin hurting?"

"A little. Why? Am I burned?"

"Does your skin feel tight?"

"A bit."

"It should. You got a lot of sun yesterday and you'll need to put more aloe on."

Dismissively, she said, "Just tell me where you keep the washing detergent."

"I should have some detergent under the kitchen sink. There's a utility drawer in the kitchen with a laundry key as well."

Sadie disappeared down the stairs, and Mac watched her go. She now looked like a roasted marshmallow on singed toothpicks. Little white blotches of skin at the folds of her arms and legs highlighted the scorched red skin. Mac shook his head and followed her down to gather the necessities for washing clothes. Then he grabbed his dirty laundry and brought it to the front door. Tiptoeing, he snuck over to the stairs leading below and peeked. Sadie had removed the blanket from the bed and was folding the sheets into a pile. Though her back was to him and blocking most of the bed, he could tell she was meticulously trying to hide something inside the folded sheets. He tiptoed back to the front door and pulled out twelve quarters, then went back to the kitchen sink and retrieved two Bounce fabric softeners. When he stood up, Sadie was at the top of the stairs with her sheets and travel outfit folded nicely in her arms.

"I'll walk down with you, Mom. It will be easier since this is a lot to carry."

"Okay."

Together, they walked down the stairs and turned left at the bottom. As they passed the garage, Mac noticed Ribbit standing there looking at Sadie's white Passat. He was holding his phone out, and the camera on it flashed. Mac stopped.

"What are you doing?" Mac asked.

Startled, Ribbit looked over. "Ah, do you know whose car this is?"

"Yeah, I do."

"It can't be parked in here."

"It's been here all week and hasn't been a problem."

"It's gotta go."

"Why is that?"

"Because it's assigned parking."

"These two spaces are assigned to me. This one and the next to it." He pointed with a bottle of detergent clamped to his hand. "So, what's the problem?"

"You need to use parking passes or we tow."

"You won't be towing any cars parked in my spaces. Passes or no passes."

"Actually, I will."

Mac took a beat looking at his mom then back to Ribbit. "Don't make me your enemy."

"Excuse me?"

"Did you talk to the neighbor because it was quiet last night?"

"No, I told you to write an email."

"Then fuck off."

"You can't talk to me like that."

"I just did. So why don't you do something productive like speaking with Penny or defending Theodore or anything else that needs addressing, which doesn't involve harassing myself or my mother."

"Like I said before, you'll have to email management."

"Let me ask you something, fuck stick. Did it ever occur to management that maybe Theodore isn't paying rent because of what's going on upstairs?"

Ribbit said nothing.

"You don't have to be *that* guy, ya know?"

Ribbit took a moment before responding. "What guy is that?"

"The guy that you are now. You can be better than that." Mac turned and signaled his mom to follow. His mom stood there looking at Ribbit until Mac coughed, then turned and followed him.

"Was that guy taking pictures of my car?" Sadie asked.

"Apparently."

Sadie frowned. "Why did he take pictures?"

Mac shrugged. "Probably was going to send it around in an email to everyone." He imagined towing was out of the question because the garage ceiling was too low to get a tow truck inside. Mac had met a few of the drivers, and none were willing to drag a hand trolly into a low garage. Tow truck drivers were usually not physical and might be somewhat lazy by nature. They generally enjoyed the perks of eating fast food. Drivers worked on an hourly wage, not by commission.

A truck company owner was different. He might walk a hand dolly into a garage to make three hundred dollars on a tow away. But again, the space was Mac's and that eliminated the tow threat, so he let it go.

"Who is he?"

"He thinks he owns the building."

"Does he?"

"No, Mom. A nice man named Reza owns the building. But since my friend Jim who was the building manager retired or fired, we've been handed this useless prick who takes pride in trying to take things away from tenants."

"Like what?"

"I don't know. You'll have to ask the other tenants. I just know the type."

"Why does he harass us? That makes no sense."

"Why people do what they do is rarely beyond me, but this fruitcake really takes one for his team. I don't get it, but I don't feel sorry for him. He's in a horrible position."

"What position is that? Wanting to own the building?"

They both laughed.

"It's a good building to own, right? A real moneymaker."

* * *

With that said, Mac turned on his heel and headed to the laundry room at the back of the building, Sadie in tow. The laundry door was a grate of meshed steel coated in black iron paint. A foot deep inside sat a squat cinder block cement wall with a step down to reach it. Mac approached, pulled a key from his pocket, and slipped it into the keyhole. When he twisted his wrist to turn it, nothing happened. Then he paused, moved the key slightly, and jiggled.

The metal door sprang open, the reverse of what should have happened. Another perk of things done cheaply, using metal vulnerable to rust instead of stainless steel. The beach life had its perks, but it came at a price. Anyone not familiar with it was either naive or so cheap their wallets squeaked in their pockets as they walked.

"The spring is broken again."

"What happened?" Sadie asked, not understanding.

"Oh, they welded it two years ago, and it rusted again," Mac replied, looking up at the broken metal. "No worries, we won't be here long."

As Mac removed someone's clothes from the washer and placed them in the dryer, Sadie stood and watched. When Mac reached for her clothes, she clung on and said she'd put them in herself. Mac obliged and added the detergent after. Then he filled the slots with quarters, turned the wash cycle to cold, and shoved the slide in. The washer sprang to life, and he turned and looked at the dryer.

"I think I'll start their load in the dryer in case they aren't coming back."

"Do you have enough quarters for our dryer?"

"I do upstairs. All good, Mom. Let's go."

As they walked back to the condominium, Mac turned to the right, away from where they'd come. But Sadie wanted to pass by and look at her car again.

"We can do that from either way, Mom. It's at the foot of the stairs, so all roads lead past the garage."

She followed, and when they got back to the garage, Ribbit was gone. Sadie leaned into the gate and checked the corners of the space.

Mac looked at her with curiosity. "Are you doing what I think you're doing?"

"You never know. He could be hiding from you."

Mac chuckled. "Maybe. He's a rat kind of guy."

Mac turned away and gestured for her to lead, but Sadie shook her head. Instead, she followed Mac up to the condo. "I think I've overdone it. My legs are really aching today. And my back."

"I'll just put some coffee on, Mom. Get you going. You need me to carry you up the stairs?"

"Oh, Mac. Don't be ridiculous."

Mac entered the kitchen and turned on the coffee machine anyway, then faced his mom arriving to sit on the couch. "What's going on, Mom? Are you really that sore?"

"My body isn't like yours, Mac. I'm a lot older, in case you hadn't noticed."

"I know, Mom."

"You pushed me too hard. I almost fell down this morning trying to go to the bathroom."

"I'm sorry," Mac replied. He knew he'd overdone it. It was obvious. He also knew there'd be an involuntary reaction she couldn't control. He'd expected it. His mom was a combination of truth and exaggeration, summoned by emotional scars deep in her history before he was born. The countermeasures he'd taken still only softened her return to what she knew.

And Mac returned to what he knew too. Defending his mom and those who could not defend themselves. And upon occasion, being ruthless. His verbal karate was a precursor to physical punishment. Skills he acquired from a very young age on the coast of Big Sur with slingshots and bullies. Then sports followed. Then the navy.

Mac was particularly fond of the tactical training the navy taught him, and he had been eager to learn. He remembered extremes and unpredictability were his best friends, constantly adapting as new regiments were implemented. And it was those adjustments that kept his mind alert and his spirit engaged. So, as he surveyed the debunked habitat, he began forming an exit strategy that would remove him from this building's equation permanently. One that involved an old teammate from the Navy SEALs named Joaquin.

"I'm going to rub your legs this morning while you drink your coffee. I'm also going to give you half a banana with some peanut butter in your smoothie to thicken it up. How does that sound?"

"I'm not a child. You're talking to me like I'm an infant."

"I'm sorry, Mom. I don't mean to do that."

"Well, you are."

Mac nodded acceptance. "That coffee is probably hot. Let me go get it. Also, take two ibuprofen with your daily medication. That will help with the inflammation and pain you're feeling."

"I've got tendonitis. And other things I can't pronounce."

"The ibuprofen will help that too."

"I can't walk today. I need rest."

"That's why I'm proposing we ride bicycles. Mix it up. Easier."

"Jesus, Mac, do you ever stop?"

"Yeah, Mom. But not today."

CHAPTER 37

Mac returned with two piping hot coffees and a glass of Horizon milk. They both poured their own milk, and Sadie took two ibuprofen liquid gels. Within fifteen minutes, her mood had shifted, largely due to Mac massaging her feet.

Mac convinced his mom to ride bicycles north along the beach path. It was the opposite end of the Playa, where they'd done yoga yesterday. The curves of the path were covered in sand and slippery. He didn't want his mom crashing and breaking a hip or femur. To make things worse, the edges of the bike path were covered in homeless tents. They had to go slowly.

Mac wondered when the police would get through the political red tape and clean the place up. It had been done early mornings when he was visiting before with power washers and street sweepers.

But there wasn't a pandemic. Not like this. Not crippling the workforce, debilitating county staff, and sickening many essential social and medical workers. Cleanup was at a standstill. So the curves were slippery.

The inhabitants living on the street seemed to outnumber the occupants living in homes. There were so many, it was nuts to him. Mac began to wonder who was paying taxes anymore with this overabundance of homeless, so he ran an imaginary calculation.

Housing taxes. Sales of whatever people consumed. He tripled alcohol due to the homeless encampments and depression. And tourism.

Which was nonexistent.

Except for Sadie and Mac, who felt very much like tourists.

He saw the final number of lost revenue in the trillions and shook his head. Like the tide, Mac knew there was an ebb and flow to the system as a whole.

Venice was built on it. The tides. They constructed the breakwater originally while the tide was out. Then when the tide rose, they'd wait until it went out again.

Same with construction. Timing. Same with cleaning up Venice. They'd let it go to a point, then come in and wash the collective scum away. And there was a lot of scum.

When the bike path straightened, Mac slowed, and they rode side by side.

"When do you think the homeless situation will get figured out?" Sadie asked.

"I don't know, Mom. But they will, eventually."

"I hope soon. Do you think it will be different?"

"Different how? With the amount of people living on the street?"

"Yeah."

"Not really. I think there will be designated areas where homeless are not allowed to gather. Like in front of our doors. Most things come back to normal if given a chance. Just takes time. Like any war zone. Some areas will fail. Most will adapt."

"I looked at the news this morning."

"On your phone?" Mac said, alarmed.

"Yeah."

Mac wished she hadn't. There was so much disinformation and stress on a daily basis he knew it had to be taking a toll on everyone's nervous system. Especially his mom's.

"There's another variant. Worse than before. It's adapting. Getting stronger."

"That's what viruses do. They adapt. Just like humans."

"We are not viruses, Mac."

"Aren't we, though?" he asked with a smug smile.

Sadie looked at him with disgust.

"Big, multidimensional, complex organisms trying to survive," he continued, removing his hands from the handles and mimicking amoebas swimming with his fingers. "One big petri dish?"

Sadie said nothing.

"Adapt or die?"

"How are you adapting?"

He returned his hands to the handlebars of his bike. "I'm here with you, aren't I?" he said and smiled with genuine care and empathy.

They peddled together, in sync. Mac was curious how the future would play out. Uncertain, but committed with his mom to a better tomorrow.

When they crossed Rose Avenue at the bike path, Mac recognized Chad, the chill Asian guy from Mariners Village. He was walking alone the opposite way of traffic on the bike path. He was shirtless and having an intense conversation.

At first, Mac thought he was on a phone call so he didn't interrupt, merely waved. But Chad didn't see him, and as he passed, Mac didn't see any cell phone or earbuds. What he overheard alarmed him.

Chad was on the brink of tears, pleading with himself. Some intense internal struggle that sounded painful. Like he was on the extreme edge, begging not to do whatever it was he was asking of himself. "No, please don't. Please. I beg you. Don't."

Mac slowed, uneasy at what he was witnessing. Looking back, he pointed to Chad so his mom would see him, but her focus was elsewhere. She was having her own difficulties navigating the turn and didn't see Mac pointing or recognize Chad.

That guy's in serious trouble, Mac thought to himself and at that moment decided not to tell his mom. After the debacle on their first morning walk and her interpretation of the crazies screaming through Venice, this was an inconvenient truth best left to Chad. Plus, they both had misinterpreted his wellness at Mariners Village as they commented on homelessness. It was embarrassingly bizarre. Maybe he was an actor, Mac hoped. But he seriously doubted it.

As they peddled onward, Mac struggled with his thoughts on mental illness and the battle he'd witnessed Chad was having with himself. He had made such a nice impression on Mac and Sadie. Both while he was alone on the beach and later at Mariners Village overlooking at the boats. And now that memory was a stain of sadness for him. He wondered how many other young people were out on the street, living hand to mouth, having fallen through the cracks.

When they reached the Santa Monica Pier, Mac pulled over. There was an outdoor gymnasium with rings to swing on. Ropes to climb. High bars to navigate. Low bars to stretch. Pointing to a square lawn behind them, he said, "Let's do some stretching over there."

"What, here? Are you sure?"

"Yeah. We've ridden about four miles. This will be a great place to stop."

Sadie followed Mac as they walked the bicycles across the sand. Mac steered them to a cement block big enough to hold the bikes. And big enough for the sleeping homeless man who'd adopted the adjacent cement block.

Mac lay his bike down first and turned to his mom. She was slowly making her way toward him, so he stepped toward her to help. "Let me take that. I'll place your bike against mine and leave the guy to his nap."

"Nap? He's been there all night, Mac."

"Kidding, Mom. Come on. Follow me."

Mac led Sadie over to the grass, and they sat down together facing one another.

"Spread your legs out, Mom. We will match each other foot to foot."

"Just a minute. I want to take a puff." She extracted a small glass stoner pipe, the same one Mac recognized from the deck, and a new lighter he hadn't seen before. Annoyed, he stepped away and slowly did some pushups. When he got to seventy-eight, she was finished, so he rejoined her.

Sadie barely got her legs three feet apart. Mac helped widen them to four, then knelt behind her.

"I'm going to help you, Mom, in little movements. We will take our time."

"Oof," she huffed. "Easy, Mac. Don't try to hurt me."

Mac eased off and patiently tried to elongate her torso. There was so much padding it was grueling. Once she appeared to get the hang of it, he put a light pressure on her lower back.

Sadie's hands touched her knees. Three minutes later they were on her shins. It was a slow, rhythmic process of deep breathing and gentle movements. Fifteen minutes later Mac sat opposite her as she held her ankles. Beads of sweat adorned her forehead.

Mac stood up. "That's really good. Let's get you some water."

"Yes, please," she said with relief.

Mac carefully unscrewed the water bottle's green cap, the tiny, little grooves exposed as he sat back down across from her. He was careful not to let his fingers touch the lower ring that locked the cap together. A safety measure ensuring the water hadn't been compromised. He was sure everything in the general vicinity had been.

The task was much easier, Mac thought, than diffusing a bomb underwater but perhaps just as lethal. The news had stated a new variant was running rampant and hospitals were filling. The graphs were spiking. One situation, you're on a ventilator suffocating a slow, measured death with an eighty percent kill rate. The other, instant explosion. Either way, with what the news had said, everyone's chances weren't good.

Death and gloom. Fear and doom.

Sadie looked at the water bottle suspiciously.

"It's safe, Mom. I was careful."

"Thank you."

"If you want, why don't we just pour our waters straight into our mouths without touching the plastic?"

"That sounds like a good idea. I wasn't touching my groceries for three days."

"What do you mean?" he asked, reaching for his bottle.

"I was leaving them in my studio so the germs would die."

He tilted the bottle, then stopped. "In your front painting area?" he asked for clarification.

"Yeah, my studio."

"What did you do with the milk?"

Mac waited for her reply. She curled her lip as she looked away. He nodded, acknowledging she'd avoided the question like he hadn't asked it. He stood up and walked over to the rope, thinking about anaphylactic shock from touching one's groceries. An image of his mom opening the Horizon milk and it exploding.

"Going forward, you may want to skip dairy and just do almond or oat milk."

Sadie said nothing.

He reached up high on the rope and did a gentle stretch. His shoulder was still bothering him. Pectoral tear and rotator cuff separation, that's all one needed to know. Say that alone, and people understood the nasty scar that engulfed his left shoulder area, which left people staring and mouths downturned.

His motion was limited, and he knew more therapy was needed to get rid of the scar tissue. He lowered himself and held his left arm high on the rope while he looked out across the bike path at the sea.

Swimming, he thought. *That's what I should be doing.* Warm water swimming. Gentle. Therapeutic. Good for his soul. Every morning moving forward while Mom slept in.

Which triggered the memory of his conversation with Nate. Nate's worried look and wanting to talk. Mac telling him a swim in the ocean would be a safe place to discuss the details. Better than in his home with Sadie within earshot.

Then the sleeping bum rolled over and farted loudly, as if on cue. It was impossible to ignore. Disgusting. His thoughts on Nate would have to wait.

He looked back at his mom, who was hightailing it in a wide arc away from the bum. "That wasn't me!" she exclaimed, continuing her evacuation from the area.

He turned away, trying not to laugh. "I'll get the bikes and meet you at the path."

"Sounds like a plan," she replied.

Mac took a few short breaths and one big, held it in, and walked over, casually grabbing both bikes as another homeless man approached. He looked disheveled and dirty. It wasn't clear whether he woke up on the sand or rolled out of bed nearby.

The Wild West of beans and bourbon, Mac thought as he rolled the bikes away, saying, "Not today, buddy. Not today."

CHAPTER 38

Ten minutes later they were peddling south toward Rose Avenue. "Let's roll past Gold's Gym," Mac said, veering left into a parking lot that butted up to the sand. Sadie followed, and they passed a brown building called the Venice Ale House. It was boarded up, protected from vagrants and flying debris that might shatter glass or steal whatever was inside.

"I wish they were open," Mac called out as Sadie followed behind.

"Did we eat there once?"

"Yes, you remember. My favorite taco place!"

Four blocks later they passed the Firehouse Cafe on the left and Rose Café on the right. Both had posted signs, "Closed for inside dining." Their outside patios were open and had makeshift setups at the curb for takeaway orders.

Mac stopped at the Rose Café takeaway stand and asked a polite, slight, and somewhat nerdy young host if they had protein smoothies.

"Yes," he replied, pointing to a posted sign. It had a big hash-coded square. "Take a picture of this graphic, and our menu will pop up on your phone."

"I don't have my phone. But why don't you tell me what you have and I'll order like that."

"Ah, okay. Um. Er. I don't know all the smoothies," he confessed, leaning forward then quickly leaning back. "Here, let me look on my phone. Just a sec."

Mac caught his mom pulling her fanny pack around to the front to retrieve her phone and waved her off. A moment later, the host was reading off the smoothie menu. Mac ordered two sixteen-ounce smoothies and paid with a card because they weren't accepting cash.

He turned to his mom. "Follow me around the corner."

They pushed their bikes to the end of the block, then jumped on and rode the long block south through a catacomb of tents. It looked like something out of a war zone. The tents spilled into the street and had all sorts of collected crates and other debris, making the areas appear to be shanty homes, with outer gardens and tunnels to more grotesque things. Dirty, used sheets were walls and open entrances to filthy mattresses and drugged-out streetwalkers.

"I don't like this," Sadie said under her breath as Mac continued forward.

"It can't get any worse."

"These people all look sick. They probably have the COVID."

"*The* COVID, Mom?" Mac laughed. "Sorry, not funny. Just keep riding."

At the end of the block, it was worse. The tents had taken over the Gold's Gym parking lot. Structures were built up against the building's walls, which were huge glass windows. They stopped in the center of the four-way intersection. No cars were anywhere in sight.

"Remind you of your time with the flying doctors?"

Sadie looked east down the street. "A little."

"It's like we've become the Third World."

They turned and looked south. Then west. Then north from where they'd come. The spectacle wasn't attractive. It made Mac a bit sad. Several homeless people moped around, swollen and dirty. They all looked like they'd eaten well beyond the limits of their credit cards. It made zero sense. Mac looked over at his mom. "Remember years ago when I brought you into Gold's Gym?"

"Remind me," she replied, her gaze following a scrounging dog entering a tent.

"Well. For one, I introduced you to some friends, and you couldn't look them in the eyes," he said, smiling. "Recall any of that?"

"What? Why would I do that?" She scowled.

"You told me the guys looked like cartoons."

"Oh!" she replied, remembering. "It was ridiculous. They lost their minds. They were gigantic, Mac! Who does that?"

"Bodybuilders, Mom. Steroids."

"You seemed really into the weight lifting back then." Her tone dropped. "Have you ever taken steroids?"

"I am sorry you have to ask that. I was into getting my body back. Rehabbing my injuries. Remember?"

Sadie remained quiet. She turned away from Mac and looked at the sprawling city of tents in all directions.

He continued, "I've never done it and I *would* never do it. Wasn't desirable in the least."

"What happened?"

"Doesn't matter," he said, dismissing it. "The guys at Gold's just do what they love. And a lot of them compete at some point."

"What? Compete at posing?"

He laughed. "You're funny, Mom. Yeah, kind of."

"You're lucky. You know that?"

"Lucky for—what exactly are you referring to?"

"I used to be worried about you."

"Why?"

"Your temper. Worried you'd get beat up."

Mac smiled. "I've been in plenty of scraps. None ever very long."

"It's all so pointless. So dumb."

"Sometimes you don't have a choice."

"You always have a choice. Run."

"Yup. You could do that. That's true." He started laughing again.

"You think the smoothies are ready yet?"

"I hope so. Let's go."

They returned to the Rose Café where the nerdy host had their drinks bagged and ready at his podium. While Mac tipped the host, Sadie ravenously tore open the stapled bag and jammed a straw into one of the drinks.

Amused, Mac watched as she stood sucking the bottom of the straw while scouring the restaurant with her eyes. "It's backwards, Mom. The fat part of the straw goes into the bottom of the smoothie, like a spoon."

"Oh," she replied, reversing it, and they drank the smoothies while watching a handful of people trying to eat food with their masks on.

"Amusing, right?" Mac asked.

"Ridiculous," she replied. Then she stirred her smoothie with her straw. "This is really good. What's in it?"

"Monk fruit, allegedly. Supposed to be ten times sweeter than sugar."

Gulp. Gulp. Gone.

Mac stood in disbelief, his drink only a third of the way empty. "You just downed that faster than a race car changes tires in pit row." He took another suck and extended his smoothie to her. "Here, finish mine."

She looked at him sideways. "What about COVID?"

He pulled the straw out of the drink. "What about it?"

Sadie took the drink, removed the plastic lid, and drank it down. Unbeknownst to her, a residue stain of a smoothie mustache was under her nose.

Mac reached into the bag, pointed at his upper lip, and handed her a napkin.

"You're a true friend."

"I'm your son."

After, Mac gave the empty smoothies to the reluctant host. When he turned, he saw his mom thirty meters away headed south toward the boardwalk and home. Like donkeys and horses do on a Mexico vacation. The hired mammals labor along to the halfway point, and something changes. A light goes off in their brain and they gallop.

Which is what it looked like from Mac's perspective. Sadie's knees riding high on the peddles. Mac didn't know what her motivation was to get home. Not yet anyway. But he did know with donkeys. Their big motivation was *get this tourist off my aching back as soon as possible.* You couldn't stop them with all the reins in the world.

That's kind of what happened to his mom. She started peddling, and Mac called out, "Not that way."

But she couldn't stop. All she could do was turn her head, and the handlebars followed. No attempt to reverse peddles or squeeze the handbrake. Just a large sweeping turn, then a panicked look of fear as she crashed through the front door of an oversized, blue homeless tent.

It was a sweeping catastrophe of screams. Both from Mac's mom and the homeless woman inside.

Surprise. Terror. Screaming.

And fear—of COVID, of typhoid, of hepatitis. And fleas. All of it.

Surprisingly, Sadie never lost her footing. She went inside. Full contact for sure. Completely out of view. In fact, Mac saw her front tire protrude against the back wall. But she didn't appear to fall down and roll around with whatever was in there. She backpedaled out almost as quickly as she'd entered.

The surprise and shock and elation from bystanders, including random homeless people, was immense. As was her priceless look of horror and disgust as she exited the tent backward, having come off the bicycle seat.

Mac peddled over, looking at the tent with concern. "Are you okay? How in the world did that happen?"

"Oh my God. I've no idea."

The homeless woman yelped again. "Ahhhhh!"

Mc was still looking at the tent, but the woman never came out. Never showed herself.

"Is she okay?" he asked, turning to his mom.

"I don't know, but I'm not going back in there to find out."

"Did you run her over?"

Sadie made an expression of uncertainty. Then a booming screech from inside the tent, "Don't come back, motherfucker!"

Wide-eyed, Mac looked at the tent then back to his mom. "Asked and answered. Let's go."

"Huh?" Sadie replied like she'd just been blasted with a fire hose.

"We have to go home right now."

"Yes, we do."

He turned back to the tent. "That sounded like the same woman from the other day. It was that big blue tent, right?"

"It's definitely the same woman!"

"Then you recognized her?" Before Sadie could answer, "You've got to get in the shower immediately. You're gonna just get in with your clothes on and everything. Just in case!"

"In case? What do you mean?"

"Fleas. Typhoid. Anything. Everything. Fuck."

"Oh, fuck. You think she's got coronavirus?"

Mac figured coronavirus might be the least of her worries. All he could say was, "We gotta go. We gotta go *now!*"

Mac and Sadie peddled side by side down the boardwalk at a rushed pace. Mac was careful not to push her too fast, but at the same time not go too slowly as to suggest no urgency.

"Thank God you had your mask on. You didn't touch the woman inside?"

"No."

"Did you touch anything else?"

"I don't think so. It happened so fast."

"I saw your tire hit the back wall of the tent. Your hands must have touched the back wall when you stopped?"

"I don't know!" she snipped.

Mac shook his head. "The air in there has to be bad. That mask is not sufficient."

"What's wrong with the mask?"

"It's not a KN95 mask."

"What does that mean? Speak English."

"It's poor quality and maybe not effective."

"Why did you give me this fucking mask, then?" she barked. "This is your fault."

Mac paused. In his mind, she was right. He rode quietly for a moment, thinking. Then, "Did you breathe while you were inside?"

"I tried not to, but it was pretty hard, Mac. We were both screaming."

"I know. We all heard."

"I did the best I could."

"I understand." Normally and under extreme circumstances, Mac had been known to be somewhat creative. Inventive, even. But what he would propose next was so outlandish, even he couldn't believe he was suggesting it.

"Well, how about I take you to a manicure-pedicure place? They can wash your hands and feet properly. And all those fumes might help clean out your lungs?"

"Why would the—" Sadie turned to Mac, her head on a swivel. "You mean like what the president suggested?" she said in disbelief.

"Kind of," he admitted, sounding dumb. "Nail salons have those gnarly fumes, right?"

"You mean nail polish remover?" she asked.

He hoped his mom was just high enough and paranoid enough from the sativa she'd smoked earlier to rationalize what he'd presented. In the far reaches of his mind, his intentions were clear, and somehow in the synapses of hers, he hoped to make a connection.

"It's worth a shot. They'll give you a new mask because the one you're wearing is probably done."

CHAPTER 39

Nails For You was located on Main Street the opposite direction of home. From the street, the storefront looked closed, so Mac and Sadie wandered around to the back of the building through the alley to see what they could find. Its entire arsenal of salon chairs, fitted with water stations and wheeled carts, had been moved outside to the rear parking lot. The chain-link fence that surrounded the lot was netted in a green mesh that downplayed its appearance. Each station was equipped with pop-up tents for shade and plastic barriers that separated the chairs. Closed in front, but definitely open for business in the back.

Two women immediately had Sadie in their clutches as Mac stood off to the side talking to an Asian stylist with fuchsia-colored hair from the studio next door.

"So you can get her in after she finishes here, Eva?"

The woman was in her fifties, efficient, and seemed capable. "Yes, sir. I'll take care of her."

"Great. Just check in with her. Make sure she doesn't start looking for me. I need her occupied." Mac slipped the woman twenty dollars and walked back to his mom. Sadie looked up. "See Eva over at the hair studio waving at us?"

Sadie looked around, a bit overwhelmed. There was a lot to see. "Yes."

"She is going to wash your hair and give you a color and trim after you finish here."

"Okay."

"I'm going to lock your bike, run an errand and grab my phone. You'll be here about two hours. I'll be back in one."

"Where are you going?"

"I'll be back after. Don't worry." Mac gestured, encouraging her to keep smelling the liquid nail remover like it was flowers from her garden. He spread his hands wide, thrusting air into his nostrils with two big head dips. "Think petunias. Biological!" he shouted before disappearing.

CHAPTER 40

Mac pushed pedals hard all the way back to Catamaran. When he turned the corner, his jaw fell open. The building was surrounded by emergency vehicles. A repeat of two days earlier all over again.

But no ambulance this time. No fire trucks either. Just the ME with the black van outside and the rest of the regulars—black and whites. Sheriffs. All the commotion was now in the first stairwell. The police tape was up at the corner of the building and stopped at the mailboxes.

Mac walked his bike past the scene to the garage and parked his bike. Then he climbed the stairs, avoiding the gathered neighbors standing outside.

Inside his apartment, he grabbed his phone off the table and called Nate.

"Hey, buddy. It's me."

Nate sounded chipper. "I wondered when you were gonna call. How is it going over there?"

"Not good. This place is an emergency vehicle zoo."

"What do you mean?"

"I just got home and there's emergency vehicles again. I think I've had it with this building. With this place."

Nate paused a moment, then asked, "What happened?"

"Not sure yet," he replied, taking a breath.

"How's it going with your mom?"

"TBD. It's only noon."

"The day's early. There's hope for you yet."

"I've got her in a salon. Can I drop her off with you when she's done? If she's not in the way. You could show her how 3D printing works."

"Yeah, sure."

"I'll swing by in a few hours. Just don't want her to see this drama."

"Do you want me to fix up lunch?"

"Uh, okay. Very sweet of you."

"Not at all."

"As you know, I've got her on this cleanse. She hasn't been eating solid foods."

"I remember. I got ya."

"Thanks."

Mac hung up and walked downstairs to a clusterfuck of drama. Neighbors gathered in small groups chatting among themselves. Others approached cautiously, asking what was going on. He hung a left at the bottom of the stairs and slid left along the cinder block wall. He found Stevo, Jizzy, and Hutch just inside the garage, out of the sun. The gate was open, and they were standing facing each other in a triangle. Stevo was fired up with anxiety.

"People are falling like flies in this building, and it's not COVID. It's from drugs!" he blurted, sounding frustrated. "And the management company isn't doing anything about it. Fucking bullshit!"

Then Hutch said, "We don't know what happened to Teddy. We don't know." As soon as Mac heard the name, his heart sank.

Jizzy nodded, and her hand reached for Hutch's shoulder.

"I don't know what really happened at your house." Stevo let the statement fall in the direction of a question. It floated, suspended. Waiting an answer.

Jizzy and Hutch looked at each other as if in a trance of nonconformance, naive and innocent, admitting nothing. She looked up when Mac approached. Hutch looked also, but Stevo had his back turned away. Mac gestured apologetically for interrupting.

"What do you think? Was it suicide or overdose?" Stevo continued with concern.

Equally curious, Mac waited for the answer.

Jizzy's chin dropped, and her eyes saddened. When she began to sob, Hutch wrapped his right arm around her tightly and consoled her with a few gently placed kisses on the top of her head. He stood a full foot taller than Jizzy, and she morphed into the pit of his arm.

Finally, Hutch said, "Stevo, come on. We've been through this already." Hutch turned toward his lower deck, the one that had been crowded with emergency staff a few days earlier. "Haroun wasn't suicidal. I don't think he'd ever even done heroin before."

"So it *was* heroin?" Stevo blurted back like his suspicions had been confirmed.

Jizzy shook her head and continued looking down at the ground. Perhaps her eyes were closed, Mac couldn't tell from his position. But he knew she was avoiding Stevo's eyes. And his—*that* he was certain.

Hutch stumbled through the next portion of his words, a rehearsal of errors and missteps with nothing solid Stevo could walk away with. A noninformational ramble, not confirming or denying. "I don't know, Stevo. They—ah, well— wouldn't really tell us anything. I don't think they'll—ahhh,

I don't know, man." Occasionally looking at Mac, he lazily shook his head from left to right the entire time, gazing low.

"But you lived with him!" Stevo demanded. His hands flipped open, palms up. "How is that even possible?"

"We're not family, and—"

"That makes no sense. You lived in the same apartment, for Chrissake!" Stevo demanded, looking at Mac with justification.

"He was like a roommate, but he had a different door. Closed off from the main—"

Now Stevo's hands were folded across his chest, closed off, not believing anything. The mirror of Hutch's free arm. Hutch's right arm still clutched Jizzy.

Stevo continued, "How is this even possible?"

Mac said nothing and peeled off in the direction of Sadie's Passat. Once out of view, he circled back and listened while taking shelter, unseen against a pole.

Hutch turned his gaze up at Stevo, then floated it away into the shadowed garage in Mac's direction. "Well, it technically is a separate unit. We rented it out to him as a separate space."

"But it has no kitchen!" Stevo challenged. "Where did the guy eat?"

"Well," Hutch continued, "Haroun didn't eat much."

Why would he? Mac thought to himself. He knew heroin would suppress a person's appetite. Wondered what demons were lurking in people to try such a heavy-duty and almost certainly fatal drug.

He'd never met Haroun and never would. He was fine with that. Plus, watching Hutch squirm hunched over Jizzy was entertaining. The sad part was knowing the old guy Teddy had died. The short dialogue they'd had was pleasant.

He didn't know what had been deteriorating Teddy other than old age and alcohol.

Hutch's eyes mustn't have adjusted to the dark garage standing out in the hot, bright sun because he didn't seem able to keep a clear focus. Maybe his blond Nordic hair and steel-blue eyes were too fragile for all the sun and flashing lights. Mac didn't know, standing quietly aligned with the garage pole.

"Really? That's odd! Coulda sworn I saw you all eating dinner on the patio a few times," Stevo blurted.

Mac watched quietly and thought they were both putting on a performance. Felt like a soap opera full of bad acting. They all were performing. Like one was auditioning for a cop role. The other, an Oscar performance of denial. And Jizzy, the one-noted silent type.

"Only once. And we'd appreciate it if you could only remember that one time too," Hutch said, locking eyes with him.

Stevo stood dumbfounded. "What's that supposed to mean?"

"Nothing. It was one time, is all," Hutch said, looking to see if any cops were within earshot. "That I remember, so I don't know what you're talking about." Hutch kissed Jizzy's hair again.

"We should go," Jizzy added, looking at Hutch for acknowledgment. He nodded.

Stevo let his arms fall to his sides as Hutch and Jizzy exited the garage, leaving him to himself.

Mac stood quietly leaning against the pole twenty feet behind him. "Penny for your thoughts?"

"Bejesus!" Stevo gasped, clutching his chest. "You scared the shit out of me. I didn't see you. You been standing there the whole time?"

Mac nodded sideways. "So Teddy died?" he asked, disappointed.

"Appears so," Stevo replied with his head down, crossing straight past Mac toward the back right corner.

"What did I miss?"

"Nobody tells me anything anymore. I need to form some sort of homeowners' association to keep informed. Where you been anyway?"

"Not here," Mac replied.

"Working-wise? Where have you been working?"

"With FEMA."

"FEMA?" Stevo replied, surprised. "How did you get that job?" he asked.

"Applied."

"Is it hard work?"

"Yeah. But rewarding. Have you been working?"

"Location supervising. No on-camera work, which sucks."

"The acting thing. Right."

They both nodded similar frustrations.

"You like working with FEMA?"

"I stay busy. You know me. Always something to do, places to go."

"Like where?"

Mac threw the answer out. "Texas. Florida. From the panhandle to Puerto Rico."

"Is that full-time work?"

"Optional for me. But right now, I'm just chillin' with my mom."

"How fun!"

Mac smiled. "What's the deal with the alcoholic in unit two?"

"Which one?"

"What do you mean?" Mac asked.

"Teddy downstairs or Penny upstairs?"

"How about both?"

Stevo shrugged. "Teddy was cool. Quiet. Kind of kept to himself. He was a medical marijuana doctor. Can you believe that?"

"He had a nice, easy vibe about him." Mac smiled. "Didn't bother me. Penny, on the other hand. Guy must be strolling home after the bars close and bringing the party with him. It's too much."

"Well, as you know, I've partied plenty on my side of the building. But I'm respectful about noise."

"I don't know. I'm never here."

"Oh, that's right."

Mac was unsettled by the comment. Had Stevo really forgotten Mac was not around often, almost nonexistent, in fact? Mac wondered how much information Stevo was good for. But he asked anyway, "Any idea how Teddy died?"

"No. But we need to know. And so will the next renter because Teddy died in the unit."

Mac paused, "Two people in a week."

"Freaking weird."

Mac nooded. "What was his full name? Do you know?"

"Theodore Wolfgang Shivelbush. I read his mail once."

Mac looked at him inquisitively.

"By mistake," he added apologetically. "That was his real name."

Now the situation had gone too far, Mac thought. *Two deaths the week they arrive on vacation?* His mom would hit the roof. Probably explode. Or maybe implode, *then* explode. It was way too much. Brain overload for her.

Then Mac flipped the idea on its head and remembered he was working his way out of the building, an exit strategy. Stevo having a less-than-remarkable memory might help in ways he hadn't expected.

He said goodbye to Stevo and stared at the ensemble of flashing lights atop the emergency vehicles, thinking about his mom back in the nail shop, oblivious. Feet soaking in warm soap suds. Calves being massaged. He found himself a bit envious. Imagined himself next to her. Probably speaking Vietnamese or Thai. Smiling as a TV played soap operas in the background. *General Hospital* or, worse, *The Bold and the Beautiful*. Maybe *Days of Our Lives?*

Then Mac snapped back to the situation in front of him. He wished the movie theaters were open. He could kill some time with his mom there. Maybe a double feature. That would be roughly four hours. Then walk to dinner somewhere not too close by. All that plus walk time would amount to six hours minimum.

That would do it. The ruckus of emergency vehicles would be gone by then. Only the tape around Teddy's door would remain. It would just be the neighbors poking around asking questions. In grief. And perhaps Sadie wouldn't notice that. Mac needed a plan.

He thought of Nate again, but for a different reason. If Sadie were exposed to COVID from the incident in the tent, he would be putting his friend at risk. Mac went back upstairs and retrieved his cell phone. Canceled Nate and called Simelane.

CHAPTER 41

Sadie sat in the waiting area reading a magazine. She looked spruced up, plump, and beautiful. Her skin was glowing. The gray hair was colored brown, blown-dry with flair. Her eyes sparkled, and her red nails on all four appendages looked amazing. Like a froufrou Pomeranian poodle all done up. But bigger.

"You look great! We're going for a boat ride, Mom. Come on."

"What?"

"Through the canals in Nate's canoe. He's lending it to us for the afternoon."

"I'd prefer if we could go back to the house and sit on the balcony."

"Too late. I already committed, thanks to Nate."

"But I'm getting hungry, Mac."

Mac pulled two pressed juices from his back pocket. "That's why I brought these. You can have one now and one later. Have you used the bathroom yet?"

"Yes, but I should go again," she said, looking toward the building. "Do you really like my nails? I wasn't sure about the color."

"They look good. We are so lucky this place was open. And that they have a bathroom, right?"

"Yes."

"Great," he replied and headed to find Eva and pay the bill.

Nate had set the boat up, though Mac had insisted he could do it on his own. A towel lay across the bench seat with an oar, and two small water bottles were placed inside. Mac was careful to help his mom board without tipping over, and when she sat down and felt comfortable, he pushed her away from the dock unscathed.

"Mac," she cried out. "What are you doing?"

"Kidding, Mom, I'm only kidding. Grab an oar and paddle back here. I've got to use the bathroom. I'll be back in a few minutes."

Before Sadie could reply, Mac was past the fence well into Nate's yard.

Sadie watched him disappear with frustration and said behind him, "Why didn't you use the bathroom at the salon?"

Instead of going to Nate's front door, Mac slipped around the side of the open yard. At the next fence, he left the gate ajar and sprinted one block right and four blocks east.

Nate's storefront sat in the middle of a one-level commercial building. The building was muted gray, and Nate's red Kapow sign was plastered at the building's center above his door. He was alone at his desk when Mac burst in, panting.

Nate looked up, surprised. "Wow. Everything okay?"

"Yeah, fine. Quick questions."

"Shoot."

"Love honesty," Mac replied, raising a finger, then caught his breath. "You could teach Mom all about scanning and printing in how long?"

"The basics?"

"Yeah."

"And you want her to be a regular professional?"

"Hardly," Mac chimed back.

"There's a lot of complicated work, but she was a photographer, so at least she'd understand the scanning part."

Mac leaned forward on Nate's desk. "You deleted the facial scan you took, right? It never went up on the cloud. All internal and Bluetooth?"

"Oh, that? Yeah. Why?"

"Not sure yet. Just need to make sure. Do a search and try to find it."

"But it's not here."

"Appease me, please."

"Okay," Nate said reluctantly.

Mac circled the desk and watched Nate go through a series of searches using different words. Then he did a dated search. Then he searched all his scans ever done under his history. Then he checked all his folders. And subfolders.

"So what am I missing here besides my mom?" Mac asked. "Because the suspense is killing me."

"I'm feeling weirded out."

"So am I. And I find it bizarre you brought this up, which got me thinking."

"About what happened?"

"About everything. Please do the search again, and expand to the cloud as well. Just triple-check to amuse yourself and appease me. It will ensure we sleep better at night."

"Okay."

"One more thing. Remember ever meeting a guy name Joaquin? Do you remember that name?"

Nate shook his head. "No. Not at all."

"Good," Mac said, nodding. "That's good. I gotta go."

The boat ride around the canals was pleasurable. Filled with the same pretty homes, but viewed from the water instead of the sidewalk, which shifted their perspective to Venice, Italy. Mac set his phone to camera then handed it to his mom and asked her to take some photos while he paddled. But she was more interested in using her own phone and told Mac he should take his own photos, which was fine by him because it extended their time on the water. She would take a photo, and he would stop paddling, reset the boat to a certain position, and take some additional photos with his camera phone.

Different birds filled their frames, along with several selfies. There were blue jays, barn sparrows, several egrets, and a crane. There was also an unknown, wild-looking black seabird that looked like it had caught a trade wind north from Central America. They summed it up as global warming migration and that bird of prey the highlight of their trip.

"Mom, do you want to paddle a little?"

"Why? For exercise?" she asked, looking back.

"Just switch it up a bit."

She mulled it over and agreed. She fanny packed her phone and took the oar.

Mac began editing his photographs and blending the images from Nadine into a digital story. He went through his music library and added some jazz from his father, then saved it in an edited file titled "Canals with Mom."

CHAPTER 42

When they arrived back at Catamaran, they approached from the northeast end of the building. The exact opposite of Teddy's unit. Sadie missed the yellow tape entirely, too caught up in navigating the bicycle into the dark garage without incident.

They climbed the stairs together, and it wasn't long before Sadie was changed into fresh clothing and puffing away on her pipe upstairs. Mac pushed open the screen door and walked out onto the deck with a pitcher of homemade lemonade.

"I bagged your old clothes and am washing your shoes in the bathtub."

"Did you not hear the commotion downstairs? I thought for sure you'd wonder what was going on," she said, refilling her glass.

"No, didn't hear anything. What's up?"

"I think there's people downstairs asking neighbors questions."

"Not sure what it's about," he replied, not wanting to upset her.

"Should I put away the smoke?"

"I don't know," he joked. "Do you have a license for it?"

"Oh, God, Mac. No! I don't want people knowing my business. I'm a private person. Don't you get that?"

"I get it. But it *is* legal now. What happens if you get pulled over?"

"I don't get pulled over," she fired back. Then she stood up and waddled over to the railing and looked down. "Oh my God. There are cops down there. Why didn't you tell me?"

"I just did, didn't I?" he lied. "Some disturbance maybe?"

"There's a cop car now. Are they coming up here?"

"Why would they?"

"I don't know, Mac. I'm just saying they are here... and what if?"

Then Mac heard faint knocking on his front door downstairs. His mom didn't hear it, so he excused himself and went downstairs.

* * *

Kootz was pissed. "You lied!" he said from the crack of the door.

"Did I?" Mac said, opening the door wider. "How so? Per your request and my preservation, I filled out a form and sent you a copy."

A taller sheriff stood just behind his shoulder in the hallway. Kootz's head lined up with the sheriff's armpit like a socket.

"You have a beef with the landlord?"

"The owner? No," Mac replied, staying focused on Kootz.

"Are you aware there's been a new complaint filed against you?"

"Is there?" Mac asked, not confirming or denying.

"It's from here in the building." They were the first words out of the big man. His name tag read "Bean." Mac could tell the cop was ex-military. Probably an MP. Maybe even a warrant officer for a time. He had that air about him.

Hard to miss. Probably left the military for better pay as a private contractor but ended up a sheriff.

"Really? Who?" Mac replied, looking up.

"The live-in building manager."

"And you've had run-ins with the tenant in unit two," Bean continued. "He claims you are aggressive with him. What do you have to say on that?"

Mac said nothing but wanted to respond, "Allegedly."

"You've got an assault and battery charge already pending. Or did you forget that?" Kootz added.

"Absolutely not, sir," Mac said, opening his door wider. An invitation to invite them inside. "Did you get the email?"

"Yeah, but we need to take you in."

"For what?"

"There's been two deaths in your building in four days."

Mac paused, information he knew. "Am I a suspect?"

"This is an active investigation," Bean shot back.

"Cuffs and everything?" Mac asked, looking at Kootz.

"Not if you come voluntarily," Bean replied.

"Because of what the manager filed?"

"It's better if you cooperate," Kootz replied.

"Am I being charged with something?" Mac asked.

Kootz didn't say, but Mac obliged. "Okay. Let me put on some shoes."

"And grab a mask. You'll need it inside the car."

Mac was more curious than anything else. His mother was deep into her paints upstairs with fresh nails and a new look. She'd be busy doing art for a while, and he figured he wouldn't be gone more than four hours. Four hours to learn what was really going on. Four hours was the limit between Mom's meals, and it was important to him to keep her regimented. He figured she'd dive into her painting and writing. Maybe even get on the internet again to look at dogs for sale. That being said, he called upstairs anyway, "Mom, I'll be out for a bit. Back in four hours." He didn't wait for a response.

The ride wasn't to downtown LA but Culver City. Mac was thankful. The short ride wasn't pleasurable stuffed into the back of the detective car on a plastic seat. But it was better than downtown LA in traffic.

He was thankful not to be cuffed though Mac wasn't exactly sure why they were taking him in. It was obvious Ribbit was doing video surveillance on a daily basis, feeding that footage to upper management and detectives biting at the bit. Mac knew he'd have to be careful with what he said. If anything at all. But he was curious too. Intrigued, even. So he'd oblige them and go for the ride.

The police station in Culver City took twelve minutes. A long, two-level rectangular structure roughly four thousand feet in size. It had a front door with four glass partitions, all bulletproof, Mac was sure. They didn't drive in through the tall gates but parked directly in front of the public entrance.

Inside, a three-foot raised platform greeted all guests, where a female cop sat perched like a turret. She was Caucasian, with a fairly short haircut. The platform had a pony wall, creating a low perimeter that provided shelter from the waist down. Anyone entering with a firearm and blasting away would have a fifty-fifty chance at striking her. She could duck below the wall and fire back, while the assailant would have zero protection.

Mac imagined the pony wall was probably bulletproofed during the nineties. A common police station upgrade stemming from the Rodney King riots back in 1992. From her position, she could see the front entrance and also turn to look directly into the squad room. There was a small door beside the desk that led to her perch. Mac wondered what other doors were at the back of the building behind the desk. He was sure he'd find out.

The rest of the greeting area to lodge complaints was basic, standard government issue. Thirty by twenty, Mac surmised. Just small enough to make it intimate and large enough to suppress a riot.

The female desk jockey buzzed them through the small door, and they walked past a bunch of desks, half empty. All had little boxed computers and lamps. Some had files, others had coffee mugs, and some had miscellaneous cop memorabilia.

Mac spotted Bean's desk plate and steered toward it.

"We're not doing this at my desk," Bean replied, extending his arm toward the back wall.

Mac looked at his thick arm. "I'm not under arrest, right?"

"Not yet." He smirked.

"I'd rather do it here. No offense, but I think you're beginning to crush on me."

"Not until we stop the spread of this virus," Kootz stated matter-of-factly. "We have to isolate indoors and wear masks unless you waive your rights."

Mac was led down a long hallway to an interrogation room. The two-way glass was so obvious it was almost laughable. Mac sat in the chair observing the two cameras overhead and waited. After thirty minutes, he closed his eyes. An hour after that, Sheriff Kootz and the mustached Bean entered. They sauntered in like they had all the time in the world. *Spokes on a wheel*, Mac thought, *here comes the circus.*

Kootz set a file on the table between them and leaned in apologetically. "We brought you in to clear some things up."

Mac looked at the file and said, "Great." He leaned on his elbow and placed his masked chin in his hand.

Bean eyed Mac like he was a piece of lint on his freshly pressed white shirt. It made him feel like he stunk, but he knew it was part of the show. Mac's eyes darted from Kootz to Bean, and he said nothing else.

Kootz continued, "We pulled your jacket. You are a lot more than you appear, Mr. MacGuffin. Is there anything you'd like to tell us before this gets really sticky?"

Mac darted his gaze back at Kootz, then landed his blank stare at Bean.

"We can clear you if you talk to us," Kootz added.

Mac's stare stayed with Bean, and he let out a slight smile.

"What's so funny?" Bean asked.

"Everything." Mac opened his hands wide and turned his palms up, sitting back. "This whole thing. I'm on—"

"Vacation!" Bean blurted out.

"Yeah," Mac replied, surprised.

"My partner told me." He scowled dismissively.

"Then you should know I am here voluntarily," Mac replied innocently. "And with my mom, I might add."

Bean continued, "Listen to me. I read all about you. Navy turned stuntman turned failure. Why those directors didn't press charges is beyond me. I would have kicked your ass and definitely pressed charges. Must be tough, huh? Anger issues?"

Mac's smile turned downward. "Sounds like you're the one with anger issues. Not me." A look of disappointment engulfed Mac's face. He gestured at Bean. "I think you've confused me with someone else."

"I don't think so," Bean blurted back. "I know your type."

"What type is that?" Mac replied flatly.

Bean pointed his finger at Mac with a mad-dog stare. "I know who you are."

Mac sat farther back and crossed his one arm across his stomach. He looked over at Kootz and let his other elbow rest on his hand to support his chin. "Who am I?" Mac asked. "Are you trying to get a rise out of me?"

"We see everything," Bean replied confidently.

"Okay."

"Okay what?" Bean growled back.

"I don't know," Mac replied, unfolding his arms. "It doesn't matter who I am. It matters who I am not." Mac's hands went up, repeating the same gesture from before, this time elbows tight to his sides. He looked over at Kootz, who remained quiet but was leaning forward slightly. Mac added, "Obviously you think I have done something."

"No shit, Sherlock. I pulled your record of service in the navy. You're more than capable of scaling the walls of that building and sneaking around rooftops where there're no cameras. You're very capable. Are you telling us you weren't on the roof?"

"I haven't said I was on the roof or I wasn't on the roof. I haven't said anything. And I'm inclined to not say anything at all and just ask for a lawyer," Mac said in a noncommittal manner.

Bean leaned in. "I've seen your jacket. I know what the navy presented is bullshit. Six years in special ops. Anything else is a complete waste for a guy like you."

Mac took a long, slow breath in and took twice as long to let it out. He could tell Bean was the push behind bringing him in. That was clear enough. So he asked, "What do you have on me or think you have on me? Give it to me straight and quit fucking around. I've got my mom at home, and I don't want to be here all day."

Bean tried to speak, but Kootz waved him off. "We got you in the garage on the first night," Kootz counted off, beginning with his thumb. "We got you climbing all over the roof at odd hours." Index finger. "We got you threatening tenants for playing loud music." Middle finger. "We got you threatening the management." Ring finger. "And we got the second victim knocking on your door at different times. Now he's dead." Pinkie finger. "I just ran out of fucking fingers."

Mac looked astonished, but said nothing.

Bean jumped in, "Then we go back two years and find you were ordered to appear in court. But you didn't show. So a bench warrant was issued. Then the plaintiff goes missing. Wouldn't be surprised if he was dead too. I wanna know why whenever you come around, people start dying."

Mac rolled his closed hands over and pressed them on the table. He looked down at the desk and thought about it. Then he looked up and said, "You don't have me climbing around the roof except when I hung the shade on the first morning we arrived. Then you have me leaning over the balcony to look into the deck of the neighbor who plays his music too loud. As for unit six, I can't speak to whatever happened. I have zero ideas."

"You wanna know when the vic died in six?" Kootz asked.

"Not really. But I have a feeling you're gonna tell me."

"Within two hours of your little late-night visit to the garage."

"That's convenient. How's that work exactly?"

"Your visit to the garage was peculiar. So we'd have you on camera?"

Mac said nothing.

"You'd already been up on the roof."

Mac thought back. He looked at Kootz and said, "No. The night we arrived, the moon was full and red in the sky from the fires. I did walk upstairs before going to bed and looked at it. And the ocean before going to sleep. But climbing on the roof? No, sir."

"We'll get back to that," Bean replied. "The excuse for going to the garage at two in the morning is a doozy."

"Bad timing, is all. I went downstairs to get my mom's typewriter."

"And you never heard or saw anyone outside?" Kootz asked.

"No. I never heard or saw anything weird or suspicious. But I wanted that typewriter for when my mom woke up. My mom's a lot of work. I've been trying to protect her from all the drama, be it on television, in the building, or the freaks living on the street. I had no idea what we were coming down to in Venice. It's like a zombie apocalypse out there. Why you can't clean it up, I do not know."

"Don't change the subject, MacGuffin," Bean scoffed back in a gravelly voice.

Mac continued anyway, "In fact, I will be putting my thirty-day notice to vacate because the vibe here is horrible.

I wish I could tell you why Ted or Teddy, Theodore, came and knocked on my door. But I don't know. I only met him once. You telling me is the first I've heard of it." Mac looked up at the ceiling. "Every day, my mom and I do some sort of exercise. Try to avoid the homeless and, frankly, most of the people in the building." He looked back at Kootz and squinted. "I hope you're recording this because that's the simple truth of it. Penny is an asshole. The manager Ribbit is a fool. But probably not entirely worthless for you. But why anyone is pointing fingers at me is beyond comprehension. As I said, I'm on vacation. I'm never here."

Kootz looked at Bean, who didn't look back. Mac followed Kootz's eyes and his gaze landed on Bean too.

"As for my time served? You don't know what I did for our government. I could have been NCIS, busting guys like who you think I am. I could have been a cook on a ship. You don't know, and for whatever reason, I have a pretty good idea that you're just fishing, Bean. I was straight with Kootz, but you're just a dick. And it ain't Tracy."

Bean's face began to boil. Beads of sweat gathered on his brow, and his jaw clenched beneath his mask.

"Did you check and see if they were sick? The vics? Everyone seems to be dying of COVID past seventy, anyway. That at least covers one of the two. But they're blaming deaths on COVID so the life insurance companies don't have to pay. Just like the health insurance companies will get let off the hook. Because whatever vaccine gets approved, it will be considered experimental. And there's a clause for that in every policy. Look it up!"

Kootz spoke first, sounding stumped. "What are you talking about?"

"Quit changing the subject." Bean tore off his mask. "You're telling us how to do our job. Is that it?" He was agitated and his arms began to tremble.

Kootz interrupted, concerned. "What are you talking about with the insurance companies?"

Mac looked at Kootz, then back to Bean. "I never met you before, Officer Bean. I've no idea how to do your job. I'm not a cop. I honestly thought you wanted to get an inside beat on the pulse of the building. Maybe find out something that wasn't obvious. But what you're doing is out of line. I'm not your guinea pig."

Kootz opened his hands wide, his questions still unanswered. "Everybody calm down here. Please! Let's make this productive."

Mac continued anyway, "I'd hoped we would talk about nonsecular stuff. Military stuff, frankly. What I know of this and that which might help. But this is not going anywhere near there. You cops are as clueless as I am on what's going on in Catamaran."

"Why do you say it like that?" Kootz asked in a disappointed tone.

"Because why, Bean? Tell me why you think I say it like that."

"Because it's a fucking zoo!" he said angrily.

The room went quiet.

Mac wasn't proud of some of the things he'd been ordered to do for the military, but he wasn't ashamed either. And, if need be, he was happy to help a fellow brother in arms if it was a good deed. But most of the military deeds Mac had done weren't good. Not really. It was all classified on a need-to-know basis. If you knew, then you knew what could be asked of you. If you didn't, you really fucking didn't. Bean really fucking didn't.

Because it wasn't public knowledge. The police weren't going to learn any classified information from the navy, and they definitely weren't going to learn it from Mac. Instead, Mac's answers would be recipes for delicious meals, but in copious amounts because it took a shit-ton of food to feed a navy vessel. You would get this recipe and that recipe with an unapologetic smile and keen stare and diversion to another subject less historic. Like the origin of where the food was grown and how. Where it thrived and what nutrients inhabited the soil.

He looked past Kootz and Bean to the back wall. It was pale gray, like shark skin. Tough and brash. Then he thought about his mom, and his ears began to hear a high-pitched piercing tone. He saw her wandering around the house calling out his name, wondering where he'd disappeared without telling her. He imagined her descending the stairs to the lower deck and not finding him in the parking lot. Then he pictured her settling down with her Corona typewriter or sketch pad and colored stencils and drawing. Probably lighting up her pot pipe.

Finally, the image went away. He switched focus and looked at Kootz.

"All this stuff going on," he said, "has nothing to do with me." Mac was cool as a cucumber.

"Then talk to us," Bean said. "What are you hiding? What do you know?" He slammed the table and belted, "Talk to us. Let us help you if we can."

It was a good proposition, Mac thought, but a little too late. Theodore was already dead, and Penny would be squelched, in a matter of speaking.

"No."

"Why not?" Kootz demanded.

"We know you've done something!" Bean shouted.

"No. You don't. Are we finished here? Because this sounds like harassment."

Mac knew he was done when Bean added, "People in the building don't like you much, do they?"

"I don't honestly know that answer. I'm not here very often."

"Why the hell not? You got a beach house."

"Honest truth?"

"Please," Kootz replied. He looked exhausted. Spent. Frustrated and done. He wanted to put all this behind him. In a rearview mirror far away.

Mac could tell Kootz didn't care about Haroun. Neither did Bean. Nor Mac, for that matter. What Mac did care about was the racial injustice that had happened to Theodore. Perhaps claimed Theodore's life. And at that moment, he felt guilt. Because Theodore had asked Mac for help, and Mac had gone soft on Penny. And Penny didn't stop his antics. Penny knew Mac would be gone in a week, so he laid low, then would return to asshole as usual.

But at that moment, Mac was wondering why Theodore had come to his apartment. Twice.

He looked at Kootz. "Did Theodore really knock on my door?"

"He did."

"At what time, exactly?"

Bean answered, "We can't tell you that."

"Okay," he said and waited a beat. "I met Theodore at the front of the building for the first time. That's when I helped him with his groceries. He appeared high or intoxicated and incapable of getting his bags from the hired car to his unit. He was kind. He was easygoing. And he needed help."

"You never met him before?"

"No, sir."

"Never been in his home?"

"No. I would have remembered."

"Why do you say it like that?" Kootz asked.

"Because it was disgusting. As if his life had fallen apart. Stuff everywhere. Super messy," Mac said sadly. "Like a disheveled genius and train wreck all rolled into one." Mac paused. "I remember trying to find a place to put his grocery bags. The counters were dirty and covered with spilt spices. Like a chef's uncleaned kitchen. Except he had more varieties of spices than I've ever seen, and I've been in a lot of kitchens," Mac finished with a smile.

"Anything else you can tell us about him?"

"He needed help. He asked for it."

"What kind of help?"

"The kind I couldn't give him because I was taking care of my mom."

"What does that mean?" Bean asked.

"I think he was sick in some sort of way. Like he had a serious illness or something. He was definitely an alcoholic. There was a lot of beer in one of his grocery bags."

"And you could have helped him with that?"

Mac looked at Bean. "Next question."

"What else can you tell us? Did he have any enemies?"

"Other than the guy upstairs? I don't know."

"Anything else?"

"He asked me to tell the guy, Penny, to stop harassing him. And I then told the manager that he should be doing his job to keep the peace in the building. And Ribbit told me to file a complaint with the management on a website."

"Did you?"

"I did not."

"Why not?"

"Because I didn't want to get involved. I don't live here anymore. LA doesn't interest me."

"But you can afford to keep a place here and not use it?"

"I do all right. Like I said, I'm on vacation with my mom."

"Yeah, you said that."

"Look, I don't know what is going on with the tenants in this building. I am rarely here. In fact, this is probably the last time I'm going to use it."

"You just let this unit at the beach remain vacant. You expect me to believe that on a military pension?"

"I don't expect you to believe anything because I can't speak for you. But maybe you can take my statement at face value and leave us alone. I don't care what happened in unit six. I barely know the couple above him," Mac gestured with his left hand. "And I never met the deceased."

"Two deceased," Bean fired back.

Kootz sat there listening. Mac could tell he was mulling it over. His forehead had a crease in it the size of the Grand Canyon. "We are asking everyone in the building to submit their fingerprints," he finally said.

"Is that a voluntary request or an order?"

"It's purely voluntary," he replied. Bean looked at Kootz with disappointment. "To clear everyone from the suspect list," Kootz justified.

Mac stayed impartial and didn't blink. Neither did Kootz. Which made him wonder what Kootz wasn't telling him. But Mac knew asking Kootz would get him nowhere and attempting to help solve the crime—if there was a crime—would only incriminate himself more. Mac had no intention of raising his value on the suspect list. "I wish I could help you, but I know nothing, and I don't really give two shits. I'm with my mom, who has high blood pressure, clogged arteries, and a new smoothie diet that gives her occasional diarrhea. You might say I'm busy."

"Or dirty," Bean shot back. "Somebody offend your mom maybe? Or you have an old beef with somebody in the building?"

Mac didn't look at Bean and said nothing.

"So no fingerprints to eliminate you from the list?" Kootz said, his attention locked on Mac.

"Or add me to the list? No. Mine are on file with the DMV. You can cross-reference those if needed or this one." Mac stood up, wiping the table he'd touched with the edge of his palms, then brought his index finger down on the file. "We're done here."

Kootz stood up, grabbed the file, then went to the door. He pushed the handle, and it opened. With no one stopping him, Mac walked out.

CHAPTER 43

No ride was offered back to the beach, so Mac walked two blocks west on Culver Boulevard, turned right up to Washington, and waited for the bus. By the time the bus came, which took an hour, then another thirty minutes riding it to Pacific Avenue, and walking the beach south, it had been well over four hours.

He spent the entire chunk of time thinking about his prior life at Catamaran. The mindset he was in.

Free from college.

Free from the military.

Single.

He remembered Jizzy when they'd first met at the Cow's End Coffee Shop down the street. She'd said they lived in the same building and were practically roommates. Unit six. That three plus six made a nine. Her favorite number.

He was attracted to her initially. A twinkle in each other's eyes. A flirtatious smile. A gaze of mutual acknowledgment held longer than a linger. Stronger than a gaze, but not staring. Just watching with mutual admiration. Smiling and curious. Flirting with the possibilities of a mutual fantasy together.

But all that was gone the minute Mac stepped out his front door and saw her. It didn't matter she was beautiful. It didn't matter she was single. It didn't matter two hours earlier she wanted to swing by and see what he'd done decorating his new place. Even the word she'd chosen, swing, was intriguing.

He remembered her coming up his stairs one slow, cataloged step after another. Almost robotic and unbalanced. Out of sync and trancelike and searching for him. She'd taken a drug he'd not known about called ketamine, nicknamed Special K. It was a medication primarily used for maintaining anesthesia in sedation. More commonly used by veterinarians on horses. A tranquilizer. She'd said, "Vets use it all the time. Are you a vet?"

And had she been sober, he would have welcomed her inside. He would have laid her across his stone mantle covered in New Zealand lambskin. He would have pressed deep and slow through the edges of her beautiful lips. He would have welcomed all the imaginative pleasures she had presented with her eyes because he was single and she was game for it.

But that didn't happen because she arrived comatose. Catatonic. Disengaged. Sloppy and worthless. It would have been equivalent to kissing a mannequin. A blow-up doll. A corpse.

So he hadn't. He stopped her at the bottom of his stairs and turned her away. But he remembered.

Maybe Haroun had done the same thing. Maybe he'd tried to come on to Jizzy. Maybe Hutch found out. Or maybe he was a drug addict. Maybe Jizzy introduced the drug to him. Maybe a lot of things. But Mac didn't know the dead guy, so it didn't matter. Like Sadie had said, not his monkey, not his circus.

* * *

When Mac returned to the building, the center garage door was wide open. Mac would have kept walking straight past it and up the stairs, but Stevo was there with boxes and asked him for some help.

Three boxes in total. All four-by-four stuffed tight and heavy. Stevo had managed to remove one from his unit by sliding it down the stairs but was stuck at the turn in the landing. "I didn't want to drag it across the parking lot into the garage."

"What you need is a dolly."

"I need a lot of things," Stevo replied, sounding disgruntled.

"What do you have in here? Bricks?"

"Tools," Stevo whispered.

"Why you whispering?"

"The cameras have microphones."

"You sure about that?"

"How else are they monitoring us? They know way too much. It's bullshit."

They picked up the box together and walked it into the garage. Stevo's minivan was in the far-right corner with the rear hatch open, facing outward. Once they got the box inside, Stevo looked at Mac hesitantly. "I've got three more. Do you mind?"

"Not at all. Let's get them."

Mac followed Stevo back outside and up the stairs past unit six. Stevo's unit was numbered five and his door mirrored unit six.

Inside, his unit was an open floor plan, spacious. Big blue serpentine two-by-two tiles lined the floor opposite white walls and a pretty, French-looking chandelier. He had shabby chic overfilled cream couches and a white dining table with two bench seats on either end. The place looked somewhat like a Tiffany's advertisement from a designer magazine Mac had viewed at the nail shop where he'd taken his mom.

Two more tan boxes equal in size to the one they'd just loaded sat in the center of the room. A partial roll of black duct tape lay on the end table of the couch.

"This here?" Mac asked.

"Yeah."

They both squatted down simultaneously and lifted the first box, then awkwardly maneuvered to the door before descending the stairs. Halfway down, Mac asked Stevo, "More tools?" Stevo laughed but held a lot of tension in his face. When they finished loading the fourth box, Stevo closed the back of the minivan.

Awkwardly, Stevo asked, "Mind if we sit in the minivan and chat for a minute?"

Mac looked at Stevo with a curious grin. "Not at all."

When they entered the front of the car, Stevo began making adjustments to his seat. First, he changed his seat proximity to the pedals. When he found the position he was seeking, he adjusted the back to a more relaxed angle, less upright. Then he insisted the windows be closed after gesturing at the camera. This involved turning on the ignition key.

Mac wondered what Stevo's process of squirming through the motions was about.

"Are you comfortable?" Stevo asked.

"Are you?" Mac returned and Stevo looked away. Mac watched his eyes look through the windshield to some distant place beyond the garage.

"He was a poofter, ya know?"

"Who?"

"The guy in six."

Mac thought it was an English term. Which triggered the word Teddy had used, "lad." "What's that?"

"Trans."

Mac said nothing.

"Transexual."

"I heard you the first time."

"So."

"So what?"

"That complicates things."

"Why?"

"Well, for one thing, I thought he was a woman."

Mac paused. "Okay."

"It's embarrassing."

"Easy mistake. Not the end of the world."

"Says you." Stevo shied away, looking down at the floor of the car, and tapped his right foot.

"Why?"

"Well, I've got gray hair, but I'm not dead, ya know."

Mac looked at Stevo, "You hit on him?"

Stevo said nothing, but the look on his profiled face said everything. Mac dropped his chin slightly, squinted, tilted his head, and waited for the answer.

Stevo's eyebrows climbed. Saying it was awkward, the least of Mac's concerns. "How far did you go?"

"Not all the way, thank goodness!"

"But you...?"

"Ahhh—"

"What did you do?"

"Keep your voice down," Stevo pleaded, his lips turned down like an unhappy child in turmoil. "I might have ki—

ki—" Stevo stuttered. He couldn't get the words out. He pursed his lips and shook his head.

Mac's empathy faded. Delicately, he reached over and lifted Stevo's chin, turning his face. "Did you kill him?"

Tears rolled down as Stevo faced Mac "No. I swear I didn't. I only kissed him. I didn't kill him."

Mac let the realization loom for several seconds. Stevo's face was a wreck, a car crash of agony. "The cops are going to want to question you."

Stevo gasped in despair.

"You have motive, Stevo. That's what they are looking for."

Stevo whined, "I think I'm fucked."

"Not if you didn't do it."

Stevo let out a whimper, his face contorted.

Mac straightened up and replied, "Don't do it here, Stevo. Do not cry here. Not for the cameras. You gotta pull yourself together and drive out of here or take it inside."

Mac left Stevo in the seat of his minivan weeping. He made a half-gesturing wave and walked away, masking the sadness he'd learned. Stevo was ashamed. And he had motive.

As he exited the garage, he thought about Stevo throwing parties years back. Always having cookouts and sports games on. Pretty people around. Friends showing up with potluck meals, eager to share and rejoice at the beach and jump in the ocean.

Then another thought popped into Mac's reptilian brain. Black duct tape and sealed boxes.

Had Stevo just made Mac an accessory? What was really in those boxes?

CHAPTER 44

Mac climbed the stairs three at a time, punched the door code into the keypad, and stepped inside. The house smelled of salt air and something else he couldn't decipher. He could hear Cuban music coming from the upper balcony where his mom was busying herself. He hailed, "Lucy, I'm home," in a Cuban accent and took another whiff of air.

He found the source of the new scent downstairs. Amongst her things, a small cone of incense burned myrtle in a small red ceramic bowl. On the nightstand was a little square bedtime book, *Remember the Night Rainbow*. It featured a beautifully drawn elderly woman with tears pouring out of her eyes. Across the top it read, "If You're Afraid of the Dark."

He turned away and climbed the stairs to the main level. He knew his mom would be hungry, so he went into the kitchen and prepared a smoothie.

Coconut milk: most hydrating natural liquid on the planet. Half a banana; spinach: because Popeye swore by it for iron. Almond butter: because it was his favorite. Peanut butter: because it was her favorite. Protein powder: because everyone needed protein. Collagen powder: to keep skin young. Maca: to boost vigor. Bee pollen: because without pollination, humans wouldn't exist.

He fired up the blender and let it rip for twenty seconds. The brown liquid frothed high in the blender, filled with air bubbles. *Delicious*, he thought as he sampled it and poured two heaping glasses. "She's gonna love it," he said to himself before climbing the stairs.

Sadie was exactly where Mac had expected, except she was leaning back in an awkward position. Her hat was off and eyes closed. The sun was directly on her face, and she appeared asleep. The music was playing a rhythmic melody, and her sketch pad had fallen to the floor, stencils scattered. The beautiful flower arrangement of plastic locked into its bracket at the table's edge was Sadie's sketch. She'd painted it fuller of life on her sketch than what the naked eye offered. Mac sat down on the outdoor couch and smiled, setting her smoothie next to the typewriter.

"I made you a smoothie, Mom," he said, picking up her sketch.

Sadie didn't reply. Didn't move at all.

"Mom? Are you sleeping?"

Nothing.

Suddenly, panic washed over Mac's face. He leaned in and touched her forearm gently, "Mom?"

She jolted slightly and lifted her head, then reached for the back of her neck. "Where have you been all day?" Sadie asked, appearing disoriented.

"Hi. Here and there," he said, relieved. "Had to take care of some stuff."

Sadie reached for the smoothie and took a big swig. "This is really good."

"Glad you like it."

Sadie took another gulp. "It's so nice up here, Mac. I really wish we could come here more often."

"Funny you should say that, mom. My time here might be done."

"What do you mean?" she asked.

"I don't want to live in LA anymore."

"But you've kept this place for eight years. It's been so good for you."

Mac knew it was seven but didn't correct her. "You ever wish you'd done something and didn't?"

Sadie looked at him and took a moment to smile.

"I'm glad we could enjoy being together regardless of the unfortunate things that have happened." He paused. "I just learned the strangest thing."

"What's that?" she replied, taking a gulp.

"The old guy I helped with the groceries died."

"What?" she replied, her jaw dropping wide open.

Mac gave a look and nodded sadly.

"When?" she replied with empathy.

"Yesterday."

"Oh, honey, that's terrible. I'm so sorry."

"He had asked me to help him deal with the loud neighbor next door."

Sadie paused in thought, then asked with concern, "How did he die?"

"I don't know, Mom. That's what the police were asking about."

"You think it was COVID? Should we get tested?"

"I don't think so. I feel fine. Do you feel fine?"

"Yeah. I feel great," she said sympathetically. "I'm sorry. Sorry for what I said. I know you liked him. He did look sick, though."

"I know. It's just, he said the neighbor was bullying him, and I could have done more."

"That jerk next door?"

Mac nodded, then laid down what Stevo had told him in the garage while they drank the smoothies. By the time he'd finished breaking it down, both glasses were empty.

"You gonna help your friend—Stevo?" she asked.

"By doing what?" Mac replied, surprised.

"I don't know, Mac. You're smart. You will think of something."

"I don't think so."

"You're not going to help him?"

"He got himself into this mess. He can get himself out."

"That doesn't sound like you."

"It sounds exactly like me avoiding all the drama from this week. You've kept me busy."

They both looked at each other and laughed. Mac blinked at her gently, his eyes filled with love. "It sounds exactly the opposite of me, doesn't it?"

Sadie laughed again. "This is true."

"I think Stevo's fingerprints are all over the bottom of unit six. I can imagine Haroun seducing Stevo as a woman and Stevo going along with it. Unsuspecting. Having a beer or glass of wine. Maybe some nuts."

Mac gave his mom a curious look.

They burst out laughing.

But having these thoughts all kinds of wrong in Mac's mind, and he knew it. He felt empathetic for Haroun being born into a body that, in his mind's eye, was not his. Growing up obstacle-ridden with sexual orientation. Being a kid going through adolescence was brutal enough, never mind being in the wrong body for your mindset.

"Do you think he did it?" Sadie asked.

"Stevo? No way. He's not the type. He might have accidentally but wouldn't be able to function post. So, he would be a dead giveaway. Given that he's only just navigated to this point, what—three, four days later? He is innocent for sure. But he will be drilled when those prints come back with him in the room. Interesting that specific camera wasn't working."

"Convenient."

"My thoughts exactly."

"Did the police question you?"

"Yeah."

"Did they take your fingerprints?"

"I wouldn't let 'em."

"Good. You need your independence, you know? Your own freedom. That's your greatest strength." She frowned, then added, "Don't get caught up in this."

"Cops look at me and they either want to question me or think I'm one of them. Been that way my whole life. I'm either with them or against them. It's like a film on my skin I can't wash off."

"You're different. No doubt about it, son. And you're my beautiful boy."

Mac smiled solemnly.

"What do you need me to do, Mac? I'll support anything you choose."

* * *

Mac retrieved his mailbox keys from the kitchen's miscellaneous drawer. Stevo taking inventory of things that needed to go away made Mac think of the backlog of mail that must be jamming up his box. The box with the new wood built by

Ribbit, which would be eaten by termites within a year. Not that he cared all that much. He wouldn't be here in a year. He thought about what could be in his mailbox. Probably all junk mail. One of the perks of going paperless. But looking into a mailbox he hadn't opened in over two years was a percolating interest just the same. So he descended the stairs and turned a corner to the little hall that housed the mailboxes and was adjacent to the storage room for miscellaneous building supplies.

The key was clean, but the lock wasn't. Salt and whatever else makes up corrosion had grown thickly in an unused keyhole. It took some jamming to get the key in and another risky maneuver of turning it in the lock not to snap it. But the key held with some finagling and fell right, releasing its tumblers.

There it was in black and white.

Get the fuck out. A three-day notice to pay rent or quit from the owner.

Immediately Mac's mind raced. This was in his mailbox. Not plastered to his front door. A way for Ribbit to avoid confrontation and another to start a restraining order against his choosing.

The notice stated the owner wanted the occupant to move out. Mac read the single sheet of white paper in its entirety, then removed the blue tape holding it to other mail. All junk coupons and solicitations. He looked at the return address. Leisure World, Reza Thaddeus. 12076 Armada Way, Seal Beach, California.

The straw that broke the camel's back. Except, it wasn't Mac's back. The notice was addressed to Theodore Wolfgang Shivelbush. Teddy was the camel.

Several red, tan, and blue rubber bands wrapped parts of the junk mail together. All old and one step away from snapping. Mac held the clump in his grasp, closed the door, and gingerly removed the key.

Lubricant needed in every aspect of this quagmire, he thought to himself. He pocketed the eviction notice and let the rest fall from his hand into the empty trash can. He was exhausted. Time for sleep.

CHAPTER 45

DAY 6

The next morning, Mac pulled his sheets from his bed and folded them in with his mom's laundry bag. Then he headed down to his mom's room and pulled her dirty laundry and bedding. At the top of the bed, tucked underneath the pillows between the headboard and wall, were some candy wrappers. Mac stood there, looking at them in shock.

Mac climbed the stairs two at a time, stepped back onto the upper deck, and looked at his mom with disappointment. "What is this, Mom? Suicide by food? We talked about this."

Sadie saw the candy wrappers crumpled together in his right hand. A guilty look consumed her face, and she jolted slightly like a small electrical shock had tased her. "How did you find those?"

"Doesn't matter how I found them. The point is I found them. What the hell?"

"You searched my things?"

"Are there more?"

Sadie clammed up.

Mac tilted his head sideways and squinted. "Are there?"

"You found those in my bed?"

"I was washing your sheets to make you a fresh bed. This is how I'm rewarded?"

Sadie said nothing.

"This is betrayal, Mom. Self-sabotage. I don't know how else to describe it."

Sadie looked down.

"This is exactly like Dad's funeral. I caught you stuffing desserts into your mouth in the middle of a speech about Dad's life."

His mom glanced away to her right.

"You were sticking chocolates in your mouth and more in the other hand," Mac said, raising his arms. "No one had touched the desserts except you. Dinner hadn't even been served!"

Sadie looked back at Mac, a guilty look on her face.

Mac relived the moment. He was witnessing the second dessert enter her mouth at his dad's funeral. His jaw hung open in shock. And like a little girl stealing sweets in a candy store, Sadie took the other hand still smudged in cream and shushed him, then licked her fingers in satisfaction.

"I felt like I'd witnessed a child push two fingers into the backside of an uncut wedding cake. As wedding vows were exchanged!"

Sadie pursed her lips together.

"That was the first time I'd ever seen you do something like that. Is this where we are now?"

"I'm hungry!" she snapped. "I've been pooping like a goat for days!"

"It's no wonder, eating like this. Candy bars and nuts clog you up. We are on a cleanse, remember?"

"When will I go to the bathroom? What am I supposed to do about that?"

"This is a juice diet to cleanse your body. You shouldn't be pooping at all by day four. We are on six. But you're messing all that up by cheating."

"I've been trying to put some food in me so I can poop. Because I can't poop. You've got me walking every day, Mac. It's exhausting to me."

"You're not supposed to poop. We are trying to burn all the food out of your body, Mom. Losing weight is eighty percent diet. This isn't going to work if you don't stick to the diet." Mac opened his hands and unraveled the wrappers. "What is this stuff? Coconut cream Twinkies and blackberry pie. Salted nuts, and I don't know what this other thing is. No wonder you've been pooping like a goat with all the roasted nuts loaded with salt. What did you expect?"

Sadie sat back in her chair, shaking her head. "I know I disappointed you. There's no excuse. I'm sorry."

Mac walked over and hugged his mom from the side. It was awkward, almost forced at first. But as he held on, she softened, and she put her right hand up onto his right shoulder. They held each other for a few minutes and rocked gently.

Softy Mac asked, "Is there any more junk I should know about?"

Sadie lowered her voice and whispered, "Maybe in the car under the seat."

"Okay. Going to donate those to the homeless," he said, standing up. "Most of their teeth are rotted already, so…" He trailed off, then added, "Like Tintin's were." He walked to the door and asked, "Can you come with me, please?"

Sadie stood up sheepishly and followed him down to the kitchen.

Mac turned and waited, taking a few deep breaths, then opened the refrigerator. "Look around my kitchen. Every food here has a purpose. Everything is nutritious or it isn't in here." He closed the refrigerator. "If you have a problem saying no, then don't let it in your kitchen at home. Be purposeful, Mom. Like your paintings. Food nutrients should be energizing, not stuffing. Enriching, not suffocating." He began opening kitchen cabinets and looking at dates on dry food and cans. "If you're not on this journey, you're on another one, and our roads will not meet up. How do you think I made it in LA for five years with all the distractions around me? By eliminating them and not making space for any of the nonsense." He dropped several items into the trash can. "Compartmentalize. I would make it a game. The practice of a system. And it works."

"It's not that easy, Mac."

"You're not a victim, Mom. You've taken the path of least resistance and chosen things you can control. That resonate happy thoughts. Your paintings are your visual expressions of happiness. When I read your poems, I see splinters of your past that are darker. Things that frighten you. But not in your paintings." He closed the cabinets he'd opened and turned to look at her. "Keep painting."

"Does this mean dinner is off?"

"You've got jokes after all this?" he said, annoyed.

Sadie made a face, but didn't say anything.

"Don't you worry, we will still get our walk in today. Just later, when it cools off. It's too hot for you to be walking now." Mac pulled out his phone and said, "I created a little video for you to watch. We can change the music if you want. Even add more photos from your phone." He hit play and stood up, handing her the phone.

"Where are you going?" she said, not looking at the phone.

"I've already seen it, and I've got things to do. Freedom is my greatest strength, remember?" And with that, Mac headed downstairs and out the door.

Mac found some salted bags of nuts under the car seat, and it pained him to throw them away, so as promised, he walked over to some homeless people in the back alley and set the nuts down by the trash bins. A scrawny, small lady with a butchered bowl haircut lay next to the trash bin. She took notice and crawled toward the pile as Mac walked away.

Mac went back around the building and looked up at Theodore's front door. The tape had been broken, and the security camera hung down by a cord, useless.

Then he went to look at the other end of the building. Unit six mirrored unit two but was the end cap of the other side of the building's south-facing side. It had a small walkway that ran the distance of the building's width and dropped you off in the alley. That was the way he approached it. The door seal was still there, stretched across the doorjamb and stuck to the door and wall. Against it was the yellow warning tape.

He climbed two steps up and looked at the camera. Its angle was different from the one at his stairway. He didn't know the angle of unit two's camera because it was hanging by its cord.

Then he walked back into the garage, jumped on his bike, and pushed pedals north.

CHAPTER 46

This time Mac rode through the canals. He passed Washington and Venice and Windward Circle into the hood. Passed Fourth Street and the avenues and beyond, to where he thought an acquaintance might be.

He circled the housing projects twice, looking into their inner courtyards past high, locked iron fences and nonexistent children jumping rope. He wondered when they would be back outside playing with one another, able to touch without concern or masks.

After that, he continued north to a milder, less rough area. Urban and chill. The homes were modern and had bigger glass and better foliage. Curb appeal. Nothing doing there either. Then he went east a mile and cruised that area too. Nothing. Ghost town.

It was on his way back down Venice Boulevard that he spotted his target riding a shiny beach cruiser. It was chromed and low with a longer frame and fake mufflers. Big silver mirrors protruded from the handlebars in a ridiculous display of a tin man's wealth.

Mac crossed the street and pressed to catch him. Joaquin slowed when he saw Mac in his rearview mirror. He wore baggy blue jeans and a white shirt with white skateboard sneakers.

"Glad to see you, Cappy. How ya been?"

"Been doin'." Mac smiled. Only those who served under Mac called him Cappy. It was a name he liked. One he'd earned. "You know how it is. I saw you coming up on me, Joaquin. Almost didn't recognize you."

Joaquin smiled. "Good I recognized *you*," he said, underlined with warning.

Mac caught a glimpse of his pupils when he leaned forward with the message. They peeked above the rim of his glasses, hollow and somewhat vacant.

"Coulda been dangerous, right?" Mac replied, making light of it.

"No doubt, hommes."

Joaquin made a double gun gesture with both hands. A rite of passage. They smiled and shook. A three-move collaborative dance of fists and wrists. Then Mac said, "I see you're still riding a tin bicycle."

"Fuck you," Joaquin replied with a glint of mischievousness in his subdued eyes.

"That how you stay low profile?"

"I got toys," he shot back. "This is cardio."

"Oh."

"I thought I'd never see you around here no more."

Mac smiled. "I'm on vacation."

"During a pandemic?" Joaquin laughed. "You always were crazy, Cappy."

"Gotta go sometime, am I right?"

He nodded and glanced behind Mac.

Mac noticed. "How's my six?"

"You're good." Then his eyes glazed over and went cold. "No judgment, man, remember?"

Mac's eyes softened. "All that training, yet here you are, full circle."

"The navy wasn't for me. What can I say?"

"And this is?"

"Wasn't for you either."

"It was for a time, but you're right. I'm out too."

"Gotta do something. This is where I grew up. Stop hating."

"I'm not hating, brother. Just observing."

Joaquin nodded, and both took a big breath of air.

Then Mac asked, "Anything happening south of Washington?"

"Oh, now you need me?" Joaquin replied. He leaned in. "You can't see what's happening on your own?" Then he leaned back. "That's funny."

Mac said nothing, but when he rubbed his chin, it meant everything. He waited.

"Yeah, I heard something died over there."

Mac nodded. "What did you hear?"

"An OD. Lots of bright lights and shit."

"Yeah."

"In your old building, hommes."

"I heard that too. Does that happen a lot?"

"Only in the hood."

"What? Rich people don't OD?"

"When rich people OD, cops care. But in the hood? They don't."

Mac paused a moment. "So north of Washington," he said flatly.

"Correcto."

"You wouldn't know anything about that, would you?"

"The hood?" Joaquin smiled.

"My building?" Mac smiled back.

He tilted his head back high, chin raised, then said, "No," with an upside-down grin that created premature wrinkles around his jaw.

"Same shit, just another day," Mac replied.

"The usual, ya know." He nodded and glanced around as if someone might be watching them. "You need me to hook you up?"

"Me?" Mac shot back, a bit stunned. "Nah, I'm good."

"We got *paca loco* shit," he justified. "Nice for the mind shift."

Mac thought about Teddy. His use to shift his mind and inevitable outcome.

"Not my wheelhouse, brother."

"Whatever, whatever," Joaquin replied. Basically, take it or leave it. He didn't care.

"Remember brother, every day above ground is a good day," Mac shot back.

"Precisely," he said, extending his hand to end the talk.

They bumped fists, another rhythmic flow, and Joaquin patted his heart with a fist.

"Joaquin?" Mac said before he turned. "They got cameras on the building now. Lotta heat. You might not wanna come around anymore."

"Yeah, I noticed that. The whole peninsula does." He took a moment to look Mac over. "You still got it, don't you, Cappy?"

"Once trained, always trained," Mac replied.

"It doesn't wash off, does it?"

Mac acknowledged this with a bitter grin. His eyes looked away then returned. "No. No, it doesn't."

Joaquin's eyes became solemn, and the wrinkles returned to his lower cheeks. "I miss it, man. The adrenaline rush.

Drugs are the closest to it and the furthest to push it away."
He looked behind him before turning and riding off.
Mac sat in his thoughts, watching Joaquin push pedals.
Then his gaze fell to the ground. He shook it off by shaking
his hands and took a massive breath and pressed exhale.

CHAPTER 47

Mac rode north away from where Joaquin had gone. He knew Joaquin meant the usual was bad-grade cocaine. Maybe Molly, Special K, and whatever else the cartel was slinging. It might be methamphetamine. Meth was everywhere and especially in the homeless encampments where people had hit rock bottom. He didn't know if crack cocaine still existed. But he could spot a meth head a mile away, and at the beach were plenty. Walking zombies all dried and spun in the hot sun until the next fix. Then they'd race out to collect more garbage for their enclave, only to rearrange everything all over again. It was a sickening cycle of nonsensical brain damage few escaped. He wanted no part of it.

At Ocean Park Boulevard, he turned west and rode all the way down to the beach path, then turned right on it. Soon he was past Santa Monica entering the town of Pacific Palisades. He turned east at Temescal Canyon Road and pushed pedals up the hill through Sunset Boulevard into the Temescal Canyon State Park. Pine trees bracketed the entrance followed by giant Sycamore trees bordering the dry creek. He rode the cement path until a dirt path appeared in a small opening of brush. He cut left and braved his bike through a bushy unused trail toward the creek.

Once at the dry creek, Mac looked up the hillside, the canyon holding sycamore trees with yellowed leaves and bleached white branches. Sage and wild brush and poison oak were plentiful. He pushed his bike into the brush and left it pitched upright. On foot, Mac traced the canyon back down to the creek, skirting the rocks below before picking his spot. Pushing the trash bag and clippers deeper into his pocket, he set off on a dense deer trail. Carefully holding branches away from his body as he passed through, he scanned the leaves of every plant and branch he passed for ticks. Around a small turn, a bush full of three-leafed weeds caught his attention. The leaves were hearty in a bloom of red, orange, and green.

Mac pulled out the black rubber gloves and slipped them on. They were small, but he managed over his thick hands and proceeded cutting the ends of the sprigs of green leaves and red leaves, leaving the orange alone. Once he had what amounted to a bunch, he removed one glove and sealed the bag. Then he removed the second glove and folded it inside the first before placing them back in his rear pocket.

Turning back down the trail, he sauntered off and returned the same way he'd came. This time the trail went quicker, and once in the clear, he checked his body for stranglers and cling-ons. Sure enough, one tick was on his ankle, and he flicked it off. Then he put his right toe to his left heel and held the end while lifting his foot. He checked his ankle on both sides, then repeated the move with his other foot. Confirming nothing had climbed down inside his shoes, he continued on to the bike he'd stashed in the deep brush.

It was dark by the time Mac returned to the condominium. Little lights in various windows lit the building except the lower units two and six. Those were pitch black and echoed of death. He put his bike in the garage and took the eastern path around the back of the building. Slow and methodical, not fast or rushed. Casually, like he had all the time in the world. He considered the task an exercise in patience. And due diligence.

He made his way to the laundry room. Inside the hallway, after placing the laundry in the dryer and checking for cameras, he pushed his hands deep into the plastic bag and grabbed hold of the green leaves inside his pants pocket. Mac gripped them tightly and started mulching them inside his palm, all while twisting dryer heat options with his left hand holding the dial. Then he pulled his right hand and gripped the security room door handle as he passed by. The moist liquid floated on the metal surface like oil on water.

Returning around the side of the building, he climbed unit two's stairs and pretended to knock on Penny's door. It was an air knock that couldn't be identified by the camera because of the depth of the door and jamb in relation to the camera's position. To cover the knocking sound, he coughed loud at the precise time of the knocks.

Three hard faked knocks.

Three hard faked coughs.

He faked a short conversation and finished with, "I'll come back later, then, when I've time." He turned and, bouncing back down the stairs after waving through the imaginary opened door, said, "No, no, no."

On camera was a good sell. Maybe a great sell. The door had never opened, no one had appeared, and no conversation had actually taken place. It was a pantomime of gigantic proportions.

Mac smiled as he descended the bottom stairs. The upper camera was still there, recording his movements. The lower camera was still hanging, doing much of nothing.

When Mac entered his home, he went straight to the kitchen and scrubbed his hands clean with dish soap in cold water. Poison oak had never been an issue for Mac. Nor his siblings, for that matter. Nor the fifteen percent of the population across the globe. It was the other eighty-five percent he was thinking about. Goats' milk and cheese as a child had sorted that long ago and made him immune. As he washed his hands, he thanked his mother for raising them in Big Sur. Another reason to appreciate his mom, which at times was really hard to do. He dried his hands and tiptoed over to her stairs and peeked down.

From the top of the stairs, he couldn't see his mom, so he slowly stepped down. When she appeared, her back was to him as she stood at the foot of the bed. She was wearing another long undershirt as a nighty, barely covering her bottom. Mac avoided looking at the dimples of her fat legs and knocked lightly on the wall. "Everything all right, Mom?"

"Oh, honey, you're back," she replied, turning around. "Everything good?"

"Yeah, Mom. Got your laundry going in the dryer. Should be ready in thirty minutes, and I'll make your bed. Do you want me to make you some tea?"

"No, thanks. I had a smoothie a little while ago."

Mac paused, a bit surprised. "Oh, good."

"I think I just want to read. Do you mind?"

"Not at all. A quiet night would be great."

CHAPTER 48

DAY 7

I t was not to be. At 2:07 in the morning, a reverb of bass penetrated the condo from the west-facing wall. It was a series of intricate finger rips that at any time other than 2:00 a.m. would have been fine.

Mac started at one hundred and began counting backward to one. At twenty going to nineteen, he heard laughing on the upstairs deck. Then it became arguing and, shortly after, something else. When he heard the girl say, "Get off me," he got out of bed.

He slipped on a T-shirt and went up to the deck, wondering why the poison oak hadn't worked. Maybe Penny was spraying his door handles with alcohol. He didn't know. Mac quietly closed the screen door behind him, then closed the regular door as well. He could hear the woman pleading to stop on the other side of the wall.

When Mac peeked around the ledge, his heart raced. Penny was on top of the girl. Mac couldn't see her face, but her voice was familiar. Then he remembered the rape conversation when he was returning from grocery shopping and recognized the voice. It was the girl who had said hello that he didn't recognize.

What she saw in Penny, Mac had no idea. But whatever it was had turned to fear, and she was doing her best to fend him off. Penny was straddling her and holding her pinned arms against the outdoor bunk bed. Her top was open as she twisted away from him. She wasn't screaming but clearly wanted him to stop.

Mac glanced into the darkness at the buildings adjacent and the deserted beach, the lone lifeguard tower silhouetted in the distance. Then he made a decision. He put his right hand on top of the wall and slipped around it to balance forty feet in the air.

Like a mountain cat, he floated through the air and landed silently on the deck barefoot. Three swift steps, the third being a leap, he swung hard and true and connected sideways with the back of Penny's temple.

Penny never saw it coming. Knuckles crashed against delicate ear cartilage and temporal muscles and ligaments, causing his brain to slam against its skull. Immediate blackout. His body went limp and flew left several feet. His hands seemed to follow the lead of his head as it bounced on fake grass at the doorway. One of his shoes came off.

Mac stood between Penny's feet and the girl. His punch had landed him there. The circumference of his swing had brought him left of her at a three-quarter angle. His bare feet were on the plastic grass, moist from the damp, warm air. He breathed lightly because he didn't want to scare the girl any more than he already had by punching Penny. He hoped she was relieved. He wasn't sure. So he asked, "Are you okay?"

The girl, maybe twentysomething at most, lay silent in complete fright. Frozen. No breath. Eyes wide open. Mouth agape. Exposed.

"What's your name?"

She blinked and looked over at Penny. She stuttered, "M-M-Melissa."

"Are you okay, Melissa?"

She nodded and softly said in a mousy voice, "Yeah."

"Am I in trouble for doing that?" he asked, pointing over at Penny.

"No," she said. "Thank you."

Mac stood still. It was awkward. She pulled her top up and covered herself. "What do you want to do?"

"What do you mean?" she asked.

"Do you want to press charges?"

She shook her head, no.

Mac waited, but she said nothing. "You should go, then," he said in the stillness.

She slowly looked at her chest, noticing her pink breast exposed. She pushed it back into her bra and took a deep breath.

"That could have gone terribly wrong if I hadn't heard you call out. It's good you fought him off."

"Yeah, didn't really help, though." She nodded, still lying back. Finally, she lifted herself up to her elbows. Like an afterthought, she added, "Thank you. I mean it."

"You're welcome," Mac replied. "And it did help because I heard you."

"I don't want anybody to know."

Mac sized her up. He wondered. "Okay."

"You didn't remember me when you saw me today. Did you?" she asked like she was ashamed.

"I'm sorry. I didn't. I don't," he returned apologetically. "When did we meet?"

"On the beach a long time ago," she said, adjusting her top. He felt horrible. "I don't live here. I'm sorry. Been a long time."

"Penny told me you guys were best friends."

"This guy? No. It's not true."

"Will he be okay?"

"He's not dead, if that's what you mean."

Melissa nodded like that was fine.

"Why don't you go to the bathroom and clean yourself up, then let yourself out? Can you do that?"

She nodded. "Yeah, I can do that." She moved like molasses. Slow, methodical, and careful not to step in any wrong areas. Like everything on the ground was precious and flowers could be crushed.

Penny was no flower. In Mac's mind, he could be crushed.

Mac took a step left and felt the edge of something soft beneath his foot. He looked down and saw a purse lying on the fake grass. "I think this is yours," he said, leaning down to pick it up. He walked forward and handed it to her.

She took it and maneuvered her way past Penny through the door to the stairs. Mac watched her the entire way. When she closed the bathroom door, Mac scanned the ground for anything else that might be hers. Then he stepped inside. He looked down at the unit. It had a canopy bed in the loft bedroom and plump brown couches below in the living room. The music was still blaring bass line rips from heavy metalheads with axes. Long hair over faces, tight pants, and silk shirts. It may have been Black Sabbath or Iron Maiden, Mac wasn't sure. It was intense, with poetry woven into the lyrics on how to navigate success in an unforgiving world.

Penny lay on the ground, unconscious, his hair looking like a fresh-greased mullet. Mac took his time thinking before bolting into action.

When the girl exited the bathroom, Penny was lying on the kitchen floor soaking in yellow dish soap. The music was turned down, and the bass had morphed into another metal song. Mac was wearing a bright yellow dish glove. In his left hand was a soap bottle. He squeezed the container with the last of the soap to add to the effect.

"You're gonna be okay?" he asked Melissa in a whisper.

"I'm gonna be okay," she replied, sounding better and less mousy. Her face was puckered, cheeks red, and hair somewhat put back together.

Mac put his finger over his lips to keep the whisper going. "I never saw you, right?"

"You never saw me," she answered quietly.

"Don't ever come back here."

"I won't."

She opened the front door and exited. She didn't close it before another idea popped into his head. It made no sense, zero, theoretically. But it was creative. Artistic, even. He looked at the front door and wondered if he could pull it off.

Mac was up to the challenge. The door was half-closed now, hanging in the balance, the young woman gone. He reopened the door and checked the hallway without leaning outside, then swung the door wide. It caught the carpet at the end of its swing where the indentation had lain.

Mac turned and grabbed Penny by his feet and dragged his limp body to the door and swung it halfway back. Then he leaned down and unbuttoned Penny's tight, slim-fit blue jeans.

He pitched him forward on his side and brought Penny's belly as close to the indentation in the carpet as possible without blocking the swing of the door. Then with the gloved left hand, he reached in and took out Penny's testicles with clinical detachment. When he thought he had everything in position, he shifted Penny's teetering weight and brought the door back to its maximum arc. With Penny's testicles pinched between the carpet and door bottom and his body in limbo, Mac stepped back.

Penny groaned in unconscious agony as the door pinched against skin and carpet. Mac imagined something in Penny's simpleton brain recognized, no matter how disconnected, something excruciatingly painful had occurred. His conscious mind was not yet firing and Mac imagined his subconscious felt a burning sensation, like exploding shrapnel on virgin skin. There was no blood, so he wouldn't bleed out, but the scarring was inevitable. Maybe reproductive ending. But not life threatening.

Mac looked at his face one last time as he placed his foot against Penny's hip and gently pushed. His body twisted back toward the kitchen and away from the door, Penny's critical organ caught under it.

Mac could see in his peripheral the skin stretching well beyond its intended range. He didn't imagine an organ could extend like Penny's had. But there it was. He didn't look directly at it—it was too grotesque.

He'd dreamed up some sick stuff in his time. But this was the kicker of kickers. Better than broken kneecaps and shoulders that never healed.

Then he wiped the door handle and, two at a time, climbed Penny's interior stairs to the upper balcony. The atmosphere was warm and balmy outside. A light wind blew salty air. Mac walked to the railing, leaped up against the wall, and slipped around the edge.

At the top of the wall, he imagined waving out into the darkness. He knew a camera somewhere was recording him. The whole peninsula was covered in them.

Then he climbed down onto his balcony and washed in the bathroom with his light off. After a meticulous scrubbing, he pulled scissors from the bathroom drawer and cut the rubber gloves into tiny bits.

Then he lay on top of his bed.

But he couldn't sleep. He thought he heard some faint sound of distress. But when the sound screeched again, he discovered it was only seagulls flying by.

He wanted to walk on the beach, jump in the ocean, and wash Penny's filth off. Minutes before, he had Penny's scalp hair beneath his nails. His body odor on his skin. And his unmistakable cologne scent on his arms.

Fuck, he thought. I still feel filthy.

When Mac was on the farm back when he was growing up, he might be dirty all day. There could be brown dirt from Sycamore Canyon under his nails. Or black dirt from the Big Sur River. Or red dirt from above Pfeiffer on the rocks. But not sand. Never sand. Sand was the elixir like the ocean, which was what he really wanted.

It cleaned nails when he surfed in it. Cleaned skin when he bathed in it. Cleaned hair when he swam in it. And softened feet when he ran on it. It was the best-known cleanser to mankind. People had paid hundreds of dollars for salt scrubs and seawater rubbed on their bodies. Mac had heard there was even a company that had it bottled and sold in high-end spas, like Big Sur hotels Ventana and Post Ranch. Body scrubs using sand off the beach he'd grown up on. Furthermore, he'd heard they were using mud from the north end of that beach as a mineral bath.

He wasn't sure what they were charging, but it was interesting to him. And he wanted to be on that beach. He wanted to be far away from this place right now.

CHAPTER 49

It was now three in the morning. Mac would have to lie in bed another two hours before dawn. Then it might seem reasonable if he walked outside to the beach. Most people weren't working, so rising this early while on vacation didn't make a lot of sense.

He lay in bed for another two hours thinking about his mom, hoping he didn't get caught and ruin the entire trip. The obvious thing to do was go straight home. Pack up and leave in the morning at first light.

But he didn't.

Instead, he lay wide awake thinking about his mom's dog, Tintin. He couldn't get the damn dog out of his mind. All the poops. All the pees in people's homes. On their carpets. On their curtains. He was a real terror.

Just like Mac.

And Mac felt no better.

Then his phone chirped. It was a coded email file from Simelane. The subject read "Leisure World."

"Who lives at Leisure World?" Mac asked himself. Sounded more like some kind of amusement park. The source of the notice to vacate had originated there. Bizarre place to have an office. Maybe it was some sort of commercial building complex.

It had been a long time since he'd spoken to the Catamaran owner, Reza. Only one time, in fact. It was seven years ago, after he learned his new apartment manager had served in the Army Corps of Engineers. When they pieced it together, Jim told him the owner was a navy man. That he'd married into a family that owned apartment buildings. They'd crossed paths one time at the Catamaran building. Brief and pleasant. One soldier to another, except it was one soldier and two navy officers having a friendly chat. Pleasantries were exchanged, everyone enjoyed meeting each other, and that was it. They went on their separate ways.

Mac didn't want to cold-call Reza out of the blue. But he did want to talk to him, and he wanted the element of surprise on his side.

Unfortunately, Jim was gone. His only real ally. Allegedly fired. Replaced by a numbnut. No, it wasn't a phone call type of conversation he wanted to have with Reza Thaddeus. He wanted to see him face-to-face.

When first light finally crept into the sky, he got up and took a walk on the beach.

And waited.

And dreaded.

He considered the possibility that Melissa might have panicked when she got home and called the cops. Or, once the shock wore off, called the cops. Or woke, felt she was to blame, and called the cops. Or told someone, and they called the cops. Or several other scenarios that all led to calling the cops.

Then there were the neighbors in unit one. Perhaps they heard something and called. Or when they opened their front door. That must have been a gruesome scene, Mac imagined. A moaning and a screech or scream.

Either way, he found sitting on the beach a better option than lying in bed waiting for the cops to break his door down. *Christ*, Mac thought. Perhaps closing Penny's door wasn't a bad idea. The exact opposite. It was wide open, holding what was left of Penny's tortured manhood.

And Penny had it bad. Pinched between the corner of the door and carpet. Multiple fractures all over the inside of his ear and a broken cock. Stretched beyond what Mac ever thought was humanly possible. Back to the Dark Ages of torture. Or, he turned in his mind, Jim Crow. That brought a smile to Mac's face. He imagined Teddy smiling too. On a slab somewhere in a crowded morgue.

Then he saw something move in his peripheral vision to his left. It was under the lifeguard tower. He knew people sometimes slept there on romantic excursions. Sort of a voyeuristic truth or dare on the seashore experience bucket list. But the homeless were plentiful too, so he was wary.

When the homeless guy rolled over and Mac saw Chad's face, he felt like an insensitive asshole again. He'd completely misread Chad twice. Once on the beach. Again at the Village near Mother's Beach. The same late-twenties, good-looking Asian man.

Homeless.

On his own.

Alone.

Not voyeuristic at all.

Chad was decently dressed. Like he'd rolled out of a suburban home nearby. Probably decided sleeping by the ocean was better than sleeping in a hot, stuffy apartment. Maybe to sleep off his evening's alcohol on the beach under the stars. But maybe the night dew made him move beneath the tower. Maybe not. Mac didn't know.

But the man said hello when he woke. So Mac replied back, "Good morning to you too."

"Going to be a beautiful day," Chad said, upbeat and positive. Almost jovial.

"God, I hope so," Mac replied, then said to himself, "Maybe I won't be going to jail after all."

"Are you swimming?" he asked.

"Yes, I am. Do you remember me, Chad?"

Chad nodded, wiping sleep from his eyes. "Yes, of course. We've met a few times."

"Yes, we have." Mac paused. "Are you homeless?"

Chad looked at Mac, an awkward expression of uneasiness on his face. "Yes."

"I feel embarrassed about what I said the other day."

"No worries. I saw your points."

Mac nodded. "How are you coping with it?"

Chad rolled the question over in his mind. "Some days are difficult for me."

"May I ask why you're homeless?"

"I have a tough time concentrating."

Mac put the pieces together quickly and garnered Chad wasn't able to keep a job. Then becoming homeless made his obstacles multiply. And maybe his personalities too.

"What if I could find you a temporary home?"

Chad looked at Mac surprised, his expression of shame turning to bewilderment. "What?"

Mac flipped his wrist open and said, "You seem like a good person caught in a difficult time. I've seen you around. It's not a hard decision for me." Mac watched Chad look up to the sky and back to him. Watched his gesture land. "You need a place, and I might know of one."

"I don't have any money."

"I think rent's been paid through the end of the year. So, no issue there. And there's a pandemic. People need housing. And you're a person. I think a good person. It'd be a shame to let the place go unused."

"Where is it?"

Mac smiled.

CHAPTER 50

Mac swam for an hour. He walked straight out into the waves, leaving his shirt on the sand and Chad with hope. The water felt warm, seventy-two degrees. Global warming was working. There was a slight swell creating waves three to four feet high. The current was strong. He felt it pulling him in different directions, swirling about his body. And kept thinking about what his mom had said. *Be free.*

Mac caught a culmination of waves before deciding he'd had enough. As he walked up the sand past where he'd spoken to Chad, nothing seemed amiss. The usual-suspect vehicles were parked in front of the building. No flashing lights. No screaming sirens. No ambulance.

He crossed the hundred-meter beach and stepped onto the asphalt. Looked left and right up and down Speedway Alley and crossed.

He climbed the stairs past his mom's room and stepped into the living room. He felt light and easy, refreshed. He could hear Sadie lightly snoring below. He continued up the stairs to his bathroom. There he rinsed off in a warm shower, brushed his teeth, and used the toilet.

Coffee, tea, or jail for me? was a rhyme that kept ringing in his head. "Coffee," he decided, having not slept all night.

He needed his brain firing faster than it already was. He needed to sort out loose ends. Mainly, he needed to have an alibi for all the times he'd been on camera with Penny. Because it was there in black and white. Maybe color. He didn't know.

So he made coffee and drank it. Lots of it. With oat milk and honey. Then he decided to take out the trash.

On his way to the back of the building, he passed Ribbit entering the center hallway. He was wearing a wifebeater tank top and looked like shit. His eyes were swollen shut like puffy, infected zits. In fact, Ribbit's entire upper torso was so blotchy his neck looked like an irritated red cord of rope ending in a knot, his face.

Mac knew the poison oak was in his bloodstream. Like someone had done a skin burn twist from grade school on his wrists and worked up. It had worked a lot faster than Mac had imagined. Ribbit had a brown paper bag in one hand labeled from the market down the street. Mac figured calamine lotion.

As they passed each other, neither said anything.

Mac dumped the trash, then slipped inside the laundry room. He triple-checked for obvious cameras and any hidden cameras he might have missed the first time around. When he saw none, he stepped to the door he'd poison-oaked a day earlier. Then he jimmied the door with a butter knife and stepped inside.

The room was small. Maybe ten feet across and six feet deep. It was as he imagined. An electrical surveillance box. One wall with camera monitors. A basic Dell computer with separate keyboard. And a CD player that burned DVDs with a memory stick portal. Standard and reliable.

The monitors, of which there were four, had split black and white screens that covered the entire building. Time code ran on all of them, and they were synced with a twenty-four-hour clock. All motion sensor recording, so it made speeding through footage super easy.

Mac knew if it had facial recognition, which he doubted, that would make it even easier. Target certain people, and it was game over.

Mac touched the keyboard, and it sprang to life asking for a password. He thought about the day he'd met Reza years ago and what Reza would have used. He thought about the information Simelane had delivered in her file. He thought about the address of the building. Using the butter knife, he pressed keys, always ending in enter.

Nothing worked. Ribbit was a mystery to him. For all he knew, Ribbit was the code master. He didn't know. But he needed to see what was on the computer, so he pressed onward.

The computer hit its lockout threshold at ten failed attempts. It was a random number that could be preset in settings. That, Mac knew. Now he'd have to wait until the keyboard unlocked. How soon it would unlock was a question only the engineer who programmed it knew the answer to. And Ribbit or Reza manning the program. Again, Mac didn't know.

So he waited for another random number to unlock the computer. He imagined it was under thirty seconds, but could range up to 99,999 minutes. All sixes upside down, never a good sign. *Ribbit the code master.* Representing the devil to the tenants, though he looked more like a troll.

He remembered Reza had a dog but couldn't recall the name. Something short and simple. Maybe from a movie or hero.

"Wait," he said to himself. *What kind of dog was it? Could the password be the breed? Could that be it?* The dog was smart, Mac remembered. Super attentive. What breed was it? White with some black on it. Not a schnauzer like his mom's. Not a Jack Russell either. *A mutt?*

Then Mac switched gears, thinking the breed was some sort of a random misfire. The password would be the dog's name. And the dog was named after a car from the fifties or sixties, Mac remembered. A rarity. Probably a car Reza's parents had when he was a kid. The automaker Ford was the most obvious, at least in Mac's mind, so he started there. But Ford model names went on forever, so it was a big list. They'd built planes that saved democracy during World War II. And now, they were building electric cars with names like Mach, to save the planet. Mach was a terrible name he thought, so he backtracked up the alphabet then down landing on T for Tucker.

That must be it, he thought.

Now he'd have to wait for the keyboard to unlock. He figured ten minutes to match the ten failed attempts. He relished the idea that Tucker could be the password. Then he wondered what else was special about the day he'd met Reza. They'd talked ships and deployment. Mainly regions they'd served. He wanted to be prepared for the face time. Reza outranked him by several tiers, and he'd have to be crystal clear in his arguments why this visit was important. Especially now. No better insult than a young, commissioned ex-captain telling an active officer that outranks him something is amiss under his command.

When ten minutes passed in Mac's mind, his back of the brain counting the six hundred seconds like clockwork, Mac tapped on the keyboard. It lit up and the cursor was ready. *One down*, he thought. Slowly Mac pushed the blunt end of the butter knife into the keys, spelling "Tucker," and hit enter.

It didn't work. Nine more attempts left.

He tried "Tucker1" Nope. Then tried "Tucker1Catamaran." Nope. Same with "Tucker1CatamaranSt," "Tucker1Catamaran1Street," and several other variations.

Mac stopped. It was his tenth attempt, and if it was wrong and didn't work, he'd lose another ten minutes.

He knew Ribbit was dedicated. Like beyond measure. And though Ribbit was itching like the son of a bitch he was, he might not be deterred for long in getting last night's surveillance footage to the police department. And Mac didn't want to be caught inside the video room by him either. He imagined Ribbit entering the small room, face covered in ointment. "What are you doing in here? I'm calling the cops!"

"What was it about Tucker, dammit?" he asked himself. Something Reza had said about his keen sense of smartness...

He was a border collie! That was it. And avidly at Reza's side.

Mac gestured as he whispered to himself. He brought his right elbow in tight against his waist, going through the body language of that day so long ago. His hand turned down as if to pet the dog, but level, parallel to the ground. *What was it about Tucker?* he wondered, as he swung his hand sideways, elbow still at his side.

"Radar," he said aloud. Almost too loud as his eyes went wide. "Tucker's radar. His keen sense of people," Reza had said.

Quickly Mac deleted his tenth input and keyed in "Tuckers Radar." Mac paused, taking a breath, and hit enter.

Password accepted.

CHAPTER 51

When Mac walked around the building, he saw Kootz's car blocking the garages. He was climbing out of the driver's side, and the passenger seat was empty. Kootz saw Mac immediately, and Mac went straight toward him. "What? No partner today?"

Kootz closed the door, favoring his right arm, and said nothing.

"You wanted to say something in the precinct, but you didn't. Why?"

Kootz took a breath and smirked. "Normally, it's the police who ask the questions, Mr. MacGuffin."

"Was it Bean stopping you?"

Kootz said nothing and began gathering his gear.

"How do you know so much about this building?" Mac asked. "It's not just the cameras at work. You guys know a lot more than normal."

Kootz said nothing.

"I'm down to burn some bridges, but you gotta level with me."

Kootz looked up, "Because of what I said?"

"No, because I've got something you don't."

Kootz stopped gathering his gear. "What's that?"

"We gotta have trust first. I'll tell you when I know for sure."

Kootz stood still, looking at Mac.

"That didn't happen yesterday because I didn't know anything until now, Kootz."

Kootz started to walk toward the stairwell. "It's Sheriff Kootz—"

Mac cut him off. "Teddy was a good man."

Kootz turned back. "I thought you didn't know him."

"I didn't. More of an instinct. Which is what you had with me."

Kootz said nothing.

"What was clear to me is that decline takes place in many forms and it was inevitable he'd die a painful death."

"Mr. Shivelbush had ALS and some other rare disease."

"He did say something about it being too late. I didn't know what he'd meant."

"There was no cure for it."

Mac nodded. "Thank you for telling me that."

"You're welcome."

"How did he die?"

"He hung himself." Kootz said flatly. No emotion. Like it had all been drained out of him from saying it a thousand times in less than a month was exhausting. A cop's job. Tough. Brutal. Bitter. "It will be ruled a suicide."

"Horrible way to go."

"It was quick."

"It's a choice."

Both held one another's stare. Kootz broke the silence. "Anything else, MacGuffin?"

"You familiar with Bell's palsy? It's often the step before a stroke."

"Mr. Shivelbush didn't have Bell's palsy."

"What do you have?"

Kootz's left lower eyelid flickered, but he said nothing. Then his right arm trembled again. Mac saw it and pushed further. "It's only going to get worse." It was a straight, non-judgmental statement, right on the chin. "What's going on with your arm?" he asked next, no spin, no manipulation.

"Nothing." Kootz frowned, defensively looking down at his arm, and began rubbing it.

"Bullshit," Mac offered with concern.

Kootz looked at him. "You a doctor? I didn't think so." It was delivered as an insult. Like the damage was done and no way of healing it. Bitter.

Mac barely smiled. "No. One good guy trying to do the right thing to help another. Like brothers in arms. That I am."

Sheriff Kootz rolled the idea in his mind of opening up. Mac could see that. He was conflicted. In pain. At a crossroad of two minds.

Kootz looked down at his notepad, then his eyes scanned the stairway he didn't want to climb. Or maybe it was the building he didn't want to enter again.

Mac recognized the hesitation. "I can offer you an alkaline water. We try this interview thing all over again without your partner?"

Kootz looked like he was at the end of his rope. "Alkaline, that's—"

"Anticancer," Mac said firmly. "Cancer can't manifest or grow in an alkaline body." He turned and walked a few short steps toward his stairwell. "Eastern medicine, Sheriff Kootz."

Mac paused, "By the way, Shivelbush was trying to burn the disease out of him with hot foods."

"What do you mean?" Koot's asked.

"And alcohol. Though that was probably more for the pain. You asked me about his kitchen. I didn't mention all the Chile's I'd seen, just the spices because, I figured it wasn't important. But then, I figured it out. I would have gone the other way."

"What do you mean?" Kootz asked.

"It's called, the water diet. Instead of burning it out with spices and chile's, you let your body eat the disease. You starve it. Ten days of fasting or longer without food. Because the body has nothing to eat, it begins eating itself. And all the impurities. It starts in the gut. Then outward through the body. If you become too weak, you can eat a one-time teaspoon of raw organic honey. That's it. And after ten days, you're rail thin, but any disease is usually gone."

"How did you learn this?"

"I met a world heavyweight boxer and trainer named Michael Kowlowski. He told me about it. He's got a video on YouTube. Something titled: ten-day water diet with coach Mike, I think. Look it up." Then Mac turned away towards his unit.

Amazingly, Kootz followed him. As he trailed him up the stairs, Mac asked, "Room temperature or cold?" barely looking back.

Kootz held his position just inside the door, looking at the red painting above the dining table. "I shouldn't," he replied hesitantly.

"You're already here, Kootz. It's just water in a sealed bottle. I don't care if you wear a mask or not. I don't have cooties. I'm gonna give you room temperature because it's better for you." Mac said convincingly because Kootz did it.

"Yeah, I seem to have read that somewhere," he replied, his voice full of gravel.

Mac opened a cabinet above the sink, revealing two cases of alkaline water plus electrolytes bottles. He pulled three bottles down, left one on the counter, and handed another to the sheriff, who took it with his left hand. Mac twisted open his own bottle and took a heavy gulp. The sheriff struggled with the twist top.

Mac stepped to his dining table, now a makeshift desk, and sat down. The sheriff held his position, back to the absent television in the alcove off the wall.

Mac studied him carefully. "So what happened?" he asked again, nodding at the arm. The sheriff finally got the plastic twist cap off with a minor grunt and took a small sip. He shook his head once almost dismissively, and words formed on his lips, but nothing came out.

"It's not your arm, is it? The cause of the injury?" Mac asked delicately.

"How do you know that?" Kootz replied cautiously with curiosity.

Mac continued, "They run electrodes through it?"

Kootz nodded lightly. "Affirmative."

"Hurt like hell?"

Kootz exhaled a waffled breath. "Yeah."

Mac scratched the back of his neck a moment, then asked, "Have you ever heard of cupping?"

Sheriff Kootz shook his head. He was looking across the room at an epoxied award encasing four FBI badges. Mac noticed but said nothing. He took another water swig, this time bigger. "Those weren't there before."

"I pulled out a few things I wanna keep."

"You going somewhere?"

"Every day," he said, then changed his tone. "Back to cupping."

"Huh?" He was still looking at the badges.

"Well, it's not related to spooning, so don't get any ideas."

"Oh?" Kootz replied, turning to Mac apologetically. "Sorry, what did you say?"

"Acupuncture combined with wet cupping. Ever hear of that?"

"Acupuncture, yes. The other? No."

"You've probably got a slight case of Bell's palsy. Is it only your arm?"

"Yeah," he said, looking away from the badges back to the painting. The room was sparse. Mac looked at Kootz and the empty dining chair across from him. The only two dining chairs in the entire home.

"It will get worse unless you do something about it. What did your Western doctor say?"

"He wants to operate. He's got me on aspirin," he replied matter-of-factly.

"This and a few other symptoms are what happens sometimes prior to a stroke. You don't want that. The aspirin is good, even baby aspirin is helpful. And taking vitamin B-12."

"How do you know this?" Kootz asked.

Mac shrugged and didn't answer. Instead, he asked, "Is it possible you have a banged-up disk in your neck that's affecting your arm? You experience any body weakness, incoordination, temporary paralysis?"

Kootz listened, but his eyes beamed acknowledgment.

"All signs of a serious neck injury. And if not treated properly, it will worsen over time."

"Yeah?" Kootz replied, concerned.

"I see your stripes, so I know you've put in time. Probably plenty on the pavement and before that in jails. Am I right?"

"Maybe," Kootz replied.

Mac was on target, and knew he could help. "Stop masking. You're conservative, and I get it. What happened down at the station is water under the bridge. Waste of time for me to be caught up in that shit. But what I want to propose could"—Mac slowed his speech—"and *would* make the rest of your time with this injury a lot more pleasant."

He had the sheriff's full attention, or at least he thought he had, so he pressed onward. "I'm suggesting you bring your medical records to a friend of mine that works on professional athletes and soldiers. Let him look at your arm. And, so you know, he'll be examining your neck, arms, back, and probably the way you walk."

Kootz frowned like he'd never heard this before. "Okay," he replied after Mac waited.

"Then he will probably give you some chiropractic adjustments before applying acupuncture needles. I don't know your deal, and telling me is meaningless. What matters is that you call my friend. He will use suction cups, hence the term *cupping*." Mac gestured parenthesis with his fingers. "This is to remove stale blood to the injured area that is blocked."

"Blocked?" Kootz asked.

"Correct. In your neck. Lacking circulation. He's gonna most likely prick you with needles to create passages for the blood to extract itself."

"I don't know about any of that with the pandemic going on. That would be illegal."

"I'm sure it could be. But what you got is very dangerous, so I'm not gonna mess around with pleasantries. You understand?"

Kootz was in agony, and the right side of his face at certain angles looked deflated. What masking he'd done looked to be reaching a precipice.

"You are at a critical point. I can tell by the way you move your head and the arm that you're struggling. It's up to you. Take it or leave it. Your choice."

Sheriff Kootz's eyes squinted, and his brow furrowed deep. He rubbed his temple and forehead with his left hand, almost spilling the water bottle he was holding.

Mac looked sadly at the motionless right hand at his side lightly holding the plastic bottle cap. "It sounds intense, but it sure beats taking pain meds and kicking the injury down the road. It will not get better."

Sheriff Kootz nodded, then suddenly his demeanor changed. His nose twitched. Kootz sniffed the air twice, lifting his head, and searched for the foreign scent. Upon recognizing it, he asked disappointingly, "Is that pot?"

Mac held his face neutral while thoughts of his mom upstairs on the deck lighting a fresh doobie darted through his mind. Mom was doing morning hits on the upper deck.

Her timing was terrible. Couldn't have been worse.

He'd brought Kootz into his home. Built a fragment of trust. Maybe made an ally. Extended an olive branch of kindness on the back of a wretched interrogation. A man he'd wished he befriended before Teddy died. Maybe it would have made a difference.

But that was all gone now. Up in smoke. His mom's smoke. Poof.

To try to rescue any sort of procured relationship Mac might have gained, he began mirroring Kootz's body language. Mac sniffed then, like he was equally stunned confirming his suspicions, added, "Yeah, probably. Unfortunately, both two and 2A are pot people like my mom... or were. Meaning Teddy is dead." Mac looked up toward the balcony. "You go up there and scare the shit out of her if that's your thing."

Kootz looked at Mac with an odd expression and said, "You're an interesting guy. You want me to scare your mom?"

"No, I really don't. But I can't help thinking about the look on her face if you were to go up there." Mac took a moment and chuckled, "Honestly, I can't stand the stuff."

Finally, Kootz nodded. "Me either."

"Makes me slow. And slow I don't do well," Mac chimed back, relieved.

"Allegedly it works for some people, for injuries I hear," Kootz replied. "I was waiting for you to suggest it to me."

Mac smiled. "Not me. I wouldn't do that."

Kootz returned the smile. "I wouldn't take it."

Mac wrote his friend's name and number on a paper sheet. Handing the paper to Kootz, he said, "Gotta pay in cash. Bu Pau doesn't take credit cards or insurance."

Kootz frowned. "No insurance. That's one of the best perks of my job," he replied.

"Do it once, you won't regret it. You don't have to thank me. I'll be gone."

Suddenly Mac changed the direction of their talk with a physical turn away from the conversation. He thumbed his right hand to the north wall. "Now let's chat about this guy. He is a constant nuisance. I'm gonna level with you, Sheriff.

I've never been a narc, and I'm not a cop. So it's hard for me to turn somebody in for anything. And our judicial system is less than adequate. But I grew up in Big Sur before pot was legal. Hell, grew up practically in a pot field."

"But you don't smoke."

"Like I said before, can't stand the stuff. The smell gives me a headache."

"I see."

"So, I wanna know if you've talked to the owner of this building. You personally?"

Kootz hesitated. "You know I can't tell you that."

"What about Doctor Shivelbush? Teddy, from unit two? Did you question him personally?"

Kootz shook his head again.

Mac nodded; he already knew the answer. "I had to ask. I figure you are close to retirement, which may have helped my situation."

"What situation is that exactly?"

"After doing the background check on me, I don't think you'll understand. I'll leave you to whatever I interrupted. I'm going to make my mom a smoothie."

Kootz looked insulted and tapped the piece of paper before folding it. "Out of curiosity, did you ever have a sword?"

Mac turned back. "I'm sorry?"

"A sword. Like a knife, but bigger?"

Mac paused at the description and gave a face of, "I don't follow."

Kootz put the folded paper into his breast pocket. "I thought I saw a sword here on that wall some years ago?" He said pointing to the wall.

Mac looked over at the wrong wall, intentionally. "I couldn't tell you. Now if you'll excuse me, I'm gonna make that smoothie. You can see yourself out."

CHAPTER 52

After Kootz shut the door, Mac raced to the bedroom to grab his phone. He quickly punched in a series of decryption codes, then scrolled through the message Simelane had sent. Then he climbed the stairs two at a time.

Sadie was at the table with her cell phone in hand.

"Oh, Mac. I found this great website with the most adorable schnauzers. The breeders are in Minnesota and the dogs are just glorious." She beamed.

"Glorious, huh?"

"I'm so excited. Maybe we can call them?"

"Sure, Mom. Did you like the video of the canals?"

"That was wonderful. I forgot to tell you I called Nadine, but she didn't pick up. She did such a great job! My home looks so nice."

"I'm glad you like it. We can call her again tomorrow on the drive home."

"We're leaving tomorrow?" she shrieked, sounding surprised.

"It's been a full week, Mom. Enough is enough. But I do need to run an errand with your car today. Do you mind?"

"Where are you going?"

"Not far. Be back in a few hours. Probably around lunchtime."

"The keys are by my bed."

"Great."

Mac descended the stairs and went to the back of his closet. He pulled out a pair of FEMA cargo pants with auxiliary side pockets. He dug deeper and found some light tan desert boots. Steel toe. Then a black V-neck T-shirt and whipped it on. After that, he went to the bathroom, opened his toiletry bag, and dug through his hygiene kit. In a black felt bag, he found his navy chain dog tags and slipped them over his head.

Mac pulled the white Passat out after crumpling a note left on the windshield he didn't read. At the corner of Washington Boulevard, he turned right and headed east away from the beach. He passed Lincoln Boulevard and kept going all the way to the San Diego Freeway and turned south before punching up Simelane's cell number. Straddling the phone and steering wheel, he hit a sequence of numbers, and a series of tones sounded. Several rings and Simelane picked up.

"How's it going down there?"

"It's been eventful. How's it going where you are?"

"We're still here."

"Thank you."

"What?"

"For letting me try this," Mac said, smiling and looking at himself in the mirror.

"Yeah. Did it work?"

"Kind of."

"It goes against everything you believe. Your core issues and all."

"I know, but it's my Mom."

"Yeah." The line crackled and a deep breath could be heard. "When are you heading back?"

"Soon, maybe tomorrow."

"That should be nice."

"You gonna be there awhile?"

"Well, we have an election coming, so who knows? Crazy country. You know how it is."

"Yeah, I do."

"Love to you both." And the line went dead.

Mac looked at the phone, the connection lost, and set it down on the passenger seat. Forty minutes later he picked it up again. This time it was a man's voice. His timbre was medium pitch, and a tractor's motor could be heard in the background.

"Where are you, Cappy?" the voice asked with an Indiana drawl.

"Seal Beach."

"In SoCal?"

"Affirmative."

"Know it well."

"I'm sure you do."

"What are you doing down there?"

Mac took a breath. "Cross-pollinating."

"Huh?"

"You still got people down here?"

"Yeah," the voice replied curious.

Both paused in silence a moment.

"Need a favor."

"Shoot."

CHAPTER 53

Leisure World was a retirement home for the military. A glorified trailer park of double-wides a mile in each direction. They had a nine-hole golf course, swimming facilities, and a bowling alley close to the naval yards and secured by active military personnel.

Driving up to the gates was like approaching any military compound. Uneventful and par for the course. The gate had sniffing dogs, bomb-checking mirrors, and four armed guards per security checkpoint.

At the initial gate, Mac was asked if he had an appointment by an energetic young private. Mac flashed his Ret. Navy ID to the private, who snapped a salute. She took hold of it and passed it to another guard, who took it and walked it over to an equally uptight and energetic corporal. Mac could see the corporal, maybe a year older, was stationed inside a four-by-four guard shack with a computer.

While they waited, Mac smiled at the energetic private. "How's it going?" he asked.

"Good, sir," she replied. "Who are you here to see?"

"Not sure," Mac replied. "It should be in the computer, though."

"Understood. Lot of unknowns right now," she replied with a frown.

Another uniformed soldier circled the car with a low-hung mirror and nodded to the corporal. "All clear."

The corporal stationed inside the guard shack whistled and retrieved the ID and two printed sheets of paper and returned them to Mac.

"Thaddeus, Reza. Retired lieutenant colonel, US Army, F23. Is that who you are here to see?"

"Yes, that's him," Mac replied.

The two guards looked at each other awkwardly, then the corporal returned to the guard shack and got on the phone.

Mac watched the private turn away from him and have a discussion with the corporal on the computer. Not a short permission-to-enter conversation, but a drawn-out, wait-for-information-and-be-given-instructions one. She nodded several times and turned away.

Mac wondered what the big deal was. When the corporal returned, he said, "I'm sorry to be the one to tell you this, but the lieutenant colonel died five months ago."

"How?"

"On the record? COVID."

Mac took a chance. "Off the record?"

The corporal looked at the private, then back to Mac.

"Let me rephrase the question. How old was he?"

The corporal did a quick calculation. "He was eighty-two."

"Understood." Then Mac remembered the date of the eviction for Teddy. Had to be less than six months or the sheriff would have evicted him. But COVID was allowing people to stay longer. He gambled again. "Any chance someone is still in his home? A son or relative maybe?"

The corporal looked at the computer screen again and confirmed it. "His son was living there for two years. As his health care provider."

"Is he still living there now?"

"I'm not sure. Let me look." He scanned the page, which took ten seconds, before hitting another page on the computer. "Yes, but he doesn't use this gate."

"I'm going to need to speak with him."

Both the corporal and the private looked a little nervous. Anything out of the playbook was usually not allowed. It might mean another phone call, and this one might not go in Mac's favor.

"I'll have to accompany you, since you're retired and technically your destination is deceased."

"I'd prefer that. I may need a witness."

"This a legal issue?"

"I hope not."

"I can call a warrant officer," the corporal offered.

"No MPs needed. Just a simple chat will do."

The corporal nodded. "Park your car there in guest parking. I'll transport you in the cart," he finished, pointing open-handed to a row of faded blue golf carts.

The fact Mac looked like a warrant officer was appealing. He was hoping it would help grease the wheels inside the gates and maybe catch Reza's son off guard.

The aluminum double-wide trailer wasn't far away. The corporal drove Mac in the faded golf cart. The vibe felt a lot like Palm Springs between the heat, the cart, and the barren mountains looming in the distance. Three minutes later and past a bunch of palm trees, they both stood outside a pale yellow double-wide. The corporal knocked on the door, and after thirty seconds the door swung open quickly.

Hamilton Thaddeus was a mixture of South Pacific and Persian. Like his father, he was tall and wiry, maybe six-two. One inch taller than Mac, if he wasn't barefoot. Hamilton was.

"Are you any relation to Lieutenant Colonel Thaddeus, first name Reza?" Mac asked, lifting his voice.

"I'm his son."

"And your full name is?"

"Ah, Hamilton Ronald Thaddeus. What's this about?"

"It's about your father."

"How can I help you?"

"I was a friend of your father's. I'm sorry to hear he passed away."

"Oh, thank you. The service was small. I'm sorry I didn't have your information or I would have informed you."

"Yeah, I would have liked to attend it. Where was it?"

"At my mom's."

"And where is that exactly?"

Hamilton's face went pale, and his eyes widened. It was subtle, but Mac caught it.

"In Twentynine Palms. Sorry, I didn't catch your name?"

"That's fine. When was it?"

Hamilton squinted again ever so slightly, his right eye twitched. He scratched his cheek.

Keep scratching, Mac thought. *This is getting good.*

"About five months ago," he replied, his mouth looking parched. "Sorry, how did you know him?"

"That's odd. I did a search in the obituaries and couldn't find any mention of it."

"Ah, strange. What was your name?"

"Not really. The military and GP usually don't interface. But I thought it was strange too."

"Well, I'll be sure to contact somebody. The newspaper maybe?"

"Unless you're trying to keep it out of the public." Mac dropped the other foot. "Or away from insurance companies, which I find extremely odd."

Hamilton froze.

"We are going to need to see the death certificate. Or I can have the MPs ten-hut over here and search the place while we wait?"

"No. That won't be necessary. I'll get it."

Hamilton retreated inside as Mac turned to the corporal. "You may want to step inside while I make sure he doesn't jump out the back."

"Good call," the corporal replied and stepped inside.

Hamilton didn't jump out the back. He handed the certificate to Mac, shaking like a nervous wreck. Mac switched it with a crumbled piece of paper he'd pulled from his back pocket and snapped a picture of Hamilton simultaneously, then turned to the corporal. "How long is he able to occupy this tin can before a staff sergeant boots him?"

"Technically six months to get his affairs in order."

"That's what I thought."

They zipped away in the faded blue golf cart back to Sadie's white Passat. As they rode, the corporal said to Mac, "Knew there was something fishy about that guy."

"If it smells like fish, it usually is."

Mac was happy he didn't have to tell Hamilton he was a tenant at Catamaran. Also that Hamilton didn't recognize him in case he was monitoring the video footage, like Ribbit had done before his eyes swelled shut.

As far as Mac was concerned, he was done living at Catamaran. They could keep all his possessions and burn the building down for all he cared. Without everyone inside, of course. On the drive back, he fished out Kootz's card and punched the number into his phone. Kootz picked up on the second ring.

"Hey, Kootz, thought you might want to know the owner of the building died several months back. I've got his death certificate in my hand."

"And you're telling me this why?"

"I am pretty certain his son has been forging signatures on a bunch of documents, including illegal evictions. He may have his power of attorney, but evictions through our court system during a pandemic have to be illegal, right?"

"In all fifty states, last time I checked."

"You may want to find out who the insurance company is too. The kid has sticky fingers."

"You sure you're not a cop?"

Mac laughed. "Positive."

"Well, I should notify you that you've been cleared."

Mac paused a beat and looked at his cell phone. "How's that?"

"You've been taken off the suspect list."

"I wasn't aware I was ever on it?"

"Technically you weren't but—just in case."

"I see. Good to know. So I guess we can leave town now?"

"Yeah, you're free to go."

Mac accelerated into the carpool lane, smiling. "My mom will be delighted. You want a photo of the death certificate or in person?"

"You can send a photo. I'll have to confirm it anyway."

"Not if I have the original. Did you call my friend I told you about?"

"Gonna see him this weekend. You really got me thinking about my health. I need to retire."

"Retire already. Quit screwing around."

"My parts done, Bean will take over the investigation."

"Oh," Mac replied, disappointed. "As long as I'm not in his sights. I'll see you around," he said and hung up. He looked at the road ahead and the cars whizzing by the opposite direction. Then he thought about Lieutenant Colonel Reza Thaddeus buried six feet under dirt in a navy cemetery somewhere. *Had he been cremated or buried in full military uniform?* He wondered.

Then he thought, *Where will I end up… and when?*

CHAPTER 54

Mac raced the white Passat back up the 405. Traffic was light as he zipped along at eighty mph. This part was called the Santa Monica Freeway. One name, one direction. A different name for the other direction. Confusing? Maybe.

When he got to the Marina del Rey Freeway, he turned west. This freeway had one name for both directions. Confusing? Not so much.

The phone chirped, and a number came up he didn't recognize. He didn't pick it up. Then it chirped again. Caller ID blocked. This time he picked up.

"You owe me," a gruff voice grunted loudly.

"Who is this?"

"This is Sheriff Bean. Kootz's partner, remember?"

"Oh. I don't like talking to you." And hung up.

Five seconds later the phone chirped again. And again. And again.

Mac looked at the phone, annoyed. "What do you want, Bean?"

"Wanted to call and let you know you owe me an answer."

"Do I?"

"I have you on camera going over the balcony."

Mac went silent a moment. "You do?"

"Yup."

Mac could feel Bean grinning on the other end of the line.

"But you were going left, which means you were headed to unit two. I want to know why."

"On camera?"

"Yup."

He felt Bean grin again. "From where?"

"Lifeguard tower."

"Didn't see that coming."

"Nope."

Mac chuckled. "I'll give it to you, Bean, you're one hell of an investigator. You do your homework."

Bean grunted, "What's your answer?"

"I saw the camera and I've been cleared."

"Not by me."

Mac let him have it. "Maybe Penny is a drug dealer. Maybe I like stealing his drugs because he's got the best stuff and that's the way it is."

Bean said nothing.

"Maybe I think he's so whacked out I'm dumbfounded that you guys haven't busted him yet."

Nothing from Bean.

"Or maybe I knew you guys were watching and I was hoping you'd bust down the door and catch me in a home invasion. Then you'd see all the narcotics and be thankful I'd led you to him. What do you think about that? Clean up some of the filth in the neighborhood for a change."

"Why you jerkin' me around?"

"Because you wasted my time, and my time with my mom is precious to me."

Bean was quiet for a moment, then replied, "Final answer?" He sounded aggravated.

"No, Bean. I get the sense you want to pin something on me that won't stick. I've got no motive, so let me break it down for you. Mr. Penny next door is a simpleton. A creep.

The solicitous, meretricious kind. Once the drugs and alcohol flow, he can't control himself. He comes home forgetting he has neighbors to consider. He cranks up the music. He bullies people. He thinks women have no value. And allegedly, he's somewhat successfully molested them for a long time. But not anymore. Any alarms going off? Am I hitting any bells?"

"Sounds like you got motive right there."

"For what? Penny is not dead. Unless you know something I don't. You've got two dead people and no connection to me. I didn't know them."

Silence on the line.

"Shall I continue?"

"Keep going."

Mac took a breath. "You're lucky I like Kootz." And paused. "Okay, the creep has got a history, Bean. Look him up. But you're so good I'm sure you already have." Mac paused again, waiting for Bean to reply. Another silence. "Are you recording this now?"

Bean said nothing.

"Because you have to notify me if I'm being recorded or this won't hold up in court."

"Go on."

"I heard a woman screaming."

"You broke into his unit without permission?"

"I will rephrase that. I heard screams from a woman needing help."

"Do you have any corroborating witnesses?"

"Aren't you the guys with the cameras and secret microphones and stuff?"

"No."

Mac paused, irritated. "The woman won't press charges."

"What's her name?"

"You tell me. You've got the camera footage."

"She covered her face when she left. You tell her to do that?"

"Don't even go there."

"Why didn't you call nine-one-one?"

"Haven't you guys been here enough this week?"

Bean let out a huff of air. "You should have called nine-one-one. Better for you."

"You are right. If it was a fire, I would have. But it wasn't. I heard someone scream from the upstairs balcony, and I went up to help."

"I'm listening!" Bean persisted.

Mac thought about it for a second. He didn't want to be involved, and he didn't want to be asked not to leave town again. He wanted to get his mom, pack their belongings, and drive away to never return. Ever.

"Tell you what, Sheriff. I'm gonna give you a piece of paper that will exonerate me from any wrongdoing. I want you to make copies. I want you to give one to Stevo in unit five first. Then give it to all the tenants. Like an insurance policy. Don't tell 'em what it is. Just give it to them."

"Why would I do that?"

"Because you need all the help you can get. You've a partner that's retiring soon."

"What's on the paper, and how's it get you off the hook for unit two?"

"Falsifying signatures for illegal evictions by the son of the deceased owner is pretty bad, I imagine. So is insurance fraud. Probably some other stuff a military court will find interesting too. But that's not your department, is it?"

"Wait a minute. Slow down. Deceased? You saying there's another dead person?"

"I'm glad you're listening. I just spoke with his son."

"Whose son?"

"The owners. On a military base forty miles south of here."

Bean paused. "You serious?"

"Very."

"I need you to come in."

"Not to the police station. Not like before."

Bean paused again. "Tell me where you are? I'll come to you."

"I'll be outside my building in fifteen minutes."

* * *

Bean was waiting as promised, parked sideways, taking up three spaces. He was standing at the front of his car deep in conversation with Jizzy and Hutch. Their body language told the story. Guilty about something and pleading they were clueless. Innocence was bliss.

Mac parked the car and handed the paperwork to Bean, disregarding sad-eyed Jizzy tucked under the pit of supporting Hutch. Bean turned and took the paperwork, pausing midsentence. "MacGuffin?"

"Yeah?"

"I still need to talk to you."

Mac turned back. "I'm sure you do," he said, then looked past him. "Those papers are an insurance policy. More of an umbrella policy, actually. Covers the tenants in the building."

Jizzy and Hutch looked at Mac, bewildered.

"Your umbrella policy? What are you talking about?" Bean shot back with disgust.

"The gentleman in unit two, Dr. Theodore Wolfgang Shivelbush. He was harassed, served illegal eviction letters, terrorized by the racist neighbor above him continually. All this undue stress while undergoing some sort of medical treatment for his failing health. His family should file a case against the owner of this building for wrongful death. The illegal eviction alone is worth one hundred dollars a day for harassment. There's no price you can put on your health, man. Did you know he was going to commit suicide?"

"No. How the hell would I know that?"

"One thing usually leads to another. Didn't you question him before he offed himself?"

Bean shook his head. "Guy was a mess!"

"Was he? Before or after you questioned him?"

Bean shifted his weight but didn't answer.

Mac read Bean's body language, disappointed. "And didn't he tell you about the bullying from the tenant upstairs?"

Now Bean was scratching his head.

Mac pointed at Bean with an open palm. "Somebody is liable for that. Let the insurance company and lawyers figure it out. I just want to go be with my mom while *she's* still alive."

Backpaddling, Bean said "I've got your number in case—"

Mac cut him off. "In case what? I'm in the wind."

Bean fumbled for words, but none came.

"You don't got shit. My friend Chad will be here after I'm gone. Please make sure *he* isn't harassed."

CHAPTER 55

Mac climbed his stairs three at a time, an undercurrent of anxiety building in him. Everything about Bean was annoying to Mac, and for good reason. A waste of manpower with a badge to nowhere.

In the kitchen, he blended a pair of smoothies, finishing off the fruit. The blueberries made the drinks purple, and he popped banana wedges on the rims of the glasses.

He went up the stairs, stood at the screen door, and watched his mom filled with joy, completely unaware of his presence. She pecked away on her classic typewriter, laughing at what she was writing. Occasionally she would call out, "Mac, are you back yet?"

Mac stepped out onto the balcony and handed Mom the purple smoothie with its banana wedge. Sadie's eyes lit up. "Wow, that looks delicious!"

"Yeah, it's loaded with goodness."

"It looks it," she replied, taking a gulp. Gulp. Gulp. Gone. "I found another Tintin and am writing about him right now. This one's in Montana. He is so precious. Have a look!"

She was happy, and that helped ease Mac's tension. "What do you think about packing our bags and getting out of here today?"

"Today?"

"Sure. After we finish our smoothies and before traffic."

Sadie held his gaze and he saw her thinking about it. "I could do that."

"I can leave if you can."

"What about your brother? We need to call him."

Mac gave a deep sigh for several seconds in sadness, scratching his head with downcast eyes, then looked up at his mom. Her eyes were bright, hopeful. "I'll call him on the drive home. Would that be good?"

"That would be great," she replied, smiling.

Mac took another breath and felt a gentle breeze against his face. The breeze blew Sadie's hair off her shoulder. "I think he is already here with us in spirit. I've always told him we got all the good days that were available."

"Oh?" she replied inquisitively.

"We can tell him about the bad music, the banana-less smoothies, and needing to poop in the bushes."

They both started laughing. Mac had to turn away to catch his breath. It took several attempts before he could gather himself.

"What about your things here, Mac? We can't fit them all in my car."

Mac looked around the deck. "Just things, Mom."

"You don't want them?"

"Nope."

"You're not attached?"

"To this place? Not at all. Sometimes the things you own end up owning you."

Sadie glanced around. "Mind if I grab a few items?"

"Fire at will. Take anything you want."

CHAPTER 56

As Mac brought his bag downstairs, he heard a loud scream. It came from the west end of the building in the vicinity of unit two. Its pitch sounded high and female, resembling shock, maybe surprise.

From the loam of his memory, Mac remembered Penny lying on the floor. The reclusive female neighbor must have opened her door and found Penny with his pinched testicles. Then as Mac entered the garage, he heard a masculine yelp from above. Mac figured it must be the neighbor's husband. The man belted in astonishment, "Oh my God! Holy hell!"

Penny could be heard moaning in agony. Then the man was saying, "Here, let me help you."

Suddenly Penny yelled, "No, no, no! Don't touch the door! Call nine-one-one! Get me an ambulance!" and began sobbing.

The woman's voice yelled again, "Alan, don't touch it! Call an ambulance!"

"I'm not touching it!" The man yelled back.

Back at his apartment, Mac quickly switched into high gear and opened the downstairs door to his mom's bedroom. "Mom, we really gotta go now!"

Sadie shuffled over with her bag. "I'm going as fast as I can."

"Hurry up," Mac said from the doorway.

"Can you help me with my bag?"

"Yes, Mom," he said and hurried over.

"Did you hear that scream?"

"Yeah. We gotta go. We don't wanna get blocked in by another ambulance."

Sadie nodded, her eyes going wide.

He grabbed her bag and the two items she wanted and set them at the stairwell. Then he helped her down the bottom stairs. Sadie asked, "Are you leaving that door open?"

"Yes, Mom. Chad from Mother's Beach is going to be here later today."

"He is?" she replied, sitting down in the passenger seat. She looked up at Mac, confused.

Mac put her seat belt on. "He needs a place to stay. I told him he was welcome here."

"How much are you charging him for rent?"

"I'm not charging him, mom."

Mac fired up the engine and quickly pulled out of the parking area. As they turned the corner, Sadie was looking up the first stairwell in the direction of the yelling. "What the heck is going on up there?"

Mac shrugged his shoulders as he checked for traffic and took the turn north. A man's legs could be seen halfway up the stairs, and an ambulance siren whined from somewhere in the distance.

As they pulled up to the stop sign at Washington Boulevard, Sadie asked, "What do you think happened?"

"Who cares? Not our circus anymore."

Sadie corrected him, "Not our monkey. Not our circus."

He switched gears and casually asked, "Shall we take the coast?"

"Sure," Sadie replied nonchalantly. "Up through Malibu sounds nice."

"You got it," he replied, downshifting to take the turn.

The fake bundle of flowers from the upper deck lay pinched in the corner between the passenger door and dashboard and, beneath it, the striped red umbrella was at her side. Mac's plaque of four FBI badges lay in the small pocket of his bag atop two cases of alkaline water. They didn't stop at Nate's home or his shop on the way out of town. Instead, they turned left at Pacific Avenue. They headed north through Santa Monica and joined PCH at the ten freeway.

Mac chose to not remind Nate of the past they'd shared with another surprise visit. Nor tell him the questions Kootz had asked. Nate wasn't accustomed to cop games, death, and violence like Mac was.

When Nate had called two years ago in tears saying he'd skewered an intruder in Mac's home, he was a mess. Crying and sobbing and remorseful. Mac was a five-hour drive away and made it to Nate in three and a half. It was after 4:00 a.m., and Penny next door was in full swing, his music thumping through the walls like tomorrow never existed. And maybe it didn't.

Mac walked in the door and saw Nate sitting on the floor in tears. Shock and repentance. The body of Brandon Peterson was upstairs in the bedroom. Mac recognized him immediately. He had a bag of fake smoke detectors with hidden cameras. Why he was sneaking into units and installing hidden cameras in the middle of the night was beyond Mac's imagination. Some sort of perverse implementation of a plan. To what end, Mac couldn't sort. Bizarre beyond measure. And hard to prove, theoretically.

Because Nate was drunk when it happened. He was still drunk when Mac arrived, memory foggy. But he'd called Mac instead of 911. He said he'd come home from the bar up the street and was climbing the stairs when he heard someone in the bedroom. He panicked and grabbed the biggest weapon he could find. A sword. The Excalibur at the foot of the stairs. King Arthur's sword of legend.

Then he called out, but no one answered. So with liquid courage, he rushed up, furious for the invasion. He wanted to be brave. He wanted to be the hero. He wanted to save the day and kill the bad guy.

And he did. Kind of.

But it cost him a piece of his innocence. And scarred his dreams forever with nightmares. Terrors of the event. Nate had to listen to the guy moan with a sword through his lung until Mac arrived and put the man out of his misery. Three and a half grueling hours.

Mac was pragmatic and relatively calm when he spoke with Nate. "Tell me about your 3D printing press. How does it work? It scans things?"

"Yeah, that's right."

"It can scan anything?"

"Pretty much. Depending on the scale."

"How big is it? Is it easily movable by yourself?"

"Sure."

"I need you to go get it. I need you to bring it back here, Nate. We're gonna scan this guy's face."

"Why?"

"Because this guy is gonna walk out of here tomorrow."

And Nate did it. He did a fantastic job. And when he returned several hours later from his workshop, he had a face to show Mac. And Mac had a clean home to show Nate.

Nate had asked, "Where did the guy go?"

"You don't need to worry about it. Less is more."

"I don't understand."

"Perfect. Do you fish, Nate?"

"Yeah, I can fish."

The 3D print was flawless. Neighbors saw Brandon walk out of the building at 10:00 a.m. the next morning, the same-looking clothes and bag of smoke detectors under his arm. Plain and simple. After the act.

And for the next several days, Mac and Nate fished off the end of the Venice Pier with chum that was individually wrapped in Saran wrap—chum frozen in Mac's fridge and thawed on the pier in the sun. They never ate the fish they caught. It was all catch and release, which had a better feel to it. Santa Monica Bay was dirty.

CHAPTER 57

The fall had come and gone and seemed even hotter than summer with the fires burning, which had been long and dry. Finally, winter was here, and the fires were out two months after Mac and Sadie's adventure. Truth being told, Mac missed his mom. After concluding operations in Florida, he flew back to California.

That morning he'd stopped by Costco and filled two boxes with nonperishable foods, tucking them alongside a red umbrella he'd bought months earlier. It would be a replacement for the tattered orange one that shaded Sadie's outdoor sitting area. Among the other items he was traveling with were two bright, brand spanking new orange traffic cones.

Clouds filled the skyline as Mac raced seventy miles south down Highway One through Santa Cruz, Watsonville, and the marina north of Seaside. A thin layer of mist hung over the artichoke fields. Gulls flew low along Elkhorn Slough at Moss Landing as geese migrated south toward warmer weather.

When he exited the off-ramp to his mother's house near Home Depot, he added a stop and three turns. At the corner of Empathy and Consideration, he exited the car under gray skies and left two food boxes to be shared by the homeless encampment living under the off-ramp.

At his mom's house, her little car was in her spot, tucked between ripe tomato bushes and the tall green hedge. Mac looked at the tomatoes, then unlocked the gate, pushed it open, and strolled in, with the umbrella in one hand and bag of groceries the other.

"Oh, great. You're here! Perfect timing," she said from her perch in the garden. "Please close the gate."

Mac reversed and pushed the gate closed with the shaft of the umbrella.

"I got a notice in the mail. Something about having to be in court. I don't understand it."

"Let me see the notice, Mom," he said, giving her a kiss on the cheek.

"I'll get it. It's on my desk." She stood up. "By the way, I can't seem to close the kitchen window. Can you help me?"

"Sure. Just take these groceries inside. I'll put up the umbrella. Rain is coming."

"I know. That's why I want to get my window closed," she replied, taking the grocery bag. She looked at the umbrella, her eyes sparkling. "Oh, that umbrella is pretty."

"I think so. It celebrates twenty years being in this home. How about that?"

"Twenty years? Impossible."

"Possible, Mom."

"Has it been that long?" she replied, looking inside the grocery bag. "Did you say hello to Phoenix? He is so sweet. He's been chasing Baju and Raazi around the garden all morning."

"Hi, Phoenix. Hi, Baju."

Phoenix was his mom's brand-new mini schnauzer. The replacement for Tintin if ever there was one. He was a bundle of joy with puppy breath and sharp teeth that caught on Mac's shoelaces. "Go play with Baju," Mac said, brushing Phoenix away.

Mac pulled the faded and torn old orange umbrella from the cement block he'd made years earlier and set it to the side. Then he slipped the new umbrella into the cement sleeve. When he opened it up, the bright red color popped beautifully against the backdrop of garden green. Vibrant and fresh, it was a big, happy statement for new beginnings. He looked up to see his mom watching him.

"Your father was such a sweet man. Easygoing and thoughtful. You're very lucky, you know that? You have all those qualities. What will you do with them next, I wonder?" she asked, crossing the garden.

Mac sat in the extra chair beside hers. He extended his hand from the shade of the new umbrella, ready to take the letter. "Have you lost weight?"

"Yes, I have. Sixteen pounds, to be exact." Sadie stood modeling her figure, arms extended. She did a slow turn, and Mac imagined the little girl in her alive and well, frisky and feisty as ever.

"That's great, Mom, I can see it. Let me see that letter."

She remained standing and handed him the letter.

It was a notice from the Santa Monica Superior Court dismissing Sadie as a witness. *A witness to what?* Mac wondered. He read the notice. The police had never interviewed his mom, but Ribbit had written her license plate down, and as one thing leads to another, she ended up in the system.

Nonsensical. Mac crumpled the notice after taking a photo and set it on the garden table. "It's nothing, Mom. You're good."

Sadie huffed and produced another piece of paper from her pocket. "Now, with all your talent and experiences,

I thought I'd write something to protect you," she replied, still standing. "You may need it."

Mac looked surprised. "Protect me from what?"

"Well, just in case you decide to start writing books. You know, your stories? I want you to include this in the beginning."

Mac looked at her with wary distrust. "You wrote a legal letter?"

"It will protect you and expunge me in case you write about me."

Mac pursed his lips, not yet taking the letter. With measured restraint, he replied, "I think I got this, Mom."

She paused, searching. "I prefer you don't write about me."

They both gave each other sharp looks and waited.

Neither budged. Both frozen.

Mac scratched his head and cautiously took the paper, his eyes darting between his mom and what lay on the pages. He could see it was written in red ink, which he found alarmingly odd. "Shall we talk about something else before I read this aloud?"

"If you must," she replied, eyes sharp as a fox seeking equal vulnerability. "What did you have in mind?"

"Remember that Bikram yoga class in LA?"

"Funny, I was just thinking about that this morning. I thought I was gonna die," she said, swallowing.

"So did I, but you didn't." He held a beat.

"Did you want me to?"

"Of course not." He held another moment before bursting out with laughter.

Sadie shot him a look and sat down in her garden chair. "It wasn't that funny."

"It was," he stated flatly. "You were in way over your head."

Sadie smirked. "I thought I was the only one in agony, then that woman near you sat down."

"I saw that. But she survived, and so did you. It was hard, but you did great. And now look at the weight you've lost. You've been drinking your smoothies and pressed juices regularly. You're on a comeback."

"It feels really good. My body aches have subsided. My joints don't hurt as much. And I think I sleep better."

Mac smiled. "You take it in steps, Mom. There's no rush, no judgment."

"I know. I wasn't born yesterday."

Mac nodded, "I'm lucky to have you. You know that? Tell me what the doctor said."

Sadie was smiling and all was good in her world again. She was holding her cat Baju tight. As if he wanted to escape. Pheonix was under her chair chewing on a toy. His nose covered in freshly rooted soil. The invisible Raazi was on an adventure. Nowhere to be seen. And Mac was in his mother's garden.

Acknowledgments

With a special acknowledgment to Talia at Palmetto Publishing, whose thoughtful guidance and uplifting wisdom gave me insight to writing tight. And my friend in Canada, Alison McBain, whose polish with grace embraces my freedom.

About the Author

Thyme Lewis spent his formative years in Big Sur, California, with his mother, Heidi Elizabeth McGurrin, and two siblings, Winona Lewis and Alistair Monroe. This is his second book in a series of adventures from around the globe. Now a full-time writer, Thyme (pronounced with the h) currently resides in Northern California's Carmel-by-the-Sea. You can visit his work online at amazonbooks.com and thymelewisbooks.com.

Jack MacGuffin returns in

Blood and Bones

Coming in paperback & eBook from
Palmetto Publishing
Audiobook from Pacific Sound Studios
Spring 2023

Special preview of the first chapter

CHAPTER 1

Miami, Florida

Mac settled in to observe the packed room full of inspectors. His seat was in the second row of the third isle, a conference room nicknamed Big Hall because of its size. The hotel was on high ground because all the low ground hotels had flooded. The room was noisy and hot and humid, standing room only.

As it was, Mac had taken the last available seat and wedged himself between a heavyweight guy wearing a Baltimore Raven jersey and rail thin man with a twangy accent and buzz cut. The heavy guy had a barrel chest much like a boxer, and a belly like a Sumu wrestler. The thin man was at most one hundred and forty pounds soaking wet, with nervous eyes. His experience when in confined spaces with strangers was to make polite conversation or say nothing at all. The group around him appeared stressed, so he chose the latter and listened. They were all eager to hear what the three men at the front of the room had to say.

The men at the front appeared to be in their early fifties to late sixties. Mac figured them for ex-vets from other military branches now working for FEMA, the Federal Emergency Management Agency. One man stood out above the rest. He held a solid stature at 6'1" with salty hair and sleeves rolled up, revealing swollen forearms like Popeye the Sailor Man. He was listening to the other two sidestepping while keeping his gaze on the information they presented him.

Mac didn't know the three men, but from what he heard, neither did the inspectors in his immediate vicinity. They knew their titles. How long the men had held those positions approximately. But they didn't know them. Not personally.

Energy radiated outward across the people in the room. Mac was no exception, yet his experience was in hearing problems and enacting solutions quickly. Sitting there in the crowded room, making observations, was intriguing for Mac.

As the inspectors talked amongst themselves, Mac's eyes scanned the Working Solution Programs posters that plastered the walls. Slogans, hardhats, and rapid deployment were the WSP theme, reasons to join, and why. But his ears informed him of a different story. The men around him weren't convinced, they were concerned. As were the three men at the front of the room.

Mac could tell. He'd been around men in power long enough to pick up minute signs and read their body language. Which today appeared clipped and tight. Heads tilted and paused, eyebrows raised and fell, and lips pressed together, rigid. Accompanying hand gestures gave dismissive flaps of skepticism and wariness.

The Popeye man turned to the audience, shifted his posture, and said, "Okay, everybody, let's get to why we're all here."

The crowd hushed and all focus fell on him.

"My name is Dan Fitzpatrick. For those who don't know me, I'm number two at FEMA. The reason I've called you here is because we've got a situation that needs to be addressed." He turned and timed his delivery with pointing at the map of Puerto Rico. "Over there."

Mac watched the backs of everyone's heads turn. Focused, probing, tilting, measuring. They were veterans, having been in the field many times. And none of them, from what Mac had learned, were soft. They were hard, pragmatic, and seasoned. Most looked like galvanized nails spit out of a Dewalt nail gun. They'd already proven they wanted to make an impact by joining WSP to combat the worst disasters imaginable. So why were they being hesitant now?

"Most of you have shown up time and time again in disasters and we appreciate you. Now, I know many of you don't speak Spanish, but many of the people that we need to help do not speak English. It's a real obstacle. So, we are asking for anyone you know who is bilingual, capable to pass the training course, to enlist and go to Puerto Rico."

Wariness and skepticism erupted through the room in a low rumble of grunts and mutters.

Mac turned to the thin man on his right and whispered, "Why don't we use interpreters?"

The man shrugged and whispered back with a twangy voice, "I don't know. I never been to Puerto Rico."

Dan hushed the audience and continued, "Now, we have a unique situation and many of you are probably asking yourselves, why don't we hire locals? The answer is this. We would prefer to use bilingual inspectors. But we've run out. So, we will be hiring to fill the gap. On a temporary basis or until deemed necessary." He scanned the audience and caught Mac's eye before continuing, "For those of you who wish to go to Puerto Rico, Harold here is going to break down what we know is happening on the ground thus far." He turned and opened his stance to the man on the left.

Mac scanned the boards at the front of the room as the man stepped through his line of sight. Each one displayed maps of Puerto Rico and the surrounding US and British Virgin Islands. Circles in red centered off the southwest coast of Puerto Rico and radiated outward in all directions, followed by rings of orange, yellow, and pink.

Harold stood at the helm telling the audience about what had occurred, in his professional opinion, and made references to tectonic plates and current seismic activity. The informational speech lasted about thirty minutes and included all the government agencies engaged in the disaster.

Mac found it odd that with all the people mentioned, FEMA was short-staffed for bilingual building inspectors. Hope for the best but, prepare for the worst. They hadn't.

After the briefing, Mac walked straight up to Dan in the hotel lobby and asked if his broken Spanish would be a help.

"Yes. But you won't get the numbers you're getting here," Dan stated, sizing Mac up. Mac seemed to have that affect when he walked into a room, and Dan had locked eyes with him three times during the briefing.

"You know what I'd do if I were going there?" The question came from the third man from the podium. Salt and pepper hair, rugged features, with emerald green eyes. "I'd rent a jeep and get a local guide. Because you're not gonna be able to use your navigation. Hell, most of the roads are blocked by power lines and palm trees. Half the island was under water and there is no electricity. Like zero. People are doing a mass exodus. It's Syria all over again. Get a local guide."

Mac nodded. "I'll go."

"What's your name, son?" Dan asked.

"MacGuffin, sir."

"What's your first name?"

"Jack. But I go by Mac."

"Very well, Mac." Dan extended his hand to shake and turned. "This is deputy director Jim Beam."

"Like the whiskey?" Mac asked, turning to the green-eyed man.

Jim squinted keenly. "That's right. How long you been with us?" And without interruption they spoke for three solid minutes. Several men waited to get Dan and Jim's attention while they talked, but Dan would have none of it and waved them off.

Mac nodded, and that was it. He was going straight to the epicenter while the world swirled around him.

Later that night when Mac got back to his hotel, a two-hour drive north, he told Ric.

"You went to the briefing?" Ric asked, sounding shocked.

"I did. And I signed up. I'll leave tomorrow or the next day."

"Shiiit. You're leaving me?" He sounded disappointed.

"You can come. Work here will last awhile, but it'll thin. Doesn't seem like it'll be thinning *there* anytime soon."

"Doesn't seem like you'll be getting anywhere there, either."

"It'll be fine. I'm not here for the money. I'm in it to make a difference. The experience will be fantastic. You should come with me. They need people."

"I don't speak Spanish."

"My Spanish only gets me around kitchens and building sites. That's enough. All we'd have to do is memorize the key questions and pronounce the options so people understand us. Everything else will come together."

"You're very optimistic."

"It'll be fun. An adventure."

"How'd you get in today? It was for WSP invite only."

"I just walked in."

"You crashed it?" he yelped with surprise.

"I did."

"What they say?"

"The guy said I'd be lucky to get three inspections a day."

Ric started laughing. He almost rolled off the bed laughing. "Three inspections!?"

"I don't care. I'll be helping people. Besides, it's Puerto Rico. What could go wrong?"

Ric rolled his eyes and threw his hands up. "They just had three hurricanes, then an earthquake! *Everything* could go wrong."